# MAUD

by

Russ Cooper

# CHAPTERS

| | |
|---|---|
| **Prologue** | **4** |
| **PART 1** | |
| Chapter 1 – A Child is Born | 15 |
| Chapter 2 – A Nefarious Rogue | 39 |
| Chapter 3 – Mischief Abroad | 55 |
| Chapter 4 – All the King's Horses and All the Queen's Men | 75 |
| Chapter 5 – The Race to Tewkesbury | 102 |
| Chapter 6 – A Tale of Two Towns | 116 |
| Chapter 7 – A National Tragedy | 144 |
| Chapter 8 – Aftermath | 159 |
| **PART 2** | |
| Chapter 9 – A Fateful Meeting | 182 |
| Chapter 10 – Ungentlemanly Conduct | 199 |
| Chapter 11 – A Haven No More | 211 |
| Chapter 12 – The Archer | 223 |
| Chapter 13 – The Tourney | 236 |

| | |
|---|---|
| Chapter 14 – Young Love | 255 |
| Chapter 15 – A Day at the Market | 269 |
| Chapter 16 – Betrayal | 281 |
| Chapter 17 – A Series of Unfortunate Circumstances | 296 |
| Chapter 18 – A Dance with Death | 313 |
| Chapter 19 – If Only... | 326 |

## PART 3

| | |
|---|---|
| Chapter 20 – Justice is a Dish Best Served Without Emotion | 344 |
| Chapter 21 – A Travesty of Justice | 356 |
| Chapter 22 – Maud's Elm | 373 |
| Chapter 23 – J'Accuse | 386 |
| Chapter 24 – Tribulation Before Trial | 400 |
| Chapter 25 – A Mockery of Justice | 424 |
| Chapter 26 – Decisions have Consequences | 444 |
| Chapter 27 – A Deathbed Confession | 459 |

**Epilogue** **477**

# Prologue

## Winter 1469, All Hallow's Eve

### Swindon Village, Gloucestershire

The storm raged, as a heavily pregnant Meg Bowen crept out of the door of her cottage.

It was a wicked night and thunder rumbled, then crashed. "SShhhush!" she admonished the weather, as she carefully closed the door, not wanting to wake her slumbering husband. She turned towards the small path that ran away from her house. Lightning flashed, illuminating the route she needed to take through the church graveyard towards the main street of the village. The howling wind was driving the rain almost horizontally. Her face was lashed, before she had the chance to draw her shawl more tightly around her head. She blinked the stinging water from her eyes and ran towards her destination.

Another rumble, another crash, the storm now directly overhead. There was no delay between the terrifying sound of thunder, and the simultaneous, deadly flash of blanket lightning. Bent nearly double against the prevailing tumult, she pushed on, determined to reach the muddy main street. Splash! She stepped into a large puddle, soaking her shoes and drenching the bottom of her skirts.

"This is madness!" she thought.

She pressed on undeterred. The cottage that she was heading for was situated, inconveniently, on the far side of the village, set away from the others, just as her own was at this end. Her summons had been precise, the time and day specific.

"The Witching Hour! On All Hallow's Eve! Whatever next? "she thought, with an equal measure of trepidation and scepticism.

As she continued running as fast as her sodden clothes and pregnant condition would allow, the now almost continuous thunder and lightning lit up the dwellings on either side of the street. As she passed, she looked at the homes of her neighbours and friends, and briefly thought "They are all safe and warm, tucked up and sleeping through the worst this weather. Here am I drowning! How much more stupid could I possibly be!"

She had pride in her village, and despite her current predicament, she still noticed that most of the homes were well maintained, being a mixture of wood, wattle and daub construction, with thatched roofs. "No rain will get into those!" she muttered, bemoaning her own saturated state as she ran. She passed the houses of some of the wealthier tenants and saw that they had some stone construction, with slate roofs. Next to many of the cottages, wicket fences penned in domestic animals, chickens, goats, the odd sheep, and some pigs. Some had dogs, but these sensible animals had all buried themselves deep inside their kennels, despite their normal ferocity, most would be whimpering with fear at the tempest that was ravaging the village. Nevertheless, she could hear some howling their displeasure at the Gods of Storms.

The road was awash with water, the rain was torrential. Large pools and ponds formed everywhere, and gushing rivulets filled the gulley's and ruts in the village throughfare and ran down its edges. Meg lifted her skirts as she ran, trying to avoid the worst of the water. Her splashing and sploshing efforts a testament to her failure, wading through puddles that seemed to be getting ever deeper. "Damn!" she cursed under her breath, regretting the fact that she had agreed to attend the meeting at Old Mother Sawyer's home. In her heavily pregnant state, she again pondered the stupidity of her decision to leave her husband asleep in the safety of her own home, to make this clandestine visit. "Why do I need to hear whatever news she is going to tell me by myself? Why did she tell me to come alone?"

The roaring and rumbling of the thunder continued unabated. It seemed that the storm had settled itself right over the village and would not move. The threat of flooding at the river and brook that skirted the village, was now a real possibility. Meg's previous experience told her that storms, normally moved through quite fast, but this one was stubbornly persistent. The lightning also continued, relentless in its awesome power.

"Goodness!" she cried as she was momentarily startled by a loud, unexpected crash just beside her. John Smith's boar pig had smashed itself in a frenzy of fear into the fence surrounding the pen. The fence shook and the pig screeched. The giant pig threw itself against the fence again, threatening to break through. The pigs were clearly unsettled by the storm, and in a state of extreme fear. With no where to find cover, they were becoming dangerously frantic.

Meg hurried on, she was now nearly in sight of Old Mother Sawyer's home, but on this night, a few minutes' walk, seemed a journey of miles. Meg was soaked to the bone, her skirts were covered in mud, her shoes drenched.

Another flash of lightning lit up the Sawyer cottage, a single storey, tumble-down assortment of wattle and daub, rickety and awry, more of a hovel than a cottage.

Meg rushed to the door and banged hard. The door opened, and from the depths of the cottage, Old

Mother Sawyer beckoned her inside. "Come in my child and get yourself warm by the fire."

Meg once again thought of the folly of her decision to agree to this meeting, but Old Mother Sawyer had been insistent, it had to be this evening, All Hallows Eve…. No other time would be possible she had stated, and there would be consequences if Meg did not attend.

Meg had been perturbed when the old lady had come up to her in the street a few days past. She had hardly ever spoken to her, and although she often greeted her out of courtesy, Meg did not go out of her way to acquaint herself with the old woman. Old Mother Sawyer was as old as anyone Meg had ever seen, and she had lived in the village before anyone could remember. Old Mother Sawyer was reclusive, but not unkindly, although she generally kept herself to herself, she greeted people and people greeted her, whenever she was out and about. As a child, Meg and her friends would tell stories and dare each other to go and knock at the door of the rotting old cottage in which the wizened old woman dwelled, but none of them were ever brave enough to go through with it. They would usually run off, laughing, having not got closer than 10 yards, frightened by the stories of curses, potions and spells that could turn a person into a frog!

Old mother Sawyer was known in Swindon village and the other villages around as a sayer of truths, and to be honest, Meg was quite frightened of her. However, if anyone, particularly women, needed healing remedies, then Old Mother Sawyer was the person people came to.  If there were accidents or maladies, Old Mother Sawyer was the first port of call.  Old Mother Sawyer helped with most of the births in the surrounding villages, and in a time of high infant mortality, the record of deaths of babies was surprisingly low.  In general, Old Mother Sawyer was quite aloof, and tended to keep herself to herself, but she was friendly and polite to everyone she met.  Every now and again, she would summon one of the villagers to discuss something of import – no-one else ever knew what was discussed and no-one ever tried to find out.  In a village as small as Swindon, that was a rarity, as almost everyone knew everyone else's' business.  She had a particular knack of always knowing when a new baby was due, and always before the expectant mother.

While the weather outside continued ruthlessly, the small dark cottage felt ominous, Old Mother Sawyer indicated to a small wooden stool next to the fire, "sit yourself down girl, I have something to say".

Meg dripping and sodden pulled back her head shawl, rubbed her freezing hands together to get some warmth back into them.  She looked around.  Despite the dilapidated condition of the outside of the cottage, everything inside was neat and tidy.  She quickly returned her attention to the old woman, "What would you have me know Old Mother?"

"Your child is in great danger!"

A startled and confused Meg did not know how to respond. She stared at the old woman in shock "How? Can you give me a remedy?"

The old woman sighed "There is no remedy for your child, other than love, and security...."

"But what does that mean? Is my baby ill? What can I do?" said Meg as she choked with emotion.

"Your child is not ill Meg. Your child is in danger from those who would do her harm."

"What? Who would want to harm my child? Why?" cried Meg.

Old Mother Sawyer did not respond immediately. She twisted a delicate chain around in her fingers slowly. She stared over Meg's head, her eyes glazed and became opaque. Meg shivered involuntarily, unsure about what she should do.

Suddenly, another loud crash of thunder reverberated outside the cottage and it seemed to Meg that the walls physically shook. She looked around, startled by the violence of the noise. When she returned her gaze to Old Mother Sawyer, the old woman was staring back at her, her eyes had returned to their normal state.

"I cannot be certain" she stated, still twining the chain around her fingers, "Your child will be born safely. My vision tells me that in her future, there are dark forces that will seek to harm her. Men, who will do her harm…"

Meg cried in anguish "But how do you know this? Who are these men? What can I do!?"

The old woman continued to coil the chain around her fingers "You will need to watch your child, protect her always! Be vigilant! I can tell you no more."

"But what about the men! Can you tell me no more about them?" Meg exclaimed "Surely, you have seen them in your vision?"

"They are shadows child; I cannot see them clearly. One is a powerful stranger, the other is closer to you…"

"Her? You keep saying 'her', will my child be a girl?" Meg asked becoming exasperated.

"Yes" the old woman replied, "She will be an exceptionally beautiful girl, and this will be the cause of her woes…."

"How can I protect her?" Meg implored.

Old Mother Sawyer looked down at her hands. She began to unwind the chain from around her fingers. "I can do little, you can do even less. Take this trinket made by the maidens of Alney, and make sure that your child has it with her always. It will help to protect her." She held out her hand, and Meg could see a small red crystal in her palm, at the end of a silver chain.

Meg took the crystal and chain and turned it over in her palm. "This is beautiful Mother. I cannot take this from you!"

"Take it Meg. This belongs to your child, not me. It has been waiting here for a long time, longer than me, longer than I have lived…."

"But how?" whispered Meg, staring at the delicate and beautiful object in her hand. The old woman looked at her with tears welling in her eyes "I do not know, child, I only know that it was meant for your child, and she must have it with her always."

Old Mother Sawyer moved slightly in her chair "If you are willing, I might be able to teach you some of our ways. This might help you in the future…."

"But I have no gifts" replied Meg "I couldn't do it."

"You have gifts child. You are an exceptional weaver…even at your young age…I feel you have magic in your fingers…"

"No!" Meg laughed despite herself, "I have no magic! Just the skills I have learned through practice."

"That may be child. Nevertheless, if you are willing, I will try to help you…"

"I will think about it." Meg responded, "But what am I to do now?"

"Go home, have your child. Love her and protect her, there is nothing more…"

Meg stood up, "I don't whether to thank you or not Mother. I am not sure that I wanted to know what you have told me, and I would have been better off not knowing."

"I know! I know child. There was never a choice to tell you. It had to be, and I am sorry to have distressed you. Whether or not my warning will have any effect, is not for me to know, but I have done what I had to do." The old woman closed her hand gently around Meg's, her frozen hands warmed immediately, "Remember what I have said and think on it. You and your husband are the protection she needs, and in order to protect her, you need to protect yourselves".

"I will Mother, I will." Meg gently pulled her hand from the old woman's grasp and turned towards the door "I must go, Will, will be waking soon." As she lifted the latch, she heard Old Mother Sawyer repeat "be vigilant child, be vigilant….."

Once outside, Meg pulled the door to and ensured the latch was set. As suddenly as it had begun, the storm had now passed, just a light spitting rain and a slight breeze remained. Magically, her clothes were dry, and her body was warm, no sense of the heavy rain-soaked, chilling garments remained. Nevertheless, Meg shivered as she set off back towards her own cottage.

# Part 1
## 1468-1471

# CHAPTER 1

## A CHILD IS BORN

### Summer 1468- Swindon Village

Swindon village was a small tight knit community sitting on the north-western boundary of the 'Cheltenham Hundreds'. It was a small parish, sitting within a larger parcel of land. The 'hundreds' were divided for ownership, tax revenue, and governance purposes as was the tradition in Medieval England.
The name of the parish derived from the Saxon language, meaning "Pig Hill", a less than salubrious name one might imagine. However, the villagers did rear pigs, and other livestock, as well as labouring on the agricultural farms around the edges of the village. In fact, the "Gloucester Old Spot" pig, which was reared on the land, was a magnificent example of its species, and the tenant farmers were rightly proud of their unique produce.
Life in the village was fair. The people worked hard but were adequately sustained from their endeavours. The village contained a manor house, a church, rectory, and about a dozen dwellings. Some were rented, and some were freehold. It was in one of these freehold cottages that Margaret Bowen lived, with her husband William. William (known to everyone as Will) was a labourer on

the nearby farm, known as Manor Farm, and Margaret (known to everyone as Meg) was an accomplished weaver, renowned for the quality of the wool she produced.  In addition to weaving wool, she was also able to make garments that were much sought after, when she had the time and surplus wool to work with.  Both Will and Meg were industrious, hardworking people. They were loved in the village by all their neighbours and known to be kind and helpful to all.
"Mornin' Meg." Mary Forrester called out. As Meg passed her cottage on her way to taking lunch out to Will in the fields, she saw that Mary was scrubbing some clothes against an old wash board, up to her elbows in frothy water, while her two infant boys, Roger and Ned, played on the floor next to her. "I'll kill them kids! I don't know how they make such a mess!"
"Morning Mary, will we be walking to the market together tomorrow?" Meg replied.
"Roger! Take that worm out of your brother's mouth!" Mary cried, rushing over to her youngest son, trying to take the worm out of his mouth and at the same time clipping Roger round the head, for feeding it to him in the first place, "Oh Aye!  Meet you by the bridge? Early mind!" responding to Mary's question.
"Of course!  Will you be bringing both the boys?"  Meg laughed, as two-year-old Roger began washing his hands in the clothes bucket.
"You little bugger!" Mary said cuffing him again.
"Hugh'll be working on the farm. So, I'll have to bring

them along..." she continued the dual conversations at the same time.

"I'll see you tomorrow then!" Meg confirmed, skipping away towards the fields. As she came towards the end of the village, she saw Old Mother Sawyer standing by the side of the road.

"Morning Mother!" she called out.

"Morning Meg! Could I have a word?" The old lady replied.

"Of course!"

Old Mother Sawyer took Meg by the elbow and drew her to the side of the road.

"How are you feeling?" She asked.

"I'm fine." Meg responded.

"Good. No sickness yet, then?"

"What? Why would I be sick?"

"Good! Good!" Old Mother Sawyer responded with a chuckle and a naughty glint in her eye.

"No!" Meg gasped. "You're not telling me.... No! I don't believe it!"

"But you have been trying?"

"Well yes.. but!"

The old woman laughed again. "Here! Take these." She said, handing over a small pouch. "Some herbs when you do start feeling sick. Take them just before you go to bed."

"Old Mother, it is too soon!"

"Take them when you need to and let me know when you need some more."

Meg took the pouch and slipped it into her sleeve. She had missed one of her fluxes but had not told anyone yet. She had thought that it was much too soon and did not want to tempt fate. The old lady gently tapped her on the back of the hand and winked at her, before beginning to walk away. Meg stood by the side of the road, dumbstruck! She knew that Old Mother Sawyer had a reputation for predicting pregnancies, but this was absurd!

As May moved into June, Meg found that she was with child. This was joyous news, not just for the Bowens, but for the rest of the village too. Old Mother Sawyer officially confirmed the news, and then of course, everyone in the village knew! Pregnancy and the birth of a child were a precious resource, and special within these communities, as they enabled the continuation of the cycle of life within the village.

Although all pregnancies were fraught with danger for both mother and child during this period in history, Old Mother Sawyer was trusted to oversee the births of all children within the parish, and she had a remarkable record for ensuring that mothers were cared for, and births were successful. She was revered and trusted in the community, and although the church might frown upon her activities, the local people, trusted her completely. All children in the village, were treated as children of the village, and became part of the extended families of all the neighbours and friends, cementing their importance in this fragile society.

On hearing the news, the Lord of the Manor of Swindon Village himself paid the Bowen's a visit.

"Mrs Bowen, I hear congratulations are in order!" Richard Moryn exclaimed. He grinned from ear to ear. "Apparently so! My Lord." Meg replied, her cheeks flushed with the attention from this important person. "Well, a little something from my wife and myself!" he declared handing Meg a beautiful bunch of wild flowers, and a bottle of dark red wine to Will. Meg did a little curtsy, and Will began to bow but was stopped by Moryn, who instead, gripped his hand and gave it a hearty shake. "Well done Will! Mrs Bowen.." and then Moryn himself, bowed down to both of them, right leg bent, left delicately straight in front of him, finishing with an extravagant flourish of the hat he held in his hand.

"Thank you! My Lord!" Meg laughed and returned the compliment with another, much more sophisticated curtsy of her own.

"Now, now! My Lord!" Will joined in the laughter, "I hope you are not flirting with my wife, Sire!"

Moryn liked Will, he was a hard worker, who was well-known and well-liked in the village. He was a huge, loveable giant of a man, whose thick blonde locks were the envy of many a woman. He would do anything for anyone. His courtship of Meg, and eventual match with her, had been the talk of the village. When they inevitably became married, it was an occasion of pure joy, rarely equalled in the tight knit community.

"I'll have you know, Mr Bowen, that I am a happily married man!" Moryn responded, "However, you are an extremely lucky man!"

Meg blushed again, and they all laughed. Moryn was an important person in his own right, but was, in truth, merely the overseer for the land, and rented his own home, from the "Over Lord", Robert de Vere, who owned lands and properties across the county, and beyond.

Richard Moryn was the local landlord, but owed his fealty to the major landowner, and was in effect, the manager and administrator of the buildings, tenants, and farms that constituted the village and its immediate surrounds. He was responsible for ensuring that the relevant tithes were collected and paid. He was known as a fair and honest man, who treated the villagers with respect and tolerance, protecting both his own interests and the interests of the villagers in equal measure. He had realised long ago that happy villagers were productive villagers, and always made a point of celebrating special occasions with his charges.

**January 1469**

"Will! Will! I think it is time!" Meg called out. It was early morning, and Will had stoked the hearth fire from the embers of the night before and was about to put an armful of logs around the lit kindling.

"Oh MY LORD!" he cried, dropping the logs and stumbling over them to reach Meg. "Oh MY LORD!"
"You need to get Old Mother Sawyer…" Meg instructed him.

"It's really happening! Oh my Lord!" Will said, bumbling about, not knowing where to put himself.

"You need to go now!" Meg confirmed, laughing at her temporarily inept husband.

Will walked towards the door, "Yes! Now! Mother Sawyer!" he said mostly to himself, before realising he was still in his under breeches and undershirt. He rushed over to Meg, and hugged her, just a little too firmly.

"Careful! You big lump!" she chuckled, pushing him away. "Thank heavens men don't have babies!"
"Thank heavens!" Will repeated, as he pulled on his trousers, and fumbled about trying to pull his jumper over his head. At the first attempt he put his head into a sleeve, and his arm out the neck.

"Come here!" Meg laughed, "Calm down!" she guided his relevant body parts into the correct holes and pushed him away.

"Mother Sawyer! Now!" he repeated, as if it were a shopping list, and moved towards the door again. "Boots!" Meg called, as he started to go out through the door.

"Boots! Right!" he said. He found his boots and pulled them on, hopping around in his haste.

"I'll have already had the baby by the time you get back, at this rate!" Meg shouted after him, as he finally left in some semblance of order.

The thick January snow covered the ground all around. A weak winter sun glistened across its surface, creating the hints of diamonds hidden just below, which disappeared as you approached them, only to reappear a few feet further on. Will trudged through the knee-deep blanket, a satisfying crunch as his boots broke the surface. When he reached the main street, much of the snow had already turned to mush, as the local people went about their business. Although, new flakes were still falling in abundance.

"Old Mother Sawyer! Now! Baby coming!" Will muttered the mantra to himself, not hearing the greetings called out to him along his journey. As he ran,

he slipped and slid, arms flailing like a demented windmill in his attempt to keep his balance.
The thatch on the roofs had a hat of snow, and all the cottages looked like little snow hills with doors in. Apart from those doing essential work, most families were huddled inside.

"Old Mother Sawyer! Now! Baby coming!", as he passed children building snowmen and throwing snowballs at each other.

With the snow still falling steadily, he finally arrived at Old Mother Sawyers cottage, He considered it to be one of the most important journeys of his life. A distance of about 300 yards….. Still in an absolute panic, he ran to her door and banged on it. Old Mother Sawyer opened the door almost immediately, and much to Will's surprise, was already properly equipped to walk out of the door. She was fully dressed and had a basket in her hand.

"Now! Old Baby Mother! Sawyer Coming!" he burbled, fluffing the most important lines he had ever needed to say….. apart from those other important words…. "I do!" – and if he had got those two the wrong way round, he would not have been in his current situation!
 "No need to make such a noise, young man!" she said, moving past him, through the door. Stunned into silence, Will turned, and mutely followed the old woman back to his cottage. Old Mother Sawyer

radiated a confidence that was hard to gainsay, and therefore Will trailed after her, prepared to do whatever he was told!

The journey back to Will and Meg's cottage was far more orderly and efficient than the expedition the other way and seemed to be achieved in a fraction of the time.

"Will. Will! Go and ask Mary to come, please!" The old lady instructed as they approached the Forresters cottage. Will complied. Old Mother Sawyer trusted Mary, and often asked her to help whenever there was a new birth. Mary left her two children with her husband Hugh and hurried to catch up with the striding Mother Sawyer, who seemed to float over the ground, and the giant windmill, that was Will Bowen.

When they arrived at the cottage, Mother Sawyer entered and efficiently took charge of proceedings. One of her first orders was for Will to make himself scarce.

"Will! Go and find some of your reprehensible friends and get them to take you to the Cross Hands!" She commanded. "If you stay here, you will frighten the new born to death! And today we are trying to achieve the opposite of that condition!!

Meg, put her hands in front of her mouth in a vain attempt to stifle a laugh. Mary just guffawed at the golden colossus who looked like a lost kitten.

"We will send someone to find you, when we need you!" the old lady stated as together with Mary they pushed him out the door.

As Will was being unceremoniously pushed outside his own cottage, he noticed a large gathering of men standing outside. When he appeared, they all started cheering. Realising that Hugh Forrester had already spread the news, he smiled and waved his hands in the air, enjoying the celebrity status. The group rushed forward clapping him on the back, shaking his hand, and commenting on his good fortune.

"I'm not counting any chickens yet!" he called out above the merry banter and congratulations.

"'Tis no matter, young Will!" one of his neighbours said, "It's an excuse to go to the Inn!"

Another added, "Aye, I don't know the last time my wife actually pushed me out the door and told me to go to the Inn!" to the laughing agreement of the rest of the crowd.

The happy group began plodding through the snow towards the Cross Hands Inn, the nearest alehouse to the village. It was only a short journey of about half a mile, and even in the snowbound conditions, it took little more than ten minutes.

The inn itself was situated at a major crossroads on the routes towards Cheltenham, Gloucester and Tewkesbury, and served weary travellers as well as being a popular haunt for the locals. It had a reputation for attracting some unsavoury characters and had been the scene of fights between rival villages on more than one occasion. The inn was a large one storey construction, with oak cross beams, and wattle and daub walls. There was a large single, entertaining room, with rooms to accommodate guests at the rear.

The family who owned the inn, lived in three rooms to the side of the building and entered it through the kitchens. In truth the building had seen better days. Its exterior walls were dirty, mainly from the mud from the road being blown against them, the thatch was in desperate need of repair, and a number of bird nests could be seen buried within it. The constantly burning fire inside had stained the walls, a deep orange, and because of the size of the main room, it was always very dark, despite the chimney opening, there was always a smoky fog inside the building.

When he arrived at the Cross Hand Inn, there was a good gathering of other local men, who were taking advantage of the inclement weather, and the impromptu day off serious work.

By mid-morning a nervous Will sat at a table towards the back of the inn, nursing a jug of strong ale. He realised that there was nothing he could do now but wait and worry. This was their first child. He knew that Meg was fit, young, and healthy, but he also knew that childbirth was precarious, and anything could happen.

Some of the other men at the inn, known to Will, came over and clapped him on the shoulder and made encouraging noises. Others laughed and joked and tried to allay his fears. "Come on Will! Get this down yer!" One local said, "Aye, there will be plenty of time to rue your freedom to come down to the Inn, after the baby is born!" exclaimed another.

On cue, several jugs of ale were passed his way, and he was encouraged to join in and forget his fears. "Wet the baby's head now, m'lad" shouted an old timer in the corner, before adding "You'll have no time once it's born!" to gales of laughter from the other patrons. Despite himself, Will was unable to refuse the kind offers, and gradually he began to relax and enjoy the atmosphere, and after a while he joined in.

His previously sombre mood was lightened by the camaraderie of his friends and neighbours.

❖

Meg's contractions were now coming more frequently. Mary was fussing around making sure that water was on the boil and fresh linen and towels were available. Old Mother Sawyer looked on, waiting for the right time to take charge.

Every now and again Mary would dab a cloth against Meg's brow, and whisper reassurances to her, "You're doing fine, my love, keep your strength up." she said. Meg panted and breathed, panted, and breathed, as best she could. In her hand she clutched a wooden crucifix. She grasped it so hard it would probably be imprinted into her palm by the end of the ordeal. Old Mother Sawyer sat on a stool near the kitchen table, doing nothing but keeping an eye on proceedings. She would be needed soon enough, but not quite yet. Finally, she judged that the time had come. She moved over to the bed with some herbs tied in a bundle in her hand.

"Shhh! now, my girl, shhhh! It is time." She shook the herbs around the edges of the bed and over Meg, and then she placed them in the hand not holding the crucifix. "Hold these dear." she said. "When it is hard to breathe, bring them up to your face, and breathe in their scent". She gently brought Meg's hand up towards her face and said, "Try now".

Meg breathed in deeply; the scent was refreshing and pure. It did help her to breathe more clearly. Old Mother Sawyer moved to the bottom of the bed, and leaned over "Mary, bring that pot over and plenty of clean cloths", with that she looked up into Meg's face "Time to push Meg, Push! PUSH!

Meg's face contorted in agony as she tried to push. It felt like she was being ripped apart. She relaxed for a short while, until Old Mother Sawyer urged her to push again. Time passed, and Meg was exhausted, but still she battled against the pain. "Push girl!" she heard from somewhere distant. She pushed as hard as she could, crying out aloud and thinking that her heart was about to burst, and then with a slippery slush, the burden was released.

Meg was too exhausted to lift her head and see what was happening. A few seconds went by, but they seemed like hours to Meg "Is she alright?" she sobbed, pushing a lank strand of hair away from her pale and fatigued face.

"There is nothing wrong, child. Everything is fine."
At just that moment a small squeal was made, followed by the screeching and wailing of the child, as it was unceremoniously brought into the world, and began to take its first independent breaths. "Hush now little one" Old Mother Sawyer crooned, "Meg you have a beautiful new daughter!"

Old Mother Sawyer swaddled the babe and brought her to her mother's breast. "There, there, relax now." As old Mother Sawyer moved away towards the hearth where she had some more herbs brewing, an exhausted Meg drifted off to sleep.

Outside the Cross Hands Inn, there was a commotion. Will, having become less morose with the aid of multiple refreshments, and slightly the worse for wear, looked up. He was having some difficulty remembering where he was and why he was here.

The door of the inn burst open, and a gaggle of young children launched themselves through the door. "Will! Will!" they cried in unison "The baby has arrived, and we have been sent to bring you home!"

A loud cheer went up within the Inn, as everyone congratulated Will, more ales were ordered, and the merriment continued. "No rush Will!" said one of the regulars "One more for the road son!" and pushed a mug into his hand. Will tried to resist, but it was clear that no-one in the inn was going to let him leave, without first being able to have a celebratory drink with him. Will relented and downed the strong-tasting ale; to be honest most of it went down his shirt. Finally, slamming the mug down on the table, Will staggered to his feet, suddenly remembering everything. He needed to get home to Meg. "Are they both ok?" he cried, as he lurched towards the door, and promptly fell flat on his face.

Members of the group picked Will up from his prone position and marched triumphantly off down the road. No-one took much notice of the sullen figure, sitting in the shadows of the far corner of the inn.

Godfrey Bowen scowled at the frivolity, with a countenance of jealousy, malice etched across his face. He was not happy that there was now an heir to the Bowen cottage.

Will gradually floated up from the depths of his alcohol induced coma. As he roused, he felt as if he was on a ship, being thrown around in a storm. He was looking up at the sky, and he could feel movement, and then lots of laughing and singing.

He realised he was being held aloft on his back, being carried by a few of his friends and fellow villagers.

He looked around gingerly, and could see from the corner of his eye, a whole crowd of happy, joyous, dancing, people around him, as he was paraded in the air, like a stricken king, being carried back to the village.

It seemed as if the whole village had come outside in the dreadful weather to celebrate! Will suddenly realised, "I am a Father!"

As the cheering crowd neared his cottage, he heard the voice of Old Mother Sawyer admonish the happy mob. "Will you keep that noise down, you drunken rabble!" she half-shouted, in an attempt to quiet down the din. The raucous group became much quieter suddenly, responding to the old woman's reprimand, although there were more than a few burps and subsequent giggles.

"The new mother is sleeping." Old Mother Sawyer whispered, bringing her finger to her lips in a "shushing" motion. "Both are healthy and fine" she exclaimed lowering her finger and her face broke out into a broad smile.

Despite themselves and their severe telling off, the crowd could not contain themselves and an enormous cheer rang out, and hats were thrown into the air. "Three cheers for Will and Meg!" someone shouted, and as the cheers echoed around him, Will was lowered to the floor, as gently as could be expected from a group of staggering drunken men. People started making snowballs and throwing them at each other. It was as if half the village had become children again. Will laughed out loud with all the joy he felt, and then threw up all over his nearest neighbour!

A slightly befuddled Will was helped into the house by the surprisingly strong Old Mother Sawyer. He looked into the gloom. The hearth was alight, and candles were place strategically around the room. He looked over towards the bed and saw his beautiful wife asleep, and next to her a small bundle, also asleep. He moved towards the bed and leaned over to kiss Meg on the forehead. "My beautiful girls!" he whispered, as tears formed in his eyes. He did not notice the red crystal pendant pinned to the shawl wrapped around the baby.

A couple of days later, after Meg had had a chance to recover somewhat from her labour, she insisted that she, the baby and Will visit Old Mother Sawyer, bearing gifts and thanks for the safe delivery of their daughter. Will had caught some rabbits, and had purchased a partridge and some decent wine from the landlord at the Cross Hands Inn. Meg had agreed that these were suitable presents for the purpose. The happy trio set off across the village, nodding greetings to neighbours as they passed.

The snow had relented somewhat and now there were just some remaining clumps scattered here and there, now more ice than snow.

They arrived at the rickety old shack that old Mother Sawyer called home. Meg knocked on the door. It opened mysteriously, and they heard the old lady call from somewhere inside "Come in, Children!" Will looked at Meg, mystified, and mouthed at Meg "How does she do that!?" Meg smiled and shook her head in wonder, urging him to go inside by gently pushing him forwards.

They both entered and saw Old Mother Sawyer sitting contentedly by her fire. She beckoned them forward and invited them to sit. Meg sat on a stool, with the baby snuggled in a shawl clutched to her breast.

"We have brought some food, to thank you for what you have done." Meg stated, "We are both so grateful!" "It was nothing child." The old woman replied, "it is always a wonder to bring a new life into the world." Will placed the offerings onto the table and looking about the inside of the cottage declared "Mother, you have some things that need to be repaired!"

"Tis of no account." She responded.

"But I would be happy to do the repairs for you!" Will stated enthusiastically "It is the least we could do!" he added, as he leaned forward and caught a drip that had fallen from somewhere in the thatching.

"That would be very kind of you." Old Mother Sawyer replied. "May I see the baby?" she enquired, looking at Meg.

"Of course!" Here." Meg said lifting the baby over to the old woman. Old Mother Sawyer held the child and looked into her eyes "Beautiful!" she crooned. She looked back down at the sleeping child, and noticed the pendant pinned to her shawl. She flicked her eyes back to Meg's, smiled and nodded her head. "Have you named her yet?" She asked, gently stroking the few golden wisps of hair, already growing on the baby's head.

"She is called Maud!" Meg replied.

They chatted away for a while, drinking a delicious broth that the old woman had made. "You must give me the recipe for this!" Meg exclaimed, licking her lips. "Of course!" Old Mother Sawyer replied. "That, and much more." She added enigmatically.

Will looked around, surveying the work that needed to be done, and could not help wondering about this strange old woman, who did so much for the village. She seemed to be part of the fabric of the village. She seemed to be as old as the village itself. She had no local relatives, and even his parents had only ever known her as an old woman. Now they were dead, and she was, still here.

He shook his head in disbelief.

Believing that they had taken up enough of the old lady's time, Will and Meg rose preparing to beg their leave, Old Mother Sawyer stayed them with her hand. "I have something for each of you." She said and wandered over to a shelf on the wall at the back of the cottage.

"Please!" cried Will and Meg simultaneously "There is no need! You have done enough!"

"They are just small trinkets." She replied, "Of no value, just charms for luck." She turned and held them out. "I would love you to have them."

She placed a delicate silver ring, in the palm of Meg's hand, and then gave Will a small silver coin. The coin looked ancient and was not tender currently in use. Meg slipped the ring onto her little finger. It fitted perfectly!

Will looked at the coin in wonder. There was a figurehead on one side crowned with laurel leaves, and on the other an emblem of an eagle clutching two spears in its claws. It was beautiful!

"I can't take this from you, Mother!" Will stated assertively, convinced of its value. As if reading his mind, the old lady leaned across to him and whispered in his ear "It is only of value to me, if you have it."

❖

During this turbulent period of history, when the fate of Kings was being decided, villages such as Swindon generally played little part in events.  Land changed hands between the great Lords, dependent on the successes of the individual 'ruler' they had supported.

However, life in the villages went on, largely unaffected by the political tumult, happening at a national level. Villagers were sometimes called upon to play their part in protecting the interests of their 'Lords' and were obliged to become part of their "armies", when disputes took place, or larger conflicts arose.  When called up for these types of duties, their role was really to bolster the size of the force, rather than to take decisive action.

Being largely untrained and with limited access to weapons, their real importance lay in maintaining the land, rather than fighting.  Nevertheless, many were skilled with the primitive weapons available to them, particularly, the bow.  However, these types of events did not happen often, and the local 'Lords' and the villagers were generally left to live their lives, ignorant of tribulations that the nobles caused for themselves. Nevertheless, the possibility of becoming embroiled in such situations was always an ever-present threat.

Unbeknown to them at this time, Will and Meg would be drawn into intrigues and acts that fell far outside their sphere of knowledge and experience. These events would resonate down the centuries.

# CHAPTER 2

## A Nefarious Rogue

### 1469 – Cross Hands Inn, Near Swindon Village

"Get me another ale girl!" Godfrey Bowen called out to the young serving girl, holding his mug aloft. The girl approached to take the mug from his hand, and Godfrey grabbed her and pulled her onto his lap, groping her as he did so.

"Let me go!" the girl screamed, wriggling and writhing to get free. Godfrey finally relented with a laugh and released his grip. The girl pushed him in the face as she regained her footing and ran off.

His friends who were sat around the table leered after the girl.

"She didn't put up too much of fight!" snorted Jack Garvey.

"Fiery enough!" Richard Wendley contended.

"She'd be too much for you, old man!" Peter Smith sneered at Wendley.

Godfrey glanced up to see the landlord of the Cross Hands Inn approaching their table. He carried a brimming mug of ale and a cudgel.

"Uh oh! Trouble coming, Godfrey!" Geoffrey Holder sniggered.

Godfrey rose from the table and turned his powerful 5'8" frame towards the threat. He brushed some strands of his long, greasy, brown hair back from his face, and stared threateningly at the landlord, who was now only a few feet away.

The landlord stopped short, reconsidering his bravado. He knew that Godfrey Bowen was an outlaw, who was known to have a violent temper and be utterly ruthless. The fact that he had four equally dangerous companions with him, sealed the decision. Retaining some of his courage, and not wanting to lose face in front of his other patrons, he leaned forward and slammed the mug down on the table, spilling a considerable amount of its contents.

"You leave my daughter be!" he declared, "or that'll be your last drink tonight!"

Godfrey looked down at the spilled ale, as it dribbled off the edge of the table, and then looked back up at the landlord.

"I think you need to top that back up." Godfrey replied slowly and deliberately, with an undertone of menace.

"I don't want no trouble 'ere t'night!" the landlord said. "We've too many people in." and he waved his arm to encompass the room. Godfrey scowled and turned his gaze to look at the other customers packed into every corner of the inn. Everyone was staring at them, keen to know what was going to happen.

Godfrey allowed his anger to subside. "We've got better things to do than create a ruckus tonight. Keep the ale coming, and you'll get no trouble from us." He said pointing down at the half-filled mug.

The landlord conceded with a nod, picked up the mug and walked away.

Godfrey looked at the faces of people in the room and stared them out, challenging someone to say something. Gradually they all adverted their eyes and returned to their own conversations.

"Useless peasants!" he muttered, "You spend all your lives working like slaves for a pittance. I will never be yolked like you!"

Godfrey was contemptuous of them all. He lived rough, in the hedgerows and woodlands around the area, often spending an entire evening and night drinking and then falling asleep in some hostelry. The owners of the local inns in the area were never happy about this, but few were brave enough to confront him, and just let him be. As the Cross Hands was his favourite inn, the landlord of this hostelry knew this better than most.

Godfrey sat back down, as the landlord brought over more ale, the five mugs expertly balanced in his arms. Holder took the top two, allowing the landlord to place the others down. The landlord walked off wearily. He sighed as he thought once again how the reputation of his inn suffered because of the people who frequented it.

"Phew! That was close!" Garvey said, the sarcastic undertone to his comment did not go unnoticed by his comrades.

"Shall we get on with it?" Wendley enquired.

"Tell us." Godfrey growled. He often worked alone, but sometimes he needed the assistance of his gang. He used them when the prize was worth it and could not be achieved by himself alone. Tonight, was such an occasion.

As Wendley began to speak in a hushed tone, the rest of the men hunched forward to listen.

"He travels from Gloucester to Tewkesbury every other day, except Sundays" he stated. "He usually travels with a group of other traders, but some days he travels alone, just him and his family." He picked up his mug and noticed it was close to empty. Looking around, he raised his mug towards the serving maid, standing against the wall near to the kegs "More ale!" he bellowed. The young woman blushed and nodded, hurrying to pour a measure into another jug.

"And what would be the takings?" enquired Godfrey "What is it worth for us?" taking a deep draught of ale from his mug, and then licking his lips.

Wendley leaned over the table, and whispered, "He trades in pennies, but I have heard he exchanges his profits into gold and silver. He wants to rent a house and land. Last I heard, he nearly has enough. He is already close enough to start negotiating for some land near Boddington," he continued, the other men leaned in closer to hear better, "He carries a purse with his earnings from the market, and always has some extra to buy more goods. If we catch him at the right time, he will have his profits from the day, plus the extra he always carries."

Godfrey belched, after draining his mug of ale, "Another for me too," he said to the young serving maid, who had arrived with Wendley's new mug brimming with ale. Godfrey waited until the girl had picked up his mug and moved away, before asking "Where does he keep his savings?"

"In a strong box, under the boards of his cart" Wendley responded.

"So, it needs to be soon then?" Holding murmured, wiping his greasy hair away from where it had fallen across his brow, before reaching across and picking up the loaf which sat in the middle of the table. He broke off a chunk of bread and dipped it into the bowl of broth in front of him, before bringing it up to his mouth and sucking on it, and then popping it into his mouth with a slurp.

The group nodded in unison as Wendley replied "Tomorrow."

Godfrey lived off his wits, he did not have a job, but generally had money. This money was earned doing whatever people wanted him to do. Together with his gang, he acted as an enforcer for local landowners, he was engaged in accessing information and selling it to whoever needed it, he was involved in theft and robbery, targeting weary travellers on the road, and he was certainly not averse to committing murder when it was necessary. All in all, he was not a pleasant person.

❖

Two nights later……..

The night was cold, and the Tewkesbury Road from Gloucester was dark and desolate. Thomas Hodgekins held the bridle of Old Bess, his faithful horse that pulled the cart laden with his goods. He crouched over, pulling his cloak more tightly around himself, trying to ward off the strengthening wind. "Just my luck." he murmured to himself, "It's going to rain, just to add to my woes!." The cart also held his wife Beth and his daughter Gwen. Both were huddled together on the bench at the front of the cart, sheltering from the brisk wind, and quietly feeling sorry for themselves.

"How are you feelin' Beth?" he asked.

"Not good Thomas. I reckon it was those left over elvers." She replied.

"Aye, I didn't eat any of them, just you and Gwen."

Having been detained in Gloucester for longer than he would have liked because both Beth and Gwen had felt ill with stomach upsets, it had been some time before they both felt well enough to leave.

He wondered if it had been the elvers they had eaten at lunch time that had caused the problems. The elvers had been left over from those he had brought from Tewkesbury to Gloucester the previous day, to sell, and he now questioned the wisdom of eating them, having sold most of them very early in the morning.

"I hope none of the customers get ill, we can't afford it, if people buy from someone else." Beth said.

"Aye, I'll be having a word with that trader, and I'll not be trusting his word again!" Thomas replied.

"I'm sorry we have made you leave so late!"

"Can't be helped my love. It's 11 miles to Tewkesbury, we've done it before. It would've been good to leave a few hours earlier."

Thomas was well acquainted with the road, and he had made the journey many times, moving as he did between the markets of the two large towns buying and selling a variety of goods.

"I don't like travelling on the road alone at night. If we hadn't held you up, we could have left with some of the others." Beth commented.

"No point in fretting now. If we stop at the Swann at Coombe Hill, we can still make to the market in time."

"Yeah! We can get some food and a few hours sleep at the inn!"

"It'll take us just over an hour tomorrow morning, so we'll have to be up bright and early!"

They really had little choice but to continue their journey. Thomas had had a good day at Gloucester market and had sold all his wares, apart from the left over elvers, making a handsome profit.

Before he had left the city, he had bought some goods to sell at Tewkesbury the following day, including some fresh fish, purchased at the docks, and pies bought at the market. If these were not ready to sell first thing in the morning, then they would turn and be inedible, so the choice had been made for them.

He had a solid reputation to keep, and so they had to leave, and make the journey towards Tewkesbury that evening.

"You get some sleep my love, we'll be at the inn in less than an hour." Thomas said.

"Alright, my darling. Wake me if you need anything." Beth snuggled up closer to Gwen and pulled the blanket tightly around them both.

They had just passed the few ramshackle homes which stood back from the road, just outside the village of Norton, and were now only a short distance from the sanctuary of the inn. The church of St Mary at Priors Norton, on the right-hand side of the road, known as the 'sinking church', just visible in the available moonlight, sank behind the hill. Within the hour, they would be sitting next to a roaring fire, with food inside them and a straw bed to sleep on.

As Thomas mused over his problems, a man on horseback dressed all in black galloped past him at speed. A short distance up the road, the rider pulled his horse up abruptly, and turned back to stare at Thomas. There was an ominous challenge on the man's face, and then a smile. Without speaking the rider turned and galloped away.

Thomas was perturbed by the encounter, "Very odd" he thought. He looked over Old Bess into the cart. Beth and Gwen were asleep, and the strange horse and rider, had not disturbed them.

As darkness gathered all around, Thomas and his family continued to trudge their way towards Coombe Hill, only quarter of a mile away...

❖

Four men sat on their horses, in the woods, just off the main road between Gloucester and Tewkesbury. The horses shuffled in the darkness but were kept under tight rein by their riders. The horses were clearly agitated, and their ears had pricked up. "Quiet girl, hush now" the leader of the group whispered to his horse.

Despite the wind, the beating sound of horse hooves could be determined, coming from the direction of Gloucester. "This should be him," Godfrey stated, looking around at the others. "About time." muttered Geoffrey Holder, to his companion Jack Garvey, "It's cold enough to shrivel my stones!" Garvey suppressed a laugh "Hopefully this will have been worth it" he replied.

They all began to advance out of the copse and onto the road. Richard Wendley, pulled his horse up at the sight of them emerging from the woodlands.

"Where have you been?" Godfrey asked his anger obvious from the scowl on his face.

"He is on his way" he exclaimed slightly out of breath, matching the panting of his horse. "He left much later than usual" he continued "But that is our fortune, because he is definitely alone."

"How far? Enquired Peter Smith.

"Less than half a mile" Wendley responded.

"Right then, Peter and you Geoffrey, go past them and then make your way back. The rest of us will approach them from this side. We need to catch them before The Leigh." Godfrey commanded.

Holder and Smith, set off down the road at a gallop, and the rest of the group cantered in their wake.

Thomas heard the sound of horses before he saw them. He had just crossed the wooden bridge across the River Chelt and was making his way along a relatively straight stretch of road, approaching the lane which turned off toward The Leigh.

The riders were approaching at speed, and Thomas moved Old Bess over towards the side of the road, by nudging her with his shoulder. Old Bess whickered, and slowly moved across.

The two horsemen sped passed without greeting, and Thomas thought no more about them. He expected to hear their hooves clatter across the bridge, but that expected noise did not come. He turned around to see the two men halted just before the bridge, turning around to face him.

Thomas began to realise that this was a threat to him and his family. "Beth! Beth!" he called out quietly "Get Gwen off the cart and into the trees! Now, woman!

Beth, who was still not feeling herself and only just waking from her slumber, was not immediately able to comprehend what her husband was saying to her, "What is it Tom?" she said.

"Men," he replied, "and they don't look like they are up to any good!" he continued. "Get out of the cart, and get the girl to the woods, quick now!"

Beth shook Gwen, and they both began to climb down from the cart.

The two horsemen were now trotting up the road towards Thomas. At the same time, Thomas heard more hooves, coming from the other direction. He could see three other horses and riders bearing down on them. "Thank goodness!" he thought, "someone is coming to help us." A moment later, his hopes were dashed as the new riders came to a stop directly in front of Thomas and his cart; the man at the front was staring malevolently at him. No help was coming from these men.

Beth and Gwen had not got any further than getting out of the cart and were cowering by the flank of Old Bess. "What's happening" Cried Beth,

"I don't know, but it doesn't look good" Thomas said as he leaned into the cart to remove his long staff.

"I don't know what you men want" Thomas challenged "but you leave us be, and no-one needs to get hurt."

Godfrey, on the horse nearest to Thomas, laughed out loud, the others laughed too.

"Take him!" Godfrey ordered, and Wendley and Garvey moved forward to confront Thomas.

"Run Beth! Run Gwen!" Thomas cried as he swung his staff towards Wendley. Beth grabbed her daughter, and Gwen shrieked in fear, as they ran off towards the edge of the road, in the direction of the woods, and possible sanctuary.

Thomas's swing had caught Wendley and put him off balance, having been struck on his shoulder. Enraged he pushed his horse closer, pinning Thomas between his horse and the side of the cart. Old Bess whinnied and began to move forward, Thomas stumbled with the sudden movement and as he did so, Wendley struck down with his sword, striking Thomas just below his head. Wendley forced his arm forward, and his sword punctured Thomas in the neck. Garvey, who had also been approaching, stabbed at the stumbling Thomas, piercing him in the stomach. "Murder!" cried Thomas, as he slid to the floor.

Beth could hear the commotion behind her but was too frightened to turn around. Instead, she ran as fast as she could, trying to get into the trees and hide. Just as she jumped off the road, with the trees only a few yards away, she was pulled up short. One of the two riders who had come up behind their cart, Peter Smith, had grabbed Gwen, and pulled her back. Beth had been brought to a standstill by the tug on her hand and Gwen was forced to release her grip. The other rider, Geoffrey Holder, stood to the side of the man holding Gwen.

"Well, what have we got here?" rasped Smith, a wide grin spreading across his face. Holder was grinning too. Beth looked at both men, terror gripping her. Neither of these men was wearing a mask……

❖

The owner of the Swann Inn was clearing up in the front yard of the inn, before closing up for the night, collecting mugs and platters.

At this time of night, he did not expect any more patrons today.

He looked down the road at the obvious clatter of horses and riders coming towards him. Five men sped past, black cloaks billowing in the wind. He watched as they turned off at the junction, down the Tewkesbury Road back towards Cheltenham, and disappeared into the distance and darkness

He shivered inwardly, as if someone had walked over his grave, "Evil is abroad tonight" he thought dismally.

❖

The following morning, just after sunrise, Wat Symonds, a farm hand, who lived in Priors Norton and worked in the fields at The Leigh, had found Old Bess and the cart on the road. Normally, he got to work across the fields rather than along the main road. It was a short cut he knew like the back of his hand.

As he clambered over the low wall to cross, he noticed the abandoned horse and cart. With his interest stirred he walked over. He hobbled the old horse and looked behind the cart. He could see pies and fish strewn all across and down the length of the road. He could also see what seemed to be a heap of clothes in the middle of it.

He wandered closer, confused and not quite able to comprehend what he was seeing. As he approached the heap in the middle of the road, he was confronted with the most grisly scene.

The contents of Wat's stomach were ejected forcefully through his mouth, as he looked down on Thomas Hodgekins body, which was lying in the road. Blood had pooled around Thomas's head from a wound at his neck, his head nearly severed from a violent blow, his intestines were extruding from his stomach.

Poor Wat looked around frantically, and noticed something else a little further down, near to the small wood. He reluctantly walked over, now petrified by what he was going to find. If he had had anything left in his stomach, it too would have been spilled; instead he made a dry wretch.

In front of him was the naked body of a young woman, battered and bruised, there was a deep gash across her throat, but that was not the worst thing, a few feet away, lay the small for of a young child, a girl of 5 or 6 years old, her head had been dashed against a large rock, and the contents of her skull had leaked out.

Unable to contain himself, Wat ran back up the road towards the junction with The Leigh "Murder! Murder! Murder!" he screamed as he ran.

# CHAPTER 3 –

## Mischief Abroad

### 1470 – Cross Hands Inn, near Swindon Village

Godfrey sat brooding. His disreputable friends listened to his litany of discontent.

"The cottage in Swindon should have been left to me!" He complained, his fists were balled in anger, as he tried in vain to keep his temper in check. "I am the oldest!"

"You've told us all this before." Holding moaned. "Your mum left it to Will because he had got married. If you had got married first, she would have left it to you…" he added, scratching the scraggly beard that grew on his pock-marked face.

"Why don't you just kill them!" Garvey interjected. Killing people seemed to be his answer to every kind of problem.

"Godfrey would be the first person to be suspected, you idiot!" Wendley countered, shaking his head with disbelief at the stupidity of his colleague in crime. "Everyone knows he wants the cottage."

"What is the problem?" Smith asked, downing the last of his ale.

"Meg is the problem." Godfrey grumbled. "She is the clever one in the family. Will is not so bright. She is respectable, hard-working, and friendly. Everyone loves her. She has Will wrapped around her fingers."

"You should have married her first…" Wendley said, between mouthfuls of mutton.

"She wouldn't have looked twice at me! Little miss perfect!" Godfrey's angry eyes flashed at Wendley, a scowl darkened his face. "The birth of her brat gives me even fewer options."

"Why does the child change anything?" a confused Garvey enquired. He was not a thinker. This wiry, spiteful little man had an attention span as short as his temper.

"They have a freehold for the cottage. The child secures the tenancy for the next generation."

"There must be something we can do." Wendley said, trying to think more positively. He was worried that Godfrey's depression, would drag them all into rash action.

"I should have got rid of my brother years ago! I wouldn't have had these problems if I had done something afore he got married…!"

"You would never have beaten him in a fair fight…. He is huge!" Wendley said.

"Why would anyone fight fair?" Garvey countered. Shaking his head at the naivety of Wendley's response.

"If I am ever to get that cottage I need to take some action.." Godfrey moaned.

The men looked down at their empty trenchers.

"We need more ale!" Holder said.

Godfrey was lost in his own thoughts. "I am industrious! I am smart! Should I have taken a different path in my life?" he mused. "No! I am my own man! I don't want to scrape a living and be beholden to some noble! I will live my life on my own terms!" he determined. Godfrey had no wife, no property, and lived on his wits. This had led to him being introduced to a variety of acquaintances based on their criminal activities. The course of his life was decided many years ago.

The group of men continued debating and considered their options. They had empty trenchers in front of them, having consumed the hearty mutton stew that had been the fayre of the evening. They also had several empty jugs of ale. Smith went to fill his mug, and then noticing that each of the jugs was empty, irritably called over to the serving girl, to get refills. While they waited, Wendley blew his nose noisily into a dirty rag, that he had pulled from his pocket, and Holder snorted and spat a thick gob of saliva onto the floor. Meanwhile, Garvey absent-mindedly picked his nose, and Godfrey ran his fingers through the thick gravy on his trencher, brought them up to his mouth and sucked on them.

When another couple of jugs had been brought over, Godfrey leaned in conspiratorially and spoke. "I need to get rid of him, and the child has become an added problem, but I need to be completely above suspicion." He wiped his hands on his trousers before raising them and beckoning the other men closer still. "I'll arrange to be with someone beyond reproach, who will be able to vouch for me." He continued.

"How many of us do you need?" Garvey asked, whilst avidly studying a juicy nose-morsel on the end of his finger.

"I reckon, three of us will be more than enough." stated Wendley with confidence.

"Three should do it." agreed Godfrey, "But you will need to be careful. He is a strong as a bull, and handy with his fists." He added "Don't take anything for granted…"

"Who's going to do it?" enquired Holder, watching in fascination as Garvey licked the green mess on the end of his finger, and then popped into his mouth.

"He's seen me with you before," he said nodding towards Wendley, "I reckon, it should be the rest of you." He concluded. The other men all nodded their agreement in unison.

When will it be?" Holder asked, pouring himself another mug of ale. Godfrey held out his own mug, and Holder poured ale into it.

"Soon." Godfrey stated, "I'll let you know."

❖

"You coming tonight Will?" Hugh Forrester called across the field. He had put his scythe over his shoulder and was calling it a day.

Will placed the last stone into the wall he had been rebuilding, wiped his hands on his trousers and looked over at his neighbour. "I think I will. It's been a long day." He replied, stretching up to relieve some of the tension in his back.

"C'mon then boys." Hugh shouted to the other men who had been working with him. "Will is actually taking a night off…. And he's paying!"

The other men cheered and downed tools for the day, looking forward to a well-earned drink. They knew that Will was not a big drinker, but he did enjoy a game of cards or dice with his friends, occasionally.

Hugh clapped on the back. "Wife and baby duties can be resumed tomorrow!" he laughed, "You don't get out enough!"

"Don't need to Hugh. I've got everything I need at home!"

"Well, a little absence every now and again, will add spice to the reunion!" Hugh grabbed his crotch and broke into a broad smile.

"Heavens help Mary!" Will snorted, "having to put up with you, and your boys!"

"Girls love bad men!" Hugh responded, tapping the side of his nose, to emphasise the good advice.

"You old rogue!" Will said, as the group joined together and marched off towards the Cross Hands.

"Let's hope the Hester's Way boys are not there tonight!" Hugh added.  Although the Cross-Hands Inn attracted some characters of ill-repute, it did also cater for genuine travellers, and all the local farmers used it as well.  The Hester's Way farmers had a bit of a reputation, especially when they been drinking heavily.

"You know as well as me, they are always there!"  Will replied.

❖

Meg had just finished her work for the day and was putting her loom away.  She had had a productive day, and part of her skill was the speed with which she was able to work.  That speed did not diminish the quality of her work, and she was able to charge a good price for her wares.

Hugh's wife, Mary had come around to visit and had brought her two boisterous progenies with her. They were fascinated by the new baby and were currently trying to tickle Maud through the bars of her crib. Maud herself was crawling around trying to keep out of the way of the annoying duo but gurgling happily at the attention.

"I hope Will does not stay too long today." Meg said.

"Well, you know that Hugh has been trying to get him to go to the Inn for the past couple of days." Mary replied, "and you know he won't give in before Will does, he's annoying like that!"

Meg laughed at her friend's description of her husband, before replying, "Will deserves a night off, he has been working so hard lately. He did tell me this morning, that he would probably go with them, this evening."

"Well, there you go then!" Mary said, "if Will didn't give in soon, Hugh said that him and the boys would kidnap him!" The two women laughed at the shared vision of anyone being able to kidnap someone the size of Will.

"It would take all the men in the village to carry him!" Meg said, and the two women fell about laughing.

When the hilarity had subsided, Meg said, "Are you going to help with the vegetables? The two lumps will be starving by the time they get home!

"Of course!" Mary said, "I brought some onions. You get the meat ready, and I'll do the vegetables." and the two women began the task of preparing the evening meal.

Meg paused for a moment, there was a twinkle in her eye. Mary caught the look and smiling said "What!"

Meg put a finger to her lips and said, "Look!." She went over to a small cupboard and pulled out the wine that Richard Moryn had given them.

"When the fox is away……….!" She laughed pouring two generous measures of the ruby liquid into some cups.

❖

As the group of men approached the Inn the sun was setting on the horizon. The sky was a palette of pink and orange. There was a warm mid-summer breeze, which filled Will felt a sense of contentment. Beside him, his two oldest friends, Hugh and Joff Gilbert joked with each other and exchanged the latest gossip. These three men had known each other since they were children and had always looked out for each other.

"After you Sire!" Joff joked, holding the door of the inn open for Will. Will stood his ground, "No! I insist after you, Sire!" Hugh bundled up behind him and pushed them both inside. "No time for courtesy, boys, I need some ale!"

They found a table close to the casks of ale, and near to the girl who was serving. Hugh signalled to her and she walked over. "Dice please darling! And ale... lots of ale!" he said, the young girl smiled and departed, returning quickly with the dice and drink.

Hugh rolled the dice to see who would start. Their game of choice was 'hazard', and before long several games had been played and several jugs of ale had been consumed. Hugh was in an ebullient mood, having just won the last two hands of dice. They were playing a game of hazard with two dice, and his eyes lit up as with his final roll of the current game, he "nicked" his previous roll of 6, by rolling a 12. "Hah!" he cried, slamming his hand down onto the table in triumph.

"Three games in a row! The luck is with you tonight!" Will exclaimed, smiling warmly at his friend.

"Well, I think that calls for another round!" Joff responded, laughing "I think Hugh is paying!" he added, lightly punching his friend on the shoulder.

"Aghhh! Alright!" Hugh replied good naturedly. He knew that none of them would be out of pocket tonight, they always found some way of evening up the score before they left.

"It'll have to be the last one for me." Will told them, "I need to get back for supper."

"Right oh!" Hugh replied, rising from the table, and edging past Joff who had him penned in.

Jack Garvey and his partners in crime, were sat over on the far side of the bar. Watching Will and his friends intently, whilst supping their own ale. They had attended the bar every evening for the last week, on the chance that Will would come in. Because it was a rare occurrence, they had needed to be patient. Tonight, it was not only Hugh Forrest's luck that was in.

Garvey got up and walked over to John Mortimer. He tapped him on the shoulder, careful not to draw any attention. "John, the bloke we told you about last week.... That's him over there.." he whispered, nodding his head in the direction of Will and his friends.

"The big one, with blonde hair?" Mortimer asked.

"Aye, that one."

"No problems, we'll sort it."

"Remember, he has to walk out of here."

"I know, and thanks for paying for all the ale this week!"

"It will have been worth it."

Mortimer was a farmhand, who worked in the Hestersway area, a short distance further south from the Inn. Mortimer and his friends were notorious brawlers, and most people kept out of their way. Many of the fights that broke out in the Inn were caused by one or other of the Mortimer gang, usually for nothing more than some imagined slight.

"You just keep out of the way for now." Mortimer said as Garvey turned to walk back to his table.

"Make it look good." Garvey responded.

A number of the Swindon village farmers had already left, and only Will and his two friends still remained in the inn.

"Right! That's enough for me for tonight." Will stated.

"Wait for a minute!" Hugh exclaimed "Just one more for the road! You know we are eating with you tonight?"

"Meg did mention it." Will responded.

"Well then, I'll get them in!"

Garvey leaned over towards Holding and Smith. "He'll be leaving soon. We'd better get ready."

The three men rose from their own table and made towards the door. As they passed Mortimer, Garvey nudged him, and Mortimer acknowledged him with a look. As Garvey and his crew left the Inn, Mortimer and his gang, approached the barrels from which the ale was served.

Hugh placed the three mugs down on the bar and called over to the serving girl.

"Three more for me and my friends! And one for yourself!"

The young woman poured the measures and Hugh dropped some coins on the counter-top, before picking up the three mugs and turning to make his way back to his friends.  As he did so he found Mortimer standing directly behind him.  Caught mid-turn Hugh was not able to stop his momentum, and ale splashed out of the over-flowing mugs straight onto Mortimer's chest and belly.  "Whoooaaa! I'm sor…."  Hugh said in shock.  Before he could finish his apology, Mortimer smashed a huge fist straight into Hugh's face.  Hugh went down, poleaxed.  He was unconscious before he hit the floor, his nose a pulp, and blood gushing from it, all over his face.

Joff who had been sat facing the disturbance, rose immediately to go to the assistance of his friend.  Will who had his back to the action, took a little more time to realise what was happening, but started to rise from his seat, having seen the look of shock on Joff's face.

Mortimer now stood, leaning over the unfortunate Hugh.  He was pummelling his face with a flurry of heavy punches. Before Joff could take a step towards the fight, one of Mortimer's associates swung a stool, and struck Joff on the back of the head. The one who had struck the blow, together with another, now began to punch and kick Joff, who had fallen to the floor.

Will did not get a chance to rise out of his chair, as another of Mortimer's gang pushed him forward, and pinned him to the table, punching him in the kidneys as he did so. Will placed his hands flat on the table, and pushed up with all his strength, and was rewarded with a punch to the back of his head, just behind his ear. Momentarily stunned, Will was helpless. He expected further punishment, and when no further blows came, he turned his head. He could see the Mortimer gang leaving the Inn, laughing loudly, and clapping themselves on the back.

The landlord came rushing over, wringing his hands at the scene before him. "Will! Will! Are you alright!" he asked, his face pale.

Will rose gingerly, and touched the back of his head where a lump was forming.

"Seem to be" he replied, looking around the Inn and noticing that the place was now deserted. The other patrons had clearly not wanted to become embroiled in the violence and had sensibly retreated elsewhere.

"Oh my! Oh my!" the landlord kept repeating, cupping his face with his hands, his shock evident.

Will looked at both his friends. Both were unconscious, and clearly badly injured. The attack had taken just a matter of moments. Will fleetingly wondered why he had got off so lightly, before saying to the landlord "Look after them."

Realising that his friends needed some medical help he added, I'll go and get help from the village!"

Although still groggy himself, Will knew he needed the help of some of the other men in the village to carry his friends, and he considered that the person who would be of most use in treating their injuries, would be Old Mother Sawyer.

❖

Along the lane that led to the village, Garvey, Holder and Smith, had secreted themselves in a small thicket. Garvey held a vicious stiletto blade in his hand, the other two carried heavy cudgels. They waited patiently for their prey. If Mortimer had played his part to perfection, and if he and his crew had managed to restrain themselves sufficiently, Will would be the only man standing, and able to raise assistance. Garvey grinned to himself in self-satisfaction "Godfrey will be pleased!" he thought.

Will staggered along, as fast as his feet would carry him. He was still dazed and unsteady on his feet and his only consideration was to get help from the village as quickly as he could. The injuries to his friends had looked serious, and he knew that time was of the essence.

The lane was pitch black, the high hedges loomed over him, and any wooded areas were shrouded with deep, impenetrable shadow. No moon was visible this night to provide respite from the gloom. However, Will had walked this lane a thousand times, and could have done it blindfolded anyway. His urgency fortified his resolve, and his physical strength kept him going, despite his own injuries.

Garvey heard Will coming, before he saw him. He nudged Smith, who was standing beside him, who in turn nudged Holder. There had been no need, as each had already heard the shuffling gait, and panting breaths of the man coming along the lane. Garvey grinned to himself, clearly Will had also been injured and that would make him even easier to deal with. A fit, healthy Will would have been a handful, but he had given very precise instructions to Mortimer, and it seemed as if he had carried out his part of the bargain exactly as they had planned.

Perspiration broke out on his forehead, and the palm of the hand clutching the blade felt sweaty. It was not through fear or worry, he had killed enough men to be able to control any anxiety. This was anticipation. He wiped his brow with the back of his hand, transferred the knife into the other and wiped his palm down his trousers, before returning the blade to his dominant hand again.

As their eyes had had plenty of time to get used to the dark, all three men were able to discern the shadowy figure who lurched along the road, just in front of them. Will was only a couple of feet away, and he had not noticed his assailants, preoccupied as he was with his mission. Holder watched as Will moved to his front, slightly dragging one leg. He began to raise his cudgel in unison with Smith and they both stepped out of the thicket and into the path of the farmer. Garvey would follow up quickly, just behind them, and deliver the fatal blow with his dagger.

Holder advanced the few short steps towards Will, his club already above his head, ready to bring it down with full force onto the unsuspecting Will. Smith was beside him, adopting a similar stance. As Garvey stepped out of the thicket just behind them, Will stumbled, and pitched forward. Holder's blow, just lightly grazed Will's shoulder, and Smith missed completely, stumbling forward, and falling over Will. Will still had no idea about what was happening around him, as his fall had distracted him. He had felt the slight discomfort in his shoulder as something had struck him but was struggling to identify what had caused it. Then someone had fallen over him. As Smith was picking himself up, Holder had regained his composure and struck out at Will again. This time he made contact, but Will had moved slightly, instinctively knowing he was in danger, he moved his head slightly. The blow glanced off the side of his head, and he slumped to the floor. Although he had been stunned, the blow had not done the damage it might have done, if it had struck on the top of the head, which is where it had been aimed.

Both Smith and Holder were now looming over Will with their clubs raised, and Garvey was leaning down with his blade outstretched, poised to thrust it into the defenceless chest of the prostrate man. Just as they were about to deliver the fatal blows, the lane around them was illuminated with an eerie light, like bright moonlight. The men found that their limbs were frozen, and they were unable to move. They looked at the source of the light, and saw a wizened old woman silhouetted. She raised her arm and pointed directly at them. As she did so, they each felt a sharp burning sensation in the hands in which the held their weapons. A searing pain ripped through each of them, and their hands opened involuntarily, as the weapons fell from them.

A deafening screech assailed their ears and caused such an agonising pain in their heads, they thought they would explode. They raised their hands to cover their ears, and realising that their faculties had been restored, the terrified men ran for their lives. Convinced they were being pursued by a demon, they ripped their way through the nearest hedge, oblivious of the cuts and scratches that were shredding their clothes and their skin they fled across the fields.

Will had not seen or heard anything of what had just transpired. Awakening from his temporary blackout, he heard people shouting and calling out his name. Within seconds, a crowd of men and women were surrounding him, and then there was Meg holding his face in both hands and kissing him all over. "My Love!" she cried "How badly hurt are you!" she wailed in anguish.

❖

Practically the whole village had turned out for the search. All, except those who had remained to look after the children. Some of the other men had helped him up, and supported him, as he returned to the Cross-Hands Inn. When they arrived and entered the bar room, Will was astonished to see Old Mother Sawyer already there, attending to the two injured men.

She looked over towards Will and said "They will be alright. They have hard heads. They won't look as pretty as they did, but they will be alright!".

As the men were fussed over and their wounds tended, Meg explained that Old Mother Sawyer had come to their cottage and told her that something was wrong. Meg had alerted the rest of the village, and the villagers had set off in search of their missing men, leaving Old Mother Sawyer behind. Mary had stayed to look after the children.

Will looked towards the old lady and thought "No-one has noticed!" and as she smiled back at him enigmatically, he wondered "How did she get here before everyone else?"

❖

The following day Godfrey had arranged to meet with his co-conspirators, at the Black Bear Inn at Tewkesbury. Both Godfrey and Wendley had spent the last evening at the inn, availing themselves of all its pleasures. Both had been loud and raucous inside the inn, making sure that everyone there remembered them. They had also secured the services of some prostitutes, with the aid of a willing landlord, to provide uncontroversial evidence that they had indeed been there all night.

Godfrey and Wendley had just settled down to a breakfast of eggs and ham, together with the obligatory ale, when three bedraggled, filthy, forlorn, men entered the inn. They both roared with laughter, when they noticed the scratches, bruises and ripped clothing the men were wearing. "Bring my friends some food, and ale!" he shouted out to the landlord, who obsequiously obeyed in double-quick time. "By all the Saints! What happened to you?" he spluttered, nearly choking on his food.

The three men looked down at their boots, too ashamed to look him in the eye. Smith muttered almost inaudibly "We were attacked by a Demon!"

"What!" cried Wendley his mirth unrestrained, his disbelief emphasised as he slammed his half-full mug down onto table, its contents splashing onto the table.

Holder bravely took up the tale "It's true, what he said. We were attacked by a Witch!"

Godfrey, who had just taken a mouthful of ale from his mug, could not help himself, and found that trying to drink and laugh at the same time, just did not work. He accidentally drowned the three men opposite with the contents of his mouth. Laughing and choking at the same time, after inhaling some of his expelled alcohol, Godfrey fell about laughing, joined in equal measure by Wendley.

When their mirth had subsided sufficiently to be able to speak properly, Wendley enquired "So exactly what did happen then?"

The three would-be assailants, reluctantly, and not a little nervously, recounted their tale of failure. When each raised their weapon hands, palms up, and held them out, Godfrey and Wendley could both see the deep and obviously painful, burn marks in the shape of an "X" that were scorched across them.

Godfrey did not get angry, instead he kept his own counsel. This was a setback, and now Will would be on his guard. However, he knew that there would be another opportunity at some point.

# CHAPTER 4

## All the Kings Horses and All the Queens Men....

"....couldn't put England together again...."

### 14 April 1471 – Weymouth

Unbeknown to the folk of Swindon Village and the surrounding area, the storm clouds of war were gathering across the country. As they went about their lives and business naively, cataclysmic events were unleashing themselves, and soon everyone would be drawn into the maelstrom of the fight for the throne of England.

Far away from the day-to-day activities of the village, Mary of Anjou, head of the Lancastrian forces had landed at Weymouth to force battle with King Edward IV, who had usurped her husband, King Henry VI, and held him in the Tower of London.

Margaret of Anjou, had arrived in England from France on the 14th April 1471. The crossing had been fraught with problems, and several previous attempts had forced her ships forced to return to France. Having finally set foot in England on that inauspicious day, Margaret received word of the rout of her powerful supporters the Earl of Warwick and his brother the Marquess of Montague, and their subsequent deaths during the Battle of Barnet, on the very same day she had arrived in England.

She considered returning to France immediately, but was persuaded by her 20-year-old son, Prince Edward, and bolstered by the news that her other allies the Earl of Somerset and the Earl of Devon, had raised an army in the West Country. However, the loss of Warwick and his Army, was a major setback. Warwick's impetuosity in leading a pre-emptive action, had led to his downfall, and severely weakened the Lancastrian cause.

If her own growing army in the southwest could join forces with the 1st Earl of Pembroke, Jasper Tudor, then she would still have a significant numerical advantage over Edward IV, who she believed had illegally pronounced himself as King of England!

Her retinue moved towards Exeter, and then to Bath, before arriving at Bristol, gathering her Army and supplies along the way. The intention of her Commander, the Earl of Somerset, was to cross the River Severn at Gloucester, to join up with Jasper Tudor and his Army before marching on London.

In the meanwhile, Edward IV, head of the Yorkist forces, had heard about the arrival of Margaret, and quickly mobilised his own army to set off in pursuit. He left Windsor on 24th April, with an army of 5,000 men, believing that Margaret of Anjou would join battle with him somewhere close to Sodbury.

## 1st May 1471 - Severn River Crossing, Gloucester

The messenger approached the Severn River crossing at Gloucester. "If I can get into Gloucester, I can rest and give the message to the governor of the city," he thought. He had been chased from Striguil Castle at Chepstow but had managed to lose his pursuers in the heavily wooded Forest of Dean. Unfortunately, this had taken up valuable time, and had taken its toll on both rider and horse.

"Halt and be recognised!" A guard near the crossing called out. The messenger tried to make out the livery of the guard and his companions. He drew a little closer, and saw that there were two archers, and two pike men.

"I have a message for the Governor of Gloucester." The messenger called back, still trying to establish who these guards were. Were they from Gloucester itself, a Yorkist stronghold, or were they one of the patrols sent out by the Earl of Pembroke?

"Come closer, so that we can see you properly!" the guard ordered. The messenger stopped his horse about

150 yards away from the guards and looked more closely at them. Each was wearing a helmet and metal breastplate, obscuring their clothes, but he could just see a flash of green and white. Pembroke's men! An advanced scouting party from the Welsh Army.

He quickly considered his options. If he was captured in possession of the message, he would not only be killed, but the contents of the message would betray the name of the spy in the Pembroke household. He did not know if these men had horses, but if he approached any closer, he risked capture anyway. He made his decision and turned his horse around and spurred her viciously "Yah! Yah!" he yelled, urging the horse to gallop.

"Stop!" the guard cried, as the two archers readied their bows.

200 yards! The first arrow zipped past, then another. 250 yards! Another arrow narrowly missed! "I'm going to make it!" he thought. A fourth arrow was loosed, whether by luck or good judgement, this one found its mark. The messenger was struck in the thigh, and nearly fell from his horse. He managed to cling on and urged the horse faster. If the guards pursued him on horses, he would be lost.

He kept the horse at full gallop for another mile, and then reined her in. There was no sign of pursuit, but now he had other problems. The adrenaline coursing through his body had kept the pain in check for a while, but now he was in agony. Blood was seeping from the wound, and the muscle around it was severely damaged.

He realised that he was now in terrible trouble. Not being able to cross at Gloucester meant he now had to travel on to Tewkesbury and double back. He was not sure if either he or his horse would make it.

He reached Tewkesbury without further incident and managed to use the ferry to cross the river. If the ferrymen had thought there was anything odd about him, they kept their thoughts to themselves.

He pushed on with his desperate mission, even though his strength was being sapped with every stride.

❖

Will was just clearing up before heading home when he heard the 'clop-clop' of horse's hooves. He looked over the stone wall and saw a man slumped in the saddle of a horse, barely clinging on. He hopped over the wall and rushed towards the stricken man. "Hey there! Are you all right?" he asked but got no response.

Will patted the horse on the muzzle, "Whoa there boy!" He could see that both horse and rider were blown. The animal was frothing at the mouth and could hardly put one foot in front of the other. Then Will noticed the arrow protruding from the man's leg and realised that he needed urgent medical attention.

He checked to ensure that the man was secured in the saddle and then took the horse's reins and guided it to Old Mother Sawyer's cottage, which was only a short distance away.

"Mother! Mother!" he called out, banging on the door.

The door opened and the old lady looked out. Immediately recognising the problem, she beckoned Will inside, "Can you get him down, and bring him inside?" she asked.

I'll try." Replied Will, returning to the horseman and easing him out of the saddle and on to his own broad shoulders.

"Gently!" Mother Sawyer reprimanded him.

"I'm trying my best! He is a dead weight you know!"

Mother Sawyer smiled warmly at him, she doubted that any other single man in the village, would have been able to carry him at all.

Will took the man inside and laid him down on the bed.

"Check the horse and then go and get Sir Richard…" the old woman ordered, as she cut the clothes around the wound to get a better look. "And can you bring Meg back with you? I'll need some help."

Will went outside and hobbled the horse, giving her some grain and water, before running back to his own home.

"Meg! Meg!" he shouted as he entered the cottage. "There's an injured man at Mother Sawyer's, she needs your help."

"Goodness!" said Meg, gathering her shawl, and picking up her daughter.

"I need to go and get Sir Richard and let him know!" said Will as they went their separate ways.

"I'll see you there in a while then." Replied Meg.

Will ran to the Manor House and knocked on the door. A servant opened it and enquired about his business. Will explained what had happened and went to fetch Richard Moryn.

"Sire, there is an injured Man at Old Mother Sawyer's cottage. He seems quite important. He's taken an arrow…."

"Thank you Will, I will be right there." Moryn replied. The servant hurried to wrap a cloak around his master's shoulders, and they departed for the old lady's cottage.

"How is he?" Moryn asked as they entered Old Mother Sawyer home.

"He has lost a lot of blood and will lose more when I take the arrow out." The old lady replied.

"Will he live?"

"I am not sure at the moment."

Is there anything we can do to help?"

"We need to get his clothes off, so I can check him for other injuries, and get a better look at the arrow."

The two men helped to ease the clothing from the messenger and laid him back on the bed. Old Mother Sawyer dribbled a potion onto his lips, trying to get him to swallow some. Meg was busy boiling pots of water.

"Should I send for my physician?" Moryn queried.

Old Mother Sawyer smiled at him. "That old 'saw-bones!" she said, "He'd chop his leg off, soon as look at it! We'll be fine…"

Moryn smiled back, he knew of the old lady's reputation, and also knew the reputation of the local physician. He decided the unknown man was better off in her care.

Whilst the old woman and Meg were administering to the messenger, Moryn searched the man's clothing to identify him and found the message. It was addressed to King Edward himself! He placed it on the table.

"Old Mother, it is vital that he survives and is able to talk to us!" he said.

"Then start praying Sire!" she responded.

Mother Sawyer determined that it was better to remove the arrow while the man was unconscious. The bodkin had penetrated right through the leg but did not seem to have hit a major artery or the bone. She snapped the fletched end, and asked Meg to hold a towel against both sides of the leg. She then grabbed the bodkin and pulled the arrow right through. The man spasmed in pain, and the old lady considered that to be a good response. Meg quickly pressed the towels into the wounds on either side of the leg, while Old Mother Sawyer put some herbs into one of the pots of boiling water. After letting the concoction brew for a few moments, she poured in some cold water to cool it down, and then after asking Meg to lift the towel on each part of the leg, administered the medicine to the affected area. The old lady then stitched the wounds, and asked Meg to hold the towels in place again while she bandaged them securely with some strips of linen. She gave the man another sip of her potion and laid his head back down.

"Now we wait!" she said.

❖

With nothing for him to do, Moryn returned to the Manor House with orders to for someone to get him as soon as the man woke up. Will and Meg remained at the old lady's cottage, to provide whatever assistance they could, and snatched some sleep. Old Mother Sawyer sat on a stool next the sleeping man.

"Mess……age! Mu g mess!" the man moaned, twisting in the bed. Sweat poured from his brow and Mother Sawyer gently mopped it with a cool rag.

"Mehess….aage!" the man said more insistently. Even in his delirium, his mission was driving him.

"There, there!" the old lady soothed.

"Hmmmm!!" the man mumbled.

Old Mother Sawyer dribbled some more of the potion into his mouth, and he calmed before drifting off to sleep once more.

"Water!" Meg woke to the sound of the unknown man's voice. She had taken over from Old Mother Sawyer to give her a chance to have some rest. "Water!" the man repeated. Meg leaned down to pick up a mug of water from the floor and raised it to the man's lips.

"Gently now! Not too fast!"

The man slurped at the water, desperate to have more. "More!" he gasped.

"Only if you slow down!" she said raising the mug once again. This time he was more relaxed. His face was showing signs of recovery and was now slightly flushed rather than pale as it had been before. "How are you feeling?" Meg asked.

"Much better."

"That's good." said Mother Sawyer, who had been awoken by the whispered discussion. She leaned over and prodded Will, "Better go and get Sir Richard!"

A groggy Will shook his head and brushed himself down, before leaving to get the Lord of the Manor.

❖

Richard Moryn followed Will back to Old Mother Sawyers cottage, keen to know what the messenger had to say. They entered the small run-down building and saw that the unknown man was sitting up in bed, having recovered significantly from his condition of the following day.

"How are you, my friend?" Moryn asked.

"I am feeling much better Sire, thanks to these people."

May I enquire as to your business?"

"Sire, my name is Henry Saville. I have been providing intelligence for the King from inside the Duke of Pembroke's army. I have come from Siguil Castle, where Pembroke has amassed an army, and is intending to join up with Queen Margaret." The man replied, "I am aware that Gloucester and Cheltenham are for King

Edward, and I was trying to deliver a message to Sir Richard Beauchamp at Gloucester."

"You are indeed amongst friends here." Moryn assured him.

"Thank you Sire, I was stopped from crossing the river at Gloucester by Pembroke's soldiers and had to go the long way around to cross at Tewkesbury. Unfortunately, I took an arrow as I fled Gloucester."

"I saw your message, but I have not opened it." Moryn responded.

"Sire, it is vital that the King is informed, unfortunately, I will not be able to ride any time soon."

"I will ensure that the message gets to Beauchamp."

"It is too late for that, the King needs to be informed immediately, I fear it may already be too late!"

"What do you suggest?"

"Someone needs to take my message to the King himself, immediately!" Saville insisted.

"I see," said Moryn, "We received word today that the King is at Sodbury, expecting to do battle there."

"Then I believe he has been deceived Sire. This makes my message even more urgent!"

"I have no men available. They have been summoned by their liege lord and will not be back until tomorrow!"

"I can take it!" Will interjected.

"Can you ride Will?" Moryn asked.

"Aye Sire, more used to riding bare-back than in a saddle though."

"You understand the importance of this mission Will?"

"Aye Sire, I will not let you down!" Will said confidently, glancing at Meg.

"Is there no-one else Sire? Meg asked, the worry etched her face.

"My love, there is no time. I will be safe, all I have to do is deliver the message and then I will come straight back."

"Be careful Will!"

"God bless you!" Saville said.

While Meg made some provisions, Richard Moryn took Will to his own stables and provided him with one of his best horses. Will took his bow and quiver, and with the message safely tucked away inside his shirt set off to find the King!

❖

## Berkley Castle 2nd May 1471

The journey from Bristol to Berkley had been arduous but necessary. Bristol had been open to their army, and they had collected provisions, cannon, and additional men. The Lancastrian Army had moved through the night, finally arriving at Berkeley at mid-morning.

"Well met, Sir Knight!" William, Lord Berkely called out to the approaching retinue, from the gate of his imposing castle. He bowed to the royal entourage deeply, "Your Majesty! It is a great honour!"

Margaret nodded "Arise Sir Knight! We thank you for your support" she replied.

Somerset jumped down from his horse, and strode across towards Berkeley, "Well Met! My friend! How are you?" he shouted effusively, grasping the other man in a bear-hug and clapping him the back.

"Everything is good. How are you? You must be weary!" he said, responding to the bear-hug in kind, before stepping back to look his compatriot.

"We are! Our men are taking some rest, but I fear we will soon need to be on our way again." Somerset informed him, wiping his brow with the back of his hand.

"Please! Come in and take some refreshment!" Berkeley exclaimed and turned to let the Royal retinue through the gates.

By the time they had arrived at Berkeley, Margaret's army had swelled to about to around 6,000 men. In the meadows around the castle, tents were hastily erected, pots put on to boil, and horse and other livestock were fed. Men, weary from the forced marches they had endured, rested while they had the chance.

In the Great Hall of the castle, a feast was being prepared. Advanced scouts from the Lancastrian army, had arrived early in the morning, and enough time had been given, for the occupants of the castle to prepare a decent meal for the Queen of England.

Whilst preparations were being made for the meal, the weary travellers were taken to rooms in which to rest. The meal was due to take place in the late afternoon, giving everyone time to eat, rest, and prepare for the night-time march.

By early evening, the meal was in full flow, and the entourage were merry and loud, having indulged in the food and especially the ale and wine on offer. All of the men, including Somerset, had slated their thirst significantly, enjoying the respite following their arduous trek the previous day.

"We have fooled him!" Somerset boasted loudly, "We made a feint at Sodbury, and he fell for it!" he exclaimed, before drinking deeply from his goblet, and holding it up to be refilled. "We have created more time for ourselves, and he is now lagging behind!" he guffawed.

A servant standing directly behind him, moved forward quickly to fill the proffered goblet, and then retreated back to his position by the wall.

"We'll not tarry long, William." Somerset said, between mouthfuls of pheasant. "We need to get across the river by midday tomorrow.

"Well, you have 18 miles to Gloucester, and more if you want to yourself secure on the other side of the river." Berkeley responded, picking up his goblet and taking a long draught of ale. "I suggest you leave before midnight, and march through the night" he concluded.

"Aye, you're right, we'll need to leave as soon as everyone has had some rest, but if we can get over the river, we can defend the other side of the bridge." Somerset replied confidently. "The Yorkist usurper will not be able to get enough of his army across, after us, and he will have his back to the river. He won't want that." Somerset continued, dropping a bone onto this plate, and picking up another greasy morsel, which then he lifted it to his mouth. "We tricked him at Sodbury, and hopefully, that will put him far enough behind us, to ensure our safe crossing. We need to join up with Jasper as quickly as possible." He said, chewing the food in his mouth, as he spoke. Somerset referred to the Earl of Pembroke, a staunch Lancastrian supporter, and half-brother to King Henry VI.  They all knew that the King was currently a prisoner of Edward in the Tower of London and were appalled at the audacity of the false monarch.

"Once our forces are together Edward's army will be no match for us!" he added pouring more ale into his goblet, picking it up, and drinking deeply from it, while still chewing on a mouthful of meat.  He swallowed and then belched, "best food I've had in days!" he exclaimed merrily.

"Aye Richard, but you need to be careful.  Edward is no fool.  We have already lost too many good men to him.  Don't underestimate him."  He declared solemnly.

"Jasper is at Chepstow, awaiting our messenger.  Once we are across the river, he will advance up to meet us, and then we can choose our ground.  He'll be no match for us then, and we can end this thing, once and for all!"  Somerset retorted, standing and raising his goblet to the crowded Hall, "King Henry!" he bellowed, "King Henry!" cheered the entourage.

❖

King Edward IV was camped at Little Sodbury and was waiting for stragglers from his army to catch up.  He was certain that Margaret of Anjou, Somerset and the rest of the Lancastrian Army, would be headed for London. His scouts had lost a skirmish, earlier in the day, and he was convinced that the major confrontation between the two armies would happen here. However, since his scouts could find no further sign of the enemy, Edward remained perturbed. Sitting in his tent with his senior commanders around him he bellowed "Where has that witch and her guard of devils gone?"

"We are scouting the area, Sire" responded Lord William Hastings replied. "We will find them soon." he made this statement with a confidence he did not quite feel. The army had made good time, and were more mobile than the Lancastrian army, nevertheless, today had been a setback, and it seemed increasingly likely that they had been hoodwinked. The King was clearly furious.

Every delay was critical, and Edward was committed to resolving the issue once and for all, at the earliest possible moment. He did not want Margaret and her son being given any more time to bolster her army with additional men and supplies or give her the advantage of setting the stage for battle.

He was determined to harry her at every opportunity and keep her on the run, until he was able to choose the battlefield himself.

"I need them found now!" he berated his commanders, with a fearsome look in his eyes. His most senior men looked down at their feet, sheepishly.

❖

Will's destination was Little Sodbury. His horse was fresh, well-fed, and watered. He estimated it would take him about 4 hours to travel the 35 miles to Sodbury. Once there he would need to find Edward's army, and he would then have the less than easy task of trying to get an audience with the King!

He moved as quickly as the road and weather conditions allowed and was making good time. However, he was well aware of the importance of the information he carried, and the urgency needed for the information to have any value to its recipient.

He arrived in the vicinity of Little Sodbury at about two in the morning. It had been a very long day, and a tiring ride to his current destination. However, Will was strong, resilient and committed, and the money he could make from this errand, would more than compensate him for any discomfort he was currently feeling. He was very aware that sentries and patrols would be arrayed around the area, for this reason, he slowed to a trot, and made no effort to prevent noise.

Soon, he was rewarded by a shout of challenge "Halt! Who goes there?" a stern voice bellowed. "Advance and be recognised!" the guard commanded.

"William Bowen, a messenger for the King!" Will responded in kind.

"William Bowen, you say! Who is your commander?" the guard queried.

"I have no commander! I bring a message from Sir Henry Saville" Will rejoined "I have important news for the King!"

"We know you not, sir!" the guard "I cannot give you entry!" he ended.

"Then you will be hanging from a tree by morning!" Will responded angrily. "If you cannot give me entry, then find someone who will! Now!"

A little perturbed by the confidence and tone of Will's response, the guard hesitated before conferring with his fellows. "I will send someone for the Guard Commander," he relented "and God help you, if you are not who you say you are!" he ended, somewhat pleased with himself.

Will waited impatiently for a while, when suddenly he heard some commotion at the picket line. "Dismount from your horse!" he was commanded.

"And who might you be?" Will questioned, calming his horse, as it skittered in alarm at the stern voice coming from the darkness.

"I am the Commander of the Guard!" came the indignant riposte.

"Thank Goodness! At last!" cried Will "Hopefully, someone with some brains!" he grumbled, as he began to dismount, tired and saddle-sore.

Four men appeared from the tree line, two carried spears and one carried a bow. The other had a sword secured around his waist. They approached as Will walked his mare towards them, his hand guiding her with a secure grip on the reins. The horse was tired and panting from the exertion of the last few hours, and Will patted her on the snout "Good girl!" he whispered.

"I am John de Lacy" the guard commander announced stiffly. "I am told you have a message for the King?" he asked curtly.

"I am Will Bowen, and I have just come from the Swindon Village, near Cheltenham." Will responded. At this the guards bristled and the two with spears lowered them threateningly. "I am a friend," Will added quickly, "and I have news form Sir Henry Saville of the intentions of the Lancastrian army." he declared.

Unknown to Will, John de Lacy had been within earshot of the King's belligerent outburst earlier in the evening and knew of the urgent need to locate the Lancastrians.

"Remove your weapons, sir." he ordered, adding "We will search you and then take you to someone who will hear your tale."

Will submitted to the search, having handed over his weapons. Content that he was safe to be admitted into the Yorkist army lines, John de Lacy said "We will get your horse fed and watered, and I will take you to my Liege Lord." De Lacy led the way and Will followed, one of the other guards took his horse and weapons away and another followed behind, his spear at the ready.

Will was taken to a tent erected around a blazing log fire. Two guards stood outside the tent and de Lacy went over to speak to them. One of the guards nodded and immediately went inside the tent. Will could hear some rustling and bustling from inside the tent, and some words were spoken, but he could not hear them. A moment later the guard came back out with another man. The man was dishevelled, having clearly been awoken from his slumber, but was alert and decisive, nevertheless.

"Go and wake the Kings squire" the man ordered to one his guards "and ensure the King is available to hold a meeting." Having given his orders, he turned to face Will. "I am Lord William Hastings," he explained, "I believe you have some news for us?" he added, with a smile on his face, steering Will away from the tent and towards another part of the camp.

Will was taken to another, larger, tent. Inside were a number of guards. Will was offered a seat and some wine, which he took eagerly. After a few minutes, an order was roared "Stand for the King!," Will jumped up, and a few seconds later, King Edward and his senior commanders rushed into the tent. Will bowed deeply, and then straightened.

Will handed over the message, which provided troop and weapon numbers, information about the state of the army and their morale, and most importantly, the intentions of the leaders. Despite the time of day, and the fact that he been rudely awoken in the middle of the night from his sleep, King Edward showed no weariness, and wasted no time, in making his plans and getting his commanders to work.

Finally, he turned to Will "Will Bowen," he said "Thank you for what you have done today. England will most certainly reward you in due course. However, I now have another mission for you….."

It was 3 o'clock in the morning of Friday 3rd of May 1471…

❖

Within the hour, Will found himself once again on horseback. He had been given a new horse, and his mission was to make haste to the city of Gloucester and deliver a message to the Commander of the City. So much for going straight back to Swindon, he thought. He had been given a fresh steed, and had been provided with food and drink, as well as provisions for his journey. He felt slightly sorry for the loss of his faithful mare, but her replacement was younger, larger stronger, and much more valuable. "It was a good exchange." He thought.

More importantly, in contrast to his arrival at Edward's camp, he now had an official duty, and carried a letter from the King himself, as well a bulging purse, and the promise of more, if he completed this mission. This letter was to be delivered personally into the hands of Governor Sir Richard Beauchamp, and Beauchamp was ordered to provide additional recompense to Will. And so, with a fit, fresh horse beneath him, Will was a motivated and content man, no thoughts of tiredness clouded his mind. There would be plenty of time to rest once he had reached Gloucester.

❖

Edward wasted no time in breaking camp, and organising his forces to move towards Gloucester, determined as he was, to catch up with Lancastrians at the earliest possible opportunity. Will's information could not have come at a more opportune time, and although the Lancastrians were now a significant distance ahead of him, he knew that if Will succeeded in his mission, then there was still a good chance to catch up, and delay the Lancastrian march. Much depended on Will reaching Gloucester ahead of the advancing Lancastrian forces.

The journey was just under 30 miles and he would travel via the Cotswolds escarpment (the same route that Edward would take). Will knew that timing was critical, and he would have to push the horse, if he was to make it in time. He had a slight fear that the horse would be blown by the time he reached his destination, but that was no matter. The roads were good, the weather was fine, there was enough moonlight to see his way, and the last part of the journey into the city, was downhill.

Will rode like the wind, his horse sure-footed beneath him.

❖

Sir Richard Beauchamp stood on ramparts of the fortified South Gate of Gloucester City. His scouts had warned of the approaching Lancastrian army, and from his position, he could see the dust clouds in the distance, and could hear the faint beat of drums.

Richard Moryn had personally relayed the message given to him by Henry Saville, and Beauchamp pondered his choices.

"They will be here within the hour." He remarked to his lieutenant standing by his side. "I am minded to let them through." He added. Although loyal to Edward, Sir Richard, had not received word of the Kings whereabouts, and was reluctant to sacrifice the city to a siege. He realised it was a major judgment call on his behalf, and he had not yet made up his mind. He also realised that the time was fast approaching when he would be forced to make a decision.

It was 9 o'clock on the morning of 3rd May 1471.

At that moment, Beauchamp was alerted by a call below him. One of his guards was running towards the gate, flailing his arms in the air, shouting "Sire! Sire! A message from the King!."

Just behind him, was a man on horseback. Both the rider and the horse looked exhausted, and Sir Richard hurried down the steps leading down from the gate. As he approached, the horseman tried to dismount, but practically fell from his horse.

The guard held out a hand to steady him. "Sire, I am Will Bowen, and I have an urgent message from the King!" he exclaimed, breathlessly. With his last ounce of strength, Will pulled out the letter with the Kings seal, and handed it to Sir Richard Beauchamp.

Beauchamp tore open the seal and quickly read the contents. "You are commanded to seal the gates and deny entry to the Lancastrian Army to the City. I am within striking distance of the City and will be in a position to reinforce you within hours." The letter was signed and dated by the King himself, and also contained the value of the reward that Bowen was due!

"Close the gates! Prepare to defend the walls" Beauchamp bellowed.  His command was followed by a flurry of activity, as his troops prepared to defend the city of necessary.

"God bless you, Will Bowen!" he shouted towards the man, now slumped on the floor.

"Guards, take this man to my chambers and give him sustenance!" he ordered, "and you there!  Take his horse to the stables!" One of the guards rushed over to take the reins of the horse and guide it away, as two others assisted the exhausted Will to his feet and supported the now hobbling man to the Governors quarters.

Will had succeeded, just in time!

# CHAPTER 5
## The Race to Tewkesbury
### 3rd May 1461

Margaret of Anjou and her retinue arrived at the South Gate of the City of Gloucester at about 10 o'clock in the morning. With Somerset in the Vanguard, and with the young Prince Edward at his side, they steadily and confidently approached the city.

Somerset began to feel slightly uneasy as he moved forwards. He could see the gates were closed, and he could also see cannon, soldiers, and bowmen manning the fortifications. Ominously, the cannon were pointed directly towards his column, and it looked as if the men in charge of those cannon were paused to fire if necessary. He knew that Richard Beauchamp was the Governor of Gloucester, and he also knew that Richard's father was a staunch Lancastrian supporter. He had not anticipated or planned for any problems entering this city and crossing the river here.

Having arrived directly beneath the solid gates, and finding them still barred, he bellowed up at the ramparts "Open the gates in the name of the King!"

Richard Beauchamp, who was standing on top of the battlements, had been nervously awaiting this confrontation, nevertheless, responded confidently.

"Sire, I do not recognise the king of whom you speak. I have received a message from King Edward himself, who commands me to deny you access to the city, signed by his own hand!"

"You insolent cur!" Somerset raged, open the gates now, or I will have your head!"

"Alas Sire, I cannot!" Beauchamp countered. "Leave now, or I will fire on your party!" he added. "The King is but a few leagues away and will probably want *your* head!" he countered boldly.

Somerset turned to the Prince, his cheeks flushed with a mixture of rage and humiliation, "Come Your Highness. We will speak with your mother, and then return to deal with this traitor!". He angrily spurred his horse away, leaving the young Prince in his wake. Prince Edward momentarily looked up at the battlements, before turning his horse and following the de facto commander of what he considered *his* army.

Somerset had expected to be let through the city and across the only bridge for miles, without any problems. Most of the south-west of the country supported the cause of King Henry and the Lancastrians, and having been greeted so warmly at Berkley, he had no reason to doubt that they would be received in exactly the same way in Gloucester itself. As he rode back down his lines, he was absolutely enraged at the humiliation.

They both headed back towards the centre of the army where Margaret was waiting. Both Wenlock and Devonshire were also in attendance.

As Somerset and her son approached, Margaret stood to receive them. "What news my Lord? What is the delay?" she enquired.

"My Lady, the gates have been closed to us, and they will not let us pass." Somerset informed her, "We should lay siege and force our way through!"

Devonshire interjected "My Lord Somerset, Edward is only a short distance away, and will be here soon." He pointed towards the east, "We will not be able to deploy our troops for siege, and defend our rear or flanks, when he arrives. We will be at a serious disadvantage."

Wenlock looked over at his commander, "Devonshire is right, My Lord. We are still ahead of the Yorkists, and if we use the time wisely, we could cross at the next point."

"And precisely, where is the next point, My Lord Wenlock?" Somerset demanded, "We have walked our troops through the night, and are within sight of our crossing!"

"The next crossing is at Tewkesbury. There is a ford, south of the town, or a bridge across the Avon, just north of the town. Either would serve our purpose, provided we make haste!" Wenlock responded, glancing across towards Devonshire.

"It is our best option." Devonshire agreed.

"Margaret spoke up for the first time, having listened to her military advisors. "How long will it take to reach Tewkesbury?" she queried.

"It is about 11 miles, Your Majesty," Wenlock informed her, "It will take 4 to 5 hours." He concluded. Margaret herself concluded that Wenlock's calculations included the time it would take to cross the river. She trusted her commanders to know the lie of the land.

Unfortunately, none of them did. If Margaret had realised that the only two crossing points at Tewkesbury were both fords, at Lower Lode and Upper Lode, and that the next bridge was at Upton-On Severn, another 7 miles north of Tewkesbury, they might have reassessed their decision.

This lack of concrete, military intelligence, was to prove costly and create problems of a magnitude that changed their position from one of having the advantage, to being placed at a deadly disadvantage.

Margaret's natural caution caused to her ask "Do we have sufficient time?" She again, began to doubt the wisdom of the entire venture, reminding herself of her reluctance to continue, and her desire to return to France immediately on hearing the news of the death of Warwick, when she had first arrived at Weymouth only a few weeks before.

"We shall make the time, My Lady." Somerset blustered, with all his customary self-confidence, even though he was still smarting at the insult he had received at the gates of Gloucester.

Wenlock and Devonshire glanced at each other, each raising their eyebrows in unison. Both had exactly the same thought at the same time "God help us! He'd better be right!"

Despite the over-confidence of Somerset, buoyed by the arrogant, enthusiasm of the young Prince, he now realised that the delay in crossing the river, had placed his forces at huge disadvantage. The subterfuge they had used to distract and confuse Edward of their intentions, had given them several hours of respite, but his army was exhausted and in desperate need of rest. He had not anticipated this delay, and now they would be forced to continue their journey, for the next several hours at least.

Somerset reluctantly acquiesced to the other nobles "By God! I will see the Governor of this city swing!" he raised his arm and pointed directly towards Beauchamp, standing at the top of the gate, just visible, some distance away. "But time is of the essence, and we must make haste!" He turned his horse and cantered towards the front of the train, shouting as he went "To Horse! We march on!"

Most of the knights had dismounted, to relieve some of the burden from their horses, and most of the foot soldiers had taken the opportunity to sit or lay on the verges of the road.  Some had removed their boots and begun to massage their aching feet.  On hearing their commander's call, weary soldiers began to form up, and knights began to remount, and take up their positions, ready to march again.

The drums began beating again, as the army once more began to march.  However, the pomp and triumphant waving of the banners, that accompanied the approach to Gloucester, was now subdued, as they were forced to walk around the fortified walls of the city, almost shamed now, by the spectacle they presented, and with no way of seeking redress, against those peering down at them from those fortifications.

❖

Edward was making ground.  Turning north, he headed for Cheltenham, keen to mirror the Lancastrian army, and run parallel with it.  Having received word from Beauchamp that the city was secure, and that Margaret had been forced to continue her journey towards the next possible crossing point on the River Severn.

He was also aware from his informants, that Somerset would have trouble getting his entire army across at Tewkesbury, and that it would take many hours, to do so.

"We should be able to make good time Sire!" Hastings called across to his King, "The roads are good, and we should be able to intercept them by tomorrow morning."

"Our luck holds, Hastings!" Edward replied, "We must continue to be bold!" the smile on his face belied the determined look he had carried all morning. "The troops are still in good spirit, though we must be sure that they are well rested before any combat." He added, solemnly.

"We're in better shape than Somerset!" replied Hastings, joyfully. "Aye, long may it continue." Replied the King ruefully.

❖

Somerset had decided to stay as close to the river as possible, in the vain hope that some form of crossing would appear miraculously. The road was poor and narrow, and the army struggled to gain any pace, becoming further and further strung out. "Damn these roads!" he muttered under his breath, his brow furrowed and his demeanour grim.

The army was weary, the men and horses exhausted.

The road was difficult, and the pace was excruciatingly slow.

He ran the back of his hand across his brow, to wipe away the sweat that was streaming into his eyes. "God's teeth! It's hot!" He blasphemed irritably, and called over a sergeant, with a wave of his hand. "Go to the back of the train and let me know how far back we go?" he ordered.

"Aye Sire!" the sergeant replied, turning his horse, and making his way back down the column. His progress was not fast, due to the space the lane provided, and it took him nearly half an hour to reach the end of the train.

Here he observed that men and horses drawing cannon were meandering. The depleted beasts, starved of water and frothing at the mouth, were plodding along at a snail's pace, and falling further behind.

"You there!" he called out towards the hapless group of soldiers accompanying the horse-drawn cannon. "You have to move faster! You are falling behind!"

The men, who were for the most part just looking down at their feet, placing one foot in front of the other, as if in some kind of trance, looked up and smiled. One of the men spoke up "If these horses don't get to rest soon, it'll be you pulling the cannons!" he said belligerently, no longer caring what punishment he might receive, for his outburst.

The sergeant looked at him sympathetically, the soldier was right, and pushing them harder would just be counter-productive.

"I understand." He replied, "But you have to make an effort to catch up." He reprimanded. The men continued plodding along at the same pace. There was nothing more he could do. These men were out on their feet!

Whilst the sergeant pondered what to do, and what to tell his commander, he suddenly became aware of a noise behind the column.

He could hear hooves, and as he raised his hand to shield his eyes, he could make out the tell-tale sign of dust being kicked up into the air, as horses galloped along the road.

As he watched, he could see a large group of horsemen approaching at speed. "Defence! Defence!" he cried out in panic, "We are being attacked!"

His soldiers turned and tried to raise their pikes to form some sort of defensive line, but they were too tired and too slow.

The horsemen were upon them in seconds, slashing and thrusting at the soldiers on foot.  The screams of dying men, mingled with the blood-curdling roars coming from the knights on horseback "For the King! Die you bastards!"

The sergeant tried to respond and drew his sword as he pushed his horse forward using his knees, but was quickly engulfed by two or three riders, and slain in his saddle.

Foot soldiers, and mounted men further up the line, heard the commotion and began turning to face the threat.

The attacking knights, having killed the soldiers protecting the cannons, turned their attention to the horse pulling them.

They slashed at the throats of the horses, killing and maiming them fatally within seconds.  Having caused their devastation, they turned and rode off back down the road towards Gloucester.

The knights of Gloucester led by Richard Beauchamp had dealt a severe blow for King Edward!

❖

About a mile further up the road, Somerset was getting impatient. He had dispatched the sergeant nearly an hour ago, and he had still not returned. He turned towards Prince Edward "Where has that man got to?" he exclaimed; his anger apparent.

"He should have been back by now!" the young prince responded equally perturbed. As Somerset considered sending someone else to see what was holding the sergeant up, he heard a commotion behind him.

Halting his horse, and in doing so, causing the whole train to come to a standstill, he looked back to see a rider urgently pushing his way towards the front of the train shouting "Make way! Make way! Get out of my way!" as he did so.

He approached his commander and shouted breathlessly "Sire, we have been attacked!"

Somerset called to his personal guard, "You! Take the Prince back to his mother and wait with him there!" indicating to one knight.

"My Lord Somerset!" the young prince interjected. "I will accompany you." he commanded.

"Sire, please wait until I have established the nature of the attack, so that I can decide what action to take." Somerset responded in an agitated manner. He did not have time for the whining of this boy, he was a head-strong youth and needed to be reined in.

"Your safety is of paramount importance and until I know exactly what has happened, I want you to be protected." He motioned towards some of his other guards to follow him, and rode off, without brooking further argument.

The army had come to a complete standstill and were moving off to the side of the road, providing as much space as they could for Somerset's retinue. As they passed Wenlock, who was accompanying the Queen, Somerset noticed that Wenlock himself was preparing to follow him. "Wenlock, stay! Protect the Queen and the Prince. I will be back anon!" he called out without slowing his gallop.

Somerset and his guard party continued down the interminably long train, passing men, horses, wagons, and cannon. Finally, they reached the scene of devastation. Devonshire, was already there, with a contingent of his own knights, and he acknowledged Somerset, as he came up beside him. "I sent some men off in pursuit," he said, "but I fear they are long gone, it was a small raiding party, probably from Gloucester."

Somerset surveyed the scene on front of him sombrely. "Seven cannon, and at least a dozen men." Devonshire informed him. "The problem is the horses," he continued, "we have no spare, and without them, we cannot move these cannon."

"Can we not save some of them at least?" questioned Somerset, his anger barely suppressed.

"If we can find any spare horses, which is doubtful, we would have to abandon something else." Devonshire responded dismally. "It will also take some time to prepare, and some of the harnesses' are damaged beyond repair." He added with an air of resignation.

"Damn these Yorkist scum!" Somerset bellowed in a rage. "This reduces our cannon by nearly half!"

With little other choice available to him, Somerset reluctantly concluded "Leave them then!" before adding "We have no time to spare, let us move on."

Devonshire abashed, stated "I will ensure we have a contingent to secure our rear."

Somerset remarked disdainfully, under his breath "Yes! That *would* have been a good idea!" not quite quietly enough, for it not to be heard by all the knights who were in close proximity.

Devonshire, who was insulted, but contrite, held his counsel, and watched as Somerset turned and led his retinue back towards the head of the column.

Tiredness, lack of food and water, and aching limbs were taking their toll. The physical fatigue was certainly having an impact, but the stress of the change of plan forced upon them at the last minute at the gates of Gloucester, was beginning to have a detrimental effect on the decision-making capabilities of the leaders of the army.....

❖

Will sat on his horse, on the brow of a hill, overlooking the valley in which the increasing forlorn Lancastrian army was moving. Having spent a few hours sleeping and recovering from his exploits earlier in the day, he had offered to monitor the movements of Margaret of Anjou and her army, promising to relay any important information to Edward's army, which was approaching from the east.

He had been aware of the Richard Beaumont's plan to harry the rear of the Yorkist train and had originally volunteered to take part. However, Richard Beaumont had wanted his knights to take the glory for this and thought that Will would be far more use as a spy.

So, Will watched from a distance, and witnessed the attack on the rear of the convoy, and had then continued to monitor their progress from a safe distance.

# Chapter 6

## A Tale of Two Towns

### 3rd May 1461

Fate was rapidly determining that it was becoming the best of times for Edward, and the worst of times for Margaret of Anjou.

Edward had made astonishing time and had closed the gap with the Yorkist army to just a few hours. Having received messages that Gloucester was secure, and about the successful harrying raid against the train on the road to Tewkesbury, Edward had clear intelligence about the position and disposition of the enemy forces.

Although his own army was slightly smaller than his foe, Edward's army was better equipped. He had more cannon, more horses, and his army was well supplied. Although his march had been no less arduous, in terms of sheer pace, than the Yorkist army, his troops were fresher, and their path had been easier to traverse.

Edward arrived on the outskirts of Cheltenham in the early afternoon, and safe with the knowledge that Margaret of Anjou was less than 5 miles away, he decided to stop for a while in the fields surrounding Swindon village, to rest his army, and ensure they had food and water. He took advantage of the short break to re-supply, discuss tactics with his other commanders, and receive intelligence reports from his spies.

The Cheltenham Hundreds, like Gloucester, were in the hands of Lords who were supporters of the Yorkist King, and Edward's arrival was greeted with enthusiasm. As much food, ale and water as could be mustered, was secured from the local area, and the short stop had the benefit of refreshing the troops and providing a significant boost to moral.

Edward held a council of war during the short stay in Cheltenham in the area surrounding Swindon Village.

Together with Richard, Duke of Gloucester, Clarence and Hastings, he planned their strategy. In the meantime, he also received messengers, and dispatched scouts to keep him informed of the movements and disposition of the enemy forces.

One of the messengers he received was Will. As he was admitted to the King's tent, he dropped to one knee and bowed his head. "Your Majesty! My Lords!" he said, "I have news of the enemy."

The King recognised Will, and remembered the service he had already provided previously, said "Rise William! Pray tell us, what news?!"

Will stood and looked directly at the monarch "Sir Richard Beauchamp has successfully carried out a raid against the foe Sire! They have lost a number of cannon, horses and men!" he beamed. "They are looking very weary, and their progress is very slow. They are struggling in the lanes, and it will still be several hours before they reach Tewkesbury." He concluded.

"This is encouraging news indeed!" exclaimed the King. Turning to Richard of Gloucester he said, "We can use this information to our advantage!"

Gloucester replied "Aye Sire! They have more men at arms, but they are mostly foot soldiers. The loss of their cannon will give us significant superiority."

Edward interjected immediately "And more Gloucester! We will use their own artillery against them! Send word to Beauchamp, to recover the Lancastrian cannon, and bring them forward towards Tewkesbury!"

Hastings took the opportunity to enquire of Will "How well do you know Tewkesbury?"

"Like the back of my hand Sire!" he responded, still beaming.

"What are the river crossings like?" Hastings continued.

"They are just ferries, My Lord. It would take many hours to get the army across, and it would be treacherous to try to do it during the night.

Clarence then joined the conversation "My King, if what this man says is true, then they will not be able to attempt the crossing until the morning."

The King looked around at his commanders "Then battle must be drawn tomorrow!" he exclaimed decisively. "We must prevent them crossing and joining up with Tudor!"

He looked back at Will. "I want you to assemble a small group of men, who are skilled with the bow, and have them join the scouting party that I am sending out. You will be under the command of one of my most trusted sergeants, Sir Walter Devereux."

Shortly after, Will was dismissed and taken to see Devereux. "Sire, I am commanded to seek out a small contingent of local bowmen, and assist you in scouting the area around Tewkesbury." he informed the Knight.

"Indeed sir." Devereux responded "You have enough such men?" he queried.

"Aye Sire" Will replied "I can have six within the hour!"

"Then get to it man!" Devereux countered "I will meet with you within the hour!"

Will turned on his heels and left at haste, a smile playing on his lips.

❖

Will made a slight detour on his way to call in at his cottage. He opened the door and startled Meg. She ran towards him and hugged him with all her strength. "Will, thank God!" she exclaimed. "You are safe!"

Will kissed her face, and held her in a fierce embrace, "I still have work to do for the King!" he exclaimed, pressing the pouch of gold that he had received for his endeavours into her hand. "In this pouch is our future," he said, "and the King has given us permanent ownership of the cottage, the pouch contains his signed parchment to prove it!" he cried.

"Oh Will!" Meg hugged him and kissed him, her face flushed with her love for him.

"I have been told that I will be knighted for my work, once the battle is won!" he told her, his face beaming. "...but I have to go, there are still things I must do."

"My love, thank you for what you have done for our family," Meg declared, "but stay safe, I couldn't bear to lose you!"

"I will be safe, my love, and when I return, our lives will be changed forever!"

"I love you!" Meg declared.

"I love you, and always will!" Will glowed as he held his beautiful wife. "I must go! I will see you again in a couple of days." He kissed her again and turned towards the door.

Meg sobbed as her husband left the cottage and made a silent prayer to protect him in the days ahead.

❖

Will made his way directly to the Cross Hands Inn, where he knew his brother would be waiting. At such short notice, the only people Will could think of was Godfrey and his friends. As he entered, he saw Godfrey and his gang sitting around a large table on one side of the room.

"Godfrey," Will called out, "Can I have a word with you?"

"Ah, Will! To what do we owe this unusual pleasure?" Godfrey replied, while his friends continued chatting and laughing.

"The King has arrived at Swindon!" he beamed, "and set a task for me!"

"And pray, how does that involve me?"

"I need five archers, and I thought of you and your friends…" Will looked around at the motley group. He had considered using some of his friends from the village, but he did not want to put them in any kind of danger. He also knew that Godfrey and his gang were cut-throats and would probably appreciate some extra coin.

Godfrey laughed, "Archers? You say!"

"I know you are all effective with a bow, and not frightened of a scrap. You will be well rewarded."

Godfrey turned to his men, who had not been listening to the conversation between Will and Godfrey. Smith ordered more ale.

"What news, Godfrey?" Wendley enquired.

"We have a task for the King, no less!" Godfrey beamed.

"I hope that task doesn't involve me being killed!" Smith added sullenly.

"Oh, I assure you, we will be in no danger!" Godfrey responded quickly, with a glint in his eye.

Holder noticing the sly look that passed across Godfrey's face, was keen to know the plan "So what are we going to be doing then?"

"We are going to do some scouting, well away from the action, and we are going to keep Will company!"

The other four men looked up at Godfrey together, each smiling conspiratorially.

"You go ahead Will. We will join you shortly." Godfrey said.

Will left to meet with Meg, and the others stayed to finish their drinks before following him.

❖

Around the village, there was a lot of excitement. All of the villagers knew that the King's army had arrived, and many people from the wider area, had come to the village to watch proceedings. All the children, and not a few adults, were fascinated by the pageantry, the drums, the knights in shining armour, the banners and flags.

The soldiers themselves were keen to take the chance to rest, and there were more than a few growls, if they were disturbed by excited children running around.

Will joined Meg and their toddler Maud, who were enjoying the spectacle. The King in Swindon Village! They would never have imagined anything so exciting! Will put Maud on his shoulders, and both he and Meg stretched and strained to look over the rest of the crowd, to try and gain a glimpse of their King!

Godfrey and his cohort were wandering around among the animated throng, seeking out Will. They knew he would be here somewhere, everyone else was!

It was Holder who spotted him, near the edge of the field. Spectators were being held back from entering the field in which the army was camped, and guards had been posted at the entry points. Will and Meg were standing next to a lower part of the hedge, with a reasonably good view of proceedings.

Godfrey, indicated to his men, that they should hold back, out of sight, while Godfrey himself went forward to meet Will.

Meg was startled when Godfrey put a hand on her shoulder and said "Afternoon, sister!" and then looking at Will "Brother." Will looked at his brother suspiciously, and replied "Afternoon, brother."

"We are ready to do our duty for the King!" Godfrey smiled.

Meg laughed at him, and lightly pushed him on the shoulder, "Don't be daft!"

"It is absolutely true, I promise!" he grinned.

Meg looked at Will, a question in her eyes. "I have asked Godfrey and his men to accompany me." Will declared.

"Seriously?" Meg asked, her whisper incredulous. "Why Godfrey?"

"He has asked me to find five men to reconnoitre the enemy with me," he said in a serious tone. "We will be safe and away from any real danger."

"There is always danger Will!" Meg admonished, "And even more so with Godfrey at your side!"

"I didn't want to use any of the men from the village..."

"So, you admit there could be some danger!" she hissed.

"The King will not want us to get in the way of his real soldiers, and tonight we are just scouting."

"I don't like it Will, you will not be safe. Why didn't you refuse?"

"Meg, you cannot refuse a King!" Will gasped.

"Are we having a family picnic, or are we going to see the King?" Godfrey interjected.

"Meg, my love, I have to go." Will said as he took Maud from his shoulders and handed her over to Meg. Meg cuddled her into her chest, as Will leaned over to kiss her. Turning to Godfrey he said, "Let's go Godfrey, can't keep the King waiting!"

As he ran off Meg called after him "How long will you be gone?" Will turned and shrugged, quite thrilled to be involved in all the excitement. "Be careful!" Meg cried, but by now, Will was too far away to hear.

❖

Will collected his gear quickly and returned to the meeting place indicated by Godfrey. When he arrived, he saw Wendley, Garvey, Holder, and Smith, already waiting. "Will." They greeted him in unison, nodding their heads as they did so. Although Will recognised these men as friends of Godfrey, as he had seen them together before at the Cross Hand Inn, he had never spoken to them, and was quite wary of their reputations. If they were friends of Godfrey, he had surmised, then they were not good people.

Will beckoned them as he walked towards a guard who was protecting the entry to the field in which the army was camped. After a brief conversation with the sentry, the group joined him, and they passed through.

Meg who was still standing behind the hedge, watched as Will joined the group of men, and enter the field. She didn't like the look of them, and she nervously twizzled the small silver ring on her finger.

Will strode across the field towards one of the tents in a confident manner, followed by Godfrey's fretful crew, who were a lot less sure of themselves. Each looked around at the hard-bitten soldiers, slightly in awe.

When they arrived at the tent, Will ordered them to remain where they were, while he walked over to the guard outside. After just a few words, he was admitted inside.

The men waited in the light afternoon sun, until Will returned in the company of a grand knight. The Knight introduced himself as Sir Walter Devereux, and he began to outline what their task was.

❖

Just over 5 miles away, Margaret of Anjou's army had arrived at Lower Lode ferry crossing, a mile short of Tewkesbury itself, and to the southwest of the town.

The Queen was extremely perturbed at what she saw. The crossing consisted of one boat that was drawn across the river by men pulling on ropes. She quickly realised that to get 6,000 men, their horses, supplies, and cannon across, would be likely to take more than a day. It was now early evening; her army was exhausted and trying to move people across the river after dark, would be treacherous. If she was unable to get her whole army across at the same time, then Edward would catch her with her army split on two sides of the river.

Frustrated and annoyed, she called her senior commanders to discuss the situation.

"My Lords, what say you?" her pursed lips betraying her feelings.

"We will not be able to cross here today." Somerset stated flatly.

"My Lord Wenlock. You told us there was a bridge to the north of the town?" Margaret asked curtly.

"Yes, Your Majesty! I was informed so." he replied.

"Then send scouts to assess the crossing immediately!" she commanded, turning, and walking away.

"Devonshire, put out pickets, we will tarry here for a while, to consider our options." Somerset declared.

Devonshire complied with his orders and left to ensure the perimeter of the army was guarded. The bulk of the army was allowed to rest for a while, and the horses were watered down at the riverside. Scouts were sent to survey the other crossings, but critically they were not asked to survey the land north of the town, in terms of its suitability as a defensive site, only to assess the river crossing.

Meanwhile, having rested for a short time, the army was moved inland, away from the river, and closer to the town. Camp was pitched, any food that was available, was eaten, and everyone waited for news from the scouts. The Queen was billeted at the manor house known as Gupshill Manor, and her army was camped around the area.

Just after dark, the scouts returned. The news they brought was not good. The next crossing, at Upper Lode, was also a ferry, and no better than the one they had seen at Lower Lode. The next proper bridge crossing was indeed to the north of the town, however, it was a further 7 miles distant!

Faced with the clear decision, that they would not be able to cross the river here and would not be able to travel on to the bridge at Upton-On-Severn, their choices were severely limited. In fact, their options had now become limited to one only. They would have to face their enemy! A battle at this location was now inevitable, and fate had conspired to trap the Queen at Tewkesbury!

❖

Edward, emboldened by the intelligence he had received, had decided to send a contingent of knights on horseback, towards Tewkesbury, and make themselves known to the enemy. The purpose being to ensure that they continued to feel under immediate threat and collect intelligence about enemy positions.

Devereux commanded the troop which consisted of a dozen knights and Will's bowmen, and they left just after dusk. The bowmen had each been provided with a horse.

Will and Devereux had the lead, but Will was given the task of finding safe passage as they approached the enemy lines. He was uniquely equipped for this task having lived in the area all his life. He knew every lane, hedge row and hiding place.

While the scouts were out, Edward packed up his camp, and moved towards his overnight resting place at Treddington. This would leave him within striking distance of the Lancastrian forces and provide him with the flexibility to respond to any strategy his foes deployed against him.

❖

The town at Tewkesbury, stands in a quite unique location. Sitting at the confluence of two major rivers, the Avon which runs across the north of the town, and the Severn, which runs to the west of the town.

Somerset and his Captains, having accepted the inevitable, decided to survey the local topography. Thus far, their troops had not had any real time to rest. They had moved from the riverbank to their present position and would soon be needed to move again to their battle positions. This was becoming a major issue, they had been on the move, continuously, for almost 24 hours, and had not had much food or drink, during that time.

Because of the time available to them, they had not looked at any positions north of the town, and the towns people had not been particularly friendly towards them.  Local support, it seemed, had ended at the gates of Gloucester.  Somerset determined that he would place his army in front of the area known as the Vineyards in front of the ancient abbey.  He had ascertained that the high ground in front of the abbey would create a decent defensive position.

Somerset had not really reconnoitred the north of the town.  If he had, he might have decided that it provided a better defensive position and would force Edward's army to come through the middle of the town and stretch them out in the process.  This might have been a grave tactical error caused by fatigue.  Instead, Somerset only looked south of the town, as he was keen to get into position as soon as possible, and give his men some much needed rest.

Somerset convened a council of war in a tent on the far side of the road from the Gupshill Manor.  The Queen and her son Prince Edward were in attendance, together with Devonshire and Wenlock.

"Your Majesties, My Lords.  We have surveyed the local area.  I believe we need to move back from our current position, three to four hundred yards." He stated confidently.

As they surveyed the map drawn by Somerset, he told them of his plan and position "This position provides protection to our left, for My Lord Devonshire's 'battle'.  There are many high hedges and ditches to our front, which will hamper the enemy advance in the centre, this will be My Lord Prince's position, with Lord Wenlock. We will place our available cannon here, in the centre." he continued.

"I will take the right 'battle' and look for an opportunity to outflank the Yorkist's from this position. Once I move, the centre should begin to move forward to engage and distract the enemy centre and ensure our success. My Lord Devonshire, once The Prince's battle is moving forward, you can then engage and take advantage of any opportunities you perceive." he added.

"We will initially take a defensive posture and try to bring them onto us. Once they do, I will counterattack against their left flank, and then we will drive home our advantage!" he concluded triumphantly.

"Are we clear?" he asked the assembled audience. Each nodded their head in agreement.

"Where will I be positioned?" enquired the Queen.

"My Lady, we will repair you to the Abbey, where you will be able to watch the conduct of the battle." He replied, bowing with a flourish of his arm.

"Let us prepare then, My Lords. I will address the men." The Queen commanded. "Let us finish this once and for all, and secure our King, and the position of my son! No quarter gentlemen!" she looked towards her son, standing proud amongst these experienced soldiers.

"No quarter!" they cheered with a unified response.

❖

Meanwhile, Will directed Devereux's command along two possible routes of advance for the Yorkist army.

As they approached along the Gloucester Road, Will spoke to the commander "This is the main route to the town. It is the most obvious route."

"They will expect us to come from here?" Devereux questioned.

"It is the most obvious route, and it will be easy to move the army along this road." Will replied. "I wanted you to see it and make your own decision."

"You have another proposal?" Devereux asked looking over at his guide.

"Aye, but I want you to be able to get a view of them from here first." He replied pointing in the direction of the distant town. "We will give them a wide berth and observe how they are positioning themselves."

They moved forward once more. They traversed Behind the Gupshill Manor, closer to the Severn River, and up into the deer park. Once they had reached the highest point on the hill, they were able to look down on their enemy. Devereux was aware that the Lancastrian commanders were likely to have patrols out but was surprised that their progress had remained undetected so far, and they had not come across any pickets.

He turned to one of his knights and said "It looks like they are keeping the pickets close in. Probably don't want to extend their lines too far."

"Aye Sire!" came the response "That's a mistake!" he added. The group of experienced soldiers all nodded in agreement.

As they continued to watch, Devereux made a note of the positions of the 'battles'. The Lancastrian's were arrayed in traditional formation, with their individual battles on the right, centre, and left. By the light of the campfires, they could also see the main positions of the enemy cannon, predominantly in the centre.

Will pointed out a wooded area to their right, lower down the hill. Devereux considered the potential advantage that the Lancastrians might have in the upcoming battle by occupying this wood. He nodded at Will "I must remember to ensure the King is aware of this."

❖

Whether or not this was an oversight by Somerset, or perhaps he felt that it was too far out from the sphere of influence of the Lancastrian lines, and troops posted there could get cut off from the main army, is not known. Somerset did not station any troops in these woods. That decision was to have devastating consequences.

❖

The Queen rode out to rally her troops on the eve of the battle. She rode down the lines with her son, and a small escort of standard bearers. As she saluted all her soldiers, cheers rang out and could be heard several miles away.

It was a stirring sight. This determined woman, who possessed such fortitude, had journeyed with her army, and suffered all the same deprivations that they had endured. She was one of them!

She stood up in the stirrups of her horse. Leaning forward she raised her arm, her fist clenched.

"My Men! My Men of England! Gird yourselves and show no fear!

We have lost great champions on our quest, and we have lost many of your brethren!" She cried out with passion.

"But we have great champions still! They lead you here!

We need have no fear of this usurper, who calls himself King!

The whole country is behind us.  These evil brothers have caused me much grief!

We will end their corrupt dynasty here! Tomorrow!

Stand Fast Proud Men!  Do not trust them to spare you in defeat!

They have shown no compassion in their dealings and will show you none here!

Pray for your King! Pray for your Prince! Pray for your Queen!

Our many destinies will be decided on the morrow!

Remain steadfast in your hearts!

Your souls will be guarded by GOD!

HE will provide us with the Victory we deserve!
Give them no quarter!

NO QUARTER!"  She screamed!

The whole army took up the refrain, banging on their shields, banging on their armour, drumming their enthusiasm for this magnificent woman on anything that would make a noise.

"NO QUARTER! NO QUARTER! NO QUARTER!" their united voices roared!

Still tired, weary, and hungry, every single one of these brave souls, were ready to give their lives for this Queen!

❖

Edward's army had left Swindon Village in the early evening, cheered off by the enthusiastic crowd.

Refreshed and rested and with their bellies full, the army was in good heart as they commenced the journey that would determine their individual and collective destinies.

They made quick progress to their "Laying Up Point" at Treddington, covering the four-mile journey within a couple of hours.

Pickets were posted, tents were erected, and welcome sleep was taken. They were now within striking distance of their uncompromising foes. They also knew that tomorrow would bring a resolution to this conflict. The Lancastrian army had nowhere left to go!

The troops were content, steeling themselves for the desperate fight that they faced in the morning.

The quality of their rest was only tainted by the battle-cry of their enemy, which could clearly be heard across the short stretch of land that divided them.

Despite their training, despite their experience, and despite their personal confidence in their own abilities, and their belief in the abilities of their commanders, and King (who had never lost a battle in England), a few of the battle-hardened troops felt a shiver go down their spines.

Edward too had heard the enemy battle cry, he smiled at his brothers. "No Quarter, indeed!" he said. "They are asking us to give them No Quarter, and we shall oblige!"

"The colour of fear is brown!" Richard replied, looking out at the campfires and tents of his army.

He knew that more than a few of these tough and dangerous men would need to empty their bowels before morning. Better now than in the heat of battle! he thought.

He knew that their sergeants would counsel them that fear was good, fear kept you alert, fear kept you alive!

❖

Devereux and his troop had also heard the roar of defiance from the enemy lines. He admitted to himself that it was impressive.

They moved from their position of advantage and re-positioned themselves to an area where the enemy might expect an attack.

Despite the fact that he knew that the Lancastrians were exhausted, hungry, and had been forced to make a stand in a place that they had not chosen, he also knew that they were committed, and were led by impressive commanders.

"We need to piss on their fire!" he told his group. "Time for you to earn your money boys!" he directed his comment towards the local archers.

Will directed them closer to the enemy picket lines.

"We'll make ourselves obvious." Devereux stated. "You create a nuisance!" he said directly to Will.

"Right-oh!" Will retorted, and the group separated.

Devereux led his troop of mounted knights and positioned themselves out of range of enemy bowmen, but ensured that their presence was known, with the moonlight silhouetting against the skyline. To ensure a response, they made a lot of noise, and were rewarded with a hail of arrows, all of which fell short, by a significant distance.

Meanwhile, Will and his group crept closer. They ensured they had chosen an angle that was oblique to the position of the enemy pickets. They quickly loosed two or three arrows each, towards the location that they knew contained the sentries guarding the Lancastrian lines.

The six men heard the satisfying sounds of the chaos their arrows had caused, and also the screams of those who had been hit. In the dark any hit was a bonus. They quickly retreated back to their horses, before any response could be initiated against them.

Re-joining Devereux's party, they moved around the enemy perimeter, causing minor havoc, and creating continued tension in the enemy lines. The enemy had no idea how many of their opponents they were facing, or where they would strike next.

When word got back to Somerset, he was extremely angry. First, he had been woken from a much-needed sleep, and second, he knew that problems being caused by the marauders would also deny sleep to members of his army.

He realised he had no choice and increased the number of horse patrols around his perimeter. The men who would be forced to undertake these tasks would be critical in the morning when battle was joined. Tiredness would severely impact their effectiveness in the trials to come. He had far fewer mounted knights than his opposition, he had far fewer cannon, and he needed all of his assets to be as fresh as they could be.

Will consulted with Godfrey, who also knew this area well. They decided that their last task would be to take Devereux along the Rudgeway. This was a decent road that travelled almost directly north, approaching the town of Tewkesbury to its eastern side. It ran all the way up to Walton Cardiff and would allow the Yorkist army to approach its enemy directly from the east. This would mean that Edward would be approaching the battle on the Lancastrian left flank, causing the Lancastrian army to look directly into the glare of the morning sun. Edward's army would still need to cross the Swilgate river, but it would provide a tactical advantage if it could be achieved. The Yorkist army would enter the battle with the sun behind them.

Will pointed out the approach, its advantages and its issues. He left it to Devereux to decide what the most appropriate direction of attack would be.

When they arrived back at Edwards camp the archers were shown to a tent. Although they knew they would be leaving in just a few hours, the men felt unable to sleep immediately. The excitement of the evening was still coursing through their bodies. Garvey suggested a game of dice to relax them, and they all agreed. They played a few games and Will's small purse had become rapidly depleted. The only coin he had left was the unique charm that had been given to him by Old

Mother Sawyer. "I'm out!" Will declared "I've nothing left."

"You have that coin." Garvey stated pointing at the charm.

"Oh, I can't use that! It was a gift!" Will retorted quickly, suddenly regretting that he had tipped his whole purse onto the table. He picked up the coin and placed it back into his purse.

"Just one more game Will?" asked Godfrey a glint in his eye.

"No. No more for me, I need to get some sleep." Will said as he rose and went over to his blankets.

Godfrey's eyes followed him, taking notice of where Will had put his purse.

The other five men continued playing for a short while, before retiring themselves. It was going to be a long day tomorrow, and if they were lucky, they would be able to get about 4 hours sleep.

Will felt a little anxious and initially struggled to go to sleep. He had seen the look in the eyes of the other men, when they had seen the coin, and it worried him. He touched the pocket where he had put his purse. To reassure himself, and then turned over to face the wall of the tent. After a while, and despite his discomfort, Will eventually drifted off to sleep. The excitement and exertions of the day had finally caught up with him.

When he heard the snoring of the other men and knew they were all asleep, Godfrey rose and crept over to where Will was sleeping. He gently removed Will's purse and removed the coin, before replacing the purse where it had come from. "Lucky charm eh!" Godfrey murmured as he put the coin in his own pocket.

Will did not stir. After all, this was one of Godfrey's great skills.

# CHAPTER 7

## A National Tragedy

### 4th May 1646[1]

Edward and his army broke camp just before sun rise to make the short 3-mile journey to the battlefield.

Armed with the information gleaned during the reconnaissance mission undertaken by Devereux the previous night, Edward moved forward with a measure of confidence. Once he could see the location for himself, he would make his final assessment and battle plan.

He had organised his forces into their battlefield formations, with the Earl of Gloucester in the Vanguard (who would take the left flank on the field), Clarence and himself in the centre, and the Earl of Hastings at the rear (who would take the right flank)

They took Will's advice and travelled up the Rudgeway, cutting west just before Walton Cardiff. He knew that the Lancastrian army was already in position, and that it would be extremely difficult for them to move, now that they had dug in. By arriving on the field at an oblique angle to the established lines of the Lancastrians, Edward wished to put doubt into the minds of their commanders.

He had also taken on board the information regarding the woods flanking Somerset's position and had called Devereux forward.

"Devereux! The woods we discussed last night, on Somerset's right flank. I am concerned that he might aim to make trouble there." he stated, "Take 200 men on horseback, plus your archers and secure this wood. If there is no ambush, then wait there for any suitable opportunity to join the battle!" he concluded.

Devereux gathered the required men, and made a wide detour, coming at the woods out of sight of the enemy, through the Deer Park. When they arrived, the woods were vacant. Devereux sent a messenger back to the main force to tell his King that they were watching and waiting. Then they sat and bided their time.

Edward also had another plan. Having arrived on the field, he ordered a significant proportion of cannon to be deployed with Gloucester on the left flank. He had been able to see for himself the difficulties that Gloucester would have advancing over the terrain, of hedges, ditches and banks, and wanted to try and draw Somerset away from his defences.

He trotted his horse over to Gloucester. "Richard, you will have the devil's own time trying to move forward. Let us try to antagonise him. He can be a hothead!" Both brothers laughed at the insult.

"Their cannon are limited, not as good as ours, and cannot fire as far." Gloucester responded. We might be able to force them to move, and then we can make a feint to draw them out." He concluded.

"Do it!" the King agreed, "I will keep an eye on proceedings over here and support you if necessary!"

Gloucester moved his cannon up on the enemies right flank, supported by archers and defended by foot soldiers, with mounted knights in reserve. The opening salvo came from the Lancastrian lines, but the intention to draw the Yorkist's forward was ineffective. The obstacles in the terrain made it suicidal for the Yorkist to move forward. Gloucester ordered the opening salvo from his own army to commence. The superior design of the guns, their accuracy and number, meant that the cannonade was devastating to the defenders, and there was practically nothing Somerset could do to counter it.

Edward had slightly staggered his battles, so that they remained off to the side and slightly behind each other, marginally out of sync with their marching formation. If necessary, they could still move forward and present a solid line. By doing this, it prevented proper engagement with the centre and left flank of their opposition and ensured that the enemy canon were ineffective.

It also had the effect of focusing the attack on Somerset's flank.

The first salvos fired by the Yorkist army came from their left flank. Although the Lancastrian army had dug in and were protected from assault by the hedgerows and ditches in front of them, the opportunities for any kind of direct assault, by either side, were severely limited by the terrain.

The Lancastrian defences, hastily built over-night, were designed to be held against an assault, and give them an advantage. However, the ploy was too obvious, and the Yorkist commanders could clearly see the folly of such a strategy. For this reason, the battle was like to become one of attrition.

The key factor was the amount and quality of cannon possessed by each army. In this regard, Edward held a huge advantage, that allowed him to deploy and begin to pound his opponents into submission, without the need for close-quarter combat. The use of archers on this flank also had a devastating impact, and very soon began to tell on the moral of Somersets men.

Somerset's position gradually became untenable. The screams of soldiers being ravaged by heavy stone shot and the volume of arrows falling from the skies. The black clouds of hundreds of yard long arrows with armour piercing iron bodkins, hissed through the air and landed almost vertically with devastating effect. Up to ten volleys every minute, gave the hapless defenders no respite, even to those hunkered down in the ditches, and together with the cannonballs smashing through the barricades, casualties began to mount.

"My Lord!" cried a Sergeant-at-Arms "The cannon shot and arrows, are decimating us!"

Somerset sat on his horse surveying the carnage and listened to the screams of men being rent limb from limb. The few guns he had were ineffective. He had to do something the change the course of the action.

"Send a message to the Prince and My Lord Wenlock. I will advance to attack their flank with my horsemen!" He cried out to his Sergeant "They will need to advance in time!"

"Aye Sire! And the rest of our troops?"

"When they see I have gained the upper hand, they are to advance with all speed!" he responded.

The Sergeant turned his horse and galloped away to deliver his message.

"To me! To me! Brave men of Lancaster!" Somerset bellowed to his fellows. He was about to split his own battle into two, in a huge gamble to gain the advantage.

The horsemen formed up and began to make their way out to their right and onto a lane, known as Lincoln Green Lane. The high hedgerows protected them from view and Somerset had surveyed the area the previous night.

He had planned to use the lane for a counter-attack once he had drawn Gloucester's battle forward.

However, the current circumstances dictated he would need to be bold, and take advantage now, in the face of the unyielding bombardment. It was his key opportunity to take the enemy by surprise!

With the sounds of battle raging all around, the large group of mounted knights trotted down the lane until they were behind Gloucester's part of the Yorkist army.

Where the hedgerow ended, Somerset found himself on a slight rise, above the enemy positions. From his position, he could see the 'battle' of the Edward himself, in the centre.

In the course of just a few seconds he surveyed the scene in front of him and considered his options. "If I can rout Gloucester, then I can attack Edward's flank. With the rest of my battle advancing, alongside Wenlock, victory will be mine!" he thought.

"Charge! My noble knights! CHARGE!"

He advanced his horse, and his cohort began moving forward at pace, galloping down the hill towards the rear of Gloucester's forces. Swords drawn, lances poised, the galloping horses and blood-curdling war cries of the mounted knights was a fearful sight to behold, and a terrifying sound to hear.

"For Lancaster! For the King!" they screamed, as they bore down on the surprised soldiers in front of them.

"They yield! They run!" Somerset cried out in joy, keen to press his advantage. The Yorkist soldiers, having been surprised by the attack to their rear, had begun to turn away and move back towards the centre of their army.  If Somerset could crash his knights into the flank of Yorkist centre, he might be able to take their King, and end the battle immediately.  "I can destroy their archers and take the cannon!" he thought as he charged.

Emboldened by the retreat of Gloucester's battle, he pushed forward.  At this time, he was expecting Wenlock and the Prince to have seen the advantage that he had created and begin to move their own troops forward and engage the enemy from the front.

Wenlock had not moved….

❖

Up on the hillside, hidden by the woods that surrounded them, Devereux and his 200 knights and mounted archers watched and waited patiently.  They had seen the large contingent of mounted knights leave the Lancastrian lines and advance along Lincoln Green Lane.

Devereux raised his eyebrows in surprise.  "If that was what they were going to do all along, why didn't they put some troops here?" he wondered aloud.

"They might have thought it was too far away." Replied the knight next to him.

"Aye, it's half a mile, but still…"

"Should we move now?" the other knight asked.

"Not yet. We'll tarry a little longer." Devereux responded, his face grim.

Godfrey, Will and the other archers, sat on their horses, filled in equal measure with anticipation and fear about what was to come. Similar thoughts filled all their heads. "I'm glad I'm up here, and not down there!" said Godfrey.

They could hear the roar of cannon, see the smoke drift across the fields. They could hear the shouts and screams of men, fighting and dying in front of them. They had witnessed the carnage being wrought on Somerset's flank and were now watching his counter-attack against Gloucester.

As Somerset launched his attack down the hill, Devereux called out "Now!"

❖

Edward's foresight, added to the excellent intelligence he had received about the lie of the land, had put him a position to be able to anticipate Somerset's tactics. He knew that Somerset was an astute commander, who was prepared to take bold and decisive action, when called upon to do so. These were the characteristics of his enemy that he knew well, and was relying on, as his own plan unfolded.

Even above the other sounds of the battle being raged in front of him, Edward became quickly aware of the clamour on his left. As he gazed across the field towards his brother, he could see the mounted knights charging down the hill towards him. Gloucester's rear seemed to be unprotected and his own flank exposed. Gloucester's soldiers had appeared to turn and run back towards the centre.

"They come!" Edward called out.

"As expected My Lord!" called his sergeant. "Move! Now!" he cried, and a large party of mounted knights turned towards the Lancastrians.

As they moved forward at pace, Gloucester's troops stopped and turned also. Pikes were placed in the ground, arqubusiers were primed and aimed, and the mounted horsemen of Gloucester's battle wheeled to face the oncoming threat.

Somerset's momentum carried into the fray. Surprise and realisation found simultaneous expression on his face, "I have been fooled!" he thought, "No Matter! The force of our attack is unstoppable! Their ruse has failed!"

The two sides clashed, blades whirled on their deadly arcs, pikes were thrust, and arqubusiers boomed their deadly cargo, smoke enveloping their shooters. Men screamed in anger and anguish as limbs were cleaved and the blood-letting began. Men, all fighting desperately for their lives, blood and adrenaline pumping, muscles being pressed to their limits.

Somerset fought on, not immediately aware of what was happening behind him. Will, Godfrey and the other archers had stopped short of the carnage occurring in front of them, dismounted and positioned themselves to fire their arrows into the rear of the Lancastrian horsemen. They did so with devastating effect, 60 arrows every minute struck the unsuspecting knights of Somerset's cavalry. The archers stopped just before Devereux and his own knights charged into the rear of the Somerset's contingent.

For a short while Somerset continued his assault. He thrashed his battle-axe right and left with furious abandon, smashing skulls and torso's as they presented themselves to him. The red mist had fallen, and he was oblivious to what was happening to his rear.

"Sire! Sire! We are ambushed!" one of his men cried out, from a short distance away. Somerset dispatched the Yorkist knight that had ridden against him and looked around quickly. Where have they come from!" he screamed, suddenly aware of what was happening.

"Retreat! Fall back!" he yelled above the din of clashing swords and the screams of injured and dying men. He rallied those that were left, quickly broke away. They were forced to continue fighting as they viciously fought their way out of the killing zone. Eventually breaking free, they made all haste back towards their own lines. His gamble had failed! "Where is Wenlock!" He fumed!

❖

With the counterattack and ambush successful, and with Somerset in full flight, Gloucester's battle pursued the fleeing knights. Edward's supporting knights returned to the centre and both he and Hastings began to advance to engage Wenlock in the centre and Devonshire on the left flank of the Lancastrian army.

The Yorkist soldiers clambered through hedges, into ditches and dykes and stubbornly made their way forward. The Lancastrian centre was distracted by what was happening on their flank, and the apparent indecision of their commanders.

Somerset arrived back at his own lines, but with startled looks on their faces his soldiers watched as he galloped straight through. Other knights followed on behind, and panic began to set in, when the soldiers realised that Gloucester's battle was flooding in after them. Their resolve broke and men started fleeing from their defensive positions.

The rout had begun. Gloucester's forces moved forward rapidly, and the Lancastrian right flank began to crumble.

Somerset rode straight to the centre section of his army and confronted Wenlock. "You traitorous bastard!" he screamed, and before anyone could react, he heaved his battle-axe and cleaved Wenlock across the neck, almost decapitating him. Wenlock fell from his horse, dead. Rage and fury were etched on the face of Somerset. The knights around him cowered.

Prince Edward stammered "What has happened?"

"We are lost! That is what has happened!" Somerset roared.

The knights quickly began to realise the import of Somerset's words and began to retreat towards the town, taking the young Prince with them.

While Gloucester's forces chased the hapless soldiers that had made up Somerset's right flank, Edward and Hastings advanced forward from their positions, scrambling through the hedges and crossing the small brooks and ditches that separated them from Wenlock and Devonshire. Brutal hand to hand fighting ensued and every inch of ground was hard fought and stained with the blood of those who had been martyred for their respective causes.

With Somerset's flank now in flight, and the Yorkist cannon now being ranged against the Lancastrian centre, Edward's army was now steadily gaining the upper hand.

On the left flank of the Lancastrian position, Devonshire valiantly fought his way forward, leading his men from the front. As his army clashed front on with the Yorkist army lead by Hastings, he tried to rally his troops "For Henry!" he cried wading into the thick of the action. His courage was not rewarded. The Lancastrian centre had now collapsed, and Devonshire's forces were completely surrounded. He found himself fighting on foot against three or four opposing knights. "Lancaster!" he cried out his last words defiantly, as three blades punctured his bruised, battered and exhausted body.

❖

On the hillside Godfrey, Will and the other archers began to follow the rapidly advancing soldiers of Gloucester's battle. They reached an area of pasture, with steep sided banks on either side, topped with hedges. This piece of land was designed to pen livestock. In front of them hundreds of men were being slaughtered. Somerset's defensive position had placed the Lancastrian army with their backs to the rivers Avon and Severn. The inability of the Lancastrian army to cross these rivers had been the cause of their woes up to this point and forced the stand against the house of York here at Tewkesbury. It was now proving to be the final barrier that gave the frightened and despairing men, fleeing from the vicious retribution of their enemies, nowhere left to run.

Many dropped their weapons and tried to remove items of armoured clothing as they ran. Some pleaded for their lives, others were resigned to their fate. The impossible choice left to them, was die where they stood, or die from drowning trying to cross the river.

Men scrambled and stumbled into the river, arrows flying after them, their armour and heavy clothing weighing them down. Their relentless, and merciless foes, following hard on their heels, continued to pursue them, baying for blood.

Around 2000 Lancastrian soldiers lay dead on the battlefield, hundreds more floated in the river or sunk to its depths.

Will stopped and stood still for a few seconds. He was shocked to his core. Watching the slaughter and butchery, taking place in front of him, it sent a shiver down his spine. Will was a strong, tough man, but the wanton murder he was witnessing, chilled him. "What is the point?" he asked himself.

As Will was distracted by the blood-thirsty spectacle he was watching, Godfrey crept up behind him. Wendley, Smith, Holder, and Garvey looked around them, checking that Godfrey was in the clear. All attention was focused on the fleeing Lancastrian army, and no-one was interested in what was going on towards the rear of the battlefield.

The battle noise still raged all around and Will did not hear Godfrey's approach. As the long, thin blade slid into his back, he turned towards his assailant.

"Godfrey! Why?" he sighed with his last breath, as life abandoned him.

# Chapter 8

## Aftermath

### 4th May 1461

Sir Walter Devereux met the five remaining archers at the camp after the battle.

Godfrey, Wendley, Garvey, Smith, and Holder had carried Will's body back to the camp and explained to Devereux what had happened.

"He was trying to stop a couple of Lancastrian soldiers fleeing up the hill Sire. We tried to get there to help, but we got there too late…" Godfrey explained.

Devereux looked at the body of the lifeless giant. "He was a good man. 'Tis a great pity." he lamented. "You men did great work, and your local knowledge made a real difference. Here is your pay, and a purse for his widow," he said handing over six purses to Godfrey. "This one here is for his widow, with something extra in it. Will you make sure it gets to her?"

Of course, my lord." Godfrey answered with an obsequious smile on his face.

"I need you to do some more tough work, digging graves and collecting weapons, are you up for it?"

Godfrey looked at his men, and seeing their greed in their eyes replied, "Indeed Sire!"

"That is settled then. Once the graves are dug you can have a couple of days to take Will's body back to his village. Then I have a proposition for you."

"A proposition Sire?"

"I need good fighting men, and I would like you to join my company of archers. I was thinking of offering the position of Captain to Will, but as he was married, he probably would not have taken in anyway. So, I thought you might want the position Godfrey…"

"Me! Captain of Archers?" a surprised Godfrey responded.

"Yes, you have acquitted yourself well, and are obviously capable of leading men. I would have your men join me too…"

"May I discuss it with them, and let you know?"

"Of course. Think about in the next few days, then if you return after taking Will home, I will know you have accepted."

"Thank you Sire!"

The five men did as they had been commanded and completed the task of clearing the battlefield, collecting weapons and armour, which were put onto large horse drawn carts, to be used another day.

Of course, like all the other soldiers, they did not baulk at taking anything of value for the bodies of the dead.

❖

"What do you think boys?" Godfrey asked, while they sat in the shade, drinking some ale and taking a breather.

"What about?" Garvey replied.

"Joining Devereux…. He'll pay well!"

"And you will be king of the castle! Captain Bowen!" Wendley replied, the sarcasm dripping from every word.

"Aye! And why would we want to put ourselves in harm's way?" Holder added, scratching his head with fingers that were still filthy from lifting dead bodies.

"Well, it would be steady coin, and regular grub!" Smith said, as Godfrey looked at him in amazement, his eyebrows arching.

"Well, I suppose with Godfrey in charge, he'll see us right!" Wendley.

"Of course, I'll look after you!" Godfrey grinned, slapping Wendley on the back.

Once the battlefield had been cleared of anything valuable, they were then given the gruesome task of digging vast pits, into which the dead would be buried.

Again, the carts were used to move the dead bodies before they were dumped into the pits.

The people of Tewkesbury were unhappy about having mass graves dug too close to their town, and therefore the graves were dug a couple of miles south of the town.

Of the 6000 troops that had lined up for the battle, the local scribes counted around 2000 dead. These were the bodies they could count.

Those that had met their deaths attempting to cross the rivers were unaccounted for and not included in the figures that were produced.

It was probably many hundreds more, whose fate was to float down the river, and probably wash on some bank towards Bristol, or simply float down the Bristol Channel and eventually out into the Atlantic Sea.

Local priests held brief masses for the dead, but did not record the locations of the graves, or indeed even know their names.

Will's body was handed to his brother Godfrey to take home to Swindon Village, along with his purse, intended for his widow. When they were out of sight of prying eyes, Godfrey distributed Will's purse amongst his men.

Godfrey had considered putting Will's body into one of the mass graves, but decided that an explanation would be required back in the village, and therefore they would return his body there.

The work they were required to do in the aftermath of the battle, kept them in the town for another couple of days.

They wrapped Will's body in hessian and left him in the cellar of a local hostelry, after intimidating the owner.

They hoped the cooler air in the cellar would keep the body fresh until they could return home. Whilst they stayed in the town, they heard about the terrible crimes that had been committed after the battle.

❖

Edward IV took swift retribution. Lord Devonshire had died on the battlefield, the Young Prince of Wales was either killed on the battlefield, or if the rumours were true – had been murdered after the battle!.

Somerset and 12 others who had sought sanctuary in the Abbey had been forcibly removed, found guilty of treason and were now in the town square, about to be executed.

Godfrey and his friends had left their own sanctuary at Black Bear Inn, and cut short their breakfast, in order to watch the macabre spectacle that was unfolding in the town square.

They pushed their way forward through the gathering crowd, to gain the best possible view. From where they were standing, they could see the raised wooden platform that had been hastily erected.

An executioner stood on the platform with his face covered. His feet were placed apart, and his broadsword was placed between his legs, so that it formed the shape of a crucifix at his waist, the tip of its blade resting on the deck. His hands rested on the pommel of the sword, one on top of the other. He was a large, powerful, looking man, with the build of a blacksmith, with a strong chest and arms.

In front of him was a wooden block, on which the unfortunate's head would be placed.

"He's an ugly looking bastard!" Wendley joked.

"Aye, "said Godfrey "But he is exactly the kind of man you'd want to be your own executioner, if you want a swift and less painful death!" he concluded grimly.

"Aye, better than the noose! But you don't want the bastard to miss with the first blow!" Garvey observed.

The five men chuckled in agreement, despite the shiver that went down each of their spines.

Godfrey and his men were stood on one side of the platform, and they could also see the array of nobles seated in front of the dais.

Pride of place given to the King and his brothers.

Richard, Duke of Gloucester, who was also Constable of England, had pronounced the sentences, and sat on the King's righthand side, and George, Duke of Clarence (who had sworn fealty to the now dead Prince of Wales, only a year before), sat on the King's left.

There was a hubbub in the crowd as they waited for proceedings to commence. It was a clear morning, the sun was shining, and there was just a slight breeze in the air.

A noticeable frisson tremored through the crowd, as the level of tension rose.

A mounted guard, led by Lord William, Baron of Hastings, followed by some horse drawn carts could be seen making their way towards the square.

Outriders guarded the flanks, and a further cohort of mounted men brought up the rear.

In the carts, the prisoners, including Edmund Beaufort, Duke of Somerset, Sir John Langstrother, Prior of the Order of St Johns, and Hugh Courtenay, cousin of the Earl of Devon, could be seen.

Each of the prisoners was standing, and clearly struggling to retain their balance as the cart rumbled towards the square.

Each prisoner was bound, with their hands tied behind their back, and a noose around their necks. Evidence of severe beatings could be seen by the bruising on their faces, and their naked chests.

"Thank God we picked the right side!" quipped Smith.

"Aye!" the Godfrey's men nodded their agreement.

A hush fell over the crowd, as Somerset was the first to brought up onto the dais.

Two guards, one on each side, held him roughly by the arms.

Richard, Duke of Gloucester stood and addressed the crowd. "Edmund Beaufort, guilty of treason!" he declared.

The executioner stood with the sword raised and poised.

Somerset was given no right of reply, no opportunity to make a speech.

As soon as judgement was pronounced, he was roughly pushed down, his head slammed into the wooden block in front of him, and the blade brought down.

It slammed into his neck, making a dull thud, that could be heard by all present, as it severed his head in a single blow, and struck the block beneath.

The body was dragged off the platform and dumped off to one side. The executioner stepped forward and kicked the severed head of the dais.

"Whoaa!" exclaimed Garvey as the head rolled away, echoing the sentiment of the crowd.

The next prisoner was brought up onto the stage. The Duke of Gloucester again pronounced sentence. John Langstrother, guilty of treason!" Another immediate blow, another headless body.

Eight prisoners in total were executed; the process took less than 15 minutes. The bodies that had been piled up next to the dais, were manhandled back into the carts, and taken away.

Due process having been observed, the nobles rose and repaired to a local tavern for lunch.

In the course of 48 hours, the entire House of Lancaster and its chief supporters had been obliterated. Edward, Duke of York was now the undisputed King of England!

❖

Godfrey and his gang had been paid and released from their duties, and having been entertained by the beheadings, the five conspirators decided to return to Cheltenham. But first they needed to recover the body of Will.

Will's body was residing in the cellar of the Black Bear, their favourite watering hole in Tewkesbury.

When they entered the Inn, Godfrey caught the eye of the landlord. "We've come to collect the body." He said soberly.

"About time! The smell is beginning to get my food a bad reputation!" the landlord replied with a scowl on his face.

"let's get to it then!" Godfrey responded turning to Garvey and Smith "Off you go then! We'll be outside with the horses."

The landlord led the two men down into the dank cellar, and the smell assailed their noses. Garvey pulled his shirt up over his face. "God's teeth!" he murmured. "Let's get this done quick!" Smith replied, "It won't be so bad, once we get him outside."

Garvey grabbed the head, while Smith picked up the feet, and they hauled the hessian wrapped body up the stairs.

Once they had him outside, the other men helped to heave him over the back of one of the horses.

Having secured their load, the group began the journey back to Swindon Village.

The small procession made their way through the streets of the town and out onto the main road to Gloucester. They had agreed to split up at the Swann Inn and leave Godfrey to make the last part of the journey alone.

When they finally reached the junction which led into Cheltenham, Godfrey waved them off "I'll see you tonight at the Cross Hands!"

❖

In her cottage, Meg had been waiting nervously. Will had been gone for three days, and although information had got back to the village about the outcome of the battle, she had had no word of her husband.

With nothing to do but wait and hope, Meg sat next to the fireplace, a stew bubbling in the pot which was suspended over the flames. Maud was cradled in her lap, asleep.

Godfrey walked his horse solemnly and slowly through the village, his head bowed. The horse carrying Will's body trailed behind him, tethered with a rope. People from the village noticed him with his sad burden and began to follow him as he approached Meg's cottage.

The grave procession was hushed as it approached Meg's cottage.

Meg herself, sensed rather than heard what was happening outside. She got up and placed her sleeping daughter in her cot, and then went to the door.

With a mounting sense of trepidation, she opened the door and walked outside.

Godfrey sat on is horse just outside, his head lowered. When he heard the door open, he looked down at Meg. "Meg, I am so sorry!" he said, "Will didn't make it!"

Meg did not really hear his words, she screamed at the sight of the sack covered body draped over the horse behind Godfrey "WILL! NOOO!"

She rushed over and started to try and pull the body down. Other villagers rushed up and pulled her away.

"Now dear, come, there is nothing you can do." Mary said, wrapping her arms around a frantic Meg and trying to guide her away.

Meg resisted; her fist wrapped in the sacking. Hugh and another villager gently prised her hand open and helped Mary to take her back into her cottage.

As they passed Godfrey, who was still sat on his horse, Meg screamed "You Bastard! You said you would keep him safe!" The crowd that was gathered were shocked at the profanity, Meg had never been known to swear, but they all understood the depth of the woman's grief.

Finally, Meg was practically dragged, kicking, and screaming back into her cottage. When they got her inside, Old Mother Sawyer was already inside. No-one thought to query how she had got there. Hugh and Mary sat the distraught Meg in a chair, and Old Mother Sawyer handed her a mug. "This will help." She said, gently bringing to Meg's lips. "Hush now child, we will get through this."

The herb potion that Mother Sawyer had given Meg, calmed her and made her drowsy. Eventually, she fell into a deep sleep, the horrors of what had happened could wait for a few hours.

Outside, Godfrey got down from his horse, and with the help of some of the other men, untied Will's body, pulled it down and carried it into the cottage. They laid what was left of Will on the table. "Leave him there!" Old Mother Sawyer ordered, "We will clean him." The men backed away respectfully and left.

Old Mother Sawyer and Mary gently removed Will's clothes and bathed his body and dressed it with herbs. They then dressed him in clean clothes and sat next to him, waiting for Meg to awake.

When removing his clothes, Mother Sawyer had found his purse. It was empty, not even the coin charm was where she knew he always kept it, in the purse. She glared knowingly at the small leather pouch. She had also noted the single knife wound, that Will had suffered, and considered that this was hardly the type of injury that would have been inflicted in the type of hand-to-hand fighting of battle. There were no other visible injuries. "Godfrey!" she muttered under her breath.

Having done his duty, Godfrey mounted his horse again, and wheeled it, to leave the village. The other horse, still tethered to his, followed. Godfrey hoped his show of grief and respect had been enough to still wagging tongues. No-one would ever know what had really happened. Once he was far enough away from the village, he allowed himself a small smile. "Now the cottage will be mine!"

❖

When Godfrey arrived at the Cross Hands Inn his friends were already there, seated at a table near the fire.

Apart from a few candles in sconces on the walls, the fire provided the majority of light in the dimly lit room.

The smoke created a pall in the rafters, and the smell of woodsmoke permeated everything.

The men looked up at Godfrey as he approached them and sat down. He smoothed his beard and wondered what the outcome of their discussions might be.

"Well brothers! Have you decided?" he asked as Garvey handed him a mug of ale.

Wendley was the first to speak up, "Pickings 'round here have been poor for a while." he said and looked at the others, who nodded in agreement, "I reckon we would be onto an 'earner' if we left with you.."

"Aye, pay was decent and taking money off of dead men is easier than robbing live 'uns!" Smith added, hefting his heavy purse onto the table.

The men all laughed, and Godfrey finished his ale before pouring himself another, "What about you Holder?"

Holder thought for a moment and then his pensive look broke into a smile, "I've always wanted to travel, and if someone else is paying, I'm in!" Holder replied, running a coin through his fingers, and then tapping it on the table.

"How long will we be gone for?" Wendley asked, looking at Godfrey. The question again elicited nods from the other men.

"I don't know. We'll be retained men, well looked after. I s'pose it will be for as long as they need us." he replied, "as long as we are being paid well, and as long as we are enjoying it..."

"I've never worked for anyone in my life!" Garvey stated, "I don't know if I can cope with someone telling me what to do every day."

"Well, it's a chance to make something of ourselves and come back wealthy men!" Holder responded.

"And if we don't like it… we'll leave, and no-one is harmed!" Godfrey said, triumph gleaming in his eyes.

He would feel more secure knowing he had his own men around him, rather than people he did not know.

"So, it's settled then? We'll try it?" Wendley asked, again looking around at his friends.

Garvey slammed his fist onto the table, "I'm in!" he declared. The other followed suit, banging on the table with their fists.

"So, it's settled then!" Godfrey agreed.

"What about that cottage of yours though?" Wendley asked.

Godfrey scowled at him, "Will is out of the way, and the cottage will still be there when I get back. It'll still be mine."

"And if we come back rich, you'll be able to pay the rent and not have to work!" Wendley concurred.

"Aye!" replied Godfrey, a grim smile played on his lips.

"Aye! But you've just reminded me of some business I need to deal with before we leave…"

"C'mon boys! Drink up!" Smith announced, "We've got an army to join!"

"You go on ahead, and I'll meet up with you at the camp at Tewkesbury later." Godfrey told them, again he smoothed his beard as he pondered his next task.

The men finished their drinks, slammed their mugs down onto the table and left the Inn.

Outside they mounted their horses and set off for Tewkesbury, while Godfrey made his way to Swindon Village.

❖

Godfrey arrived at Meg's cottage and walked straight in without knocking.  Meg was sitting next to the fireplace with Maud on her lap, gently rocking her.  Old Mother Sawyer sat across from her, knitting. Godfrey grimaced at the smell of herbs and fragrant flowers that hung in the air, and thought to himself, "Changes need to be made in here!"

"What do you want?" Old Mother Sawyer asked, rising from her chair and standing in front of Godfrey.

Godfrey ignored the old woman and addressed Meg directly, "Evening sister. I thought I would stop by and see how you are." he said.

Meg did not respond, she seemed to be in a sort of trance. "I don't think she is well enough to talk at the moment." Old Mother Sawyer responded.

Godfrey turned his attention to the old woman, who was still blocking his path to Meg, "Well, when do you think she will be well enough?" he queried.

"Give her time Godfrey."

"There are things that need to be discussed, Mother." He retorted "Things that cannot wait for ever."

"She will be ready, when she is ready."

Godfrey looked around the room and noticed that Will's body was no longer in the cottage. He looked at the old woman. Sensing what he would ask, she said "Will is in the church waiting to be buried tomorrow."

"Ah!" he replied. "I am leaving for a while, and I need to discuss the cottage with Meg…"

Old Mother Sawyer looked at him. There was a hardness to her eyes. It sent a shiver down Godfrey's spine.

Ignoring her, Godfrey continued, ""Meg, my brother had freehold of this cottage, and now it should be mine!" he started, without even making greeting.

Meg awoke from her trance at Godfrey's words, and stood up, "Sit down Godfrey!" Meg shouted at him. Her anger at his lack of respect and the timing of his visit was clear in her tone. Meg did not easily lose her temper, but she had to stand up to this obnoxious man!

"This house is mine, as it should have been mine before it was given to Will!" Godfrey continued his tone aggressive and intimidating.

"The house is not yours Godfrey and will never will be!" Meg responded in a resolute manner, without raising her voice. She was determined not to drag herself down to his level.

"We shall see about that!" Godfrey said, his anger conveyed by reddening of his face and the raising of his own voice.

"There is no need to shout, Godfrey!" Meg retorted calmly. "This cottage was given to Will, and now it is mine. After me, it will belong to Maud."

"I have a right to this hovel!" Godfrey stated, unable to lower his voice.

"You may come and go as you wish Godfrey..." Meg replied, "But you will behave yourself!"

"I will have it!" Godfrey shouted.

"You will have use of it if you need to. But it will still belong to me! Would you have Maud and me on the streets?" she asked.

"I will do whatever needs to be done!" Godfrey responded with venom.

"Then you will fail!" Meg answered defiantly. "Will has been dead for only a few short hours, but you are unable to control your greed and selfishness!"

"You will see what greed and selfishness can achieve, woman!" Godfrey snapped back. He glared at Meg and saw that the two women glared back at him, determination and… something else in their eyes.

"I will have this cottage!" he roared, "I am leaving with the army for a while, when I come back, I will finish this!" With that he turned abruptly and stormed out of the cottage.

Meg knew that she would have a battle on her hands. Godfrey was a dangerous man, and Meg considered her options. She felt that Godfrey would soon get bored of living a domestic life in the cottage, and then he would probably sell it anyway. Meg needed to protect her daughter's inheritance, and she would fight with everything she had to, to do that.

❖

As Godfrey made his way along the dark lanes towards Tewkesbury, little moonlight to illuminate his way, his horse became startled and reared up. Godfrey was thrown from the horse and injured his shoulder and wrist. Godfrey was not a believer in the supernatural, but he momentarily perceived the silhouette of a woman, backlit by a bright light. He was not seriously hurt but bruised and shaken. Such a fall could have been much worse. As he shook himself off, and remounted, he wondered if it had just been his imagination.

❖

Will's body, having been cleaned and dressed was buried in the church yard, after a short mass given by the local priest. The whole village, including the Lord of the Manor of the village, Richard Moryn, attended.

As the body was lowered into the ground, Meg stood gripping the hand of her two-year-old daughter. Meg was all cried out, her grief written across her pale and drawn face. She had no thoughts, her mind was still in shock, her body numb. She simply stared at the proceedings, unable to take in what was happening around her, no longer feeling alive. She was a living corpse, dead inside.

Old Mother Sawyer looked after Meg and her child for many weeks. Living in their cottage, making meals, and provided Meg with calming draughts to help ease her pain. She knew that Meg was resilient and would eventually come through this. She also knew that the pain would fade, but never go away completely. Will's death was devastating, but Meg had a young child to look after, and her natural instincts would give her the strength to carry on. Until Meg was strong enough to get on with her life, Old Mother Sawyer would be there to comfort her and support her.

# Part 2
## 1484-1485

# CHAPTER 9
## A Fateful Meeting
### May 1484 – Swindon Village

As the hot and heady days of summer approached and the evenings grew longer and warmer, Meg sat outside of her cottage with her daughter Maud.

They were preparing fleeces before spinning. This preparation was an important part of the process for making the quality yarn that Meg was renowned for.

She had learned long ago that if she took the time to make sure that the fleeces were properly washed and dried before spinning, the yarn would be finer and would be easier to spin.

These were Meg's trade secrets, but nothing could make up for the care and concentration needed to clean the fleece properly. Many other spinners did not take such care or time and as a result the quality of their produce did not match Meg's.

Meg was gently pushing a mesh bag containing some of the fleece into hot water to remove grease, dirt, and vegetation from it. Depending on how dirty the fleece was, this might need to be done several times. This was a delicate process, and if the water temperature was too hot, there was a danger of the fleece 'felting' and being ruined.

Meg watched Maud, as she layed the cleaned fleece onto a drying board, to allow it to dry naturally in the warm, earlier summer breeze.

"That's a pretty tune your humming." Meg called over to her daughter.

"Oh! Yes, I make them up all the time." Replied the young woman as she looked over at her mother and smiled.

"Beautiful and talented then!" Meg observed her beautiful 15 year old daughter. The setting sun created a halo around the edges of her long golden hair, reminding Meg of Will.

Maud's complexion was slightly tanned from time in the sun, her high cheek bones and delicate nose complimented the other features of her face. Her lips were full enough but not excessive, and her smile, not too wide, lit up her face.

But it was her eyes that caught the most attention, they were a startling blue/grey. The unintended intensity of her gaze could melt any heart, she thought.

Maud was a strong girl, her 5'8", her slim frame belied the grace and power of her movement. Meg considered that her beautiful child was becoming a stunning woman, and worried about the warning given to her by

Old Mother Sawyer many years ago. "Who would harm such a beautiful creature" she wondered.

"Once these are dry, we'll need to start spinning." she said, "but let's have something to eat first."

"I'll just finish putting these on the rack, and then I'll help you." Maud replied, bending as she collected some more soggy fleece. "The one's we put out this morning should be dry by now."

Maud and her mother regularly worked long into the night. They would happily chat and sing songs, as they spun the yarn and knitted the garments.

Waking early and usually falling into bed late in the evening, they did however, find some time during the day to relax and enjoy themselves in other ways.

Life without Will had been tough to begin with, but as the years passed, the pain ebbed. Meg was eternally thankful that she at least had her daughter to remind her of her husband. She often talked to Maud about her father, so that Maud would understand what a special and irreplaceable man he had been.

❖

Maud was awake early the following morning and she leaned over Meg's shoulder to see what was cooking in the pot.

"Ma, smells good!" she said, "I want to get my chores finished early today, so I can spend some time in the meadow!"

"See if you can find some pretty flowers to hang on the door." Meg replied, as Maud squeezed her in a hug. Meg nuzzled her daughter's face and smelled her freshness. "You smell good too!" Meg exclaimed.

"That's the scent we made! We could bottle it and sell it!"

Meg smiled at her daughter with pride. Maud was always coming up with new and clever ideas.

"Well, come and eat, and then we can get cracking!" Meg said, placing two bowls of soup on the table.

Maud bent over the bowl and savoured the aroma, "Mmmmmm!" she breathed, before picking up the loaf of bread, ripping some off and dunking it in the sweet-smelling broth.

With her chores completed by mid-morning, and the sun climbing high in the sky, Maud removed her apron and left the house. Her mother called after her, "Don't go too far, and don't' come home late!"

"I won't" the young woman called back, as she skipped down the path through the graveyard. Maud enjoyed going into the meadows and woodlands whenever she had some free time, but she would always bring home some mushrooms or herbs for her mother. She would often take some time to sit in the meadow, pick flowers and watch the wildlife around her.

As she ran through the village, her hair blowing in the wind, she turned the heads of everyone she passed. Young and old, male and female, all admired this athletic young woman as she rushed past. She especially turned the heads of all the young men of the village.

"Morning Mr Forrester!"

"Morning Maud!"

"Morning Jeb!"

"Morning Maud!" the young man responded with a flush creeping over his face.

"Morning Mrs Jones!"

"Morning young Maud!"

She greeted everyone along the street, happy and carefree. As she came to the last house, she saw Old Mother Sawyer.

"Morning Mother!" she cried.

"Good morning, Maud. Do you have your pendant?" the old woman asked.

"Right here!" Maud replied lifting it from under her blouse and holding it up.

"Good girl!" Mother Sawyer replied watching the retreating back of the young girl as she ran out of the village.

❖

Walter Gray walked through the woods towards one of his snares. He had laid a few the night before and was now collecting the profits of his endeavours. He had already collected two rabbits and was hoping for a few more before returning home. He had also shot a couple of fat pigeons with his bow, and they were sitting snuggly in the pouch which hung from his shoulder.

"Ma and Pa will be happy with these!" he thought, as he bent down to remove the hedging which secreted his snare. In it was another rabbit, already dead. He removed the snare and reset it, before tying the rabbit to the others he had slung over his other shoulder.

Walter lived at the House in the Tree, an Inn at the junction of the Gloucester Road and Withybridge Lane. His father was an ex-soldier, and his mother was French. They had met when Walter's father had been on campaign in France. They now owned the Inn, and one of Walter's jobs was to forage and hunt, to provide fayre for their travelling guests. It was a task he loved, and he travelled quite far around the area to find new hunting opportunities.

He was a tall, muscular 18-year-old. Standing at 6 feet 2 inches tall, he was tall for his age and the general population, his long, dark hair was tied up behind his head to stop it getting in his eyes. He strode through the woods, no longer worried about keeping his presence quiet. Having checked all of his traps he had collected enough meat for the Inn's needs and was now making his way home. As he left the trees he came out into a wide meadow. The tall grass was billowing in the breeze and the whole meadow was abundant with all the colours of spring flowers. He stopped for a moment to admire the view. He breathed in deeply, smelling the scents and watching the bees buzzing and flitting across the landscape.

"Wonderful!" he thought as began running into the sea of green.

Maud was laying down in the grass, staring up at the sky and enjoying the warmth of the sun of her face, when Walter, literally stumble across her, or actually stumbled over her!

Maud had not heard him coming, and Walter had not seen her in the long grass. "Whoaa!" Walter cried, as he tried to avoid falling right on top of Maud. "My goodness!" cried Maud as she rolled away from the hulking beast who was threatening to over-topple right onto her. Walter stumbled and fell, falling just to the side of Maud. Dead rabbits flew into the air, and his bow clattered off to the side.

They both looked at each other in a state of shock before both burst into fits of laughter. Recovering from their mutual shock, they both sat up and looked at each other. "And who might you be?" Maud grinned.

"Well, I be Walter Gray, Mistress!" Maud could not help but giggle at him "Mistress? There is no Mistress here!"

Walter coughed, rose, and began to brush himself down, "Didn't mean to be rude…. What should I call you then?"

"Well, you could call me by my name" she chuckled, raising her face to look at him again.

"Well that would be all and good….. if I knew your name!" Walter bristled, a flush appearing on his cheeks.

He was becoming embarrassed to look at her, she was the most beautiful girl he had ever seen. His cheeks reddened further, and he had difficulty in looking directly at her, as he thought how stupid he must look.

"I am Maud" the young girl declared, clearing a stray strand of hair from her face, she looked down avoiding his gaze, as she could feel a blush coming to her own cheeks.

"Well Maud" Walter exclaimed "Laying there in the grass might get you stamped on!"

"… and stomping about without a care in the world, will get you falling into a ditch! She retorted, throwing her hands in the air.

"No ditches across this meadow" he replied shuffling about on the spot.

"Can't a person have a sleep in the meadow, without being accosted by a gallumping heffer!"

"A what?" Walter laughed in spite of himself. Here was a beautiful young woman, laying in the grass, insulting him, and here he was actually acting like a "gallumping heffer!"

Maud laughed again at his obvious discomfort and began to get up herself. As she did so, he held out a hand to help her up. "Thank you, kind sir." she smiled. Once on her feet, Maud was able to see him more clearly. She was tall for a girl, but this lad, stood a half a foot taller than her. He had dark, tousled hair, and a strong, handsome face, with the beginnings of a beard growing on his face. His shoulders were broad, as befitted a true bowman and he stood tall and slim. Maud felt herself blushing again. She had taken all this in, in a matter of seconds, and she had startled herself with her forwardness.

Quickly changing the subject, she asked, "So, you have been hunting then?"

"Aye, taking something back for dinner tonight" he replied, looking around for his catch. Seeing the two brace of rabbits tied together with twine, just a short distance away, he bent down to pick them up.

"... and as a great hunter, do you often walk right into your prey?" she laughed at him.

"I do not! I'll have you know I am an excellent hunter!" he challenged "I can stalk something for days, and they would never know I was there!" he challenged.

Maud looked at him, and could not help herself, and burst into laughter again. Walter looked aghast, and responded "If you don't believe me, I could show you."

"I might take you up on that offer" she replied, "But right now, I have to get home, my mother will be looking for me." She turned to leave, the blush returning to her face. "Maud" Walter said, "Will I see you again?"

"Well, you might" she replied, "I come here quite often, you might be lucky, if you keep a better eye out!" she laughed as she skipped away through the grass and the meadow flowers.

Walter stood transfixed by the vision of the young woman skipping away from him. Her long, blonde hair flowing in the breeze, her slim frame rising and falling, as she went from heel to tip-toe dancing and twirling through the meadow. "Tall for a girl" he thought to himself, smiling.

As Maud approached her home, she could see her mother outside sitting at a table, gently weaving some wool. Meg glanced up at her daughter,

"You've been having some fun?" her mother asked. Maud was sure she could see a twinkle in her mother's eyes.

"Yes mother, the meadow was lovely, and the weather is lovely too" she replied at the same time thinking "She can't possibly know about Walter, could she?"

She shook her head at the thought, it was impossible, but her mother seemed to be able read her moods and mind sometimes. It could be very disconcerting!

Maud joined her mother at the table, "So what's for dinner" she enquired.

❖

The following day Maud managed to escape again for a short time and decided to go down to the brook and sit on the bank. She found a spot under a large, leafy tree, and after removing her shoes and rubbing her aching feet, she leaned back against the solid trunk.

She dangled her toes in the lightly flowing water of the Brook. After flinching at the initial chill of the water, it soon becoming a relaxing foot massage, as her feet became accustomed to the temperature. Sunlight glinted through the leaves, and the surface of the gently babbling brook was dappled with both the sunlight and the shade from the trees.

Maud leaned back and closed her eyes for a moment, basking in the serenity and peacefulness of the moment. The only sounds she could hear were the happy chirping of the birds, the rustling of small woodland creatures, the bubbling of the water in the brook and the gentle sound of the breeze rustling the leaves of the trees.

The day was idyllic as was the scene of this beautiful young woman reposed under an ancient tree. The sight was almost hypnotic, as she rested, with her legs stretched out, her feet submerged beneath the sparkling, bejewelled, surface of the water. She dreamed of all the things young women dream about, not a care in the world, for these precious few moments.

She was completely unaware, that deep in the woods, eyes were watching her. These were not the eyes of some woodland creature, and her stalker was another type of creature all together!

Rudely, she was awakened from her rapture as a number of birds flew out of the nearby trees, screeching and fluttering. They had obviously been startled and alarmed, by something, that had put them into a panicked flight.

She looked around her, quickly coming out of her solitary revelry.

She heard a commotion, off to her left and an anguished cry "Whoa! Agghh!", and a crashing as a branch snapped. A figure in a green surcoat, suddenly appeared, hanging onto a slim extended branch, balancing precariously over the softly undulating water of the brook. Clearly, the branch (which was more of a twig, if truth was told!), was not strong enough to resist the weight and force arrayed against it by this large, hulking individual.

The branch snapped! There was a great flourish and much flailing of arms, and then a further cry "Oh No!", before the young man (for by now, it was clear that it was a young man!) fell, with a gigantic splash into his watery doom!

Maud, equally startled and alarmed as the local birdlife, stared in shocked amazement at the scene unfolding before her.

She quickly recognised the "gallumping" form, splashing and floundering in the water. Who, after initially becoming completely submerged for a few seconds, was eventually able to sit up, spluttering as he spat out the residue liquid that had found its way into his mouth, most of which he had unfortunately swallowed!

"Oh my Lord!" exclaimed Maud. "It's you! You have been spying on me!" she cried.

"No! No! I wasn't!" Cried Walter, still spluttering and trying to rid his mouth of the brackish, and unpleasant taste of the brook water he had swallowed. Despite his denial, his cheeks reddened, into a deep and incriminating crimson blush.

"Well, it certainly seems so! What other possible reason could there be?!" she responded in a reproving tone, as she collected her shoes and began to put them back onto her feet.

"Please let me explain" said Walter, as he put one hand behind himself into the water in an attempt to push himself up. His attempt failed miserably, and as his hand slipped, he once again became briefly submerged.

Despite herself, Maud burst out laughing at the sight of the large youth, thrashing about, trying to stabilise himself on the rocks and mud at the bottom of the brook.

Removing some stray strand of hair from her mouth, which had been blown across her face by the breeze, she giggled as she thought "If this is a dangerous stalker, he needs to get a new job!"

Now standing, Maud went over the edge of the brook, where the hapless young man was still struggling to get to his feet. She looked around and found a sturdy branch, which had broken from one of the trees. She picked it up and held it out towards Walter. "Here, take this" she offered, laughing at his struggles, and obvious humiliation.

Walter was mortified, as he groped out to catch the proffered branch. "What is it about this girl, that every time I see her, I end up on my backside!" he muttered to himself, "...and each time, it gets worse!" he thought.

After a couple of failed attempts, Walter finally managed to grasp the outstretched stick, and tried to pull himself up. "Oh No!" cried Maud, as she began to slide down the bank, under the weight of the young man pulling from the other end. In a last desperate attempt to save herself, Maud let go of the branch, but it was too late, and she slid unceremoniously down the bank and into the water.

Now completely drenched, Maud sat in the cool water, and looked over to the source of her predicament. Walter looked back at her. They sat there for a few seconds, and then both of the young people erupted into gales of laughter!

Eventually, they both managed to scramble and crawl their way to the edge of the brook, and claw themselves up the bank, by grabbing various roots, to pull themselves clear of the water.

Slightly breathless, they collapsed in a heap next to each other. "We have to stop meeting like this!" they exclaimed in unison!

And so, Maud and Walter met. Over the coming months, they would meet whenever they could, sometimes in the meadow, and sometimes at the edge of the village.

They spent as much time as they could together, meeting secretly, enjoying each other's company, and most of all laughing about everything.

Walter, would often, whenever his other chores allowed, walk with Maud to the Cheltenham Market.

He would pull the cart, and they would enjoy each other's company.

Maud's mother, Meg, had been reluctant initially to allow her daughter to go to the market without her, but as Maud grew, Meg knew that she needed some freedom and responsibility, and had gradually acquiesced to her daughter's demands.

It also gave her much more time to do other work.

Walter would also hang around the market when he could, to keep Maud company, but as he also had work responsibilities, often had to leave after seeing her safely into Cheltenham.

In much the same way, he always tried to be there at the end of the market day, to walk back to the village with her.

Maud and Walter had been seeing each other in this way for a number of months.

Many of Maud's neighbours had seen them together, particularly during the walk to market on market day. It was inconceivable, that Maud's mother did not know about this budding relationship, but thus far, she had not said anything.

That was about to change…….

# CHAPTER 10

## Ungentlemanly Conduct

### July 1484 – Oxenton

Robert de Vere was the true "Lord of the Manor" of Swindon Village. A distant cousin of the Earl of Oxford (now banished from the country for his involvement in the Lancastrian cause against the King), he owned properties across the county, and also rented other properties. Swindon Village itself, was owned by The Priory of Sion, in Gloucester, and they rented land for payment to a range of nobles, and Robert de Vere rented the village from the Abbess of that Priory. In turn he rented the Manor House in the village to the Moryn's and they managed the land for him. De Vere took his tythes, and in turn, paid a portion of these tythes to the Priory.

De Vere was a busy man and spent his time travelling around his various different properties, ensuring that they were well managed and productive. He was not a pleasant man, prone to violent outbursts, he was not a man to cross. He visited Swindon rarely, as it was quite small compared to his other holdings.

Whenever he travelled, he was accompanied by a group of retained knights, all of whom were battled-hardened veterans, who had seen combat in a number of campaigns. They might have been described as nothing more than thugs, as their primary source of enjoyment appeared to be crushing skulls, drinking and whoring, and generally bullying everyone they met. De Vere himself was such a man and had much in common with his entourage.

The de Vere Family heritage could be traced back to the Norman Conquest, and although the de Vere family themselves, were comparatively minor nobles. They nevertheless had held significant power and sought to wield it whenever they could.

Whenever de Vere was in the Cheltenham area, he tended to stay at his manor house in Oxenton and toured his local estates from there.

He had a habit of turning up without notice, and then expected everyone to rush about, and attend to his every whim. In fact, he enjoyed the chaos, and particularly the fear he was able to instil in his underlings.

If anyone failed to please him, he had no hesitation in meting out punishment, which could range in severity from a flogging to hanging, and on certain occasions, decapitation! He was a thoroughly unpleasant individual, and the worst kind of bully.

De Vere enjoyed his reputation, and in common with other major landowners, was able act with impunity on his own lands.  His word was law, and no-one had the courage or authority to stand against him.

The other landowners were not interested in what happened on someone else's property, and some of the other Lords had equally fearsome reputations, in any case.

Nevertheless, de Vere was a particularly nasty specimen, and was not afraid to protect his own interests.

He was known to covet and claim properties that were not owned by him that lay close to the boundaries of his own land, particularly properties that were remote, and easy prey.

As a result, he had been involved in a number of skirmishes with his noble neighbours.  However, he was always careful not to antagonise the Lords of larger estates too much.

Men like de Vere were men of power, and men of war.  They took what they wanted and were prepared to kill, to achieve their aims.

Ironically, one of the major roles of these Lords was to maintain law and order on their estates and ensure justice was meted out to miscreants, a task that they enjoyed immensely.

Nevertheless, his own actions, were above the law, and could not be criticised.  Short of being accused of treason, and attracting the wrath of his King, he was secure to do as he pleased. To all who knew him, he was seen as arrogant, self-important, over-privileged and heartless.

As a result, his subjects dreaded his arrival, and silently cheered his departure. The irony was, that there was very little crime or disorder around his lands, except those crimes that he sanctioned.

❖

De Vere strode into the Great Hall of his manor. His two large Wolfhounds at his side.

"Food and wine!" he bellowed to no-one in particular.

Two serving maids who were in the process of cleaning the room, looked at each other. The older of the two, nodded at the younger woman, and she ran off to the kitchens, clearly relieved to be the one who was able to escape the presence of this over-bearing and frightening man.

De Vere continued to advance towards the High Table at the end of the hall, his hounds loping along beside him, tails wagging. "You girl!" he roared at the other woman, "Come here!", he said pointing with his hand to a place just in from of him.

The young woman stayed where she was, for just a second too long. "You dare to defy me, bitch!" he snarled. "I'll feed you to my dogs!" His faced was flushed with anger, and fury was written all over it.

The young woman whimpered and dropped her broom, rushing towards him, and throwing herself at his feet. "I am sorry Lord. I didn't mean to...." Her pleas were cut off suddenly, when de Vere grabbed a handful of her hair, and dragged her to her feet. The girl involuntarily raised her hands to her head, to try and relieve the agonising pain of her whole body being dragged upwards, just by the grip on her hair.

De Vere was incensed by this display of impudence, and struck her viciously across the face, leaving a read weal across her cheek.

Still held up by her hair alone, the woman tried to get her feet underneath herself, to be able to support herself, and relieve the pain. However, de Vere's grip kept her off balance, and she struggled to stand, feeling her hair, being ripped out by its roots. She cried out in agony, "Please my Lord!"

This only incensed de Vere more, and he struck her again. "Shut up! You WHORE!" he shouted. This time, the blow was so hard that she momentarily lost consciousness and slumped to the floor.

The weight of her body became too much to be supported by her hair alone, and finally a clump of her hair was ripped out. De Vere was left holding it in his fist.

Livid, he shook the hair out of his hand, and wiped his hand on his trousers, in disgust. He viciously kicked her prone body as it lay on the floor, causing the girl to groan in pain, and curl up into a ball at his feet.

De Vere leant forward over her, and grabbed her roughly by the collar, pulling her up forcefully. Once she was standing, he again grabbed a handful of her hair at the back of her head and pulled her face toward his. He smiled and pushed his face onto hers kissing her roughly.

When she did not respond as he wanted, he bit into her lip, drawing blood, and threw her down to the floor, in revulsion. "You smell worse than my dogs!" he scowled "Get out of my sight!"

The terrified girl scurried away from him on her hands and knees, and when she was out of reach of his cruelty, mustered enough strength to raise herself to her feet, and rushed out of the hall, the dark bruises on her face already revealing themselves.

De Vere slammed himself down into his chair at the High Table, "Where is my food!" he thundered.

The other serving girl rushed up to the table and placed a large plate full of portions duck and a jug of ale in front of him. After hurriedly dropping into a curtsy, she retreated immediately, bolting out of the room, before he could say anything else. De Vere picked up a leg of duck and sniffed at it derisively, before biting off a large chunk, and noisily chewing on the greasy meat.

Having devoured the meat, he belched loudly, and threw the bones over his shoulder. He smiled to himself as he heard the snarls and growls of his two wolfhounds, fighting over the morsel. He wiped his greasy hands on his doublet and refilled his mug with more ale.

❖

De Vere looked up as someone entered the hall.

"Good morrow Sire!" A giant of a man, with a huge beard, called out to him. "I hope all is well?"

"Good morrow, de Crecy. All is well." He replied to his Master of Arms, Hubert de Crecy.

"Sire, I have a man that desires to meet with you. He and his men are hoping for employment." de Crecy beamed, as he approached the long table which de Vere was sitting behind.

"What man? What kind of employment?"

"I think he could be of use to us Sire. He is a military man with some experience. Would you see him?"

"Why not." De Vere replied, "Fetch him!"

De Crecy left to collect the visitor and returned within a couple of minutes with a motley crew of men.

"So, tell me about yourself. What is your name?" de Vere asked of the man who stood in front of the others.

The man bowed deeply and said, "Sire, my name is Godfrey Bowen, and I come from near here. For the past 13 years I have been employed as Captain of a company of archers for Sir Walter Devereux. With the recent death of the King, we have been disbanded, and I am now seeking new employment."

"Where have you seen action?"

"I fought at Tewkesbury Sire, where I was commissioned as Captain of Archers. I have served in France and fought against the Scots. I have also done a lot of peace-keeping." Godfrey said trying to keep the smirk from his face.

De Vere noticed and replied, "So you are a proven leader of men? I have need of such men. Can you vouch for the others?"

"I can Sire. They are bloodthirsty bunch of mongrels, but they will do as you say."

De Vere looked at de Crecy and nodded.

"You have horses?" de Vere asked.

"Aye Sire."

"Good." De Crecy grinned, "We have some sport planned for today, and we can test your mettle!"

De Vere looked at his Master at Arms, satisfaction glowing on his face, "Show them to their quarters, and then make sure they are ready to leave with us."

❖

"The horses are saddled and ready to go, and that motley crew, are chomping at the bit Sire!" said de Crecy as he re-entered the hall.

"As we discussed last evening, the men need a distraction. They have been following me about for the past week visiting my outlying properties and sitting around watching as I undertake the tedious task of collecting tythes, and checking records," de Vere mused.

"Aye Sire, they need some sport, to vent their frustrations."

"Well, we did deal with some of the lazy bastards on my lands."

"Sire. We needed to make an example of some of them." De Crecy agreed.

De Vere grinned as he recalled some of the punishments, he had meted out to some of his hapless workers, "Aye, but we need to be careful. Their labour is a valuable commodity, so I can't do too much damage in my own backyard."

De Crecy looked over at his master, "We need a different type of physical exertion that will keep them sharp."

"Sit de Crecy!" his Master responded, "Take some ale and some duck, man. It's left over from last night, but still just edible!" he said as he placed his mug back on the table.

"Thank you, Sire!" de Crecy replied, grabbing a handful of greasy meat and pushing it into his mouth, bones and all. He leaned over to pick up a mug, and filled it to the brim, from the jug on the table. As he raised the mug to his lips, he spat the bones out of his mouth, onto the floor.

De Vere smoothed his own impressive beard with his hand, "So, what sport have you in mind today?" he grinned at his closest friend.

"Well Sire, a couple of the lads went out scouting last night, and they came across a small haven, just north of here." he replied, waving hand in a vaguely in a northerly direction, whilst raising his mug with the other. "Just a couple of dwellings, farmers who raise cows by the looks. They have a bull as well!" he chuckled. "Bengrove, they said it was. I reckon those dwellings are on your land, and I don't think we've collected the tythes!", he said slyly, picking up another piece of duck.

"Well, I think your right! We will need to resolve that." De Vere replied, picking up two more pieces of duck himself, and throwing them straight over his should towards his dogs. They both laughed at the battle being raged behind the table as the dogs clashed over the food. "Daft dogs!" exclaimed de Crecy. "Are they coming with us today?"

"Certainly," de Vere said, "They are getting as fat as you lot!" he grinned, and de Crecy spluttered, nearly choking on the meat in his mouth.

De Vere rose from his seat at the same time as de Crecy and made his way over to his friend. Clapping him heartily on the shoulder, as he passed. "Come on, you old bastard, let's get going!" he said, and the two men strode out of the hall. "Come hounds!" he called, and the dogs bounded after them.

Outside, in the courtyard, de Vere's entourage was lined up on horseback, six knights and a handful of squires had been joined by Godfrey and his men. The knights wore the accoutrements of war, mid-armour, hauberks of chainmail, with padded jupons bearing the de Vere crest. helmets, swords, maces, and battle-axes. The squires wore breastplates and caps, and Godfrey's men wore their archers leather jerkins and wrist braces. They carried their unstrung bows at their sides and two quivers holding 12 arrows each, they also carried short swords.

One of the squires held the reins of two spare horses. He released the reins to his Master and the large knight by his side and helped them climb up into the saddles. The squire raced over to the horse and cart, which was to be his transport for the day, and climbed up onto the bench.

"Bowen!" de Vere called over at his newest recruit. "Today we will see what you are made of. If I like what I see, you can stay!"

"Thank you Sire! You'll not be disappointed." Godfrey called back, before turning to his men and giving them a 'thumbs up.'

De Crecy lifted his arm in the air and waved it forward, "Let's move out!" de Crecy called out to the small army of men.

De Vere rode out of Oxenton with his Master at Arms on his left, and his entourage following behind, heading north towards the unfortunate haven of Bengrove. His intention on this day, was not to survey his own lands but to terrorise small a farmstead on the edge of what could not legitimately be called his land.

# CHAPTER 11

## A Haven No More…….

Ben Lesly farmed the small-holding in the haven of Bengrove. He had a herd of 6 cows, and his prize possession "Grump" the bull, and of course "Patch" his small terrier dog.

He had paid a lot of money for the belligerent bull, but it had provided him with extra income each calving season.

He was able to butcher the calves and sell the veal, a delicacy that was much sought after by the manor houses all around the area.

For the rest of the year, he lived by selling fresh milk and cheese to the local markets.

Ben lived with his wife Lizzie, and their eldest child, a daughter, Madge. Although in her late twenties, Madge had never married. Ben did not mind one bit, Madge was a hard worker around the farm, and the extra pair of hands were really useful.

Both Lizzie and Ben, were not getting any younger, and Madge was the guarantee that they would be looked after, in their old age.

The only other occupants in the haven were Jem, his son, junior to Madge by three years, his wife June, and their two-year-old son, Kit.

They occupied the only other dwelling. Kit was a precious child, as all children are, but Kit was extra precious, as June had three miscarriages before Kit was born.

Mother, father, both grandparents, and his aunt all doted on him. He was the future of Bengrove, and he was treasured.

Jem helped his father with the herd, moving them to new pastures, and with the milking and butchery when required.

The women tended the small garden plot, filled with all manner of vegetables, and also worked together to make the cheese. June also kept chickens.

Their life was hard but comfortable, tucked away in a forgotten part of the county, just over the border from Gloucestershire, on the edge of Worcestershire.

"Jem! You bringing those cows down?" Ben called out to his son, from under the awning of the cowshed, which also acted as the milking shed.

"Coming now!" Jem shouted, prodding the animals through the gate and into the courtyard. "Come on girl," he said to a particularly intransigent heifer, who had decided to eat some grass just inside the gate and had blocked the way for the others.

The cow made a low moan of discontent as he swatted it across the backside with his switch stick but moved forward anyway.

He moved the herd across the hard-packed soil, dried out from the summer sun, and avoided the 'pats' the cows left as they walked.

He smiled at his father whose hand was raised above his eyes to block the glare of the sun, "The gate needs seeing to Pa!" he said, "I'll fix it later, otherwise these ladies will be wandering off down the lane!"

"Oh my Lord!" Ben laughed, "We don't want a repeat of last year! You remember trying to get old Grump back in!"

"Aye, it took all of us! And he wasn't happy!"

"Well, he wasn't until we took daisy out to him!" Ben recalled his wife bringing one of the cows out of the field to entice the bull back. "Then he came back right enough!"

"Aye! No-one can refuse a woman!" Jem said, and they both laughed at the memory.

Ben brought one of the cows into the shed and sat down on his stool, before grabbing the teats and massaging the milk out into a bucket. Jem guarded the others just outside the door of the structure that had been built to house the cows in the winter, and which they also used the space inside for milking, as well as the initial stages of butchery.

The shed was behind the dwellings, close the pasture, but far enough away from the cottages, to ensure that the families were not disturbed by noise of the cows during the night. Jem was keeping the rest of the herd nearby, each cow, anxiously waiting for their turn to be milked. Patch was curled up contentedly, on a small patch of hay, away from the door.

Lizzie, Madge and June were in the kitchen of Ben's cottage, churning milk, chatting and singing songs. It was a strenuous job, but they had all be doing it for many years and were used to the exertion.

Kit was playing with a small wooden horse that had been carved by his father.

It was a fine, sunny day, and all was right with the world.

❖

De Vere and his company turned off the road leading to Evesham, into the lane that led down to the haven of Bengrove. They were now only about half a mile away.

He put his hand in the air, "Halt" he bellowed, and the entourage came to a standstill. He indicated, with a flick of his hand, for two of the squires to move forward. There was no need for speech, the whole party were well drilled in the process.

The main group waited while the two squires moved further down the lane. Presently, they were out of sight because of the thick hedgerows. After a short while, the two squires returned at a canter. The first to arrive back, called out, "All quiet, Sire! We think they must all be inside, 'cos we can't see anyone about."

"Good, good." Murmured de Vere, glancing at de Crecy. De Crecy nodded, raised his arm, and beckoned the party to move forward.

❖

The ears of Patch the dog pricked up. He gruffled, and then sat up and started barking.

"What is it, boy? Ben said to the little dog. Patch continued to bark, "We got visitors then?" he asked, releasing the cow's udders and standing up.

"You stay there girl." He told the cow, gently slapping her on the rump, "I'll be back soon." He continued.

"Come on Patch, let's see what all the fuss is about!" he laughed. Ben was curious and Patch was excited.

"Yep! We don't get many visitors down 'ere." he said and made to leave the barn. At the movement of his owner, Patch shot off towards the front of the cottages, barking for all he was worth.

Outside, he looked over to his son. "You wait there a mo' Jem. I'll see what this is all about and be right back. Probably someone wanting some cheese, I reckon, and Lizzie will be able to sort that.", Jem nodded and continued talking to the cows, trying to keep them calm, and in one place.

As he reached the rear of his cottage, and was making his way round to the front, he could still hear Patch barking away. Then there was some strange growling, a yelp of pain, and then silence. "What's bloody dog done to 'iself now?" he muttered and increased his pace round to the front of the cottage.

When he arrived at the front, he stood open-mouthed in shock.

A large group of armed men had entered the courtyard and were arrayed in a line outside his home. "What the…?" he exclaimed. One of the men was holding Patch aloft, and blood was pouring from the little dog. The dog made no sound or movement. Two large wolfhounds flanked the horseman in the middle of the line, their mouth's dripping with blood.

"Thank God for that!" exclaimed a man dressed in all the regalia of a knight, sitting on the horse, next to the other knight who was holding his dead dog. "I thought the mutt was never going to shut up!"

"You bastard!" Ben shouted, as he rushed forward towards de Crecy, who was holding his lifeless dog. De Crecy nonchalantly threw the dead dog towards Ben, and the bloody remains hit him in the chest, covering him in the gory remains, of what had until a few minutes ago, been his beloved terrier.

The gore splashed over his face. As Ben continued to run forward, he wiped a hand across his eyes and mouth.

Clearing his vision, he launched himself at de Crecy. De Crecy drew his sword, in one swift movement, and brought the pommel directly down onto the head of the furious, and distraught farmer.

Ben, fell back, stunned by the force of the blow, blood pouring from the wound on his head that the vicious strike had caused.

Hearing the commotion, the women in the cottage had come outside, and witnessed the assault. Lizzie, closely followed by Madge, rushed over to her prostrate husband "Ben!" she screamed, and then looking up at the men sitting impassively on their horses, cried out, "What have you done?"

She bent down and helped her groggy husband to his feet, with the help of a distraught Madge.

June had waited by the door of her mother-in-law's cottage holding Kit in her arms. She looked on in horror at what was happening, "Who are these men?" she thought, "and what do they want from us?"

Jem, who was too far away to hear what had happened initially, heard Lizzie's scream, and ran towards the cottages, collecting his staff which had been propped against the back wall as he went.

As he reached the courtyard, he could see Lizzie and Madge helping Ben off the ground. He looked around for his wife and saw her standing in the doorway, Kit cradled in her arms. "Get inside and bolt the door!" he called. June did as he had ordered, running back into the cottage, and securing the door.

She put Kit down, and told him to go upstairs and hide, and then went over the small window. She pushed the curtain aside and looked out.

Jem approached the line of men. "Pa! Are you alright?" he asked warily, without taking his eyes from the men on horseback. "Aye." said the older man, still feeling groggy, and struggling to stay on his feet, "I'm fine. You take the women back inside. I'll deal with this!" he commanded.

"Pa, you're in no fit state to deal with anything." Jem responded, looking at his father, and noticing how pale he had become. "You go back inside with Ma, and I'll speak to these men."

Ben was not really in a fit state to argue, but did not want his son to get involved with these dangerous men. He took a step forward, and staggered, nearly falling.

The men on horseback all laughed, and he finally accepted his son's advice, and reluctantly leaned on Lizzie and Madge, who turned to take him back towards the cottage.

"Hold fast, old man!" de Vere shouted down. "Stay where you are! I haven't finished with you yet!"

Ben turned with the help of his wife and daughter. "What is it you want?" he cried.

"You owe me a tythe!" de Vere exclaimed.

"What!" Ben responded, "We pay our tythes every month, to our Lord!" he continued, not understanding what was going on. "We have already paid this month!"

"Well, I am your new Lord. If you show any more insolence, you will have yourself to blame for the consequences!" de Vere bellowed, getting more and more weary of this situation. "What can you pay me?" he enquired.

"We have little left, Lord" Ben acquiesced, realising that he had no control of this situation, and needed to do anything, to make these men leave, before his family were endangered. "We can give you milk, eggs, and some cheese…"

"Milk, eggs and CHEESE!" de Vere countered, his anger evident. "You think that is sufficient?," he continued in disbelief.

"De Crecy! Take the men and look around this hovel! See what they have stashed away!" he said looking at his right-hand man. De Crecy signalled to the troops, and they dismounted. The all looked eager to become involved in the sport.

Jem, having seen enough, moved forward, and shouted at de Vere, "You have no authority here!" De Vere looked at the young farmer with a look of utter amazement at the temerity of the man. "I warned you about insolence!" he spat, turned to look over at Godfrey and nodded his head.

Godfrey raised his bow, already notched, and fired an arrow directly into the chest of the young man. Jem was stopped in his tracks, shocked. He looked down at the arrow, protruding from his chest, and fell forward.

Mayhem ensued. Lizzie and Madge screamed at the tops of their lungs. Ben fell to his knees sobbing "No! No!". June ran from the cottage shrieking out her husband's name. Kit hearing the screams, followed his mother, leaving the safety and sanctuary of the cottage. Lizzie ran over to her son and flung herself on is body weeping hysterically. Madge stood transfixed with terror, unable to move.

"Hunt!" shouted de Vere to his dogs, and they bounded off in search of their prey. June who had nearly reached the carnage, watched as the large dogs sped passed her, and looked behind to see her son halfway across the courtyard. "NOOOO!" she screamed, "RUN KIT! RUN!" The little boy looked at his mother in confusion for a second, and then responding to the tone of her voice, ran off around the corner of the cottage towards the paddock, with the dogs in pursuit.

June tried to follow her son but was roughly pulled back by one of the knights who had grabbed her by the hair. He began to drag her towards the cottage.

Another knight approached Lizzie and the prone body of her son. He drew his sword and plunged it into her back. The thrust was so powerful, it went straight through the woman, and into the body of her son as well. The Knight pulled the blade slowly out of the bodies, laughing maniacally.

Madge, still unable to move from her spot, was cut down by another knight, who slashed her across her throat with his blade, then without breaking his stride, moved towards Ben's cottage. Inside, June devastated by what had happened, her mind shattered, submitted to her fate, without a sound.

Two other knights made their way towards the other cottage, and kicked the door in, before entering.

De Vere nudged his horse forward motioning for de Crecy and his squires to follow. As he passed the kneeling form of Ben, he indicated to two of the squires to collect him and bring him with them. The two squires roughly manhandled Ben to the rear of his cottage, passed the small mangled and bloody heap that was what was left of his grandson, and propped him up against the gate of the paddock.

He was forced to watch as each of his cows was struck down by spears, Godfrey and his men used his bull for bow practice, and finally both cottages and the cow shed, were set to flame. Unable to do anything but watch the scene of utter devastation, Ben wished himself dead.

De Vere finally walked over to Ben and thrust his sword into the chest of the broken man. Ben slumped forward, finally released from his pain. De Vere wiped his blade on the clothes of the man he had just killed, before walking away towards Godfrey. He looked Godfrey in the eyes, appraising him. "Bowen! You have down well…. You can stay." he said.

De Crecy moved to his side and de Vere smiled at him, "Looks like we won't be collecting any tythes after all!" he howled with laughter, and he strode back to his horse.

# CHAPTER 12

## The Archer

"Pies! Pies! Bet you can't take your eyes off my pies!" the buxom female stall-holder cried out to the throbbing masses of people, as they passed her stall.

"I'll take one!" a young man said, placing his coin on the table in front of the stall, "They look delicious!"

"They taste even better!" the pie-woman beamed, "Here Kat!" she called out to the young girl serving at the stall, "Find a nice juicy one for the young man!"

The young girl selected a fat, golden-crusted pie, and held it out to the young man.

"Do you think "The Archer will be here today?" the young man asked.

"You can never tell, but I think it's likely. It is one of the biggest tournaments." The pie-woman responded.

"Well, I hope he does!" the young man replied, as he took a large bite from his pie, causing thick gravy to squirt everywhere.

"I hope he does to, always better for trade!" the pie-woman responded wistfully, as her daughter giggled at the sight of the young man with gravy running down his face and over his fingers.

"Me too!" the young man said as he began walking away, "Delicious pie! By the way!"

Another young man was making a reputation for himself around the wider area. Known to many traders at the markets of Gloucester, Prestbury, and Tewkesbury, for providing high quality meats, including a surfeit of rabbits, partridge, pheasant, and also venison and boar.

None questioned where he acquired such delicacies, as everyone knew that poaching was a potential death sentence. Nevertheless, they purchased his wares with enthusiasm, and sold them on to their discerning customers discretely. The customers, in turn, were also discrete, not wanting to deprive themselves of such excellent fair.

This person, who guarded his identity intensely, became known simply as "The Archer." Deals were made, and monies paid, without anyone seeing his face, for he always wore a hood, pulled down to conceal his identity. These deals were always conducted after dusk, thus preserving his anonymity.

This person also competed in local archery competitions and had gained an outstanding reputation. His trade deals and his competition successes were never linked.

This person was a ghost, and although many people wanted to know his identity in order to employ him because of his prowess, no-one was able to find out who he was or where he came from.

"The Archer" had joined the Tourney circuit only a year before. He had begun entering competitions, starting with the preliminary rounds, and fighting his way through to the finals immediately. He was a phenomenon, and quickly attracted a large following.

In competition circles, the mysterious young man entered competitions under his pseudonym and was renowned as being an expert in his art.

Many local landlords wanted him on their payroll, and many knights and other archers both despised and envied him. All wanted to know who this person was.

"The Archer" was able to conceal his identity by entering competitions, at the very last minute, collecting his purse, and then disappearing into obscurity, until the next challenge was presented.

Many competitions were arranged, in the hopes of enticing him to enter. In general, he only entered those competitions where he was ranged against the best in the region, but he intentionally did not attend every competition.

Whenever, a competition was organised, those who were tasked with the organisation, prayed that "The Archer" would attend. His appearance increased the numbers of people who would come to watch, and subsequently increased the betting, and the winner's purse.

Should his attendance become general knowledge, then those who were not local, would be more likely to bet on one of the more pompous looking competitors, and could be easily fleeced. Whereas those who were local, and more knowledgeable, would be unlikely to bet against "The Archer." Those who did bet would find the odds cut to the minimum.

❖

In another part of the field two nobles were conversing about the upcoming competitions.

"I hope 'The bloody Archer' stays away today!" Robert de Vere scowled at his companion.

"Aye Sire! I fancy my chances today, if he doesn't show." Godfrey smiled.

"Well, I want to see you beat him. Have you found out who he is?"

"No Sire. I have out word out, but no-one will say a word."

"To be honest, I don't think anyone knows. I don't know if I want to employ him or kill him!" de Vere grimaced.

"He would probably be a good asset, but also likely to be a pain in the arse!" his new Captain of Archers replied.

"Do we even know if it is the same person each time?"

"No Sire. He could be anyone."

"Well, he can't keep hidden forever. He'll make a mistake some time."

"Aye Sire!"

"I suppose, I'll need to get to the betting tent, to place a bet on you!"

"Aye Sire!"

"Well, if he shows up, I might take a bet on him as well!" de Vere laughed at the stricken face of his knight.

"Aye Sire!" a disgruntled Godfrey responded.

Large landowners would always be encouraged to bet on their own champions, and could not, without huge embarrassment to themselves, refuse to back them.

Local rivalry was fierce, reputations were on the line! Accordingly, the nobles would always bet enthusiastically, hoping that on any given day, their bowmen would best "The Archer."

If "The Archer" did not appear then their bets were as good as anyone else. If he did appear, and they bested him, their winnings would be astronomical!

"The Archer" was revered as a hero, by local people, who all acted to protect his identity, and facilitate his escape from unwanted attention, when required.

❖

The Tourney had been organised to take place on the meadows on the outskirts of Gloucester.  The challenge had been circulated to all the great houses in the county.  All the great and good were here.  The de Clifford's, the Beauchamp's, the Berkeley's, all out in force, along with many other noble families.

The entertainment would include some jousting, horse racing, demonstrations of hand-to-hand combat, and of course, archery.

Messages had been sent out weeks ago, and all the local Lords had received invitations to enter their champions. They were able to enter candidates in a variety of challenges, the ultimate challenge being the "Champion Archer" competition.

Such tournaments were important in developing and maintaining the skills of the men-at-arms, who were retained by the local Lords, including the archers from across the county.  For the nobles themselves, winning was often less important, than the development of the archery skills of local men in general.  However, the prestige of having a "Champion" within your household was always a source of local pride, and the ensuing "bragging rights", ensured that fierce competition remained, between households.

The transfer of the knowledge and skills of the champions was also important in developing the expertise of younger men, through tuition and training.

The tournaments provided an opportunity for each and every archer to test their metal in competition, and for local Lords to assess the competency of their own local talent against their neighbours.

This knowledge could be useful when called upon to settle local disputes!  It also provided much needed entertainment for local people, and each village supported their local heroes, as well as ensuring a continuous source of recruits for local militia, whenever required.

These tournaments were always well-attended by the gentry from miles around, their entourages, and any local people who were able to attend.  As such they attracted many trades people, selling all manner of wares, including food in all its varieties.

These events were fayres, with all kinds of attractions, and a cause of celebration.  Betting was another source of entertainment, both amongst the nobles, where substantial sums would be wagered, but also for the locals, where more modest amounts of coin could change hands.

❖

The Archer approached the Tourney area through the tents and stalls that lined the route. The sights, smells and noises assailed his senses from every direction. As it was a festival day, labourers, farm workers and other trades people were all given the day off, and the excitement in the air was palpable, the holiday atmosphere added to the sense of enjoyment and anticipation.

He walked past a stall selling freshly cooked pies and could not resist the delicious aroma wafting away from the stall. He drew a coin from his purse and held it out towards the young serving girl.

Without looking up, she took the coin and put it into a pot beneath the table, before selecting a large, juicy looking pastry. As she leaned across to hand it to him, she raised her eyes to his.

She gasped, and almost dropped the crusty goodness. As she continued to gape, the Archer chuckled, and took the pie from her shaking hands, and as he did so, gently placed another coin into her palm "For you, fair maiden!" he said.

"Oh my!" she crooned quietly, raising her hands to her face, clearly beside herself "It's you!" she continued, a deep flush appearing on her cheeks.

The young girl recovered some of her composure, as if waking from a dream, and turned to look over towards her father. His back was turned as he continued his work of heating pies over a brazier behind the stall.

"Pa!" she called out "Look!" Her father turned at the sound of the strange, almost rapturous tone in his daughter's voice, and as he did so, the young girl pointed towards the front of the stall.

"What is it my love?" her father asked, not understanding what had come over the girl.

"Look!" she said again, continuing to point, as she turned back towards to where the tall mysterious stranger had been standing just moments before.

The Archer had vanished into thin air.

"The Archer!" she whispered, "He was here!"

"What? Where? What did he look like?" her father questioned in a rush, looking all around.

"I don't know!" the girl replied despondently, all she could remember was the captivating twinkle that had shone from his eyes, where the sun had caught them. No other features had been visible, his face obscured in the deep hood of his cloak. She turned back to her father, the blush on her face still apparent, she had fallen in love……

Her father, having shaken her, and questioned her, until he was convinced that she was telling the truth, rushed off to the betting tent……

❖

Despite his clothing, the enigmatic Hooded Man, did not stand out. The people he passed did not seem to notice him. He stopped behind a tent, to take a bite out of the pie, bringing his other hand up quickly to catch the delicious, hot, thick, gravy juices that had gushed out as the crust was broken. He licked his fingers and savoured the spicy meat and vegetable in his mouth, as he chewed ravenously.

He had enjoyed the encounter with the young serving girl, and it brought a smile to his lips. He was well aware of the effect that he had on people, when he allowed them to get a glimpse of him, but their reactions never ceased to amuse him, and it pleased him that he had a positive impact on their day. It raised his spirits and helped him to prepare for the competition ahead.

As he finished his meal, his hunger satiated, he made his way around the back of the other stalls, towards the

Tourney tent. He slipped inside and stood behind the man who was busy organising the names of the challengers and collecting the fees that were required to participate.

Strangely, apart from the two of them, the tent was empty. This tent was normally a bustling centre of activity, but the organiser was happy to have a few minutes respite, which allowed him to prepare the challenge lists.

He was so wrapped up in his work, that he had not noticed the tall, cloaked figure looming over him.

Suddenly, some sixth-sense alerted him to the fact that he was not alone. He turned, a startled look on his face, he glanced over to the main tent opening and at the two guards stationed there.

They were clearly distracted by the entertainments going on around them and were completely oblivious to what was happening inside the tent.

Anticipating that the organiser was about to cry out, the Archer brought his fingers to his lips "Shhh!" he said.

 The organiser looked up, having recovered from his initial shock, he now had another shocking realisation. "The Archer!" he whispered, leaning forward "You are entering?"

The Archer responded by pulling a small piece of red ribbon from under his cloak, together with a small purse of coins. He placed them on the table in front of the organiser.

The organiser picked up the ribbon and studied it. At the bottom were three small, embroidered, gold circles. This was the secret authentication known only to certain people, to prove that this was indeed "The Archer" himself! "The archery competition starts at noon." The organiser informed him.

"You, of course, will not need to enter the opening rounds." He added, picking up the purse.

Ribbons were used to identify the participants; each had their own unique colour. The ribbons would be drawn from a bag by one of the noble ladies to signify which combatants would face each other. Well-known competitors would only take part in the latter stages of the competition, after lesser skilled hopefuls had been eliminated. Everyone knew that the red ribbon represented "The Archer."

Business concluded; the Archer slipped away as silently as he had arrived.

The organiser realised he had been given a unique opportunity. "Guards!" he called out.

The two guards briefly looked at each other guiltily, shaken from their preoccupation, before rushing into the tent. "Stay here and guard everything!" the organiser ordered "I will be back shortly!" he continued, as he rushed from the tent.

He knew that people could place bets on anyone, but if the person they had betted on did not show up for the tournament, then the bet was forfeit. He also knew that the odds were better, if their bets were placed before all of the competitors were confirmed. He wasted no time at all in deciding that this was the opportunity of a lifetime and was determined to get to the betting tent and place his bet, before it became common knowledge that "The Archer" was competing.

# Chapter 13
## The Tourney

Like everyone else in the village, Meg and Maud had taken the opportunity to attend the Tourney. They intended to enjoy the day with everyone else, but they also wanted to take advantage of the chance to sell some of their wares, knowing that the Fayre would be packed with people from all around.

They had left shortly after day-break to ensure they arrived in good time, and found a good pitch for their stall.

Because the tournament had been organised some time ago, many of the best pitches had been taken days ago, and the stalls erected in advance.

Unlike many of the larger merchants, Meg and Maud could not afford the time needed to do this and had taken the chance of turning up on the day, and seeing what was available.

Business had been brisk, and because of the quality of their wares, the two women had done well. They had turned a good profit so far, realising that they could charge more for their goods at events like this, than they could at the local market, due to the fact that there was a more diverse clientele, with so many important families in attendance.

Old Mother Sawyer had come along with them and was sitting in the shade of near-by tree, knitting contentedly. Meg had worried about the old lady making such a journey, but she need not have worried, as Old Mother Sawyer had shown remarkable fortitude and sprightliness, and had made the journey without any complaints whatsoever. In fact, she had arrived at the fayre as fresh as the moment she had left the village.

Close to noon, Maud was working alone at the stall, serving a customer. Meg had left for a short while, to buy some food and drink for them. They had not brought anything with them, other than a flagon of water, as they wanted to enjoy the rare opportunity to taste some of the pies, pastries, and other delicacies on offer. After all this was a holiday!

"This wool is gorgeous!" the well-to-do lady exclaimed in delight. "Where do you normally sell your wares?" she enquired of Maud.

"We normally sell at the Cheltenham market, My Lady." Maud replied happily, "We make our wares in Swindon Village, just outside Cheltenham, and Cheltenham is the nearest market."

"Well, I shall have to tell my husband to take me there then!" the lady effused. "I'll take these." She added, showing Maud what she had in her hands and handing coins over to Maud. "Oh! And this too!" she said, picking up another ball of wool. "Have I paid you sufficiently?" she enquired.

Maud looked down at the silver coins in her hand and replied "My Lady! This is too much! Let me give you some change!" Not knowing if she had enough change in her box to cover the difference.

"No matter! Please keep them!" the lady responded laughing, as a broad smile lit up her face, and she began to turn away from the stall, before calling out over her shoulder "I will bring my friends to Cheltenham and expect a substantial discount!". Robert de Vere's pregnant wife handed the goods to her serving girl, and flounced off, delighted with her purchases. Maud giggled to herself, pleased with the prospect of sales to come. "My World!" she thought looking down at the coins in her hand "This is more than we earn in a month at Cheltenham!"

❖

Meg had not been so fortunate. Whilst walking amongst the food stalls, she had been grabbed roughly from behind.

"Goodness!" startled, she turned and saw Godfrey holding her arm in a tight grip.

"Hello Meg!" he grinned. "I'm back!"

"Unhand me!" Meg cried out, drawing looks of concern from other stallholders and members of the public alike.

Godfrey released her, not wanting to draw attention. "I am back, but not home." he stated. "Home is the cottage, and I intend to have it!"

Meg looked at Godfrey and was surprised with how well he was dressed. "Done well for yourself then, I see?" she said.

"I have, sister. But there is still more that I want."

"We have spoken about this before, and nothing has changed." Meg spat with defiance. "You are welcome to visit and eat with us, but the cottage will never be yours!"

"We'll see!" Godfrey snarled.

"Over my dead body!" Meg responded.

"If necessary!" Godfrey laughed and walked away.

❖

Unbeknown to Maud or her mother, another shadowy figure had been observing them for some time. The Archer stood back from the hustle and bustle, and quietly watched the beautiful young girl who was working on the stall. He had noticed her earlier while passing and had been captivated by her. While he had been looking, he had also been listening, and had been able to discern, that the women were mother and daughter. He had also been able to determine from the conversation that the young woman had engaged in with her last customer, where she lived. He stored the memory away for another time.

Old Mother Sawyer remained under the tree. To anyone who looked at her, she appeared to be dozing.

However, appearances can be deceptive, and the old woman was well-versed in appearing to be something different to what she was. She opened her eyes and stared across Maud's stall, across the road that separated the stalls on the other side, and into the deep shadows beyond.

The Archer stared back, even though he knew he was completely out of sight, he could feel the old woman's eyes boring into his. She knew he was there.

Whilst Maud was distracted by another customer, the Archer left his concealment and crossed the road, all the time aware of the hawk-like eyes of the old woman who followed his every move.

As he moved quickly over towards the stall, he glanced up at the old woman, and she acknowledged him with a barely perceptible nod of her head, her eyes like flint. A message had been passed between them. Without any words, a deal had been struck, and both knew what that deal entailed.  He swiftly approached the stall and then just as quickly, moved silently away.  Maud never even noticed him.

Having finished her business with the customer, Maud bent down to put the money from the transaction into her box.  As she did so, she noticed something fluttering on the top of her cart.  She straightened and reached over to pick the item up.  She ran the red ribbon through her fingers wondering how it had come to be there.

❖

The preliminary rounds of the archery tournament had been completed.  Those skillfull enough to pass into the final stages preened and accepted the praise and congratulations offered to them.  They all knew that they would have earned decent purses today, through their success, and also that they would have earned a few more coins, from betting on themselves.

Now was the serious business, however.  This was the stage when the favourites joined the competition.  The targets were smaller and further away.  The competitors who had taken part so far realised that they were unlikely to progress to the big money, but they lived in hope.

A knight, resplendent in full, burnished armour, riding a similarly, magnificently attired warhorse, approached the lavish tented construction that accommodated all the great and the good from across the county.

The knight halted and lowered his lance towards Lord Berkeley. Attached to the end of the lance was a silk bag. The knight lowered his head and Lord William Viscount Berkeley detached the bag, opened it and held it out at arm's length towards his wife. She in turn, closed her eyes and put her hand into the bag. She briefly rubbed her fingers over the silk ribbons inside the bag, to make sure she only pulled out one, and then removed her hand and raised the ribbon she had selected aloft.

The crowd cheered, and the level of excitement and anticipation was elevated. She had selected the yellow ribbon, the colour of the de Clifford family of Frampton, fierce rivals of the Berkeley family. Lady Berkeley placed her hand inside the silk purse once again and drew a brown ribbon. As she raised this aloft, there was an audible groan of disappointment from the crowd, she had selected the colour of one of the minor challengers.

Meg and Maud, accompanied by Old Mother Sawyer, had found themselves good positions in the field, and were able to watch the spectacle unfold. Both Meg and Maud were surprised by the enthusiasm the old woman had for the competition. They had never seen her so excited and animated, and it was her that hurried them along, pushing other people out of the way, to find the best position possible.

As expected, the Frampton representative sailed through his round, and retired to the applause of the raucous and increasingly inebriated crowd.

Round two, round three and round four passed. On each occasion the favourite was victorious. The Archer watched impassively from his concealed position, as the rounds passed. Apart from the organiser, and anyone he had passed the information onto, not everyone in the crowd knew that "The Archer" was competing. A soon as word got around, the betting odds would drop dramatically!

The draw for the penultimate round was about to take place. The Archer watched. He knew that he would either join in the challenge this round, or the next. The honour in making the draw had fallen to Isabel De Vere, the pregnant wife of Robert de Vere. The crowd erupted into a frenzy of cheering, and the de Vere contingent hooted deliriously, when she raised the green ribbon above her head. She had selected the de Vere champion!

The level of anticipation was palpable, as she placed her hand into the silk purse for a second time. She paused for a moment, as she looked up and smiled at the enraptured audience, the tension was too much, and the crowd thundered its displeasure. She withdrew her hand, and without looking at the ribbon, she stretched her arm up to the limit of her reach and triumphantly waved it in the air. The crowd erupted and roared in expectation. At the same time as the crowd exploded, de Vere groaned outwardly. His wife was waving the red ribbon!

The excited crowd started chanting for their hero "The Archer! The Archer!" they cried in unison.

❖

Just outside the arena, and out of sight, The Archer removed his cloak and turned it inside out. Having done this, he put it back on. He was now dressed in a striking red robe, the well-known attire of his alter-ego "The Archer." "The Archer," now entered the arena. No-one had really noticed where he had come from, but when they saw him striding towards his mark, the cheers and chants erupted again.

Godfrey, De Vere's man stood at the other mark, with a scowl on his face. Although Godfrey was a Captain of Archers and highly skilled with this weapon, he was worried about the reputation of his opponent.

He had only been matched against "The Archer" on one previous occasion, and he had lost. He had been so angry, that he had broken his bow across his knees. This made him even more angry, as the bow had been very well made, and was expensive to replace. Godfrey did not take defeat magnanimously. Few men had ever bested him, and even fewer had lived on to boast of the exploits, most had ended up dead in a back street with a dagger in their guts.

Generally, although he might be annoyed in the immediate aftermath, he was not particularly worried about the local archery competitions. He was not the best in the area, and he knew this. His purpose was to maintain his skill with the bow, which was not his forte, and to judge those skills against the best in the area. As such, it was more of a hobby than serious work for him.

However, Godfrey abhorred "The Archer." He thought that the very name was pathetic, and he hated the adoration the man attracted. He desperately wanted to cut this swaggering, over-confident fool, down to size. For him, this was a grudge match.

The first targets were set at 100 yards. Although this was not a particularly long distance, archers in military campaigns relied on the volume of arrows falling in a specific area to do damage, rather than individually aimed shots. Therefore, these competitions really were feats of enormous skill.

The targets were man-size dollies made of straw. Each had three targets on them, a large torso target, a smaller target centred on the heart, and an even smaller target on the head. One point was scored for the torso, two for the heart, and finally three for the head. Each archer had three arrows per target.  A surer shot was generally the torso, with a reasonable chance of hitting the heart.  The head was generally avoided, as it was far easier to miss the target altogether and fail to score a point at all.

As they prepared to begin, Godfrey turned and glowered at his opponent.  "You piece of shit!" he declared angrily "Hiding behind your hood!  You're not man enough to show your face!"

"The Archer" ignored the jibe, merely nodding to his opponent, offering him first shot.  However, he did decide to teach this foul-mouthed fool a lesson in humility.

Godfrey fired his arrow and scored a solid shot in the torso of the target.

"The Archer" followed and placed his arrow in almost the identical spot on his target.

"One apiece!" the Marshalls shouted.

The other shots were fired in turn, each time "The Archer" replicated the shot from Godfrey.

At the end of the round, the scores were precisely the same.

❖

Meg. Maud and Old Mother Sawyer watched the ribbons being selected by Isabel de Vere. Maud recognised her as the noble lady who had paid her so well for the woollen garments.

"Look!" said Meg with a look of distaste on her face, "That is your Uncle Godfrey..." she pointed towards the archer who had been summoned into the arena.

"Uncle Godfrey!" Maud exclaimed, "He has returned?"

"Yes." Said Meg, "Unfortunately for us..." remembering her recent altercation with him.

Maud had not seen her uncle since she was a very young child and did not recognise him. "He is working for Lord de Vere?" she asked.

Meg scowled, "I know." She looked at Old Mother Sawyer, "I saw him earlier, he is up to no good again! I hope he gets beaten!"

Maud looked around at the crowd. Everywhere she looked, people were wearing or waving red ribbons. She turned to her mother, and asked "What do the red ribbons signify Ma?" Before she could answer, Old Mother Sawyer interjected "They are the colours of the competitors. The red signifies "The Archer"!" Maud suddenly remembered the ribbon that had been left at the stall and removed it from her pocket. Lifting it up towards her mother, Maud said "Look Ma! Someone accidently left one of the ribbons on our stall."

"Stupid girl!" exclaimed Old Mother Sawyer to Maud, causing both her and her mother to raise their eyebrows in shock. "It was no accident! "The Archer" left it for you!"

"How do you know?" questioned Meg sceptically.

"Yes! How do you know it wasn't just dropped by accident?" Maud added dubiously.

"Look closely at the ribbon, tell me what you see?" stated an exasperated old woman.

Maud and Meg both looked closely at the ribbon and noticed the three small, golden circles embroidered on it. "Nobody knows about those, it signifies that it comes from the man himself!" the old lady said.

They looked up at Old Mother Sawyer in awe, and speechless. "That, and the fact that I saw him leave it!" She added.

❖

For the second round, the targets were moved back to 125 yards. Again, each shot was matched. Godfrey was starting to feel confident.

During the third and final round the targets were set at 150 yards. Godfrey again had the honour, and his arrow struck the heart of his target. He roared in delight, and the crowd followed suit.

He turned to "The Archer," "Now I will show you who is your better!"

"The Archer merely nodded. Godfrey annoyed at the apparent lack of fight in the other man added "Let's make this personal!" and threw a purse of gold coins on the floor. "The Archer, bowed deeply, at which the crowd cried out his name, and took a similar purse from inside his cloak. He threw it next to Godfrey's.

"The Archer" took aim and struck his target in the head.

The score was three point to "The Archer" and two to Godfrey.

Godfrey took aim with his second arrow and fired. It hit the torso of his target. Three points apiece, and "The Archer" still had not fired his second shot.

He aimed, and fired, striking his target in the head for the second time. The crowd roared its delight.

Six points to three. Godfrey needed to hit the head target, just to have a chance of a draw. He fired and missed! He had lost! While he was still considering this fact, "The Archer" fired his final arrow, and struck the target in the head for the third time. The crowd almost became a riot as they cheered, and shouted and chanted their delight.

"The Archer bent and picked up the two purses and bowed theatrically at his opponent. Godfrey realising that he had been deliberately fooled, and therefore humiliated, let out a furious roar and charged towards his opponent.

"I will kill you! You scum! I will cut your head off and then everyone will know who you are!" A number of Marshalls who had been strategically positioned in case things got out of hand, intercepted Godfrey, and although he fought them off, and left each one battered and bruised on the ground, "The Archer" was nowhere to be seen.

❖

In the enclosure occupied by the nobles, another person was fuming. De Vere felt the humiliation of the defeat of his champion, every bit as sharply as Godfrey. His stupid wife had pulled out the red ribbon, and waved it around, without the slightest idea of the implications, and had even cheered the red robed opponent! He had also heard the sniggers of the other nobles and their ladies around him, as they first laughed at his misfortune of being drawn against "The Archer", and then again, as the humiliation of his household was completed.

He vowed to pay "The Archer" back by exposing him and killing him! Not necessarily in that order.

He pushed his way through the tangle of bodies and out of the rear of the enclosure, intent of seeking out the humiliated Godfrey.

❖

"The Archer" had secreted himself and become the invisible Archer once again.

He realised that he had probably over-stepped the mark, and this close to home, it was not a good idea to antagonise important local families. Unfortunately, their responses would be entirely predictable, and their self-importance and pride, would no doubt, require them to come after him.

He considered leaving. After all, he had already won a fair purse from Godfrey. After due consideration, he decided it would not be fair on all those who were supporting him, especially those who could not afford to lose their bets. Despite the risks, he would finish the competition.

From his secure vantage point, "The Archer" watched the second semi-final, as the Berkeley Champion, narrowly defeated the Frampton Champion, another fractious rivalry, although each party kept its composure on this occasion, as they had both already won in some of the other competitions.

A break was called before the final, and the Archer looked over at the still excited crowds, who were jostling about around the ale and food stools. As he watched, one girl stood out, Maud! A broad smile crossed his face, as he noticed she now had his red ribbon pinned over her heart! Another reason for him to continue in the competition!

❖

De Vere predictably, found Godfrey and the rest of his archers in one of the ale tents, helping to drown their respective sorrows, after they had all performed poorly in the Tourney.

As Godfrey saw his Lord and Master approaching through the crowds, he stood and collected a second mug of ale as he did so. When de Vere arrived, Godfrey passed him the extra mug, with ale sloshing over the rim, and onto his hands. De Vere grabbed it and took a long draught "Ahhhhh!" he exclaimed, and then tipped the rest of the drink over the head of his Captain. "You fool! You humiliated yourself, and worse you humiliated me!"

The other men, looked down at the ground, abashed at the treatment of their Captain.  Other people in the tent, laughed in astonishment at the way in which de Vere was treating his own staff, creating more gossip, and heaping more humiliation on himself.  This would be talked about for months!

"My apologies, Lord.  I thought I had the beating of him!" Godfrey spluttered, his face crimson with embarrassment and shame.

"I want you to find that insolent brat, and bring him to me, so that I can chop off his fingers!" de Vere declared.  "You had better not fail!" he added, before turning and storming out of the tent.

Godfrey and his compatriots left the tent shortly after, the embarrassment of remaining simply too much to bear.  They found a space away from the stalls, and out of general earshot.  He indicated for his companions to sit down, and they began their council of war.

Each man was given a post around the arena, to watch after the final had begun.  From there they would follow "The Archer's" movements and subsequently capture him.  Godfrey made a grim smile and thought "You will suffer, you bastard!"

❖

The time for the final arrived, and the Archer, once again changed his appearance surreptitiously, and appeared in the arena.

Godfrey's men were stationed at their watch points, not taking their eyes off their target for a second.

The competition was quite close, with "The Archer" winning in the end. He had not over-exerted himself, not wanting to do more than win, without upsetting another powerful family today. Besides, the Berkeley Champion had been courteous and a decent sport, and deserved some respect.

In the crowd, Maud and Meg were enthralled by the spectacle, the atmosphere and the tension of the competition. As "The Archer's" final shot was released, there was a collective holding of breath. As it struck true and the Champion was declared, Maud and Meg, along with hundreds of other spectators, jumped for joy, screaming gleefully. They had not noticed that Old Mother Sawyer was no longer with them.

"The Archer" quickly moved towards the prize table, collected his purse from the noble official, who was conducting the service, and turned and made a deep bow to the crowd, before moving swiftly out of the arena.

Godfrey's men began to move quickly towards the direction that they had seen "The Archer" leave the arena.

One of the men was positioned directly in the path that "The Archer" was travelling. He knew that the man would have to come directly passed his position and was waiting just out of sight to catch him unawares. He could hear the rustling of a cloak and the approach of a person. This was his chance! He raised his club, ready to strike!

"Young Man!" he heard a voice behind him, he turned around, and saw an ancient old woman stood there. She looked deep into his eyes for a few moments.

"The Archer" came round the corner and saw the thug standing transfixed. He glanced at the old woman and they exchanged a knowing look, before he continued on his way.

The next moment the thug was surrounded by his fellows, asking him where "The Archer" was. He looked around in a daze, the old woman was nowhere to be seen, and there was no sign of "The Archer."

# CHAPTER 14

## Young Love

One evening, after all the chores and work had been done, Maud said to her mother, "Ma, I am just going out for a walk, it is a fine evening and I want to smell the air."

"You be careful Maud! Don't go too far, and don't be out long!" her mother called back.

"You know I won't!" Maud retorted as she grabbed her cloak and slipped through the door. She scurried across the churchyard, and down through the trees, towards the secret meeting place, next to the stream that ran along the edge of the village, known as Wymans Brook.

This became their favourite place to meet in the evenings due to the fact that this was where they had both had their mishap, and fallen in. In this strange way, it held a cherished memory, and that is why it was their 'special' place.

As Maud neared the familiar spot, she called out "Whoooohooooohoooo!" in imitation of a single owl "hoot," to let Walter know she was coming. Within seconds, she heard a responding "hoot," and moved closer to the sound.

There, in the gathering gloom, under the trees, near the bank of the brook was Walter. He was leaning into the brook, doing something. She walked over to take a closer look. "Stay low!" he whispered, beckoning her to drop down with a nod of his head. Maud giggled at the absurd sight of the young man leaning over the bank, bobbing his head up and down like a woodpecker.

"Fishing for trout" he explained, as she crept towards him in a hunch and drew almost level with him. Suddenly, he threw his arms up, splashing her with cold water. She flinched and turned away "if this is your idea of a joke, I'm going to get you back!" she cried out laughing as the frigid liquid splattered over her face and shoulders.

As Walter brought himself back from the edge of the brook, a broad smile lit up her face, as she saw him holding a decent size trout with both of his hands. He threw it over his shoulder with a "whoop" of triumph, into the woods behind him. He then scrambled to his feet towards the flapping fish. Grabbing it again, he dashed its head against a nearby rock, and the fish stilled.

"There you go, supper!" he exclaimed. "For me?" she said, "I can't take it! How will I explain it to mother?."

"Ah... I didn't think about that! Could you say you found it?" He replied with just a hint of mischief in his eyes. She laughed back at him "How do I explain that it is raining fresh fish, and one just happened to land in my hands?"

He turned towards her, wiping his hands on his trousers as he did so. She noticed that he was looking at her earnestly. A little apprehensively she moved closer to him, and he drew her into a strong hug "Your very special, you know" she whispered to him, as she stretched upwards to place a gentle kiss on his cheek.

"You know I love you Maud, don't you?" he whispered back. "I know" she responded in kind. "So, do you love me too?" he asked a little dejectedly. "I think I do" she replied so quietly, he hardly heard her. "Did you say what I thought you said?" he cried. "I think I did" she giggled back.

For a short while after, they sat cuddled together on the bank of the brook, talking about the future, and their hopes and dreams. Walter covered them both with his cloak, and they huddled in the warmth of both their bodies.

❖

Maud crept around the side of the cottage and arrived at the front door. She stopped, with the fish wrapped in leaves in her hands, she held her trembling breath, and listened. "How am I going to be able to explain this?"

she mused, looking down at the leafy bundle. With her heart beating so fast, it seemed her blood was boiling in her ears, and she struggled to hear anything. She put her ear to the door... nothing, it was deathly quiet.

Normally, she would be able to hear her mother singing to herself while she weaved the wool, for which she was renowned. She waited but could still hear nothing. It was far too early for Maud's mother to have already retired to bed. Maud gingerly placed her hand on the latch and lifted it, trying to make as little noise as she could. Gently pushing the door open, she entered to find the cottage empty. "Strange" she murmured. Where was her mother at this time of the day?

Slightly relieved at not having to have an immediate confrontation about the provenance of the fishy gift, Maud sighed "Thank Goodness!" She placed the fresh trout on the kitchen table and looked around the cottage. The remnants of some weaving materials sat next to the stool near the hearth, and nothing seemed out of place, except the absence of her mother.

Wherever her mother was, Maud realised that she was going to have to explain herself... and she had not even managed to think of a single reason for having a fresh trout in her possession!

Deciding that whatever would be, would be, she went over to the pot above the hearth and leaned over to take in the smell of the broth still simmering away "delicious!" she exclaimed to herself, suddenly feeling ravenous! She took a bowl from the mantel above the hearth and ladled a bowlful for herself. She then grabbed the loaf of bread from the kitchen table, and plonked herself down on the chair next to it. She tore off a hunk of the bread and dipped it into the aromatic broth. She sighed deeply as the dripping bread entered her mouth, and leaned backwards against the chair, suddenly realising how famished she was!

"Is this what love does?" she thought "It makes you hungry!" she laughed out loud, hungry, delighted, slightly ashamed, and slightly scared. Whether she was scared of her mother, or what was happening to her, she was unsure…. Probably a bit of both, she concluded.

❖

Walter crept away from where he had left Maud. They had walked back into the village, and he left her at the corner of St Lawrence church. He was smiling from ear to ear and was as happy as any man could be! He had been in love with Maud since the day he had first seen her… she was pretty, funny, exciting, daring and much more! And she loved him! She loved him! It was more than his heart could bear. He was beside himself with joy. He almost skipped along the road, past the pig sheds, south of the manor, towards the bridge across the River Swilgate.

His joyful musings were brought to an abrupt halt as a hand shot out from behind one of the sheds and grabbed him around the collar. He pulled up short, choking against the firm grip. Falling backwards from the shock and the restriction around his throat, he completely lost his balance, and ended up on his backside.

"What the…!." Walter croaked, looking around in confusion.

"And just who do you think you are?" a stern voice admonished him from above, a dark shadow looming over him.

He turned and looked up, recognising the person standing over him. It was Meg, Maud's mother! "Oh No!" he thought, scrabbling away from her, in a most undignified manner.

"You have got some explaining to do boy!" Meg scolded, her voice serious and ominously threatening, as she advanced on him again.

"I do?" he replied rubbing his throat as he tried to think of some way of extricating himself from his predicament.

"Yes, you do!" Who are you? And what are you doing with my daughter?" Meg said with an intimidating edge to her voice.

"Me? Nothing, honest.." he whimpered, desperately wanting to get up and run away, but compelled to remain as he was, as if by some unseen force.

"Hiding, and sneaking around, is not what I would call nothing, Boy!" Meg leaned down and brought her face within a couple of inches of his own. Walter knew Meg by reputation to be a kindly and pleasant person, who would do anything to help anyone. Everyone in the village loved and respected her. He also knew Maud herself loved this woman unreservedly. However, the woman standing over him was nothing like the Margaret Bowen so revered in the village. This woman was like a menacing harridan, ominous and full of barely suppressed threat.

"I…. I… love her" he blurted "..and she loves me…" he cried, and then immediately thought "Oh No! that's not what she wanted to hear.". He cowered on the floor, now not daring to look into the eyes of Maud's mother.

Meg took a small step back and raised her face away from his. "Is that so?" Meg stated with a menace that made Walter begin to shake despite himself.

"I….. I do…truly" he whimpered "I would never harm her, ever." he added meekly, still refusing to look up and meet her eyes. He felt totally embarrassed, totally terrified, like a small child confronted by some monster from the most dreadful nightmare!

Meg's shadow seemed to grow bigger until it loomed above him, blocking out all light. "If you ever did, you would regret it forever!" She replied, "I would make sure of that, Boy!"

Walter did not know how to respond, and so he stayed silent, not wanting to dig a bigger hole, than he was already in. He certainly had no doubt about the veracity of her words!

Meg remained silent for some time. "Well, I think I need to know more about you, and your intentions then" Meg stated in a slightly softer voice, adding "And you need to know more about me" she added more ominously.

"Get up! You and me will talk again. Soon!" before adding "Be gone! I will find you and speak to you again." Her declaration was made with a certainty that chilled Walter. Walter did not move and did not look up for some time. When he did, he found that Meg Bowen had disappeared as quickly and quietly as she had arrived.

Walter stood up and shook himself down. "What just happened?" he asked himself, "And how did she do that?" he mused, as he thought about how a woman less than half his size had managed to put him on his backside so easily. Finally, he thought "Where did she even come from?" as he began to walk away, he grinned, although with a level of embarrassment about how he had been ambushed "That's where Maud gets her spirit from!" he concluded to himself.

Walter slipped away into the darkness and made his way home, thinking about when, and more importantly, what was going to happen when he next met Maud's mother. It was something he was not looking forward to, but even so, nothing could change his euphoria about his budding relationship with Maud. Maud's mother was an inevitable obstacle, which would have needed to be addressed at some time, it was just going to happen much more quickly than either he or Maud had ever imagined…….

❖

After finishing the soup, Maud had dozed off in the chair at the kitchen table. She was awoken with a start, as her mother came in through the door.

Maud tried to gather her thoughts, "How long have I been dozing?" she asked herself, as she watched her mother remove her cloak and hang it behind the cottage door. With some trepidation, she called out to her mother "Where have you been?"

"I have been checking on some things" her mother replied mysteriously and without clarification.

Deliberately changing the subject, Maud said "Is there anything left to do tonight, before bed?" twiddling her thumbs, and deliberately trying not to look at the Fish parcel, sitting on the table.

"No love. Not tonight. I have a few things to clear up, and then I will be ready for bed too" Meg responded, as she walked straight to the table and picked up the fish and placed it over by the hearth. Maud stared in disbelief at her mother's actions, it was as if she expected the fish to be there and it was a completely natural occurrence.

A short time later, Maud was even more astonished as she was sure she heard her mother say "At least he is good for something!" under her breath. Maud sat, opened mouthed, unable to say anything. Her mother turned away and began to pick up the weaving remnants on the floor, and then sat down on the stool near the hearth. Maud was sure she could detect a sly grin all across her mother's face.

❖

Walter did not have to wait long for his next meeting with Meg, and this time she had brought reinforcements!

He was making his way back from a particularly successful hunting trip, where he had managed to bag three pheasants. His intention was to give them to his mother, so that she could give any travellers eating at their Inn this evening a fine meal. Knowing he would be in serious trouble if he was caught in possession of them, he was keeping a low profile, stooped down, and stealthily walking along the hedgerows, and through the woods, keeping an eye, and an ear out for any signs of other people in the vicinity.

As he was walking through a patch of woodland, densely populated with large, tall trees of all types and species, he came across a huge oak tree. From side to side, it must have spanned at least ten feet. Such trees were not common in the area, and one as magnificent as this would surely be well known. It would probably even have a name, but he did not recall anyone, ever mentioning it. Although he had come along the same route many times, he could not remember seeing it before. He thought that was strange, as the tree was such an imposing specimen.

With these thoughts distracting him, he walked around the tree, trying to remember its location for future reference. He strode past as sure-footed and silent as he had been during the previous part of his journey home, never even breaking a twig.

"Oh! There you are!" he heard a familiar voice call out from behind him. He nearly jumped out of his skin! As he turned, he saw Maud's mother bending down to pluck mushrooms from around the base of the huge tree, and put them in a basket. Standing next to her, holding a basket of her own, was a frail-looking old lady.

"We've been waiting for you!" Meg stated, as if their meeting was as natural as bumping into someone along a main road going into any town.

Walter stood like a statue, too shocked to move, and dumbstruck! His heart was beating like it was going to burst from his chest, but he managed to mutter "What!" Wondering at the same time, how they could possibly have known he would be coming this way! Then another thought came unbidden into his mind "The colour of fear is brown!" This was an old military adage that his father had told him about a few years ago. It referred to the terror of combat that could literally make even the most battle-hardened warrior shit themselves! He now realised, that this was exactly how he felt at this moment!

Taking a deep breath, his heart rate nearly returning to normal he confronted the two women, who were acting like it was any other, normal foraging day in the woods. "How did you know…..?" he blurted.

Meg plucked a juicy specimen of fungus from the ground, popped it into her basket and then straightened to stand side by side with the older woman.

"This is Mother Sawyer." She replied, ignoring his question. "We have some questions to ask you!" Walter moved forwards and sat down in front of them, exactly in the place where Meg had indicated with a wave of her open palm.

The two strange women interrogated him for about an hour, asking all manner of questions. Walter responded to all their queries as honestly as he could. Finally, they both appeared to be satisfied, as Mother Sawyer turned to the younger woman and nodded, "He is alright." she stated gravely. Walter sighed with relief as both women looked at him directly and smiled. He seemed to have passed the inquisition, and the verdict was positive!

With the ordeal apparently over, he began to get up onto his feet. Meg leaned forward and offered him her basket. "These are for you." She declared "We have what we need." Walter looked down at the basket he had been offered, and saw a range of beautiful, delicate mushrooms. He also glanced at the other basket being held by Mother Sawyer. It contained other types of mushroom, coloured red, yellow with white spots, pale blue. He didn't fancy the look of those! He took the proffered basket, gratefully and thought "Pheasant and mushroom! Our guests are in for a treat!"

Meg and Mother Sawyer bade him farewell, and he continued on his way, still bemused by his encounter. Just before entering a denser part of the wood, he turned back to look at them one more time. He could no longer see the two women, or even the tree that they had sat beneath for more than an hour!

# CHAPTER 15

### A Day at the Market

After his strange encounter with the two women in the forest, Walter felt more able to woo his love more openly. He was still reluctant to call at Maud's cottage, but he met with her every day, and did his best to be available to escort her to and from the market each week.

As it was only one day a week, he rarely missed the opportunity to be able to spend as much of the day as possible in her company.

Meg had begun allowing Maud to travel into the market by herself about a year previously. She had originally ensured that Mary and her sons would keep a close eye on her, and since young Walter had come onto the scene, she was happy for him to take the role of her protector. He seemed likeable and capable, and there was something about him, that gave Meg confidence in his ability to look after Maud. It was more than just the fact that he was obviously completely smitten with Maud, there was something, hidden from plain sight, but there, nevertheless. Meg was convinced that Walter would protect Maud with his body and soul.

On one particularly sunny day, Maud had just arrived on the Runnings Road, pulling her little cart along, when

Walter jumped out of the hedgerow just in front of her. "Yaaaa!" he cried out in an attempt to scare her. She was momentarily startled, and then could not help but burst out laughing as the stupid boy, was pulled backwards sharply, and fell back into the thorny bushes.

As he had jumped out, his shirt had got caught on a branch and his momentum had been immediately checked. Losing his balance, he fell backwards. "Aggggghhh!" came his second cry.

Maud, stood and watched the hapless youth, thrash about for a few seconds, trying to extricate himself from his prickly dilemma. Eventually, having pity on him, she went over to help. "Stop moving!" she scolded. "You are only making things worse!"

"Ow! Ow!" Walter cried out.

"Here let me help you!" Maud called "Grab my arm." Walter, who had bramble tines and thorns stuck everywhere, was struggling to put his hands down anywhere where there were no spikey bits. Maud held out her arm, and with great effort, she first managed to get him into a precarious and slightly undignified squatting position, and then once he had achieved some semblance of balance, she was able to pull him forward and up with little further effort on her part, however she said "Ooof! You are a great lump! Aren't you!"

Walter brushed himself off, on the bits he could reach, and Maud pulled twigs and tines, from the back of his shirt and out of his hair. He had a number of nasty scratches on his arms, and Maud dabbed at them with a damp piece of rag, that she had taken from her cart and doused with water from her flask.

"You are daft!" she laughed, and Walter caught between a grimace and a smile, responded "Why is it that this always happens when I meet with you!" Walter's face was red like a beetroot from yet another humiliating episode, with this young woman he wanted to impress so much!

She leaned forward and lightly kissed him on the cheek "There! That will make you feel better!"

Walter looked into her eyes and said "You know, you're right! I actually do feel better!" Maud had no time for her deep blush to develop, as Walter grabbed and planted a big smacker on her lips. She pushed him away good naturedly as Mary Forrester and her youngest son Ned, began to pass them on the road "Ooooh-Errrr" Ned shouted boisterously. Now Maud's blush had free rein! "Stop it, Ned!" admonished his mother, adding mischievously "Let the young lovers be!"

"We're not.....!" both Maud and Walter exclaimed simultaneously.

"Yeah! Yeah! Yeah!" Mary and Ned sniggered as they continued on their way.

"See what you've done now!" scolded Maud. "We'll be the talk of the village, and my mother will be furious!"

She looked at her young man, and the frown turned to a grin. She just could not be angry with him for long.

Walter, looking slightly dishevelled, with ripped shirt and breaches, grinned back. He should have felt abashed, but he couldn't, he was full of joy, despite the discomfort his minor injuries were causing, just to be with Maud, he would gladly suffer any form of ignominy!

He picked up his bow and quiver from the ground just in front of the hedge and put them in the cart on top of Maud's goods, and then picked up the poles of the cart and began pulling them along, "Come on you! We'll be late!" he called, as he began to run with the cart.

"Stop! You fool!" she screamed in delight, running to catch up "You'll be worn out in a hundred yards!"

Walter slowed to allow her to catch up, and they walked on, chattering happily about this and that. They waved to friends and neighbours, who were also walking to market, and to other people who were acquaintances who they only ever saw on market days. Some stopped to chat, and they exchanged news and gossip. Everyone was happy and looking forward to selling their goods.

As they got closer to the market square, the road began to fill with people, excited trades people bustled to reach their usual spots. There were never many problems with people getting the same pitches every week, and it was important that your customers knew exactly where to find you. Most people knew their neighbours at the market and would protect their pitches if anyone was running late. The traders prided themselves on looking after each other, after all, the success of the market was important to everyone, and the quality of the goods that could be bought there was a further source of pride. Occasionally, itinerant traders would pass through, and they were supported by the local traders to do so, as they were always interested in new products, and gossip and news from outside of the area.

❖

When they arrived at the market square, there was an energetic buzz, as stalls were set up, people exchanged recent gossip and discussed recent happenings from far and wide. Fires were lit, and all manner of smells emanated across the square. Delicious food smells wafted across as roasted pigs caught the flames, pies began cooking, and stews bubbled in their pots. These mingled with the smell of hay and horses, herbs and vegetables, and all manner of other things.

Maud's stall did not take long to set up, especially with Walter's help. The cart was tipped backwards, so that the wares were exposed and easily reachable for customers, and a sturdy woollen covering was attached to the cart poles, and then to two other poles tied off with twine. This provided Maud with some respite from the sun or rain. Under this she had her stool and her small folding table, under which she placed her money box, a covering was draped over the table, concealing the money box. Maud did not carry much money, and most of that she carried on her person, to give change to customers. It was generally at the end of the day, when she would put her day's takings into the lockable box and secrete it in her cart.

Thefts did occur, but very rarely at the marketplace itself. As all the traders looked after each other, it was highly unlikely that any thief would get more than a few yards before they were apprehended and given a severe beating, by a dozen or more stall holders.

Soon, customers started to arrive. There were those who always got to market early, some even before the stalls were set up, in order to get the freshest produce, or buy something of quality. They knew that if they waited until the end of the day, they would have to buy what was left, and although there might be a few bargains, as stall holders looked to sell the last of their wares, the choices would be limited. Even so, there was a steady stream of customers throughout the day, with some having to travel further than others, and then there were the stragglers, whose sole purpose was to buy the last of the goods at a knock down price. This was especially true of the food products that trades people were very reluctant to take back home with them. The truth was that the food traders would often go around the other stall holders, and give their leftovers to them, sometimes for a trade, but often for free.

Maud got down to the day's business, and business was brisk as always. In between customers Maud and Walter would natter about all manner of things. Generally, Maud was busy for most of the day, and the products she sold were sought after.

Around mid-morning, Walter got a little bored and decided to take a walk around the market to see what was happening. He wanted to give Maud a surprise, and thought he knew just the place to find one.

He wandered through the market until he came to the place he had been looking for. The stall sold mainly fruit, and they had some huge, juicy looking pears for sale. Walter bought two and began to make his way back to Maud.

❖

Robert de Vere had accompanied his wife to the market at Cheltenham. Although it was a task he abhorred, his wife always insisted, and as it was one of the very few excursions she had a chance to make, he felt obliged to accompany her. She often met with her friends, who were the wives and daughters of other local nobles, and it would be bad etiquette for a local Lord to simply hand over the responsibility for the protection of his wife to his soldiers. It was also an opportunity to meet with other landowners and exchange news. Sometimes the men would retire to a local tavern for a while and discuss business matters.

On this day Lady Isabel de Vere was with a couple of her friends. She particularly wanted to find the stall run by the pretty blonde girl who she had seen at the Tourney a few weeks ago and show its wares off to her friends. Trailed by their husbands, and at a more discreet distance by the guards, they wandered about, as Isabel tried to remember where the girl had told her the stall would be. Although Cheltenham market was one of the closest, they very rarely came here, and most often went to the larger markets of Gloucester, Tewkesbury, or even Prestbury. However, Isabel was so enamoured of the products sold by the young woman from Cheltenham, that she had not only persuaded her husband to bring her to this market, but also her friends and their husbands too!

"Ahhh! There she is!" Isabel called out to her friends, pointing in the direction of Maud's stall. "I know it doesn't look much, but you will love it!" she added confidently. The women bustled with excitement towards the stall, while the men looked at each other with raised eyebrows!

Maud immediately recognised the heavily pregnant young woman approaching her stall. She was surprised and delighted that the Lady had two other similarly noble looking companions in tow. "Good morrow, My Lady!" she called out "You found me!"

"I found you!" Lady de Vere replied.

"Not long now?" Maud ventured, nodding at the large bump, "I hope all is well!"

"Never better my dear, everything is progressing wonderfully!" the slightly older woman gushed.

Turning to her friends, Isabel enthused "See! Didn't I tell you!"

"Look Evelyn! Isn't this precious?" she exclaimed to her friend, pointing at the garments on the cart "and these?" she said, picking up other items and showing them to her companions. The women fussed over the various wares that Maud had in her cart and after some time held them out towards Maud. "I want these!" Lady Evelyn Charteris said.

"...and I want these!" called the other companion Lady Mary Braceley.

"And I will take these!" stated Isabel de Vere, handing her purchases to Maud. Maud calculated the cost of the items and told the women.

De Vere and his acquaintances had been watching the spectacle of their wives shopping from a short distance away. Each of the men had secretly glanced at each other when they had seen the young woman. Each had fallen a little in love.

Each of the three noble ladies turned around to their husbands and fluttered their eyelids. Each husband dutifully stepped forward and paid the beautiful young stall holder.

As de Vere handed over his silver, his hand rested on Maud's for just a fraction longer than necessary. This caused her to look up at him. She smiled, because smiling was the most natural thing in the world for her. De Vere was captivated. "What is your name, young woman? He asked.

"Maud Bowen, My Lord" Maud replied with a little curtsey.

"And where do you come from?" he continued, interested in her surname.

"Swindon Village, My Lord." Maud responded lowering her eyes under his piercing gaze. De Vere smiled to himself. Surely, it was too much of a coincidence! He thought of Godfrey, his Captain "They must be related!" he thought. He threw his hands up in the air, in delight. "Swindon Village!" he cried to his fellows. "She comes from Swindon Village! One of my Manors!"

The men smiled in knowing acknowledgement, but the women looked at each other in confusion. "What on earth are you on about?" Isabel asked.

"Oh! Nothing m'dear! Just the fact that such fine produce is being made on our lands!" he smiled and winked at his friends.

"Fine produce indeed!" Braceley muttered under his breath.

De Vere spun around to face his group. "Today has been better than I expected!" Having made their purchases, the group turned and sauntered away. Lady Isabel turned briefly and gave Maud a little wave, before turning back to her group.

Maud watched them go, very happy to have found some wealthy new customers. She smiled to herself as she heard Lord Charteris bellow "Food! We need food! I saw a pie stall over here, it smelled wonderful!" as he pointed in the direction of a stall further into the market and began to shepherd the group towards it.

Maud was distracted by another customer and did not notice de Vere stop for a second and stare at her, neither did she see the flash in his eyes, before he quickly caught up with the rest of his group.

Walter had returned from his foray, and sneaked up behind Maud, "Who were they?" Walter asked when she had finished serving her customer.

"Goodness!" she cried out "I didn't hear you come back!"

"Hahaha! I brought you a present!" he said holding out two fat juicy pears.

Maud grabbed them both and took a bite from each. "Hey!" Walter reproved.

"My present!" Maud laughed, holding one out to the pouting Walter "All right then, I'll let you have one!"

"Well, only one was supposed to….Oh! Never mind!" Walter gave up, his face smiling from ear to ear, and accepted the proffered pear. Walter would give up anything for this feisty maid. A bite of his pear was a small price to pay for that beautiful smile!

# Chapter 16

## Betrayal

Since his return Godfrey had avoided visiting Meg. He was still plotting to try to find a way of taking the cottage from her. He was obsessed with the thought of it.

Tonight, he had a plan. He would take a different approach and would see what transpired. Godfrey turned up at Meg's cottage out of the blue.

He arrived bearing gifts. Meg was surprised, and Maud was suspicious. Her mother had warned about her uncle and told her that his previous visits had been acrimonious and threatening.

"I've brought dinner and wine." Godfrey declared. He walked over to the table and unwrapped a cooked pigeon and placed it on the table. Next, he placed a capped flagon of wine down, together with a jug of ale.

"Godfrey, we have a broth cooking!" Meg responded, unsure why Godfrey seemed so happy and generous.

"I know you have been through a lot, and I wanted to make amends." Godfrey said. "I want to help and support you where I can."

"Why the change of heart?" Meg retorted suspiciously.

"I want us to get along and resolve our differences." He replied glibly, wiping his hands on his trousers, "A peace offering?" he pleaded.

"We can put the bird with the broth." Meg conceded.

Maud watched the exchange, unconvinced by Godfrey's generosity. She held her tongue.

"Come! Let's eat! Before it gets cold!" Godfrey exclaimed enthusiastically.

Meg split the bird, poured the broth into the bowls and the extended family sat down to eat. Godfrey eagerly poured the wine, "Drink!" he commanded, "It'll be a long time before you taste wine like this again!"

Meg supped the thick, rich, dark red wine. "Godfrey! This is lovely!" she exclaimed in delight. Despite her natural aversion to her brother-in-law, and her suspicion about his motives, she felt that Maud and herself would be safer if they could remain on friendly terms with Godfrey. She felt herself thawing with every sip.

"Told you! It's from Burgundy!" he smiled, lifting his own jug of ale to his lips.

Maud was more circumspect. She tried the wine, but being unused to its taste, it did not really appeal to her. She pretended to drink to keep up appearances but restrained herself from drinking it all.

She indulged in eating the meat and broth, as did her mother and Godfrey. The meal was delicious! Maud greedily ate the succulent meat and drank the earthy vegetable soup. Her mother was clearly enjoying the treat and was soon drinking her second mug of wine. Godfrey refilled her cup as soon as Meg had finished it. He offered Maud a refill, but she refused, still suspicious of Godfrey's intentions.

With the food eaten, and the flagon of wine nearly empty, Meg was feeling drowsy. She smiled contentedly at her daughter and then turned towards her brother-in-law. "That was lovely Godfrey, thank you!" she said.

"My pleasure!" Godfrey responded.

Meg started to rise from the table and stumbled. Maud immediately rose to aid her mother; she gripped her mother's arm. "I don't know what has come over me!" her mother exclaimed. "That wine is powerful!" she added. Godfrey did not move to help, but sat back in his chair, a smile of contentment, and something else on his face.

Maud helped her mother towards her bed, she moved the coverlet aside, and gently laid her down. "Thank you, my darling." Her mother said, as Maud plumped her pillow, and set her head upon it. "I don't know what has come over me." She said, as her eyes closed. Maud pulled the blanket over her mother and bent down to kiss her on the head. "I love you, Ma." She whispered.

Maud returned to the main room and sat down opposite Godfrey. He seemed to be very happy, and Maud felt vulnerable in his presence.

Godfrey poured the last dregs of the wine into Maud's mug, picked it up and stretched out his arm, offering it to Maud. Maud accepted the proffered cup and took a sip. "This taste really grows on you!" she thought. Just with a couple of sips, she felt drowsy.

Godfrey grinned, the first part of his plan had succeeded, "Maud, now that we are alone, I have something important to ask you..." Godfrey began.

"What could you possibly ask of me?" Maud asked, feeling a little weary, her eyes beginning to droop.

"I would ask you for your hand in marriage...." Godfrey responded, leaning towards her, and taking her hand in his.

Maud was immediately repulsed by the very notion that Godfrey could consider her as a wife and pulled her hand away. More than that, she was disgusted! He was older than her mother! He was older than her father! But more than anything..... "But you are my Uncle!" she cried out. "It would be a sin!"

"Maud..."

"No! No! Never!" she cried "I could never even consider you as a husband!"

Godfrey's face reddened with anger.

"I hate you!" Maud screamed.

"You bitch! You are just like your mother!" Godfrey bellowed at her. His face was a torment of anger, flushed deep red and etched with fury. He grabbed her arm roughly and squeezed. Maud slapped him across the face, and he released his grip. Maud ran from him into her room, terrified.

Godfrey did not pursue her, but slammed his fist down onto the table, spilling the remnants of the meal and drink onto the floor.

He stood, threw his mug into the fireplace, and stormed out of the cottage. His ploy had failed miserably.

❖

Godfrey was determined to pursue his claim. He was infuriated by Maud's rejection and sought to raise his claim with the Lord of the Manor in Swindon Village.

He petitioned Richard Moryn and requested an audience. Moryn, who knew the Bowen family well, was very reluctant to become involved in the dispute. He knew that Will had been a well-liked and hardworking member of the community, his death had had a major impact on village life, and many of the villagers were still angry about the lack of an investigation into his death, despite the many years that had passed. Will's wife had asked for more information, and she was supported by the other villagers.

Her request was given additional impetus by the fact that Will had been the only casualty from the village, and the group he had left with, had already had a bad reputation. He also knew that Meg Bowen was an industrious and a popular personality within the village, and the welfare, happiness and well-being of the village was a key factor in ensuring that productivity was maintained.

Moryn did not want any disruption to the status quo, and he was convinced that Godfrey would not be welcome. Godfrey was a known troublemaker and if the rumours were true, something much worse. Having had such a tragedy in their lives, he also worried about the welfare of Meg and her young child. He knew that many families did not survive the death of the man of the family. The whole village had been in mourning, and he considered Godfrey's insistence, and timing to be misjudged and lacking in empathy for his sister-in-law.

However, Godfrey's claim needed to be heard and a judgement made. As a result, he reluctantly decided he must consult his over-lord, Robert de Vere. Moryn expected de Vere to be angry about the imposition on his time, dealing with a local issue. He was shocked and surprised in equal measure, when his messenger to de Vere returned commanding that an immediate appointment be made to hear Godfrey's petition.

❖

De Vere met with Godfrey at the manor house in Swindon Village. De Vere could not care less about Godfrey's claim, but his interest in the village centred on a young blonde woman, who he had seen at the market, and he wanted to know more about her. He saw the interview with Godfrey, as an opportunity to learn more about her.

"So, Bowen, What is your complaint?" de Vere asked impatiently.

The cottage in the churchyard is owned by my sister-in-law Margaret Bowen, My Lord." Godfrey replied. "It was handed down from my mother to my brother, and now he is dead. The cottage should revert to me."

"Margaret Bowen? Who is she?"

Richard Moryn replied "She is a widow, with a young daughter, Sire."

"How old is this daughter?"

"Nearly sixteen, Sire."

"Sixteen, you say! What does she look like?" de Vere enquired further.

"She is tall and strong. She has blonde hair." Moryn answered.

De Vere's eyebrows rose involuntarily at this information, "Bring them to me Moryn, I will hear their side of the story."

"Aye Sire!" Moryn left the room to find a servant to fetch the Bowen women.

❖

A short while later the group reconvened with both Meg and Maud now present.

De Vere looked at the two women, and instantly recognised Maud as the young woman from the market. He felt a sweat break out on his top lip, and he quickly wiped it away. "So, this is Bowen's niece?" he thought. His face flushed a little, but no-one noticed as they feared to look him directly in the eye.

"Godfrey Bowen claims ownership of the cottage." De Vere stated. "What do you say?"

Meg curtsied and indicated to Maud to do the same. As she rose, she said "The cottage belonged to my husband, who was killed fighting for the King. It was passed down to him, by his mother, and it is my daughter's inheritance! We have a letter signed by the Kind himself giving me ownership!"

"I see." De Vere responded. "And what say you, Moryn?"

"They are both hard working, and well-liked in the community. I would support their claim." Moryn answered.

"Well then, Bowen." De Vere said looking over at Godfrey. "The cottage has legally passed to your brother, and then to his wife. As her daughter is the heir, then the wife has legal right to ownership."

Godfrey waited for a 'but', but it never came.

"That is my decision. Margaret Bowen retains possession of the cottage, and her daughter remains the heir. Your claim is dismissed, Bowen!"

Godfrey stood, rooted to the spot, he was fuming, but unable to gainsay the Lord of the Manor. "Very well, Sire." He answered as politely as his anger would allow.

De Vere looked at him and thought about the advantage this situation had placed into his hands. The cogs and wheels turned in his mind, and he plotted his next step.

With the meeting concluded, Moryn dismissed the two women and Godfrey, and they turned to leave.

"Bowen! Tarry awhile, I would speak with you privately. There might be something you can do for me." Said De Vere.

Godfrey waited outside the manor house, still angry at what had transpired, and also concerned about what the Lord of the Manor wanted of him. Godfrey knew the man's reputation and despite working for him, he was not keen to spend any more time around him than he needed to.

"Ah Bowen!" de Vere called out as he left the main entrance of the Manor, pulling his leather riding gloves onto his hands.

"Sire!" Godfrey responded.

De Vere came closer to him, and in hushed tones said "Your cause is not necessarily lost. We might be able to be of service to each other."

Godfrey was shocked, "What on earth could I have that he needs?" he thought "And why on earth would someone as powerful as de Vere offer to do a service for me?"

De Vere was aware of his Captain's reputation and recalled the briefing that Moryn had given him. It was one of the reasons he had employed him in the first place.

"I will arrange a clandestine meeting between the two of us. I don't want us to be seen together locally, but you may still earn that cottage you desire. De Crecy will make the arrangements soon."

"As you will, Sire..." Godfrey responded, bewildered at this turn of events.

❖

Hubert de Crecy, walked into the Cross Hands Inn, and looked around. He knew that this was where Godfrey and his men spent time together, when not on duty. He was wearing peasant garb, so that he did not stand out. Since de Vere had employed him, de Crecy was wary of Godfrey and his men. They did a good job, and generally did as they were told. De Crecy had worked with many cut-throats like Godfrey and was comfortable commanding them. However, he would never turn his back on a man like Godfrey. The two men had a mutually uncomfortable relationship.

Eventually, his gaze fell upon the motley crew sitting at a table in one of the corners of the dark room, and he saw them for the type of characters they really were, common robbers and cut-throats. De Crecy, a decorated knight in his own right, despised these types of people and thought that they all looked similar anyway. He had been in Inns and Taverns across Europe, and archers always looked the same, unshaven, unkempt, and unclean, the scum of the earth. He walked straight over to their table and enquired of the group, "Godfrey!"

Bowen looked up at the burly man standing next to their table. "Sir Hubert, what brings you here?" he said with a faint air of contemptuousness.

"Your Lord and Master demands your attendance!" de Crecy ordered, irritably, thinking to himself "Who does this peasant think he is! He needs taking down a peg or two!"

"Ahhh! Why don't you keep your voice down!" Godfrey retorted, "There is no need to let everyone know our business! Especially here!"

"Come!" de Crecy ordered, as he turned and strode towards the door.

"Godfrey muttered to his companions "Who the hell does he think he is?" he did not enjoy been shown up in front of his friends. He remained seated and picked up his mug to drain its contents. "He can wait for a few more minutes!" he laughed.

When he finally did decide to get up follow the knight outside, de Crecy was not impressed. "You think you are clever Bowen? You might think differently when Lord de Vere realises you have kept him waiting!"

"Well, you should have been more discreet! No-one orders me about in my own Inn! Many have tried, none have succeeded! I have a reputation to uphold, and you just barge in and try to embarrass me!" Bowen chided him.

"Damn peasants!" de Crecy huffed, and Godfrey chuckled. "One up to me!" he thought.

❖

De Crecy took Godfrey into the heart of Gloucester and stopped his horse outside the New Inn. De Crecy dismounted and handed his reins to a stable boy, Godfrey did the same.

"My Lord is inside." De Crecy stated and indicated the door to Godfrey. Godfrey entered the Inn and saw de Vere sitting at one of the tables eating. De Crecy entered behind him and seated himself at a table just inside the door, with a group of tough looking men. Godfrey could see that de Crecy's position gave him a commanding view of the inside of the tavern.

Godfrey walked towards de Vere's table. As he approached, de Vere said "Ahh! Bowen, sit!"

Godfrey sat down at the table, and de Vere ordered more food and wine for Godfrey. Once the food had been delivered, de Vere poured them both a glass of deep red wine.

"I have a proposition for you" de Vere began.

"I am all ears!" Godfrey responded.

"You want the cottage, yes?" Godfrey nodded.

"I cannot legally give you the cottage at the moment, but if circumstances changed, then it might be possible…"

"What circumstances?" Godfrey asked.

"If your sister-in-law did not have an heir, then I could reclaim the cottage under the law of escheat."

"So, you mean we get rid of the girl?" Godfrey queried.

"Not in so many words.." de Vere continued "I want the girl!"

"You want her? In what way?"

"I desire the girl Bowen! I shall take her away." Godfrey could see the man's eyes gleaming with yearning.

"As in kidnap her?"

"In a manner of speaking. I will take her to one of my other properties and keep her there until I get bored with her."

"But if she disappears, I will be suspected!" Godfrey retorted.

"Not at all Bowen!" de Vere said slyly. "I am the Lord of the Manor; I will say that you have been with me. No-one will gain-say me!"

"So, what do you need me for?" Godfrey asked.

"I need you to help me plan the abduction!" de Vere stated. "I need you to tell me when the best time would be, and make sure that everything is in place."

Godfrey considered what was being asked of him, before replying "There is a boy who follows her around all the time. We would need to get him out of the way."

"What would you propose?" asked de Vere, stroking his beard.

"He is an innocent. If we kill him, we make things more complicated. I will arrange for him to be taken care of on the day."

"Good, we have an agreement then! I get the girl and you get the cottage!"

# CHAPTER 17

## A Series of unfortunate occurrences

"Hurry, girl!" her mother called to Maud "You will be late for market, and you will miss your normal spot." Meg called in exasperation.

For some inexplicable reason, they had both slept in this morning, and now she would be late leaving. The scarves, woollens, blankets, and headscarves they had been making during the past week, still needed to be packed into the cart, and she needed to get going!

Maud grabbed the hairbrush from the small table next to her bed, and roughly scraped through her long blonde locks, she did not have time for anything else this morning, she had to get going! As she drew the brush one last time down through her hair, it caught something. Thinking that it was nothing more than a tangle in her hair, Maud pulled a little harder, and the brush came free. Hurriedly, she threw the brush back on to the table, pulled the curtain that separated her room from the rest of the cottage, and rushed over to her mother.

She did not notice that the brush had caught her pendant, and ripped it from her neck, so delicate was the chain. The brush missed the table, and rolled under the bed, hiding the pendant from view.  Maud was in too much of a rush to worry about the brush on the floor and gave no further thought to it.

As Maud entered the main room, Meg indicated to the food she had prepared and placed on the table, "Here child, eat this or you will be hungry for the rest of the day" she said as she handed Maud a piece of loaf with some cheese on it "I have put some more bread with pickles and a piece of ham out for you, it is in the bag over there!  Meg pointed to the small linen bag sitting on the far side of the kitchen table.  "Don't forget it or you will starve out there all day!".

Maud smiled at her mother, who was busily folding the wares that Maud would sell today, laying them on the table next to the Maud's lunch.  Her mother was a magnificent woman, Maud could not have loved her more.  After the death of her father, Meg had worked harder than ever to provide all that they needed as a family.  Even having her uncle staying with them occasionally, was bearable, as Meg and Maud together worked to make a success of their small business, weaving, knitting, darning, and dyeing.

Briefly, Maud wondered where Godfrey was.  It was likely that he had not returned home the previous night.  Maud had told her mother about the disturbing night she had spent with Godfrey, and what he had said, and although Meg was still wary of him, she had explained that keeping Godfrey sweet would benefit them in the long run.

Godfrey did not appear every night, he often had duties to perform at de Vere's estate, and even when not on duty, he was often out all hours of the day and night, sometimes returning falling-down drunk, after meeting with his nefarious friends and associates.

Maud did not really know what Godfrey got up to, and she did not really care. In fact, the more he was out the better, he demanded money from her mother and never seemed to do any work. He came home to eat and sleep, and take money, then he was out again, doing Lord knows what!

She never liked being in the cottage alone with him, and the way he looked at her sometimes, disturbed her. She tried not to think about what he was thinking, when he looked at her like that. Whenever her mother was around, he ignored Maud completely, unless it was to order her to get something or do something for him. Maud was glad that he was out nearly every day and every night, and her mother seemed for more relaxed and happier when he was not around.

Meg helped her daughter carry the bundles of wares outside and gently place them into the small cart that Maud used to carrying the goods to market.

Maud stared into the distance towards the main road into Cheltenham, and she smiled to herself as she imagined Walter waiting for her on the edge of the village. He accompanied her most market days, and when he could, he would stay at the market and help

Maud to sell her wares. He would also keep her company and make her laugh. Maud hid a small giggle, as she thought about what her mother would think about her spending so much time in the company of a young man!

Meg, who was not as daft as she was cabbage looking, had noticed her daughter's dreamy countenance, and knew exactly what was going through her mind. "Who are you looking for?" her mother queried, shocking Maud out of daydream.

"No-one" Maud exclaimed quickly, a blush coming unbidden to her face, knowing she had been caught in a lie.

"That's right eh?" her mother replied, surreptitiously grinning as she bent down to place the final bundle in the cart. Meg was anything but a stupid woman, and she knew that Maud had been seeing the young man from outside the village.

She had seen him furtively hanging around, thinking he hadn't been spotted, on many occasions. Meg had never discussed the young man with Maud, and had certainly not told her about their encounter, and their subsequent understanding.

Maud seemed very happy, and Meg felt that the young man seemed pleasant enough and harmless. Meg thought that Maud deserved some joy, and if this young man made her happy, then that was fine with Meg, although she would never let her daughter know that!

With everything ready, Maud set off pulling her cart along the track, as her mother waved farewell "Don't tarry on the road back Maud!" she called to her daughter.

"I won't Ma, I'll be back as soon as I can" Maud laughed in reply.

It would normally take Maud about an hour to pull the cart the 2 and ½ miles from the village to the marketplace in Cheltenham, if Walter was with her, he would help pull the cart and they could make it about 45 minutes.  Maud was strong, but slender, and she enjoyed the exertion of pulling the cart.  She never rushed but spent her time on the road enjoying the nature she saw all around her, the flowers, the trees, the birds, and every now and again, a fox, or a badger, and plenty of rabbits.

The sun was rising in the sky, and the temperature was warm.  It was a pleasant day, and although Maud had set off later than usual, she was certain that she would arrive in plenty of time to set up her stall.

During the previous week Maud and her mother had been working hard to produce as many goods as possible for the weekly venture to the market.  Although the market sold food every day, clothing, pottery, and other types of products, were normally reserved for once each week.

This made her market day very busy, with people coming into the small town from villages across the entire area. Even the fine lords and ladies from the various manors came into town, and sometimes, people came from as far afield as the City of Gloucester itself. These types of people only came to the town if the quality of the wares was good enough, and those that Meg and Maud made were known around the area as the highest quality. Together with the quality of the goods, having a beautiful young woman selling those wares also attracted plenty of attention.

Maud was generally innocent and unaware of the attention she provoked. She had heard some comments and would blush deeply. At home they did not possess a mirror and so she did not really have much of an idea about how she looked to other people. Most of the time she would ignore the occasional crude observations of others and dismiss them as typical of some of the uneducated and lecherous men who had nothing better to do than embarrass a young girl. Despite these occasional remarks, Maud had always felt safe, and had never really had any cause to worry about her safety.

Normally, someone would be around, if it were not her mother, it would be Walter. Also, there were always plenty of other people from around her village, who all knew her. People were friendly and helpful, and probably the person she least trusted was her own uncle, Godfrey. Usually, Meg would insist that Maud travelled with other people she trusted from the village, but today, because she was late leaving, everyone else was well ahead of her.

In the past, it was Meg herself who used to travel into Cheltenham for the Market, and Maud would tag along. However, as Maud got older, Meg had reluctantly allowed her to manage the market side of the business and was pleasantly surprised at the success Maud had in selling their wares. Maud almost never came home without selling everything they had made.

As Maud approached the edge of the village, along the Manor Road, she looked around for Walter, but he was nowhere to be seen. She was not bothered, as Walter was not always able to meet her, even though he did try his hardest. Sometimes he had to work with his father, who ran an inn on the road to Gloucester, known as the "House in the Tree". She had never been there, but Walter had described it as a small hostelry that provided food a drink for weary travellers along the Gloucester Road, situated at the cross-roads for Gloucester, Cheltenham, Boddington and further to the North, Tewkesbury.

Maud had dreamed of visiting Gloucester or Tewkesbury, although she had attended the 'Tourney' in the meadows just outside of Gloucester, she had never visited the city itself, and she wondered about what exotic things she would be able to find in the markets of these places, with hundreds of people milling around. She had visited the May Fair at Prestbury once with her mother, but these other places held a mystery she was keen to explore. Walter had promised to take her to Gloucester, but she wondered when she would ever have the time to do so, and how would she ever be able to sneak away from her mother? She laughed inwardly as she thought of ways she could escape the ever-loving, but slightly stifling shield her mother placed around her.

Maud had never really understood her mother's protectiveness but had accepted it. She was after all an only child, and she supposed that that was the reason her mother was so protective of her. Bringing her up after her father had been killed, Maud was all she had. Maud realised she knew very little about the world, and despite her mother, she wanted to learn new things and experience everything the world could offer. She was certain that as she got older, her mother would begin to release her grip, and Maud herself would have a greater say in what she wanted and eventually gain more freedom.

Maud crossed the wooden bridge that crossed the Swilgate River that took her out of the village and onto the road known as The Runnings. The Runnings ran alongside Wymans Brook, a tributary that joined the Swilgate River at the bridge. Today, the river and brook were bubbling away pleasantly, but in bad weather, both could be treacherous, and prone to flooding.

❖

Despite arriving later than usual, Maud had made good time, and was in the marketplace, before it got really busy. Mary Holmes had arrived on time, and had secured Maud's usual place, next to her. Mary had brought fresh cuts of meat with her, from the pig her husband had killed and butchered the previous day, and cured meats, prepared from the offal of the pigs killed over the past months.

"Thank you, Mary! You are an angel!! Maud called over, as she set about getting her stall ready.

"'Tis nothing dear! I knew you'd be along shortly" she replied, pushing her youngest son away from her stall, as she caught him trying to steal a morsel of cured meat from the cart.

"Ned! Off with you! You devil!" she scolded, with laugh, as she clouted the hapless 18-year-old about his head "You'll be the death of me!" she added, as she looked over towards Maud and raised her eyebrows and rolled her eyes, a broad smile growing on her face.

"Ha!" laughed Ned, as he ran around the cart, out of arm's length of his mother's vicious swipe. "Just a little bit of sustenance to keep my strength up!" He continued, looking confidently over towards Maud, while he lifted both his arms and showed off his impressive biceps.

Maud blushed and looked down, mildly embarrassed by the clear display of masculinity, and Ned laughed again, proud, and arrogant in his youth.

"You leave that girl alone!" Mary admonished her son, knowing both her sons had a shine for Maud, "You're embarrassing her!"

Maud was mortified at the attention, both from Ned and his mother, and the small crowd who had gathered and were clearly amused by the entertainment being played out before them, and it showed on her face.

"Fine boy you have there, Mary!" laughed one her regular customers, who was enjoying the spectacle.

"He should be working with his father and Roger," Mary replied to him, "but I need to him to pull the cart, now that I am getting on!" She added with a secretive grin, as she stooped over to give the impression of an old crone.

Maud smiled at Mary, who she knew to be as fit as a fiddle and was reassured by the friendly banter of the market, even though she was the subject of the fun.

Maud knew from her conversations with Mary of previous market days, that she loved having her boys around her, and although she was perfectly capable of pulling her cart herself, would use any excuse to spend more time with her sons.

If it was not Ned coming into town on market day with her, it would have been Roger her oldest son, who, like Ned was a strapping young man, a year older than Ned. Mary had had two sons just over a year apart and wanted more, but work and the will of God, had not provided her with anymore. It was clear she absolutely doted on her family and loved them all dearly. Maud also knew that Ned would soon get bored after helping his mother set up her stall and would leave to go back to the farm and help out with his father and older sibling, hopefully with some stolen sausage inside him! Normally, one or other of the brothers would return at the end of the day, to escort Mary home, and pull the cart for her.

"Where's that young man of yours?" Mary called over.

"Shush, Mary!" Maud responded, her face flushing a deep red, as she brought her finger to her lips, imploring the woman to keep her voice down. "He isn't my young man!" she whispered loud enough for Mary to hear response. However, thinking about Ned pulling his mother's cart, reminded Maud about Walter, and again she wondered where he might be. "Maybe he will put in an appearance later." She thought, "He normally does!" she smiled.

❖

Where was Walter indeed! Walter had been arrested!

He had intended, as he usually did, to meet up with Maud, just outside the village, near the Manor bridge. He had left in plenty of time, having completed his early morning chores, and assuring his parents, that he would be back around noon, to help with the customers, he took his usual route towards the village of Uckington.

He preferred going across the fields and through the woods, because it often gave him an opportunity to hunt, and bag some rabbits, or possibly pigeons, on his way. Depending on how many he caught, he would often give at least one to Maud, and he would take the rest back to be used at the inn.

As he made is way across the fields, keeping mainly to the hedgerows, on the off chance that he would flush out a rabbit, the morning dew dampened the lower part of his trousers. He did not mind, his trousers were thick and warm, and a little water was not going to cause him discomfort.

He avoided the small collection of cottages, that made up the village of Uckington itself, to the south, not wanting to get waylaid by anyone, in case he would be late, meeting up with Maud. Walter was well known in the villages around the area, not least because his father ran the inn on the Gloucester Road.

As he approached the Tewkesbury Road, intending cross over directly, and continue on his way through the fields on the other side, he noticed three men on horses, who had stopped at the end of the lane leading to Uckington, where it joined the Tewkesbury Road.

The men seemed to be discussing something and were looking up and down the road. Walter did not take too much notice of them, they looked a bit rough, and he did not want to tarry.

However, the horsemen clearly had something else in mind, and when they saw him, they immediately began to canter towards him.

"Hold fast! Young man!" one of them called out. "Wait, I say!"

Walter, not really wanting to engage with these men, but having no reason to be rude, stopped, and waited for them to reach him. "Good morning, sirs." He greeted them.

"Aye, it's a good morning alright!" another of the men said. Walter thought that he sounded a little strange but let the comment pass. "Where have you come from, and where are you going?" the man asked.

"I am off to Swindon village." Walter replied, becoming more suspicious, and worried about the intentions of these men.

"Are you indeed!" The third man said.

The leader of the group was Richard Wendley, and his compatriots were none other than Jack Garvey, and Peter Smith. Walter vaguely recognised them but did not know their names.

Wendley and Garvey dismounted from their horses, passing their bridles to Smith, and approached Walter. "What have we here then?" Wendley demanded, pointing towards Walter's bow, "Out for a bit of poaching on the Lords land, eh?" he enquired with an edge of menace to his voice.

"No sir!" Walter responded hastily, wiping his hand across his mouth nervously. "This conversation is taking a bad turn!" he thought, and then added "Just getting some rabbits for the pot, sir."

"Well Jack," Wendley said, turning to his companion, "I think we've found ourselves a poacher! Don't you?" he declared.

"No doubt about it!" Garvey responded. "In that case, I think we need to detain him, and bring him before the Lord of the Manor!" he snorted, as if this was a great jest.

"No sir! Please sir! I haven't done anything wrong!" Walter pleaded.

"Well, we'll see about that anon, young lad, when the Lord of the Manor, interrogates you, won't we?" he announced with glee, as his two companions laughed out loud at what they clearly thought was a hilarious remark.

Walter did not think that the conversation was humorous at all! In fact, he was now genuinely scared "Who are these men?" he asked himself. "And what do they want with me?" he wondered, backing slowly away from them.

He was just about to make a run for it, when Wendley shot out an arm, and grabbed him firmly, "Oh no you don't!" he admonished. "You are coming with us, boy!" he added, as Garvey caught his other arm. Wendley quickly and expertly tied Walters hands behind his back, and they marched him off back up the road towards Tewkesbury.

After a short distance, they moved off the main road, and walked towards an old, abandoned cottage. Walter twisted and turned in fear. He did not want to remain with these men. Garvey's response to his resistance, was to cuff him roughly around the head. "That's enough of that! Anymore, and I will stab you!" he shouted, as he pulled a long, thin dagger from his belt, and pressed it against Walter's neck.

Walter relented, realising that trying to escape was hopeless.

When they arrived at the old cottage, Walter saw that It was dilapidated, and part of the thatched roof had fallen in.

"This'll do for now!" Wendley stated, and Walter was pushed inside the doorless entrance, unceremoniously. Once inside, Wendley roughly shoved Walter onto the dirt floor, in the corner of the room, and secured his feet and hands with a length of twine, he then placed a rag in his mouth held in place with another piece of twine.

Smith threw Walter's bow and quiver onto the floor next to him. "You stay there and be quiet!" Wendley ordered viciously. "Our Sire will be along shortly!" he grunted, with a broad smile on his face, clearly amused at his own wit.

The men went back outside and began to build a fire. Once it was lit, they sat around it, having removed some flagons and some sausages from a bag on one of the horses, they set to drinking and cooking the sausages by spearing them onto the ends of their knives.

Walter was beside himself with fear. These men were clearly very dangerous, and if the Lord of the Manor was going to arrive soon, as the men had told him, then Walter knew that the penalty for poaching was death. Often the sentence was passed summarily, and he would likely be strung from the nearest tree, without any opportunity to defend himself. His thoughts were dark and fearful, as he huddled in the corner of the dank, run-down building. "Nobody knows I am here!" he thought ominously.

Hours passed and the men were obviously getting very drunk. No-one else had arrived, and Walter again began to fear what might happen next. His nerves were taut, and adrenaline surged at every small sound, as he imagined the men were coming to get him. Walter was becoming desperate and realised that he needed to try and escape. He wriggled his hands, but the bonds securing his hands were very tight. He looked around the room to see if there was anything he could use and noticed an old broken shovel propped up against the far wall.

He scooted over on his backside and positioned himself so that he could rub the binding against the blade of the shovel. Unfortunately, the shovel was nor secure against the wall, and it fell over, making a sharp noise, as the blade dropped against a large stone on the floor.

Garvey, having heard the sound, immediately rushed into the room, "You little sod!" he shouted, and swung a brutal kick at Walter's head, catching him under his jaw, and rattling his teeth. To add insult to injury, Walter fell back and crashed his head against the wall. He fell onto his side, unconscious.

Garvey, turned to go back outside, just as the other two men were coming through the door, "Don't worry," he said, "He isn't going anywhere!"

# CHAPTER 18

## A Dance with Death

Maud enjoyed the early summer day. The sun was out, the market was busy, very busy; and people seemed to be enjoying themselves.

There was plenty more banter during the day, both between the stall holders, and with customers.

At the beginning of the day, her cart had been fully laden with yarn, balls of wool (dyed in a whole manner of colours), and various garments that Maud and her mother had made together. Maud had become an inspiration for her mother, often suggesting new styles of garment, based on the clothing she had seen people wearing in the market. Maud had quite an eye for fashion, and the garments she and her mother made, although not quite as fancy as the fine ladies and gentlemen who attended the market wore, were nevertheless, popular with the less sophisticated customers.

Trade was brisk, and Maud was busy throughout the day. Although many people would pick up her wares and study them before deciding to purchase, one particular man had attracted her attention. He was well dressed, although certainly not one of the gentry.

However, he appeared to be a man of means, and Maud's interest was aroused. During the course of the day, he returned a number of times, picking up yarn and wool, looking closely at it, and them putting it back, and walking away. On one occasion, Maud tried to engage him in conversation to try and make a sale. "That is the finest weave, sir," she started, "I can explain how we make such fine wool," she continued.

The man held his hand up, and stopped her mid-sentence, "Looking, just looking…. and thinking…" he replied mysteriously.

Maud was taken aback and did not know quite how to respond. "Well, if you need any more information, please just ask." she said meekly, turning to another customer who was holding out a ball of wool towards her, obviously intending to buy. Maud dealt with the customer, momentarily distracted with the transaction, when she looked up, the man had disappeared.

❖

Godfrey Bowen was also in town today. He had inserted himself at table, at the very back of an inn, close to the market, and was supping a jug of ale. He looked around warily, keen not to be noticed or recognised by any of the patrons.

The Inn was called the Kings Arms, although, because no "Arms" were displayed outside the Inn, which King was supported here, was a cause of conjecture

A couple of days ago, Godfrey had met with another reprehensible character, at his favourite haunt, the Cross Hands Inn, and had explained the task he wished this person to undertake on his behalf. This individual was not the rogue that Godfrey could be described as, but he was a useful contact, and Godfrey had had a number of dealings with him.

Godfrey had done work for this individual for payment, in the past, which might definitely be described as "nefarious", and now Godfrey was keen to involve him, for modest payment, in his own dubious activities. Godfrey had plotted and planned and the involvement of this individual, who was to play a minor but key role in the execution of Godfrey's scheme, would now unfold.

It is without doubt, that if the man had truly known the extent of the plot into which he was being ensnared, or if he had any notion of the potential consequences, even this man of low morals would have refused to become involved. This individual was underhand, keen to take advantage, and even prone to undertake some minor, criminal activities, but he would have refused point-blank to become involved, if he had any idea, of the events which would subsequently transpire.

As his acquaintance entered the inn, and looked around, Godfrey rose from his seat, made himself known, and beckoned the man over.

"Ah! Bernard. Welcome, please take a seat." Godfrey indicated to the seat opposite and at the same time, indicated with a raising of his hand to the serving girl standing by the kegs of ale. As she approached, he said to her "two jugs of ale, girl!." She nodded and went to pour two fresh jugs.

"You understand the task?" Godfrey resumed, when the serving girl was out of earshot.

"Yes." Bernard replied. Bernard was a Flemish merchant, who traded in the Gloucester markets, and was quite successful. Godfrey knew that Bernard was an expert in his trade, who had good contacts in a number of markets, including Bristol and Bath, as well as on the continent. His knowledge of the wool trade was an important part of why Godfrey had chosen him for this task.

"You simply need to distract her and detain her until well after the market has finished. It is essential that she is the last to leave the market, and that no-one else is around when she leaves." He confirmed what they had discussed at the Cross Hand Inn, two days hence.

"I understand completely," Bernard replied, "What I do not understand, is why a poor market wench is so important to you?", Bernard said looking up as the serving girl arrived with two full jugs of ale. She placed them down in front of the two men and withdrew quickly. She had intended to ask if they wanted any food, but the scowl that Godfrey had given her, clearly indicated to her that her continued presence was not required.

"That is not your concern. It is a simple task that I am asking you to do, and your payment should cover any problems you have!" Godfrey responded, at the same time, dumping a heavy pouch of coins on the table in front of him.

"Understood." Bernard responded, he still wondered what was so important about this girl, but he also realised that pushing the issue could be dangerous. He lifted his jug to his mouth and drank greedily.

He acquiesced "I am being paid well for such an easy task," he thought, "Whatever this is about, it is no concern of mine." he concluded privately, as he placed his empty jug on the table and lifted the pouch from its position next to where he had placed his jug. He weighed it in his hand, and with a satisfied smile, he secreted it inside his cloak. "I will do as you ask. Should I meet you later?" he queried.

"No need. If you do what I have asked, then your part is finished. Go on with your business, and forget everything we have discussed, and you have done..." Godfrey said, looking Bernard square in the eyes, with a menacing look on his face.

Bernard realised that the meeting was concluded, he rose, leaving the table, and made his way out of the busy inn, and across the packed market square. As he made his way towards his target, he shivered involuntarily, "Something is wrong here!" he thought.

❖

Bernard visited Maud's stall four or five times during the day. His primary purpose was to catch her attention and intrigue her. He had used this tactic successfully on a number of occasions, when trying to secure deals for his trading purposes.

He knew that many local traders were naïve and did not understand the true value of their wares. Bernard knew what the value of quality produce was, and what profit he could gain from selling it in larger markets. He also knew that volume was important and had negotiated a number of deals with local weavers that exceeded the profits they realised from local markets, but also made him substantial additional profits, when traded at the larger markets. The trick was to pay a little above the average price they expected and charge a substantial mark-up at the major markets in large cities. Quality fabric was much sought after in his home city of Bruges, and widely in Europe, and he exported and imported such produce across the channel regularly.

Bernard was an expert in his business, but when he first approached Maud's stall, even he was astonished! The quality of the weave was exceptional! When he inspected the produce, he thought "Ah! I know what is afoot here!" thinking that Godfrey was interested in exploiting this young woman.

As he moved away, he thought "If Godfrey is aware of this quality, why is he involving me?" Absent-mindedly, he pondered his own question, as he approached a pie stall. The delicious smell overwhelmed him, and he momentarily forgot his train of thought. He bought a pie and devoured it within seconds. Having satiated his hunger, his thoughts returned to Maud.

He did not know her name, Godfrey had merely pointed out the stall that was of interest to him, but in particular, it was obvious that his main interest was in the outstandingly beautiful young woman that sold her wares on that stall, and not the produce she was selling.

Bernard could not help but be intrigued, "What was so significant here? The wares the girl was selling, or the girl herself?" Bernard thought about his own business and concluded that both would be profitable in their own right, but together! What an opportunity this offered!

And so, Bernard was distracted from his purpose. He was enthralled by the beauty of the young woman who was selling the produce, and at the same time, he was captivated by the quality of the produce that was on offer! In all his professional business dealings, he had never been exposed to such an opportunity!

"Whatever Godfrey wants," he considered, "I will certainly take advantage here!"

Bernard returned to the stall. He wanted to engage with the young woman, but he was still conscious of the fact that he had been paid to do a job. So, he reluctantly resisted the opportunity to speak with the girl himself.

On one occasion she had tried to engage him in a sales conversation, and he had with great personal fortitude, unwillingly thwarted her attempt. As he walked away, having abruptly dropped the wool he was admiring, he began to feel foolish.

"What is going on here?" he thought, "Why do I need to wait until the end of the market to detain her?" he mused. "Why can't I just make the proposition and be done with it?" he questioned. But as he made his way through the throng of people attending the market, back towards Maud's stall, once again, he cupped his hand around the heavy purse at his waist, and concluded, "Once this is over, I will make my own approach, whatever Godfrey's intentions are…"

❖

Maud had sold everything! She was overjoyed! It was very late, and as she looked around, she realised that everyone else was packing up, and preparing to leave. Mary was ready to go, having packed everything up some time ago.

Maud smiled as Roger Forrester came into view and approached Mary's stall. "Hi Mum!" he called out, winking at Maud as he did so. "I've come to drag you home!" Mary ran to him, and crushed him in a huge hug, "Thank you darling!" she exclaimed, burying her head in his broad shoulders. The young man picked her up, and spun her around, as Mary shrieked with delight. "Right, let's go, Dad is starving!" he stated firmly, and moved towards the handles of their cart. Mary put a hand on his shoulder, and looking at Maud, asked "Maud, should we wait for you?"

"No Mary, you get going! I'll be along shortly, and I'll catch up with you on the way home." She replied, "I'll never live it down if Hugh and your boys don't get fed on time!" Mary and Roger laughed in unison "Aye, you're right there Maud!" Roger said with a twinkle in his eye. "You be careful, and we'll keep an eye out for you, on the road back."

As Mary and her son moved off, Maud began to pack up her own stall.

"Young mistress!" a man called, causing Maud to stand up from picking the cart cover, from the ground under her cart. As she rose, she saw the strange, well-dressed man, who had visited her stall on numerous occasions during the day.

"I'm really sorry!" Maud remonstrated, "I've sold everything, you are too late!"

"Far from it, young lady! I am interested in far more than what you had for sale today!" Bernard replied.

Maud was immediately taken aback, "What on earth do you mean?" she countered, more intrigued than ever, having recognised the man who had visited her stall countless times during the day.

"Allow me a moment of your time," he asked, "I am sure it will be of benefit to us both." He declared, and Maud was captivated.

"Who is this man?" she thought, "and what does he want?

"I have a proposition for you..." he stated.

The aim of Godfrey's plot was complete, but neither Maud, or Bernard realised the consequences...

❖

Back at the run-down cottage, Wendley was getting agitated. He leaned towards Smith and Garvey and said "Right! I've had enough of this!"

"Surely, we have held him long enough?" Smith responded.

"Aye, time for us to go, I think." Wendley said, rising to his feet and dusting off his clothing.

"What about the boy?" asked Garvey, "Shall I finish him?" he queried grimly, pulling his blade from his belt, and watching it glint in the light from the fire.

"Godfrey just said to hold him up, and make sure he didn't get to the village. He told us to hold him for the day until after the market was finished. He didn't say nothing about killing him." Wendley countered.

Although Wendley was the nominal leader of the group, in the absence of Godfrey, he was reluctant to make any decisions that deviated from the express orders he had been given. Although the boy had seen their faces, Godfrey had not given him any instructions about what to do with the boy at the end of the day, and therefore, he would just do what he had been told to do, and nothing more. Wendley, did not want to get on the wrong side of Godfrey!

"He's a lucky boy then!" Garvey smirked, "Didn't know you had a heart!" he laughed, jumping to his feet.

Without further conversation, the three men packed up their things, mounted their horses and rode off. The truth was that Godfrey would not have cared what the men did with Walter at the end of the day, and had they killed him, Godfrey would not have given the matter a second thought. Walter was indeed a lucky boy!

When Walter awoke, he could tell it was getting very late in the day. His jaw was very tender, and at first, he could not remember where he was, then the memories came flooding back to him, and he held his breath, and stared through the gloom inside the cottage, and listened. He could not hear a sound. He waited for some time, frightened to move. His head hurt and he felt a little dizzy. Through the door opening, he could not see anyone, but he could see that the fire had been put out. He waited and listened some more.

After a while, he managed to convince himself that the men had gone. He gingerly made his way to the opening and looked around. No-one was there. Suddenly scared that they might return, and this would be his only chance to escape, Walter scuttled across the floor of the cottage on his backside, over to the shovel and began frantically scraping away at the twine binding his hands. With fear and adrenaline combining to give him strength, he finally managed to free his hands. From there it was a short time before he was able to untie the rest of rope that had restricted his movement. As soon as he was free, he grabbed his bow and quiver, and ran like the devil was after him!

❖

Another person had observed the goings on at the derelict building, watching, and waiting in silence, in case it as necessary to act. The Archer had taken note of everything that had been said, and everything that had been done. He was now keen to find out why?

# CHAPTER 19

## If Only...

Maud was a little perturbed. She had been much later leaving for the market this morning than was usual, and now she was very late leaving for home. She had packed up her little stall as quickly as she could, and having sold everything during the day, had little to put back into her small cart.

The man has talked to her about making products directly for him, and not needing to sell her produce in the market place, he had told her that she could make a lot of money working with him, and might even be able to travel to Europe! He has said that he admired the quality of her wares, and the demand for such products in Europe was high. Maud, in her innocence did not really understand what he was saying but agreed to meet him again at the market the following week, with her mother to discuss his proposal further.

She was excited and worried at the same time. Most of all she wanted to discuss the events of the day with her mother. Nevertheless, she was concerned that it would be dark, before she arrived home, and her mother would be worried about her. The strange encounter with the merchant was bothering her, and he had delayed her to such an extent, that she was now very late.

The sun was low in the sky, and a breeze was beginning to blow. Today, it seemed, everything had conspired to make things difficult, "Great! and now it looks like it is going to rain, just to make things worse!" she chided herself, as she looked up at the darkening sky.

"It doesn't matter." she thought "I have sold everything, and mother will be pleased, and I'll be home within the hour, and everything will be fine." she concluded as she pulled the cover over the cart, in preparation for the journey home.

She pulled her cloak firmly around herself to ward off the chill that the stiff breeze was now creating and walked to the front of the cart. She grabbed the handles determinedly and began to pull. "I wonder where Walter was today?" she mused, "It is very strange that I have not seen him at all." She pondered as she set off for home.

As she walked, she noticed that all the inns in the small market town seemed to be packed, and there was a lot of raucous noise coming from them. Clearly, people were celebrating a good market day, either happy with their purchase, or their sales.

Despite the din from the ale houses, the market square and surrounding streets were almost empty, just a few stragglers, who very quickly went into houses and cottages, leaving Maud alone on the street.

Her neighbours and friends from the village had left almost an hour before Maud, and although a couple had offered to stay behind, she had not felt right about imposing on them in such a way, and denying them the opportunity to get home, and have their suppers.

And so, Maud came to be alone, as she left the dwellings of Cheltenham behind, and moved along the bumpy road out into the countryside.

❖

Maud pulled her small cart along the dusty road towards home. It had been a long day, and although she had left much later than usual in the morning, a kindly neighbour had kept her place at the market, and so she had been able to set up at her usual spot.

The market today had been teeming with people and Maud had sold all her wares. As a result of the volume of people, and the extra goods she had for sale, she had made a good profit. She felt contented and happy, and she sang a pleasant ditty to herself as she walked. The sun was beginning to set, and the breeze was getting much cooler, a gust blew and ruffled her long golden hair.

She smiled to herself, "Mother will be pleased," she thought "if we could make more, we could certainly sell more." She mulled over how her mother and herself could make more of the shawls, blankets, and headscarves, which were clearly popular.

"Maybe we could make something different?" she imagined as she tried to recall what she had seen the fine ladies wearing around the marketplace today. She considered a lighter weave, might allow them to make skirts or bodices. She would need to discuss it with her mother when she got home.

She also thought about the market at Gloucester, which was larger and had more people attend. Could they charge a higher price there? It would certainly mean that they might not need to produce more. She thought about the merchant, and what he had proposed, could it be possible?

Her happy thoughts were jarred a moment later. As she walked along the hedged lane, she was so familiar with. She thought that despite the hour, she would normally have seen at least some more people making their way home from the market at this time, but today it was deserted.

Fate had conspired…

❖

De Vere and his guard had arrived at the spot in Hyde Lane, where he had arranged to meet Godfrey. He ordered them to stay there while we went forward to meet with Godfrey, a short distance farther on near the junction with Church Lane.

He saw Godfrey waiting and moved his horse forward until they stood side by side. "Is everything ready?" he queried.

"Yes, my Lord." Godfrey replied.

"And the boy?"

"He has been delayed...." Godfrey replied with a sly grin.

"I don't know why we needed to go to that trouble?" de Vere countered.

"We don't want the chance of any witnesses." Godfrey replied.

"We could have just gutted him!" De Vere responded viciously.

"And then we would have more problems, and more people being suspicious..."

"We could make it look like a simple robbery..."

"It is done now My Lord. Let us let fate take its course..."

❖

Back at the cottage, Meg was clearing up her work for the day. Having put everything away, and just before beginning the task of preparing the evening meal, she went to Maud's room. Because Maud had left so late that morning, she had not made her bed, and Meg went over to it to pull the coverlet up, and make it look presentable.

She saw the hairbrush on the floor just under the bed and bent to pick it up and replace it on the table next to Maud's bed. Her heart stopped! As she picked up the brush, she saw the thin chain of Maud's pendant, as she rose, the small red crystal revealed itself "Oh No! Oh No!" Meg cried, desperately pacing around the room "Maud has been without her pendant for a whole day!" she screamed.

Meg rushed into the main room, and frantically pulled her cloak from behind the door, before rushing outside. In her panic she did not see Walter coming around the side of the cottage, and the two collided.

"Whooa there!" exclaimed a shocked Walter, quickly noticing the look a pure terror on Meg's face "What's wrong?" he cried. Meg raised her fist and unclenched it; within her palm she held Maud's pendant.

"Where is Maud?" she cried out "Where is Maud? Why aren't you with her?" Meg's stricken look, chilled Walter to the bone. "I was stopped and held prisoner by some men who claimed to be working for the Lord of the manor! I haven't seen her at all today!" he exclaimed. "Isn't she home yet?

"No! She isn't back yet; I have to find her!" Meg screamed at him.

A number of people had gathered after hearing the commotion "What's going on Meg?" one her neighbours, Hugh, asked, looking at the stricken pair.

"Maud is not back from the market!" Meg cried.

"I'm sure she'll be ok Meg" Hugh responded.

Meg turned to Walter "Find her!" she sobbed, before turning back to Hugh and giving him a look that could chill the dead.

Hugh and the other villagers crowded around Meg and urged her back into her cottage. "Now, now Meg, calm yourself, Maud will be alright, you'll see. If she is not back shortly, we'll go and look for her."

Meg tried to resist them, but she was exhausted and distraught, and she was no match for the good-intentioned folk, trying to support her.

"Come on now Meg, let's sit you down, and you can tell us what has happened" Hugh said comfortingly.

Meg tried to turn and flee the supportive grip that held her, but she was firmly pushed into her cottage, followed by two or three of the large men from the village.

"So, Meg, what's put the wind up you? Hugh asked gently, as he sat her down in a chair.

"God help my child!" Meg wept.

Walter shot off, all thoughts of his throbbing head forgotten, gripping his bow, he ran as fast as he could, out of the village towards the road that led to Cheltenham.

"Meg! Meg! Wait for me!" he beseeched as he ran.

❖

Robert de Vere and Godfrey had just crossed the bridge across Wymans Brook on their horses and were trotting down Wymans Lane along the route that they knew Maud always took. A short distance away, they saw her approaching them, pulling her little cart.

"What a sweet innocent child!" Robert sniggered, a smirk on his face.

"Aye, but not for much longer!" Godfrey responded, with an evil glint in is eye "Fucking wench has everything" he muttered bitterly.

The two horsemen halted just across the bridge and waited as Maud approached. Recognising her uncle, and then realising that the man with her uncle was the Lord of the Manor, Lord Robert de Vere, she waved happily "Uncle, what are you doing here?" she called out.

"Waiting for you, child" he retorted.

"But why? I will be home soon" she said, now only a few yards away, from the two mounted men. Robert and Godfrey dismounted from their horses and tied them to the bridge.

Maud was beginning to feel uncomfortable; Lord Robert began to approach her. He was leering at her.

"What is this? What do you want?" Meg stammered as she began to tremble with trepidation.

Her sixth sense screamed at her "This is not right! Something is wrong!" With Godfrey just a short distance behind his Lord, Robert lunged at Maud. She evaded his grasp and ran.

She was not fast enough, and having only escaped a few feet, she felt strong hands grab her cloak and pull her back.

"Take her man!" de Vere shouted at Godfrey, and then she felt her uncle's hands upon her, as he dragged her back up towards the bridge.

"Hold her!" de Vere raged, as he ripped off her cloak, and tore at her outer clothes.

Held firm by Godfrey, Maud tried to kick out, screaming as she did so "Help! Help!" she yelled at the top of her voice.

De Vere laughed as he exposed her "I like the noisy ones!" he brayed. "No-one to hear you scream at this time of the day!" he snorted, as he pushed her to the ground. He unbuckled his belt, while Godfrey held her arms in an iron grip.

Holding one hand across her mouth, de Vere used his other hand to push her thrashing legs apart. Maud fought with everything she had, but the two men were far too powerful for her. As Godfrey held her down, De Vere forced himself on her, grunting as he did so, like the animal he was.

Once he had finished, de Vere stood and buckled himself up, "Your turn!" he said maliciously, looking at the grinning Godfrey. Maud lay on the road within a few yards of him, all the fight gone from her.

❖

As he moved quickly amongst a nearby copse of trees, 'The Archer' heard the wretched and anguished screams of a young woman. He sprinted to the edge of the tree line and saw the distressing scene. A young woman, only partially clothed, was being dragged onto the bridge by a man. Close by, another man was mounting his horse, having untied it from the bridge. Another horse was still tethered. The man on the horse, leaned across and untethered the other horse, holding its reins in his hand. "Hurry up Godfrey!" the man shouted, "Get it done! Bring her, and let's be gone!"

The Archer quickly placed an arrow from his quiver, and onto his bow, aimed and released. He was furious that he had not arrived early enough to protect the young girl from the assault, but now the least he could do was ensure she escaped.

The arrow sped unerringly towards its target and struck the man called Godfrey in the chest. It sliced into his body and pierced his heart. He fell back, still clutching a piece of material torn from Maud's clothing. The mounted horseman, seeing the arrow in the chest of his companion, turned, spurred his horse and fled back across the bridge, fearful of being the next target. He had turned around a bend and was out of range before the Archer could restring his bow.

Having, been released from Godfrey's grip, Maud recovered her sense and ran away along the line of the brook, clutching her torn and ragged clothing around herself. She ran in a complete panic, fear and terror propelling her along, seeking the sanctuary of her village.

'The Archer' watched her run. He heard de Vere screaming for protection from his men, "Help! Get him!" He heard the stamp and clatter of hooves as de Vere's bodyguard raced towards the bridge, and towards his position inside the tree line. As the other man had made off, he was certain that Maud would reach the safety of the village shortly.

De Vere's guard quickly dismounted, drawing their swords, and spread out, moving towards where the Archer was hidden. He raised his bow and fired a couple of arrows towards them to slow them down, his aim was deadly, and had the desired effect. The Archer, aware of the hue and cry that was being raised in the village, realised that the area would soon be full of men searching for a culprit, and he didn't want to have to explain himself, especially as he had recognised the other horseman, and knew that whatever he said, a tyrannical overlord would be certain to be believed over a peasant. He had also killed at least three men. He ran, knowing he could not afford to be caught anywhere near here.

"There will be another time de Vere!" he declared solemnly, as he made his way swiftly and silently through the woods away from the scene.

❖

Robert de Vere had panicked at the bridge and screamed for his guards. As they sped passed him, he called out to them "He is in the woods, get him!"

Having escaped from the immediate danger, and calmed down somewhat, he realised that the girl would be able to recognise him. Also, Godfrey's assailant, might also be able to recognise him.

Although the word of a peasant girl, was unlikely to have much influence, the accusations of two witnesses, might create some problems that he could do without.

"Damn that girl!" he thought. He turned off the lane and into the trees, dismounting and tying his stallion to a nearby branch, out of sight of the road. "I have to get to her before she reaches the village!" he scowled and began running back towards the brook in an attempt to cut her off. He was now on the other side of the brook but envisaged no problems in getting across at some point. After all, it was only a brook, a couple of yards wide at most.

He rampaged through the woods, listening out for any tell-tale signs or noises. After a short while he could hear whimpering and the sounds of someone crashing through the woods. "I have you wench!" he exclaimed under his breath, increasing his pace, as he homed in on the sounds.

He knew that the only other crossing point was further up the brook, as it joined with the River Swilgate. She probably would not be able to get across the river, except by the bridge that ran up towards the manor, but she might try to get across the brook at some point before that.

As he closed in on the desperate girl, he heard splashing sounds. There she was, coming across the brook, she obviously knew a short-cut. He rushed towards the noise, and emerged from the trees, onto the bank, as Maud was frantically thrashing through the water towards the bank on which he was standing.

Because she was making such a noise crossing the brook, she did not immediately see him standing there. When she did sense something, and look up, she cried out in panic and immediately turned and tried to make it back to the other bank.

"Oh no you don't!" de Vere called out, as he jumped down the bank into the water. Maud screeched as she reached the other bank and desperately tried to scramble up the other side. It was not to be...

Today, fate had conspired to defeat poor Maud, she missed her footing in her desperation, and slipped back into the water. De Vere had waded across, the water reaching his knees, and as he reached her, he leaned forward and pulled her back.

She let out a stifled scream as de Vere clamped a hand over her mouth and dragged her backwards, she lost her balance as he pressed her down into the water.

With both his hands, he held her head in a firm grip and pushed it under the water. Maud flailed her arms and legs, splashing and thrashing for all she was worth! "It is no use!" she thought, as she stared up into the manic face of her assailant looming above her, his cheeks flushing red with the exertion.

As the urgent need for oxygen betrayed her body, and she could resist no longer, the last bubbles of her life escaped through her nose, and her mouth was forced open and brackish water flooded into her lungs. A look of serenity appeared on her face and her last thought was "Oh Mother! Oh Walter! I am so sorry! I loved you both!" As blackness engulfed her, her body relaxed, and the life fled from her body.

The beautiful Swindon Maid was gone.

❖

Walter ran back into the village, exhausted from his exertions, he made straight for Meg's cottage. Blasting his way through the door, "Meg!" he cried "Is she home?"

He noticed a couple of local women sitting close to Meg, comforting her.

Meg looked up, her eyes full of tears. In her hands she held Maud's pendant, and she was running its chain through her fingers. "She's gone." she moaned, a sound so full of grief and conviction, that all who were gathered burst into tears.

One of the other women, Mary moved close to Meg and hugged her "We don't know that Meg" she consoled her, "The men are out looking now, I'm sure that will find her soon."

Meg exhaled a mournful sob, and brought her hands to her face, her anguish clear, on a face that had aged considerably, in such a short space of time. Her radiance, her kindness, her empathy, her lust for life, had ebbed away. Gone forever.

Walter shook with barely controlled rage "It can't be!" he shouted, "She should be here by now!" and he turned and ran back out the door.

By now darkness had set in, and Walter could hear the sound of men calling out "Maud! Maud! Where are you?" He ran towards the woods at the edge of the village, where he could see the light from the torches of the villagers searching for Maud, moving through the woods, down near the brook.

He ran into the woods and confronted one of the search party, grabbing the man's torch, he ran towards their secret meeting place, not stopping to explain or bothered by the reaction of the villager concerned. The others followed.

As he reached the spot, he stopped dead. Looking down into the brook from the bank above, he could see his beloved resting in the water.

The rest of the search party had caught up and looked down in horror! Walter jumped down, sinking into the water, and gently raised up the inert body, cradling her in his arms and wailing his grief to the world "Oh no! Maud, NO! my love!"

The eyes of the men present, men whose characters had been forged by war and hard labour all their lives, were filled to the brim with tears.

Their beautiful Swindon Maid was dead!

# Part 3
## 1485

# CHAPTER 20

## Justice is a Dish Best Served Without Emotion

The Archer sat in one of the corners of the House in the Tree Inn. The shadows in the dark corner obscured him, and no-one else in the Inn seemed to notice him. If they could have seen his face, they would have seen that his features were grim.

The Inn was busy, with various groups of weary travellers sat at the tables eating and drinking. News of the murders the previous day in Swindon Village were the source of heated debates.

However, none of these groups held any interest for The Archer. His attention was taken by four men who were sitting just a couple of tables away. He knew three of these men. They were the men who had waylaid Walter on his way to meet with Maud on the day that she had been murdered. They had only arrived a short time before but were already halfway through their second flagon of ale. They seemed to be agitated, but the beer had loosened their tongues and their conversation was tense. Although they were talking in hushed voices, The Archer could clearly hear everything they said.

"Godfrey is dead!" Smith said, "All over that girl!"

"What was he thinking?" Wendley added slamming his mug onto the table,

"Bloody stupid, and he's dragged us all into the mess!" Holder exclaimed angrily; his hands balled into fists.

"If the boy puts two and two together, we'll hang!" stated Garvey. The men nodded their agreement.

Wendley put his hand to his chin and rubbed it thoughtfully, before saying "Well he didn't see you, Geoffrey." All eyes moved to look at Holder.

"But they know we ride together." Holder retorted.

"Aye, but the boy only saw the three of us…" Garvey stated, picking up the flagon and pouring more ale into the nearly empty mugs.

Still looking at Holder, Wendley said "Well, I'm wondering if someone sold out the plot!" he glowered at Holder, as he picked up his ale, and drank thirstily.

"Why would someone do that?" Holder queried, and then realising where the conversation was going, looked at his companions in shock. "What! You think I had something to do with it?"

"Well, it crossed our minds." Smith interjected.

"Well, you can uncross your bloody minds!" Holder retorted angrily. He knew how dangerous these men were, and what they would do, if anyone crossed them. "I offered to come, but you didn't need me!"

"So, what did you do on the day then?" Smith asked threateningly.

"I stayed in the Cross Hands and got pissed!"

"And who did you meet there?" Wendley queried.

"No-one! I swear!" Holder responded becoming increasingly frightened of the direction the conversation was going. "Ask the landlord!"

"Oh, we will." Wendley responded, his features as hard as flint.

"So, what was the plan?" Holder asked, trying to steer the exchange away from himself. "Godfrey, never really told me."

"It was all to do with that cottage that his brother owned. He needed to get rid of the girl, so that he could inherit."

"But what about the wife, she's still alive?" Holder asked in confusion.

"Escheat. He did a deal with the Lord of the Manor." Wendley informed him.

"Escheat?" Holder asked, with the other two men looking over at Wendley, clearly as uninformed as he was.

"When someone does not have anyone to inherit, then the lands are forfeited back to the Lord of the Manor. Godfrey made a deal to get the girl for the Lord, and in return he would get the freehold of the cottage…"

The men stared at Wendley for a few seconds, before the recognition began to dawn. "Oh!" they said in unison.

Wendley continued "The problem is that someone saw what happened and killed Godfrey in the process. That means they saw the Lord of the Manor. And he knows about us!"

"We should have tied up loose ends at the time!" Garvey specified. "I wanted to off the boy, and we should have done it. He's another loose end, that we will have to explain…"

"Yeah! We need to tie up as many loose ends as we can." Wendley concluded. Holder looked down at his hands which were placed on top of the table. They were shaking, as he wondered if he was one of the loose ends that needed to be tied up.

The Archer had heard all he needed to hear. He got up and went to the door of the Inn and walked outside. The men at the table were so engrossed in their conversation that they did not even notice him.

❖

Wendley and his cronies stayed at the Inn for another hour. They had gone there to identify the whereabouts of Walter but had been unsuccessful. All of the men were deep in their cups and had considerable difficulty mounting their horses. Wendley could not get his foot into his stirrup, and after several unsuccessful attempts called Garvey over to help. Garvey who had already mounted his own horse, having had a battle to get the horse to stand still, reluctantly got back off his horse and went over to help Wendley. After a few heaves and puffs, Wendley finally gained his seat. Garvey then had another pantomime, but eventually managed to get up onto this horse. Smith tittered at their antics, and Holder just wanted to get away as fast as he could.

All mounted, Wendley turned to the group. "We'll meet here again tomorrow night, same time. If we can't find the boy then, we'll need to change the plan. We can't be seen here too many times…"

Having agreed to meet the following day, the men departed. Wendley, Garvey and Smith, turned up the Withybridge Lane, and Holder made off up Hayden Lane in the opposite direction.

❖

The Archer stood off the road in the cover of some bushes, under a large oak tree.  The night was cooling, and there was a stiff breeze.  Stars twinkled in the night sky, and the moon was large and bright.  He listened to the sounds of the night, the scurrying of night creatures, the grunting of a hedgehog nearby, and the haunting scream of a fox in the distance, marking its territory.

Then he heard another familiar sound.  The sound of trotting hooves, their "clip-clop" on the packed earth of the road.  He waited as the horse drew nearer.  When he could hear it's panting, he stepped out on to the road, and stood silhouetted by the moonlight.

Holder, still suffering from the effects of his earlier imbibing, did not immediately see the man standing in the road in front of him.  When he did, it took him several seconds to respond and react.  "A robber, robbing a robber!" he giggled to himself, either unaware of the threat or more likely confident in his own ability to deal with it, even in his inebriated state.

Holder was not frightened of many things, and he had dealt with his fair share of dangerous situations in the past.  He certainly did not consider a single man capable of bettering him.  "That's just insulting!" he thought.

The man stood there, not moving, not speaking.

"Well! Are you just going to stand there or are you going to do something?" he called out belligerently, "'Cos' if you are not going to do anything, I have better things to do!"

The man just stood there, not moving, not speaking.

Holder, now getting frustrated by the stand-off drew his sword. "Well! You asked for it!" he shouted and spurred his horse viciously forward into a gallop.

The man just stood there not moving, not speaking.

Now very angry, Holder forced is horse to go faster, raising his sword, intending to bring it down in a killing blow. As he passed the man, he swung his sword violently towards the man's head, expecting to feel the familiar "thock!" as it made contact with muscle and sinew.

Nothing happened!

He rode passed the impact point, and reined his horse savagely, wheeling it at the same time.

The man was still standing there, not moving, not speaking.

Only this time he had a bow raised, and an arrow knocked.

Now beyond furious and determined to slay this individual, Holder once again spurred his horse into action. In the back of his mind, he heard the twang of a bow release. The arrow took him in the throat, and as he fell backwards, the horse reared up, throwing him from its back.

The horse bolted as the man strode over to him. He leaned forward and pushed back the hood from his cloak.

"For Maud, you bastard!" he said.

Holder looked up into the face of the man. Because of the damage to his throat he could not speak, but as his life drained away, from the blood gushing from his neck, he recognised his assailant and thought "It's you!"

❖

Wendley, Garvey and Smith had trotted a little way up Withybridge Lane, before halting and holding a beggar's parliament. None of them were as drunk as they had made out, and in reality, they had already decided on the fate of their friend Holder, before meeting at the Inn. However, they felt that they would give him a chance to come clean.

"It must have been that little shit!" Garvey exalted.

"Aye, I agree!" stated Smith.

"He was certainly at the Cross Hands, on the day. And he did get pissed. The Landlord confirmed that much…"

Wendley concurred. "But we don't know where he was for the rest of the day, and he didn't tell us." He concluded.

"Right then!" Garvey said, "He's had his chance. Let's go!"

The three men turned their horses and pushed them in the direction that Holder had taken.

The gang took the cross-roads past the House in the Tree Inn at a gallop and crossed into Hayden Lane. They expected to overtake their former compatriot within a short distance.

They slowed to a stop when they saw a horse bolting towards them and managed to slow and then tame the frightened beast.

"It's Holders horse!" Smith called out, holding the reins of the animal and trying to calm it.

"Hmmmm! There is something not right here!" Wendley murmured. "Garvey, we'll take the horses forward, but you go through the hedges. We'll see what's waiting for us ahead!" he ordered the other two men.

Garvey did as he was told, moving swiftly and silently into the hedgerow.

Wendley and Smith waited for a couple of minutes to allow Garvey to get into position, before they proceeded forward at a slow and deliberate pace, looking and listening for signs of danger. The clop of their horse's hooves rang through the night air.

Garvey had moved forward about two hundred yards ahead of the two mounted men. He drew his sword ready to spring into action at the slightest sound. The only sound he heard was a "swish!" as an arrow took him through the eye.

As darkness beckoned and light dimmed in his brain, he thought he heard someone whisper "For Maud!"

❖

Wendley and Smith moved forward cautiously. They knew that Garvey was somewhere over to their right-hand side. They were now on a straight piece of road, and they could see a large elm tree by the side of the road just ahead. The tree was silhouetted by the moonlight.

As they stared at the tree, they could see what looked like two bodies swinging from nooses, gently moving in the breeze. When they came up next to the tree, they were able to recognise the two suspended bodies. One had an arrow through his throat, and the other an arrow through his eye!

"God's teeth!" cried Wendley.

"Garvey only left us a couple of minutes ago! How did he get up there!?" Smith cried out in alarm.

Both men looked around them for any signs of the danger they knew was out there somewhere. Their horses snickered and pranced, alerting them to something in the distance.

A man had stepped out of the hedgerow and was standing in the middle of the road. With adrenaline already pumping through their bodies, the two men took no time in jumping into action to respond to the threat the man posed. Both jabbed their horses with their spurs and sped towards the silent, immobile shadow in front of them. Swords raised they each took a side of the road.

A bow hissed and Garvey was struck through the mouth. The arrow passed through the back of his head and severed his spinal cord. He fell backwards off his horse, dead before he hit the ground. Wendley heard the man with the bow say, "For Maud!"

Wendley pressed on, his rage and anger spewing out along with the spittle from his mouth. "I will kill you, you bastard!"

An arrow struck him in the shoulder of his sword arm, the force spun him around in his saddle and he lost his grip on the weapon. It clattered down onto the road. Still, he pressed forward, trying to get his knife out of his belt, and losing the reins of his horse in doing so. He intended to run the man down with his horse and then finish the fight with his knife. A second arrow struck him in the other shoulder. It unbalanced him, but fury drove him on. He was nearly upon his assailant!

A third arrow hissed towards him, and he heard the man say, "For Maud!," before the arrow struck him in the middle of the forehead, shattering bone, and imbedding itself into his brain.

'The Archer thought to himself, "Walter is safe for now."

Ten minutes later, four bodies swung from the oak tree. They swayed in time with the breeze. Each had arrows buried in them. Each arrow had red fletching and three golden dots on the shaft between the feathers. The Archer had declared war! If you listened carefully as the breeze whispered through the clothing the dead men wore, it seemed to say, "For Maud!"

# CHAPTER 21

## A Travesty of Justice

The bodies of Maud and Godfrey were taken back to the village. On hearing that the men had found Maud, Meg had rushed to the scene, to see Walter sitting in the brook, cradling the body.

Her heart was broken, both for her beloved child and the young man who had loved her.

Maud's body was borne on a palette carried by the men from the village. In her grief, Meg did not realise that Walter was not among them. All of the villagers formed a solemn procession with torches held aloft and walked with their heads bowed in respect and grief for the loss to the village of such a vibrant, beautiful, innocent and vital member of their wider family of the village. Maud had been part of the future for the entire community.

Like any child or young person, her welfare was of paramount importance to the continuing success of the village as a whole. The contribution that Maud and her mother had made with their industry and quality of their work was renowned at local markets and had raised the profile of the village across the county.

Meg walked at the head of the procession. She was a broken woman. The death of her husband had been a devastating loss, and it had taken Meg many years to come to terms with that loss.

She had found the strength to pull through, because of her daughter, and had devoted her life to educating Maud and giving her the opportunities to become the delightful and hard-working woman she was on the threshold of becoming.

Ultimately, Maud's beauty and talents, along with the success of their business, and their ownership of the cottage, had become the factors that had attracted the avaricious and relentless greed of men.

Despite the warning that Meg had received so many years ago, and the protections she had sought to place around Maud, Meg had failed.

That failure had destroyed her. Her dreams had been shattered; the world was an evil and remorseless place. She had lost her faith and her desire to live, her pain was unbearable, and if it was not a sin, she would willingly give up her own life.

In her own mind, she had no future and no purpose. Her life had ended with the death of her child.

The procession stopped at Meg's cottage, and the body of the young woman was taken inside. Old Mother Sawyer was present, having walked with the procession from the site of Maud's death. The men carrying the litter gently removed the girl from it and placed her on the table. The six men, who had transported her body on their shoulders, bowed respectfully before moving backwards and out through the door. Meg stood silently, while Old Mother Sawyer and Mary Holmes who had both been present at her birth, now administered to her dead body.

Meg was coaxed to assist in the cleansing of the young girl's body, and as they washed her, Meg carefully stroked her daughter's hair. Meg was numbed, but became more involved, wanting her daughter to be presented at her burial as the devastating beauty she had been in life. She lovingly soaked her child's remains, removing the soil and river detritus that had stained her body from its submersion in the local brook. She helped to apply rouge to the pale skin of her face, rubbing in the make-up that would give her the semblance of life, exposing her beauty for the last time. They washed her hair in herb-scented water, to bring its lustrous shine to life for one last time. They applied scent to her body that Old Mother Sawyer had made, obscuring the smell of death. Finally, they dressed Maud in her finest clothes. Maud looked as beautiful in death, as she had in life. Distressed as she was, Meg had performed her duty in presenting her child for her final journey to the afterlife.

❖

In complete contrast, Godfrey's body was taken to one of the stables at the Manor House. Apart from the men designated to convey his body, no-one followed his journey. Every single member of the village community was attending Maud's solemn procession. No-one cared what happened to the evil, corrupt, and murderous villain who had defiled and destroyed the young life which should have been the future of the village.

The body was dumped on a bed of straw and left unceremoniously. The villagers who had been tasked with the onerous duty of transporting him there, exited hastily, not wanting to remain in the presence of someone who they considered to be evil and a threat to their mortal souls.

They left his remains to be administered by the clergy from the local church of St Lawrence, who were equally appalled at being given the responsibility.

The monks did what was needed, and nothing else. They washed the body and clothed it. Godfrey was to be buried in the clothes he had died in, as no-one knew where any of his other clothes were. Under normal circumstances, someone from the village might have donated some clean clothes, but these were not normal circumstances, and not a single villager wanted to become involved.

Once the monks had finished what they had to do, they wrapped the body in a shawl and left it in the barn, awaiting further instruction.

❖

Early the following morning, de Vere arrived at the Manor House and convened a hasty inquest, he had brought with him a man from the district to act as coroner.  The local coroner was a beady little chap with some odd mannerisms, he seemed very nervous in the presence of de Vere, and constantly dabbed at his sweaty forehead with a small square of linen.

The inquest was heard in the Great Hall of the Manor House, and a number of people were invited.  This included de Vere as the major Landlord, Moryn, as the landlord overseeing the village and its surrounds, the villagers who had discovered the bodies as witnesses, and some other senior villagers.  Their roles were to provide evidence and witness the proclamations made during the procedure, and to sign and validate the process, for legal purposes.

Meg supported by Old Mother Sawyer was also invited, due to the personal tragedy she had endured, and because of that, her presence was vital to the credibility of the proceedings. Her face was deathly pale, and her eyes red from crying, but she was able to keep her composure for the sake of her child. In reality her presence was a formality, and her influence on what was about to happen was negligible...

A notable absentee was Walter, who had no official standing, and was probably too distraught to attend anyway.

The coroner invited evidence, first from one of the witnesses who had discovered Maud's body.

"Hugh Forrester? I understand you were one of the men who found the girl's body? Please tell us in your own words what happened." The coroner said, inviting Hugh to the front of the gathering.

Hugh bowed his head and began speaking, "Well Sire. Meg was very upset and asked us to go and search for her daughter. I got some men together and we split into two groups and then went to search the surrounding area."

"And what did you find?" the coroner asked.

"We arrived at the brook and found the poor girl in the water."

"What did you think had happened?" the coroner prompted.

"It looked as if she had drowned, Sire."

"Thank you, Mr Forrester." Hugh was invited to return to the group.

"James Peabody?" the coroner called out.

"Sire!" Peabody answered from the back of the room.

"Please come forward." The coroner directed.

Peabody shuffled his way forward as the crowd parted before him, until he stood in front of the table at which the senior people were seated.

"I understand that you found the body of Godfrey Bowen?" the coroner asked.

"Aye Sire." Peabody responded.

"Please explain in your own words, what you saw."

"Well, Sire, me and the other men went in the opposite direction to Hugh." Peabody muttered, he felt very nervous talking in front of so many people, …Mr Forrester, I mean" Peabody corrected himself.

"You will need to speak up, Mr Peabody! We cannot hear you!" the coroner admonished him.

Peabody repeated what he had said, slightly louder this time.

"And what happened next?" the coroner urged.

"Well, we found Godfrey's, I mean Mr Bowen's body on the bridge."

"And?"

"He had an arrow in his chest, and he was holding a piece of rag in his hand."

"Rag?" the coroner queried.

"Yes Sire, it looked like it had been ripped from a women's blouse. White linen it was."

"And what happened next?"

"One of the men ran back to the village and got some sacking, and we carried his body back in that."

"Is there anything else? The coroner asked.

"When we got 'im back to the village we could see that he had long scratches on his face."

"Thank you, Mr Peabody, that will be all." The coroner concluded.

Peabody shuffled back into the crowd, as the coroner continued, "It has been noted by this court that during an inspection of the girl's body, that the young woman had skin scrapings under her fingernails."

The arrow was admitted as evidence. It was about a yard long and was fletched with red feathers. The witnesses observed that there were three small golden circles etched onto the shaft of the bow.

"The arrow is quite unique," exclaimed the coroner, "Does anyone know who might use such an arrow?

The villagers all bowed their heads, reluctant to speak.

"This arrow is one of the type used by a man known as 'The Archer'." De Vere stated loudly, so that everyone in the room could hear, "I am aware of this, as are many others, because this individual, who disguises himself, uses these arrows in local tournaments." He declared. "Both the individual, whose true identity is not known, and his arrows are well known." He concluded. De Vere looked at the cowed heads of the villagers.

"If anyone knows the identity of this individual, they should declare so now!" the coroner stated flatly. "Failure to do so will draw substantial punishment!"

No-one responded, although there were a few mutterings in the audience.

"Quiet! Quiet!" the coroner commanded. "If no-one knows the identity of this person, then we shall proceed with the next piece of evidence..."

The piece of clothing that Godfrey had clutched in his hand was presented.

"I understand that this piece of cloth has been examined and it matches the clothing the dead girl was wearing?" The coroner asked.

Moryn nodded his agreement, and the coroner wrote something down on his parchment.

I also understand that this piece of cloth matches the shape and size of the cloth missing from the girl's bodice?"

Once again Moryn nodded and presented the clothing that Maud had been wearing. The clothing and the ripped cloth were compared for everyone to see. It was a clear match.

"Finally, Godfrey Bowen was carrying a purse at the time of his death." The Coroner stated. The Purse was presented to the witnesses. Moryn emptied its contents onto the table. A couple of coins fell out, together with the silver charm that had belonged to Will.

Meg and Old Mother Sawyer sucked in their collective breaths, realising the significance of the charm. Meg turned to Mother Sawyer and said under her breath "He has taken everything from me!" Mother Sawyer put her arm around Meg's shoulder and gently squeezed her "Shhhh!" She soothed, "It will do no good to dwell on that here." she said. A tear dropped from Meg's eye and wandered down her face.

"If that is all the evidence, we shall move on to the dead girl." The coroner stated, having made another note on his parchment.

"The dead girl was called Maud Bowen. Is that correct?" He asked.

Everyone nodded.

"And she has been identified by her mother, who is present, I believe?" he asked as he looked around the room, his eyes settling on Meg.

"Aye." Confirmed Moryn "She is known to everyone in the village." He looked and Meg, and Meg nodded her thanks, for his intervention, which meant she did not have to speak up.

"She had just come into her majority and was aged sixteen? And she was found in the brook known as Wymans Brook?"

Heads nodded in agreement.

The coroner then examined the evidence of the witnesses who had found Maud's body and the circumstance surrounding their discovery.

"When her body was examined, there were injuries consistent with an assault?"

"That is correct." Stated De Vere.

As Meg started to rise, Old Mother Sawyer gripped her arm and stayed her in her seat. She whispered "what we know has no value here… it will do you no good to protest."

"However, the injuries the young woman sustained were not fatal, and she is presumed to have drowned in the brook?" the Coroner continued.

"That is correct." De Vere answered again.

The little man scribbled onto the parchment some more.

"We have concluded the inquiry and examined all the witnesses, including the physical evidence that was available. We will now adjourn to consider the facts that have been presented and come to a verdict." He declared, rising from his seat.

"Court dismissed!" he called out.

The room cleared and de Vere, Moryn and the coroner convened to discuss the verdicts, and take some refreshment.

❖

The court was reconvened about an hour later. It was de Vere's desire to get this over and done with as quickly as possible.

The witnesses all shuffled back in, eagerly awaiting the verdicts.

The coroner commenced proceedings. "This inquest has been convened at the behest of the Lord of the Manor Robert de Vere. The inquiry has been held in accordance with legal requirements of the Sheriff of Gloucestershire and the Lord High Constable of England. Evidence has been presented by all relevant parties and has been considered in determining the verdicts. I now defer to Lord Robert de Vere as the legal entity for these estates."

De Vere stood and delivered his first verdict.

"I declare that Godfrey Bowen was killed by a single arrow, which had punctured his heart. His death was a criminal act. The arrow that had killed him had distinctive red fletching with three golden circles etched into the shaft. These were known to be used exclusively by individual known as "The Archer." This individual is hereby declared to be a criminal across the whole of England, and guilty of the murder of Godfrey Bowen. I command that he be arrested forthwith and hanged. Anyone assisting him or harbouring him, will also be hanged. That is my first verdict." The crowd murmured at the judgement but did nothing more.

De Vere continued.

"Bowen also had some scratches on his face which were consistent with someone trying to fight him off. Also, there was the piece of clothing torn from Maud's skirt that had been found in Godfrey's hand. We have concluded that Godfrey Bowen had raped the young woman and had been killed by a person unknown. Therefore, his death was declared and an Act of God, and despite his crime, he is to be given a Christian burial, as God has already punished him. That is my second verdict." The crowd began to murmur again, this time there were more signs of discontent with the judgement. They thought that had Godfrey been captured alive, he would have been hanged and left to rot, not given a Christian burial.

"My third verdict concerns the girl Maud Bowen. There was evidence that she had been sexually assaulted, but apart from this, there were no other visible injuries on her body. Our conclusion is that she had a secret assignation with her uncle, Godfrey Bowen. Both had arranged this assignation, and both attended freely."

This statement drew muted cries from the audience and whispers of "No!" could be heard around the room. De Vere continued regardless,

"We believe the girl had agreed to meet with Bowen willingly, but then something happened, and she tried to back out of their agreement. Things got out of hand, and Bowen ended up raping Maud Bowen, his niece. She tried to defend herself and scratched his face before running off."

The displeasure of the witnesses began to get more vocal, and the guards in the room began to jostle people, forcing them to desist from their objections.

"The girl fled the scene in shame. Overcome by the dishonour she had brought on herself and her family, she then threw herself into the brook, with the deliberate intent on killing herself by drowning!"

The crowd erupted, and de Vere was forced to temporarily pause his discourse.

"Silence!" The coroner called out but could hardly be heard above the sounds of anger and disbelief being noisily expressed by the villagers. Moryn held his head in shame, he did not believe in the verdicts that were being delivered, but he was powerless to prevent de Vere from iterating them. During the meeting directly after the enquiry he had voiced his objections, but with the coroner siding with the Lord of the Manor, he was defeated by a majority of two to one.

The guards became more physical, and the coroner bellowed "Silence! Or I will clear the court! If there is any more trouble, then the individuals concerned will be severely punished for contempt!"

The crowd gradually hushed, and their anger subsided in the face of the threats.

De Vere waited patiently for the noise to abate before continuing,

"As suicide is a crime against God, and a sin, the Bowen girl cannot be given a Christian burial. She will be buried at midnight tonight at the nearest crossroads according to custom. No service of any kind will be permitted at her graveside. That is my third verdict!"

There was a distinctly hostile atmosphere building in the hall, but the guards stood in front of the witnesses and looked at them with grim and threatening countenances. The crowd muttered and mumbled, but each realised they had no power to change what was happening. Thinking that the proceedings had come to an end, they began to shuffle towards the doors of the Great Hall.

De Vere called out "There is a fourth verdict!" he exclaimed loudly. The group of villagers turned in surprise "What more could there be?" they asked themselves.

"As Margaret Bowen no longer has an heir, and no other family that can claim ownership of her cottage, I claim the right of 'Escheat'. Ownership of the cottage will revert to me, and Margaret Bowen must give up the freehold and leave the cottage today! I have taken this step for the moral welfare of the village, because her daughter has brought dishonour not only on the mother, but the entire village! That is my final verdict!"

The court exploded. "Injustice!", "Travesty!" people cried, as they pushed their way towards the dais. Meg had fainted and was helped from the room by Old Mother Sawyer and some other villagers into the fresh air. The guards reacted violently against the rebelling villagers, clubbing them, and pushing them back.

Moryn ushered de Vere and the coroner out through another door and closed it behind them. He bowed his head as he thought, "Why does this man have to create such unnecessary misery everywhere he goes?"

De Vere was wiping his hands down his trousers and had a broad smile on his face "That went better than anticipated!" he exclaimed gleefully.

"You'll need to put those insolent peasants in their place!" he declared to Moryn.

"Flog a couple of them as an example, and that should deter the rest!"

With that he flicked his hand towards the coroner, "Come man, we are leaving!"

The coroner scuttled after his paymaster out of the building towards the stables where de Vere's own company were waiting with horses saddled.

Poor Moryn was left to pick up the pieces...

❖

Godfrey's body was interred immediately after the court of enquiry. No-one from the village attended. The only people in attendance were the priest and a couple of monks, who muttered some perfunctory prayers. They only did that because it was their job to do so....

# CHAPTER 22

## Maud's Elm

Meg was evicted from her cottage at the same time as de Vere's men had come to take away Maud's body. It was just before midnight. Six knights from de Vere's retinue had arrived along with four local men.

The knights were rough and uncouth. Maud's body had been prepared for the funeral that her mother had expected, and she was dressed in her best clothing. She looked beautiful. However, her innocence and chastity were soon abused by the knights.

The six men burst into the cottage and Meg was roughly pushed aside. One of the knights held her firmly against the wall, while de Crecy and two others walked over to the body lying on the table.

They cut off the girl's clothing and exposed her naked body. Meg tried to fight off the guard holding her and screamed "Leave her alone!" The guard cuffed her around the head, and grabbed her by the jaw, squeezing until she thought her teeth were going to crack. "Shut up, you bitch! We have come to collect your whore daughter!"

Meg tried to find a weapon feeling with her hands for anything that she could use against this monster, but he was too strong, and there was nothing in reach. "I'll gut you if you try anything!" he said viciously smashing her head back against the wall.

The three men around the table and the other leered at the naked dead body on the table. "What a waste!" one of them said. The others laughed.

"I still would!" another smirked.

"Dead girls are the only kind you could get anyway!" de Crecy countered. The men all laughed again, clearly finding their disrespectful jokes the height of hilarity.

Meg could do nothing apart from watch with wide open, hate-filled eyes at the desecration of her daughter's memory. Her struggles were useless.

"Come on! You've had enough time to gawk!" de Crecy said. "Let's get this over!" he turned to the guard next to the door. "Bring them in!" he ordered.

The four villagers including Hugh Forrester entered. He passed a sorrowful look with Meg, and then noticed Maud's naked body. "For the love of God!" he exclaimed, "Cover her up."

"She's a whore, and will be buried naked, like the judgment demanded!" de Crecy stated menacingly.

"Well, we won't be able to carry her half a mile like that! We'll need something to carry her in." Hugh retorted.

De Crecy relented in the face of clear logic. "All right then, find something!" he demanded. Hugh went over the bedroom and pulled a blanket from the bed. He then went over to the young girl's body and wrapped it. As he did so, he looked at Meg again, and she indicated with hers eyes her gratitude for finding a way to give her child some dignity in death.

The four villagers took the now covered girl in her makeshift litter and left the cottage.

The six knights then began to ransack the cottage, throwing Meg's possessions around. De Crecy took great pleasure in smashing her looms with his club. When they had thoroughly trashed the place, de Crecy stared at Meg and said, "Not much of value here!"

Meg stared but did not respond.

"Take what you can carry and get out!" With that the guard holding Meg's face released her and pushed roughly forward. She stumbled nearly falling but put out her hand to regain her balance on the table that only minutes before had held the body of her child.

"You've got one minute, then we are putting you out!"

Meg gathered up some clothes and other belongings before she was man-handled out of the door.

"I wish we could burn it!" de Crecy exclaimed, but the Lord has other tenants for it!"

Meg stumbled through the village, cold and afraid. She did not know where to go. In the course of just 24 hours her whole world had been destroyed.

As she wandered in the darkness, she saw a shape in the shadows.

"Come with me!" Old Mother Sawyer said.

❖

Hugh and the four villagers formed a sad procession, disgusted but the events of the day, and what they had witnessed at Meg's cottage, they did their best to carry Maud's body in a dignified manner, and trudged along to her final resting place. Two men each carried the body, the other two carried spades. When one pair got tired, they swapped over their duties. It was tough work and they had quite a distance to travel, the escort provided by de Vere offered no help, and sat on their horses making crude remarks about the poor dead girl. As far as they were concerned their job was to make sure that this burial was done by the book. The peasants could act as beasts of burden.

When they arrived at the designated place they were met by de Vere, Moryn and the coroner who had come to see that the burial was undertaken correctly. The knights lit torches so that the scene could be viewed, and the villagers had enough light to work with. The four men began their task and their spades dug into the soil. The pit was dug deep enough to stop foraging animals from digging the body up.

Once this task had been completed, two of the men carried the shrouded form of the young girl over to the pit. Hugh and the other man had the precious bundle handed down to them, and laid her at the bottom of the grave, as gently as they could.

"Hurry up Man!" cried de Vere, you should have just tipped her in!"

Hugh and his companion ignored the unnecessary and callous words.

"Just make sure the shroud is removed!" de Vere ordered.

Hugh gently unravelled the material from around the girl's body and held it up to the other villager who was standing above him on the grave's edge, he then carefully arranged her hair and her body, with her arms crossed over her chest. He took a brief look at the angelic face of the young girl who he considered to be like a daughter to him and whispered a quick prayer for her soul. As he did so, a tear dropped from his eye, and onto Maud's lips. "God bless you child!" he whispered before climbing out of the pit.

The four villagers bent over to retrieve their spades, ready for the task of covering the body with soil.

"Wait!" commanded de Vere, as he removed a stake made out of the wood of an elm tree and a mallet, from one of his saddle pouches.

The four men looked over at him in astonishment, as he strode over to the grave and jumped in. He stood astride the body of the young girl and briefly looked at her face, looking serene as if she was asleep. He then placed the pointed end of the stake against her chest, and struck down violently with the mallet, driving the spike deep into her chest. Then he struck again, and again, until the stake had penetrated through her body and embedded itself in the soil beneath her.

Pleased with his work, he again glanced at the girl's face. Her eyes were open, and a smile danced on her lips. He shuddered, before being aided from the pit by de Crecy. "I am sure her eyes were closed when I jumped into the grave!" he mumbled to himself.

As this was not a Christian burial, the body was not even allowed to have a shroud, and therefore the young girl's naked body was committed to the ground. Again, according to local custom and superstition, a stake made from the wood of an elm tree was driven through her heart and impaled her to her resting place. This custom was designed to prevent those denied a Christian burial from rising from the dead. However, having just had such a disturbing experience, he was now unsure if the custom had any validity!

Thus, innocent Maud's body was interred without ceremony or mourning, but only in shame, disgrace, and dishonour. Meg was prevented from attending the burial, and the only people allowed to be present were de Vere, Moryn, the coroner and the men who had dug the grave, along with his retinue of knights.

❖

With no income or means of earning an income Meg became a beggar. She had no abode, and wandered the lanes in her grief, accepting alms from those generous people that she met occasionally. Meg was rarely she was seen in the village, as it held too many memories for her. However, when she did wander through occasionally, she was welcomed by those who saw her, and always offered food and drink.

Meg's grief was mirrored across the whole community, and the anger and resentment caused by the judgements made by de Vere still simmered. Richard Moryn tried to mend the wounds, but was mostly ineffective, as the villagers blamed him for not sticking up for Meg. Moryn deeply regretted what had happened but was in an impossible situation. He could no more defy his Liege Lord than any of the villagers, and he suffered from his own remorse. He felt that the heart of the village had been ripped out by the death of such a poor innocent girl and the aftermath had caused a rift so deep that he knew it would take many years to recover. What had once been such a happy, peaceful, and connected community, now seethed with bitterness and fear.

Whenever Meg did visit the village, she invariably visited Old Mother Sawyer. The old woman comforted her and supported her as best she could, but even Mother Sawyer's skills could not fully mend a broken heart. In the absence of Meg, Mother Sawyer often ruminated on her part in the events that had taken place. She felt that she had done as much as she could have done, but there was still a nagging doubt. "Was there ever really an infallible solution to the evil that men do?" she wondered.

❖

Of course, there was one place that you could guarantee to find Meg. She could be seen every single day at the grave site of her daughter. Rain or shine, spring, summer, autumn, winter, Meg would be there. She would stand at the site, with her head bowed; sometimes she sat next to the grave and talked to her child. Most often she would be seen crying, her grief overwhelming. She would cry floods of tears, until there were none left. Her tears flowed onto the grave, day after day after day.

One day a small shoot appeared in the soil. It came out of the ground directly above where Maud's heart was buried. Watered by the tears of a grieving mother and sustained by the rotting flesh of the murdered girl, a tree began to grow. Although Elm trees are known to grow quickly, the growth of this particular tree was remarkable. In just a few short months, the tree had grown to stand over 7 feet tall. The tree was lovingly tended by Maud and stood as a monument to the death of innocence. The tree became a landmark in its own right. All the local people around the area called this tree 'Maud's Elm.'

Meg's presence at the tree was a sad sight; the villagers would pass her on their way to market and remember the vivacious young girl who used to do the same.

❖

Walter also grieved. He grieved for his lost love. He grieved for his failure to be where Maud needed him to be on the day of her death. He grieved for his own loss of innocence. He also grieved for Meg, and her loss. As a result, he often joined Meg at the gravesite, and sat with her for hours, until his duties called him away. Sometimes they would talk, but often they would just sit in silence contemplating a life that could have been.

Walter did manage to gradually coax Meg out of her grief; they sometimes discussed the fact that he could have become her son-in-law, and that made them both cry.

Although it was some distance away, and Meg was not getting any younger, he did persuade her to come to his parent's home at the House in the Tree. There she was looked after, given food and water, and somewhere warm to sleep. Walter's parents had been aware of his budding romance and were deeply affected by his heartache at the loss of his first love. As a young man, they expected him to recover in time, and move on with his life. They hoped that time would heal him. Although, they sometimes thought that his relationship with Meg was holding him back from moving on, they had accepted and loved Meg as a member of their family and gave both as much support as they could.

So, Meg had a variety of people who looked after her. In truth she did not really care, her life ended the day her daughter died. People sustained her and gave her shelter. She had contemplated taking her own life but knew that this would be an unforgiveable sin. Knowing how her daughter had suffered as a result of the false allegations made against her, she knew she could not do anything like that. She now had only one purpose in life and that was to protect and nurture the tree that had sprouted from her daughter's body and ensure that Maud's Elm became an everlasting monument to her memory.

There was another who protected Meg. He was another who grieved. He was another who was angered by the injustice of death of Maud and the unfairness of the accusations levelled against her. He was also angry that having vowed to protect her, he had failed. He had arrived too late to protect her from the assault by de Vere, and he had arrived too late to kill him. He was angry that his misjudgement and belief that the actions he had taken were enough for Maud to escape, had been proven to be devastatingly wrong, and he was to blame for that. He had vowed to protect Maud with his life, and having had the opportunity to do so, he had left her to her fate. His grief was a mixture of a loss of love, and the guilt he felt at his personal failure. The pain he felt was every bit as deep and overwhelming as that felt by Meg.

"The Archer" had made a second vow, one that he would keep until death. He would protect Meg from harm, whatever the cost.

"The Archer" was always present wherever Meg went anywhere. Whenever Meg was wandering the byways, or sitting under Maud's Elm, she would always have a silent and unseen protector hiding in the shadows nearby. "The Archer" was determined to do for Meg, what he had been unable to do for Maud.

❖

One evening when Meg was sitting under the now substantial tree, the murmuring and shuffling feet of people approaching her along the lane. Meg paid no attention, used to the fact that Maud's Elm was on a stretch of road which was regularly used to travel to Cheltenham.

As they got closer to her, one of them asked, "Sister, may we sit with you awhile?"

Meg looked up and saw eight women, dressed in shawls.

Meg noticed that one of the women was Old Mother Sawyer. Mother Sawyer knelt in front of Meg and placed a gentle hand on her shoulder.

She looked Meg in the eyes and said "We are eight and should be nine. We cannot replace what you have lost, but you can replace the one we have lost."

Meg looked at the group of women, a confused look on her face, "I have nothing to offer. How can I help you?"

Mother Sawyer replied, "We are the Maids of Alney, we ask nothing of you. Join us and together we will seek to right the wrongs you have suffered; and try to protect others who might suffer like you."

"What would you have me do? Meg asked.

"Come with us, and we will sustain you." Mother Sawyer replied.

The group of women gathered around Meg as she rose from the ground. They helped her to her feet and started to move away from Maud's Elm.

# CHAPTER 23

## J'Accuse

Robert de Vere was dressed in all his pomp, and his beaming wife, Isabel stood beside him proudly holding out her first-born child to its Godmother, Amelie Moryn. Richard and Amelie had been delighted to have been given the honour of acting as God Parents for their Liege Lord and knew that this honour was a significant one for their own status.

The church at Bishops Cleeve was full to the rafters with noble families from across the area. De Vere wanted this to be a huge celebration for his son and heir. He had been reluctant to ask any of the more senior nobles to act as God Parents and, knowing his own reputation amongst them and he did not wish to give them the opportunity to refuse. This would have been a huge embarrassment, and he did not want any form of bad feeling to sour this momentous occasion.

Amelie was beckoned forward by the priest. Richard touched the infant on his right shoulder to indicate that this was the child to be baptised. The priest nodded to Amelie, and she approached the font and held its head over the ancient stone receptacle. The priest dipped his hand into the holy water and poured it over the head of the child. "Ego te baptizo in nomine Patris," he intoned.

He dipped his hand once more into the font and poured more water over the baby's head. "Et Filii," he then repeated the ritual for a third time. "Et Spiritus Sancti." Having completed the baptism ritual, the priest continued with his incantation in Latin.

"May the Almighty God, the Father of our Lord Jesus Christ, Who hath regenerated thee by water and the Holy Spirit, and who hath given thee the remission of all thy sins, may He Himself anoint thee with the Chrism of Salvation, in the same Christ Jesus our Lord, unto life eternal."

He then placed a small white linen cloth on the baby's head and completed the catechism. "Receive this white garment, which mayest thou carry without stain before the judgment seat of our Lord Jesus Christ, that thou mayest have life everlasting."

The priest nodded again, and Isobel stepped forward to receive her son from the arms of Amelie. She looked down at him with a broad smile on her face. She was so proud that he had not made a sound during the baptism.

The priest completed the ceremony, by handing a lighted candle to de Vere.

The parents, God Parents, and assorted guests filed out of the church to the peal of bells and the haunting chant of the choir. De Vere's knights in their finest armour, stood resplendent as they formed a guard of honour, with their lances held over the heads of the people as they walked from the church. Outside it was warm and sunny, and the large group of nobles mounted their horses and carriages to form a procession that would proceed through the local towns and villages and end up at the Manor in Swindon Village, where the Moryn's had prepared a celebration feast.

The procession departed the church with flags and banners waving in the breeze. It was an impressive and spectacular sight that brought many people out onto the streets to watch.

The route of the procession had been planned to let as many people as possible see the new heir to the de Vere estates. It would also announce to everyone that the de Vere dynasty would continue.

They proceeded through the streets of the village of Bishops Cleeve, and then through Southam, into Prestbury, and finally Cheltenham, before taking the last leg of the journey to Swindon Village itself. The feast would go on well into the night, and the following day, de Vere had organised a hunt for the male guests.

De Vere was bursting with pride and happiness, and he held a broad grin on his face, which was a rare event, because his normal expression was a scowl. He was determined that nothing would affect this joyous and important day.

He did not know that his own actions on this day, would turn joy to the bitterest sorrow, and tears of blood.

❖

With a little over half a mile of the excursion left the pageant approached the crossroads dominated by the large elm tree. De Vere did not know it was now known locally as "Maud's Elm", and no-one felt the need to antagonise him by informing him of the fact. Despite what the law and the church said, local people respected this site as a place where a great wrong had been committed.

De Vere sat at the head of the column with Richard Moryn at his side, and Hubert de Crecy just behind.

As the procession drew closer to the tree, de Vere noticed what appeared to be an old woman standing close to it. Although she was standing there innocently enough, she was standing in the road, and creating an obstacle for the passage of the parade. Her position made the road more narrow than it should be.

"What is this!" de Vere uttered looking down on Meg. "A beggar defiles our path!"

"It is just Margaret Bowen tending her child's grave, Sire." Moryn responded.

"Move her! She is a disgusting and pitiful sight and is spoiling our day! I thought the woman was long dead!"

"Mrs Bowen! Moryn called out. "Please move out of the way, you are holding up the procession.

Meg did not look up or move. She stood hunched over crying onto the base of the tree.

"Damn the woman! She deliberately insults us!" de Vere shouted, his faced flushed with anger. In his mind, this woman was intentionally and wantonly defying his authority. She was embarrassing him in front of the cream of society from the wider area.

"We can try to go round her Sire!" Moryn interjected.

"Go around her! Gods Teeth man! I don't go around anyone!" de Vere shouted angrily. He could hear the shuffling and confusion behind him, as people commented and queried what was causing the hold up. It had been a warm day and the procession had taken a number of hours to get to this point. The nobles who had attended the ceremony, were getting hot and sticky, and were looking forward to refreshments a little more than ten minutes away.

De Vere's anger finally snapped. "This Hag! Fiend! Witch! Has ruined the day and humiliated me!" he thought. "You have come to cast a shadow over my son's Christening Day!" He bellowed, no longer in control of his emotions.

"I'll have you caged and whipped! I'll have you lashed until I can see your bones! Get out of the way, you crone!" He screamed. Tears began to form in Isobel's eyes, as she sat in her carriage next to Amelie. As she listened to her husband ranting in front of her, she could also hear the barely concealed giggles and sniggers from their esteemed guests, turning into full blown laughs behind her.

Meg neither moved nor looked up. She stood like a statue made of granite, with her head bent, crying over the grave of her daughter. Her tears dropped onto the roots of the enormous tree.

Richard Moryn realised that Meg was oblivious to what was happening around her and was not deliberately disobeying de Vere. In the madness created by her grief, she did not know or care what was happening, or even realise that other people were nearby. She was lost in her world of pain and sorrow.

Moryn began to dismount, keen to sort out this unnecessary situation and return to some semblance of sanity. De Vere's behaviour was unwarranted and obscene. "I will move her." He said plainly.

"NO!" De Vere thundered. Moryn stopped his dismount. De Vere turned to his Master-at-Arms "Hubert! Drag this witch out of the way, she defies her betters. See her punished for her insolence!"

❖

Deep in the woods by the side of the road, someone was observing the events at the cross-roads. "The Archer" watched and waited, hoping that the scene unfolding in front of him would resolve itself without any harm.

Unfortunately, that outcome was becoming more and more unlikely as de Vere's temper took control of him.

"The Archer" became increasingly concerned for Meg's safety and began to prepare for the worst.

He saw de Crecy dismount from his horse and advance towards Meg. He could see the determination and anger on de Crecy's face, and it was clear he was in no mood to be gentle with Meg. In "The Archer's" eyes, de Crecy did not seem to be a man who had any more patience or compassion than his master.

As he approached with his mailed fist curled into a ball, it was clear that he intended to strike Meg. Meg stood as if turned to stone and made no attempt to move. De Crecy's fist swung towards Meg's face.

"The Archer" drew back his bow string and released his arrow. Before the huge man's fist could land its blow, an arrow punched through his breast plate and went directly into his heart. Hubert de Crecy fell to the floor dead, before his head hit the ground.

As de Crecy lay slumped on the ground, an arrow with red fletching and three golden circles etched on its shaft, quivered in his chest.

❖

De Vere sat on his horse momentarily stunned. His eyes gaped and he had some difficulty in believing the truth of what he was seeing. His face turned deathly pale as the blood left it.

After just a few seconds he came to his senses and realised the panic that was spreading throughout his cortege. Horses were skittering, women were screaming. Men were shouting.

Finally, recognising what the arrow signified he screamed at his guard "The Archer! The Archer! Get him! Kill Him!"

His knights whose primary role in the procession was to protect the exalted guests, had also regained their composure and charged towards the wooded area that the arrow had come from. The density of the trees made it difficult to proceed on horseback, and they were forced to dismount and lead their horses through the packed trees. De Vere looked on aghast, the ignominy of the embarrassing spectacle added to his humiliation even more.

But worse was to come. He saw the procession breaking up, as nobles in their carriages began trying to turn them around in the narrow road, and the scene of chaos was complete, as they left to go their separate ways, either in fear of further attack, or to protect their womenfolk, fury at the disgraceful conduct of their host, and their own humiliation at being involved in such a farce! They all knew that gossip surrounding this affair would amuse the peasants for months, if not years! They were also certain that de Vere's shame would resound in the halls of the great houses for at least as long!

❖

After a short while, de Vere's knights returned, their heads bowed.

"We could not find him, Sire!" one of them admitted bravely.

"What! A whole troop of knights cannot chase down one man!" de Vere screamed and struck the man across the face with a stinging blow. "You useless bastards!"

Totally unmoved and unaware of the chaotic scene around her, Meg remained where she had been standing. Still with her head bowed, still crying. After berating his men, de Vere once again turned towards the woman who had caused his shame. The venom in his stare was an indication of the absolute fury and hatred he held towards this woman. She had completely destroyed what should have been one of the greatest and most important days of his life.

He would make her pay dearly for her behaviour!

"Drag that witch over here!" he commanded his soldiers. "De Crecy is not the first to die at her hands! She is in league with the fiends of Hell!" he cried.

The soldiers grabbed Meg roughly and brought her in front of their lord. "Take her away to Gloucester Gaol, she will be tried as the witch she is, and burn as punishment! I will make sure you suffer bitch!" he screamed in her face.

As she was dragged away, Maud began to struggle and kick out at the men who held her. "NO! NO!" she screamed in defiance fighting with all her strength. The men handled her roughly and did not release their grip. De Vere laughed as he thought that what he had said had got through to the demented woman. However, Meg was not screaming and fighting against her captivity or fate, she was screaming because she was being taken away from the grave of her child…..

❖

"The Archer" had quickly left the area. Although he did so reluctantly, he knew he still had a mission to accomplish. He also knew that he would not have stood a chance against so many armed men, and it would not have been possible to provide any more protection for

Meg than he had already accomplished. When he started observing her, he had expected to defend her against vagabonds and thieves, and not to have to face down an army of trained knights. To be captured now would do no-one any good.

He ruminated briefly over whether or not he should have put an arrow through de Vere but knew he would not have had the time to escape if he had. "I will come for you de Vere! And I will kill you!" he vowed.

He moved quietly and swiftly through the woodland, along the hedgerows and away from the pursuit. There would be searches made of the local area, and he needed to be well away from the trouble that was inevitably coming.

❖

With the day destroyed, the guests departed, and the disgrace he had suffered, de Vere's anger had not abated. His wife was distressed, as was the baby.

He vowed that someone would pay for what had happened today, and as de Crecy was dead, someone else would need to suffer. He decided that it would be the insolent knight who had told him that they had failed to capture "The Archer". He would have the man flogged to within an inch of his life for his impertinence, and as a lesson to the others that failure was not an option.

Moryn was still sat on his horse, wondering about what had actually happened. He was convinced that if he had been allowed to deal with the situation, things would have turned out very differently. He was wary of approaching de Vere in his current state but realised that he needed to know what his intentions were. "My Lord, what do you want to do now?" he asked.

"I have some retribution to take, Moryn! That is what will happen next!" he snapped angrily.

Moryn shuddered involuntarily, expecting in some way to be the subject of de Vere's ire. "We can still go to the Manor and have some refreshments Sire; it is all ready for you."

"No Moryn, "de Vere responded morosely. "I have had enough for one day. We will return to my Manor." His response was made in a resigned tone, he looked like a deflated and defeated man, now that his anger had subsided, and his impotence had sunk in. "Give the food to the pigs for all I care!"

Although Moryn had gone to a lot of expense and trouble to impress his Liege Lord and the other nobles, he smiled secretly to himself. He was glad that he and his family would not have to put up with the company of this obnoxious man any longer than necessary. Nevertheless, as he considered the events of the day, he felt sorry for Meg Bowen, and concerned for de Vere's wife and child.

"Sire, even if you do not wish to stay, your wife has been through a most distressing experience. As God Parents to your son, we would be honoured to have her and the child to stay with us for a few days. She could rest and you would be able to conduct your business without concern for their welfare."

"Thank you Moryn. That is a very kind suggestion, and I agree. What with the birth of the child and what happened today Isobel deserves some joy. I cannot provide that at the moment, and she and Amelie are great friends. I think she would enjoy being your guest. Thank you." De Vere said.

Moryn was delighted and surprised. His surly, easily angered, and quick-tempered lord had never spoken to him in such a way, and although he knew that his elevation to God Father to de Vere's child was mostly as a result of de Vere's lack of choice because of his reputation amongst the other nobles, he felt a pang of sympathy for this difficult man. He realised that this man did not look at the world the way that he did, he was a violent, dangerous warlord who knew nothing better. Nevertheless, de Vere's compassion for his wife displayed a rarely viewed side to his character. Moryn had a tendency to try to view the better aspects of everyone he met. He was not a warrior; he was an administrator.

"We would be overjoyed Sire!" Moryn gushed.

De Vere said, "Good! That is settled then." He did not care about his wife. She was just a vessel for his heir. He had more important things to do, including destroying a witch, punishing his ineffective knights, and catching a criminal, but not necessarily in that order……

❖

Isobel de Vere enjoyed a relaxing couple of days on the Swindon Village estate. The company was pleasant, the food was good, and she and her baby were able to relax, away from the continuous stress that her husband's behaviour caused her back at her own manor.

She was able to take an afternoon nap each day, secure in the knowledge that she and her baby would not be disturbed, and that she would not have to suffer any tantrums.

On the second day of her sojourn, she had retired to bed in the afternoon. Her boy was fast asleep in his cot, and she contentedly drifted off.

She did not notice the old woman who appeared in her room, and snipped a locket of hair from her, and then snipped a locket of hair from her son….

# CHAPTER 24

## Tribulation before Trial

Meg was taken under escort to Gloucester. She was loaded onto a cart and tethered to it with a rope around her neck, her hands were bound behind her back. She was made to stand for the entire journey of about 11 miles, which took more than 3 hours. The road was rutted, and she struggled to keep her balance. Whenever she fell, the cart was stopped, and she was beaten until she stood again.

As she was paraded through the city, people who were aware that she had been accused of witchcraft, because of the town cryer, threw rotting fruit and vegetables at her, so that by the time she arrived at the gaol she was filthy and smelly, and her hair matted with the detritus. Her condition made her look more like the sorceress she was accused of being, and accordingly the ignorant people stepped away in fear.

When they arrived at the gates of the castle, the captain of the guard called down from the ramparts above the gate. "Who goes there?"

"The guard of Lord Robert de Vere!" the knight responded.

"What business do you have here?"

"We have arrested a woman accused of witchcraft! We have brought her here to be incarcerated until she is tried." The knight called back.

"Open the gates! Allow them entry!" the captain called down to the men charged with protecting the gates.

The gates were opened, and the escort entered the confines of the castle that defended the southern approach to Gloucester.

Meg was dragged roughly from the cart and stumbled as she hit the ground. One of the guards kicked her roughly in the ribs and she doubled over in pain. The captain pulled her up by her hair and spat in her face "A witch eh!" he said staring at the forlorn and dejected woman. "Filthy old hag!" he said, releasing her hair and pushing her away in disgust. His hands had become sticky from the smelly fruit juices that stained Meg's hair, and he wiped them repugnantly on his surcoat. "Dirty bitch!" he concluded.

"We can take her from here." He said turning to de Vere's man.

"You're welcome to her!" he said, spitting at her feet.

"Take her down!" the captain called to two other guards. They both grabbed Meg by the arms and hauled her away. As her feet dragged along the cobbles, one of her shoes came off, and her foot became cut and one of her toenails broke.

The guards dragged her through an entrance and down some stairs, into a narrow hall. The walls were dank with green slime from the water that dripped down them and pooled on the stone floor. Their way was lit by fluttering torches, secured in sconces at regular distances. Meg was dragged down to the end of the hall. One of the guards let go of her and rattled some keys into the lock of a cell, Meg sagged and was pulled up roughly by the other guard. "Get up, you crone!" he shouted, before cutting through the bindings on her hands and throwing her into the cell. She fell onto the damp floor which had a covering of dirty hay, her battered and bruised body screaming in agony at the privations she had suffered during the long journey.

The guards slammed the cell door shut and walked away.

❖

Meg just lay on the floor for a long time. She was tired, hungry, dirty, and cold. The damp atmosphere of the cell seeped into her bones. She was thoroughly miserable, her arms hurt, her ribs hurt, her legs and feet hurt. She had cuts and bruises all over her body, with scrapes to her elbows and knees, which she could do nothing about it. Eventually she uncurled herself and sat up to look around. The cell was very small, about six feet deep and four feet wide. The door was made of heavy oak wood and braced with iron work. There was a small window in the door with small iron uprights, which prevented anyone in the cell even being able to put their hand through. A very small amount of light came through from the torches in the corridor.

With nothing to do but wait, exhaustion finally overcame her, and she fell asleep.

❖

A number of hours later Meg was woken by the sound of the cell door being opened. A bowl half-filled with a thin vegetable soup was thrown in along with a mug of water. The way the bowl had been thrown meant that most of the contents ended up on the floor. Meg greedily drank what remained and also finished off the water.

She realised that she would need strength to endure whatever was going to happen next, and so she determined to eat and drink everything they gave her. She was not yet ready to allow her daughters murderer to defeat her, and the tree above her daughter's corpse needed to be tended. These were the thoughts that sustained her and gave her the courage and fortitude to face the future.

❖

It was only a short time later, that the cell door was opened again, and Meg was dragged out of the cell and taken to another room along the corridor. She was taken inside and placed on a stool. In front of her was a table, on the other side of the table sat two monks. One of the monks dismissed the guards and the door was closed behind them.

"Margaret Bowen, you have been accused of witchcraft. What say you to the accusation."

"I am not a witch, Sir."

"The accusation has been made by a very powerful man. You say you are not a witch. In which case, you are saying that he is a liar?" the monk said and arched his eyebrows.

"He must be a liar, because I am not a witch." Meg responded, her hands were trembling with fear.

The other monk who was acting as a scribe, wrote something down.

"A witch would accuse someone else of lying, wouldn't they? Are you able to prove you are not a witch?"

"How would I do that?" Meg asked, her confusion showed clearly on her face.

"If you are innocent, as you say you are, you will find a way."

"Isn't it for you to prove I am a witch? She stated with a defiance she did not feel.

"No."

"What evidence do you have against me?"

"We do not need to disclose that to you."

"What do you want me to do?" Meg cried out with exasperation.

"Show us that you are not a witch."

"I don't know what to do!"

"Will you consent to an examination?"

"Yes!" Meg said, eager to do whatever they wanted her to, just to be able to prove she was not a witch.

The scribe wrote some more.

The monk held up his hand and called for the guards who were standing outside the door.

"Have this woman washed and cleaned. Then bring her back for examination." He ordered.

Meg was taken from the room and back to her cell, and the door was slammed violently behind her.

❖

A few minutes later the guards reappeared and opened the cell door. They carried pails of water.

"Strip!" one of them demanded.

"Please!" Meg said in distress.

"Strip! Or we will rip your clothes off you!"

"Please turn around then." Meg begged.

"Not a chance! We know your game witch!"

"I am not a witch!" she retorted.

"Well, you look like one to me!" He laughed.

Reluctantly Meg undressed from her ragged clothes and submitted herself to the leering scrutiny of the two guards.

Both guards picked up pails and tipped them over Meg. She jumped with shock as the freezing cold water splashed against her body.

"Turn!" the guard ordered.

Meg turned as commanded and tensed as two more pails of icy water were poured over her.

"Dry yourself!" The guard instructed her, throwing a cloth towards her. She grabbed the cloth from the air and rubbed her body and then her hair dry. In doing so, she managed to remove a lot of the dirt and grime that had accumulated and felt a little better for it.

"Scrubs up well, doesn't she!" one of the guards laughed.

Meg bent to pick up her clothes. "No need for that! You won't need them!" the guard told her. Meg stood up and tried to cover her nakedness. She realised that she had no power to avoid the indignity and humiliation she was being subjected too.

"Follow!" the guard commanded, and she walked out of the door behind one of the guards, the other followed behind. She shuddered with cold, and her wet feet slapped against the damp cobbled floor.

She was taken back to the room with the monks and told to sit on the stool again. Shivering and embarrassed Meg did as she was told.

❖

"Place your mark here." The chief monk said, pushing the parchment across the table towards her, and pointing to the spot he wanted her to sign. Meg had been taught to write her name, unlike many peasants and wrote "MEG" in scratchy writing. As she did so, the thought that she had taught Maud to write her name flashed across her mind.

"You have consented to be examined." The monk stated. "There are a number of parts to the examination process."

Meg nodded, nervously, wondering what she had signed up to.

"The first part is a physical examination. We will look for signs on your body that are irregular and record them. This is not a pleasant process, but be assured that is as onerous for us, as it is embarrassing for you!" The faces of both monks clearly displayed their disgust at the prospect of looking at a woman's body. "Please be assured that a woman's body is offensive to us." Despite her circumstances, Meg was encouraged by this, and considered it far better than being ogled at by the guards.

"First we will examine you standing." The monk specified. "Please stand."

Meg stood, and held one hand across her breasts, and the other covering her other private areas. The monks came around to her side of the table. The scribe removed the stool and put it in the corner of the room.

"Please put your hands down by your sides." The senior monk said, and Meg complied.

The two monks took some time walking around her. Without touching her, the senior monk pointed out any blemishes on her skin, and the scribed nodded and recorded them.

"Please lift your arms" the monk ordered.

Shivering with cold and humiliation, Meg raised her arms until they were both above her head. The senior monk moved his head towards her armpit and examined it closely. He then did the same thing on the other side.

"Please bend forward." He asked, despite the humiliation Meg leant forward and rested her hands on the table on front of her.

The monk completed his examination and then said "Please lay on the table and raise your legs. We are required to examine your secrets."

Meg did as she was told. She had never suffered from such embarrassment or shame, and her face flushed with humiliation.

The monk prodded and probed with a metal implement, and finally having concluded their examination, she was ordered to get off the table and sit back down on the stool, which the scribe had replaced in front of the table.

"You have borne children?" The monk asked.

"A daughter, Sir." Meg replied.

"Please cover yourself." The monk said, handing her a thick blanket. Meg gratefully took the proffered cloth and wrapped it around herself.

"You have willingly submitted yourself to physical examination, without complaint or fuss." The monk said. "That is in your favour."

"Did I pass the inspection?" Meg ventured. She was keen to know more about her situation.

"What we saw and recorded is for the court, not you." The monk responded blankly.

"You will now be returned to your cell. You will be fed. Tomorrow, the second stage of the examination will take place."

"What will be required of me?" Meg asked.

"You will find out tomorrow." The Monk replied.

❖

De Vere visited the gaol early the following morning. He was keen to know what the monks had discovered about the woman he hated more than anyone else in the world.

He had believed that Meg would have died before now, through grief, starvation, or a combination of both.

Surprisingly, he harboured a guilty conscience about the fate of the girl. Her immediate death had not been part of his plan, his intention had been to enjoy her for much longer than a single, hurried encounter, but circumstances had denied him this opportunity, and more than this, had created potential witnesses to his crime. He had thought that by destroying the mother, and deflecting attention away from himself, his problems would recede. However, every time he saw the mother, it brought back memories of a plan foiled.

He also retained the anger that had overtaken him, on the day of his son's christening. The arrogance and disrespect the woman had shown was unacceptable, and the death of de Crecy highlighted his own continued vulnerability.

He met with Richard Beauchamp and the two monks who had been appointed to investigate the case.

"What have you learned?" he demanded of the monks.

The senior monk stood and responded to the question. "Sire, we have completed the physical examination. There are no marks or blemishes worthy of note."

"What else?" de Vere asked, his irritation apparent.

"She is well educated for a peasant. She can write her name. She is an intelligent and resilient woman." The monk replied.

"Does she admit to being a witch?" de Vere demanded.

"She denies the accusation, Sire." The monk responded.

"So, she dares to call me a liar!" de Vere fumed.

"She does Sire."

"Enough!" de Vere shouted, "The insolence of this woman is beyond countenance! How dare she gainsay me!"

"Sire?" the monk asked.

"What is next?" de Vere demanded.

"Questioning, Sire." The monk responded.

"And what does that entail?" de Vere asked, his anger at the bland responses he had received was evidenced by the flush that had risen on his face.

"It depends on what is authorised, Sire."

"Authorised! What does that mean?" De Vere fumed and looked at Beauchamp.

Beauchamp looked at this dangerous, volatile, and powerful local landowner, and considered his relationship with the man against the life of a local peasant woman.

"Why is this so important to you?" Beauchamp asked.

"This devil-woman has destroyed my reputation in the county, she destroyed my son's christening, and she killed my Master-at Arms! What more do you want?" he bellowed in response.

"How did she kill your Master-at-Arms?" Beauchamp queried.

"She used her familiar, "The Archer!" de Vere boomed.

Beauchamp looked at the two monks. "You are authorised to do whatever it takes to get a confession."

"I want her destroyed!" de Vere screamed and stormed out of the room.

❖

Having been returned to her cell, Meg put her ragged clothes back on, and sat in in a corner, with her back against the damp wall. The guards had opened her door a few minutes earlier and given her food and water. She ate what was provided and drank all the water.

As she sat in the wet and dank confines of her incarceration, she contemplated her life, and her future. She reflected on the humiliations she had been subjected to and wondered if she should she give in and succumb to her fate here, or should she fight on and ensure her life retained meaning by ensuring that the enormous elm tree which stood over Maud's grave survived? Maud's life was gone, but she determined that her memory could not be allowed to die; she vowed to herself that the giant tree known as 'Maud's Elm' would thrive and become a living monument to her daughter. She would continue to fight, and she would find a way of ensuring that her nemesis, de Vere would suffer for his evil actions.

Meg was startled from her ruminations by the appearance of a bright light that came through the small aperture of her cell door. Her first thought was "The Virgin has come to claim me!" However, she then heard the clanking of keys and then the cell door opened.

A dark figure was silhouetted against the open door. Old Mother Sawyer entered the cell, and the door closed behind her.

"Mother! How...?" Meg exclaimed in wonder.

"Hush child! I have little time!" the old woman responded.

The old woman administered to Meg's injuries and provided her with a herb drink. The sweet taste revived her flagging spirits and rejuvenated her.

As she combed her hair the old lady said, "I cannot release you from your torment." Meg did not respond; she was still stunned by the appearance of her friend. "But I can give you some options." The woman continued. "The decisions are yours to make, and I cannot guide them. The decisions you make will have consequences, that you alone must bear."

"What options? What consequences?" Meg implored.

"I have done what I could to protect you and your family." Mother Sawyer stated. "Everything I have done, has failed." she continued.

"I have fretted over my actions. Should I have done things differently? Could I have done more?" The regret and pain the old woman was feeling was etched on her face.

"I sought to protect an extraordinary child. Maud." she said. "Maud was an angel, who would have transformed the lives of the people of Swindon Village!" The old lady's face was animated by her conviction.

"Ultimately, the evil of men in this world, triumphed over my modest attempts to prevent this tragedy." She said morosely.

"My attempts to influence fate, and balance what I thought was fair and justified, did not take into account the capacity of greedy men to dominate what would happen." She continued with regret.

"I sometimes fear that evil, greed and ignorance combined, will always defeat compassion, love and decency. I could have, and should have done more, but my faith in humanity blinded me. I am so sorry!" Mother Sawyer wept before the astonished Meg.

"Mother, you did what you could! You were never to blame!" Meg pleaded.

"I am totally to blame Meg." The old woman admitted. "If I had done things differently, history would have been changed!" as she sobbed uncontrollably.

"I cannot believe that anything you could have done would have changed what happened!" Meg beseeched the shattered women in front of her. Meg had always looked up to the advice, guidance, and certainty of the old lady. She had complete faith in her decisions and judgements. Seeing her in such a state of despair was a shock.

"Mother! What can I do?" she asked.

"You have a choice child." Old Mother Sawyer stated. "Everything I have taught you has led to this moment. I have two more tasks to complete before I hand over my mantle to you. One of those tasks will be influenced by your decision alone!" Old Mother Sawyer held out both her palms and revealed in each some hair clippings.

"What are these?" Meg asked, looking at the locks of hair that were being presented to her.

"These are the future of the de Vere fortunes. The fate of his wife and child are yours to decide!"

Realisation of the decision that the old woman was asking her to make resonated with Meg. "An eye for an eye!" she exclaimed.

"It is your decision and will sit on your conscience!" Mother Sawyer responded with a solemn tone.

"They are innocents, like Maud!" Meg countered.

"Exactly!" was all the old woman could say.

"I want to make him suffer! I want to destroy him and his dynasty!" Meg shouted with conviction. "He has destroyed my family, and I will destroy his!" She commanded, with a determination born out of a hatred that could only be held by a parent who had survived the trauma of a murdered child.

"It is your decision..." Mother Sawyer replied, holding out the cuttings to Meg.

Meg touched them and rubbed them through her fingers. "Do it!" She said. Everything she had suffered and endured was emphasised in her response. The love, understanding, and empathy that Meg felt for others was completely obliterated by her hatred for the man who had conspired to destroy her life, and murdered her child, for no other reason than the fact that he had the power to do so.

Evil needed to be confronted with evil, and she was prepared to accept the consequences that such a decision demanded. After all the torments she had suffered Meg declared "You cannot negotiate with a Demon, when your head is in its mouth!"

❖

The unexpected visit from Old Mother Sawyer, had revived Meg's spirits and made her more determined than ever to survive whatever torments she still had to face. However, she could not have imagined in her worst nightmares what she would now be subjected to……

Early the following morning she was awakened and led to another room. With her escort she passed the room in which she had been examined by the two monks. Instead, she was taken further along the corridor, and down some more steps. She arrived in a large room, in which the two monks were present sitting at a table, and there was another individual present also. This man had his head covered in a macabre black mask. His stature was huge, and he was heavily muscled. He stood amongst an array of terrifying machinery. Hooks were suspended from the ceiling, heavy iron rings were bolted into the wall, and large tables with winding machinery stood against the walls.

Meg was marched into the centre of the room and ordered to remain still. Having delivered her to her place in the room, her two guards remained inside the room, and stood next to the door.

The senior monk who had presided over her humiliating examination the previous day spoke. "Today is the second part of your examination." He said gravely. "You have previously consented to such an examination."

A truly frightened Meg asked, "What is this examination?"

"All will become apparent in time." The monk informed her, and then continued:

"You have been unable to prove your innocence of the accusations laid against you. As a result, we will now seek a confession."

"A confession of what?" Meg screeched, "I have done nothing!"

"Today we will seek to ascertain the veracity of your claims." The monk intoned.

"Your examination will involve pain, and through such pain, we will be able to assess the truth." the monk continued.

"Bind her!" he ordered, and the two guards moved forward and grabbed her by the arms. The man in the mask tied her hands behind her back, and she was dragged beneath one of the hooks suspended in the ceiling. A rope noose was placed around her feet and she was hoisted into the air.

The blood rushed into Meg's head as she was lifted upside down.

"Why are you doing this?" she cried.

"We need your confession." The monk replied.

"I have nothing to confess!" Meg screamed.

"That is what all witches say at the start!" the monk replied.

"Make your confession!"

"I have nothing to confess!" Meg repeated desperately.

"So be it! Proceed!" the monk said, nodding at the masked man.

The masked man selected a thick birch wand, it was about five foot long, and half an inch thick. This was the beginnings of the 'rule of thumb' law that allowed a man to beat his wife for any reason, and which was adopted into law in subsequent centuries.

The man drew back his arm and delivered the first strike across Megs back. She tried to recoil against the excruciating pain that lanced across her back, but her bindings resisted her movement.

"CONFESS!" the monk demanded.

"I can't!" Meg whimpered.

The birch struck her again and again, after each stroke the monk demanded the same thing. "CONFESS!" Meg was struck around her body, front, back and each side. The masked man was very professional and ensured that each blow struck a new area of her body to ensure that numbness, inflicted by previous blows did not affect the pain he inflicted with the next strike.

Eventually, Meg succumbed to the pain, and fainted. The monk who acted as scribed recorded that she had made repeated comments stating, "I have nothing to confess."

Fainting did not delay Meg's torment. A bucket of water was poured over her head to revive her, and the inquisition continued.

During the following days she was subjected to a variety of forms of torture. She was placed faced down on a table, and had the bottoms of her feet beaten, she had nails removed from fingers and toes. Throughout the ordeal, and despite the excruciating pain, Meg remained stoic in her refusal to admit the allegations made against her.

❖

After five days of torment, Meg had not relented, and as requested, de Vere had been informed of progress on a daily basis. Having reached the limits of the very narrow boundaries of his patience he demanded more extreme measures. Both Beauchamp and the monks objected, but de Vere would not be denied.

"What more can be done?" he demanded.

"There is a trial known as 'floating'." The monk stated.

"What is that?" de Vere asked, as a smile crossed his lips.

"She will be submerged in water. If she survives, she is a witch!" the monk declared.

"Then we shall 'float' her!" de Vere commanded.

Beauchamp looked horrified and the two monks bowed their heads.

"As you wish, Sire!"

On the sixth day of her incarceration Meg was taken outside the prison walls. Her strength and resilience had been noted. Whether or not this went in her favour, was a matter of conjecture. Her battered and damaged body made it difficult for her to proceed unaided. As a result, she was carried to the banks of the River Severn, the river that had served as a significant defence to the city.

With a rope tied around her neck, she was subjected to the ordeal of "Floating." Two guards threw her into the river and waited for her to sink. Meg who had never learned to swim, thrashed in desperation, and her natural will to survive took over. She went under a number of times but managed to struggle back to the surface. Long billhooks were used to push her under the surface, but each time, she struggled back to the surface. Finally, gasping with the last efforts of her breath, she was dragged by her neck out of the water.

She was laid on the bank like a drowning fish wheezing for air.

On the bank, the monks, accompanied by de Vere, and Beauchamp, and other witnesses, looked on.  De Vere looked directly at the senior monk and questioned him with his stare.  The senior monk noted the unasked question and declared "This proves she is a witch!"

# CHAPTER 25
## A Mockery of Justice

Meg's trial was set for the following day. A witch's trial was a rare occasion and the Town Cryer's announcements would be sure to draw a large audience.

On the morning of the trial, the hall was packed with members of the public, including town dwellers and nobles alike. No-one from Swindon Village was allowed to attend, de Vere had forbidden it. Richard Moryn was tasked with ensuring that none of the villagers could sneak in and ordered his guards to look out for anyone who might disrupt the proceedings.

De Vere was determined that this trial would be concluded without mishap, and he had instructed the guards to deal harshly with any sign of disorder.

Richard Beauchamp sat as presiding judge, in his role as Governor, and Constable of Gloucester.

De Vere acted as Chief Prosecutor.

A local magistrate had been appointed to defend Meg; his name was Edward Manning.

In an ante room away from the main hall, de Vere had arranged a pre-trial meeting with Manning.

"Manning! You understand what is required?" de Vere asked.

"Sire?"

"Your role is simple. Do the minimum required to do your job, but do not try to be too clever. I am paying you well for your services!"

"I am at your command, Sire!" Manning responded.

"The evidence is overwhelming and there is no point in delaying the inevitable!"

"I agree wholeheartedly Sire!"

❖

In the cells, Meg had been given an opportunity to bath, and had clean clothes prepared for her. She had also eaten. Although she was accused of being a witch, de Vere had calculated that the evidence that he had prepared, would be enough to convict her, and did not want the audience in the court to have any excuse to feel any sympathy for her. Her injuries were covered by her clothes, and she would be presented in her best condition.

The senior monk who had presided over Meg's examination, entered Meg's cell.

"Kneel child!" he said. Meg knelt on the hard stone floor and bent her head.

The monk put a hand on her head and muttered a brief prayer, and then beckoned her to stand.

"Would you like to profess your sins child?" he asked.

"No thank you, Father. I don't think God resides here!"

"You still have time to admit the accusations and offer your soul to the protection of God."

"My fate will not be judged by God, father, but by evil men..."

The monk crossed himself and said, "God help you child!"

The monk exited the cell, followed by Meg. Behind them two guards escorted them to the court room.

❖

As Meg entered the courtroom with her escort the excited hubbub quieted for a few moments, while people tried get a look at the witch! They had wondered what a witch looked like, and the general consensus was disappointment. The conversation resumed as they discussed the fact that Meg did not look like the description of the depraved harridans they had been exposed to from the pulpits of their churches by the local clergy.

What they saw was a woman standing proud and tall. De Vere looked over at her, and momentarily wondered if he should have presented her as the crowd expected to see her. He shook his head to dispel his own doubts and nodded towards Beauchamp. They were ready to begin.

"Order!" Beauchamp bellowed bringing gavel down onto the table at the same time. "The court is now in progress. Once again, the audience hushed, as they strained to hear the evidence against this woman.

Meg was also interested in the evidence, as this would be the first opportunity that she would have to hear it.

De Vere began to lay out his case. He began by describing the events on the day of his son's christening.

The audience did not seem to be overly impressed by de Vere's own sense of self-importance and entitlement.

"My Master-at-Arms was killed by this witch's familiar!" he exclaimed, and paused to allow the statement to sink in.

"Yes! Her familiar! An entity known only as the "Archer!"

The crowd murmured their surprise. Everyone had heard of "The Archer!", all of a sudden, this case had become much more interesting!

He described the circumstances in which de Crecy had been killed, including the unique arrow that was used. He held up the arrow for the audience to see.

"She summoned this demon to kill my knight! Despite an immediate search of the area, he had simply vanished!"

The excited atmosphere in the courtroom grew.

"Everyone knows about this entity... I will not call him a man, because no-one knows his name, no-one has seen his face, and no-one knows where he comes from!" de Vere was enjoying his own performance.

"He appeared at the precise moment that this woman, needed him!" he continued.

"I submit that he cannot be anything other than the spawn of the Devil! Conjured by this witch for her own protection!" and with a flourish he pointed directly at Meg.

The crowd gasped.

De Vere moved onto the examination conducted by the monks and called the senior monk as a witness. After formal introductions, and identifying the credentials of the monk, de Vere asked,

"You examined the witch?"

"The accused, Sire!"

"No matter! Did she admit to her crimes?"

"She did not Sire."

"I take it she was subjected to a 'Vigorous' examination?"

"She was Sire," the monk answered.

"And still, she did not admit to her crimes?"

"No Sire, she was remarkably resilient…"

"No Father! I put it to you that she was protected from pain, by the Devil himself!"

The monk paused; he knew that Meg had suffered severe pain throughout her ordeal and had felt sympathy for her.

"I couldn't say Sire." He said non-committedly.

"Have you ever known anyone else that has been subjected to such an examination, to be able to resist providing a full confession?"

"Never, Sire."

"And there you have it! Proof positive that she in league with the Devil and is protected by him!" He extolled with glee.

Once again he pointed towards Meg, drawing the attention of the onlookers to her.

"Look at her! Demure, innocent-looking, butter wouldn't melt in her mouth! She is not what you would expect a witch to look like, is she?" he said, and the courtroom was captivated by his logic.

"If you were the Devil, would you give people what they expected to see? Why would he make it that easy? He would disguise her, so that she could do his bidding without drawing attention!" his rhetorical questions demanded no answer, just agreement, and the crowd murmured in confirmation.

"There is another piece of evidence, that is indisputable!" he called out. He again addressed the monk.

"Did you submit the witch, sorry accused…" he paused and turned to the audience raising his eyebrows as he did so. His performance drew the mirth form the onlookers that he had wanted, peals of laughter filled the room.

"Did you submit her to the process of 'floating'?" he asked.

"We did Sire."

"And this process was witnessed by an authority?"

"The Governor of the City, Sire!"

"The Governor of the City, no less!" de Vere pointed towards the man who was presiding as judge. Beauchamp raised his eyebrows in response to de Vere's theatrics.

"Please describe this process." he requested.

The monk coughed, before saying, "The process is known as 'floating', Sire. The accused is thrown into water. Everyone is expected to sink, and if that is the case, the person cannot be a witch." De Vere nodded his head in understanding, and encouragement.

The monk continued, "If the accused floats, then the Devil is aiding them, and helping them to rise to the surface."

"I see," said de Vere, rubbing his chin with his hand to create the impression of being deep in thought. In reality, he was trying to raise the tension, and allow the audience the time to let the information sink in.

"I understand that she was given multiple opportunities to be able to prove she was not a witch?" he inquired.

"Yes Sire." Came the reply.

"Even to the point of pushing her under using billhooks, is that correct?"

"Yes Sire." Came the reply.

"And yet she rose to the surface, time and time again?" he asked incredulously. "What, therefore, is your conclusion?"

"According to the procedure, then she is a witch!" the monk concluded with a note of regret in his voice.

"She is a what?" De Vere pressed.

"A witch! Sire!"

"A witch! A witch! You have heard it from a man of the cloth! Who amongst you can hold any doubts? This woman is a witch!" He exclaimed loudly, with a delighted expression on his face, as he turned and invited the crowd to dissent.

There was a deafening silence.

"I rest my case!"

❖

Meg stood and listened to the evidence against stoically. She was not invited to speak during the whole spectacle and would have had nothing to say on any case. The magistrate appointed to defend her, played his role in perfunctory fashion, and did nothing to challenge any of the evidence that had been provided.

"Your name?" he asked.

"Margaret Bowen." Meg replied.

"Do you work?"

"No Sir."

"Where do you live?"

"I have no home sir."

"You have no employment, and no abode! How do you survive?"

"I beg for alms sir." Meg said, not wanting to involve any of her friends in the proceedings.

"So, you are a homeless, unemployed, beggar?"

"Yes sir."

"Some might call you a wart on the backside of society! You rely on the generosity of others for your continued survival!"

The audience growled their discontent at these revelations. Any empathy they had, had now vanished.

"But you are not a witch?"

"No sir!"

If the crowd had been hostile to Meg after hearing de Vere's evidence, they had no sympathy whatsoever for Meg after the intervention of her defence.

"The representations on behalf of the defence are concluded." The corrupt magistrate finished.

Meg was returned to her cell to await her judgement.

❖

An adjournment was called, to allow Sir Richard Beauchamp time to take refreshments and mull his decision. He was not personally convinced that Margaret Bowen was a witch. He was an intelligent and educated man, and despite de Vere's theatrics, which had played on the fears and gullibility of the audience in the court, he found it difficult to give any of the evidence that had been provided any credence.

"Demons! Familiars!" he laughed at the notion, whilst sucking on a chicken bone, "Superstition, and nonsense! Designed to hold authority over the masses!" he thought to himself. "And 'Floating'!" He mused, "What a ridiculous idea! Whoever thought that one up possessed a truly twisted and perverse logic!"

However, he realised that he would never be able to openly convey such thoughts, especially in a court of law! It would be considered to be blasphemous, and besides he reflected, keeping people in check by playing on their fears, was what held society together, and he had no issues with that concept.

He picked up his goblet, and drank some wine, "No!" he said to himself, whatever sympathy he had for Margaret Bowen was irrelevant. He did not know what was driving de Vere's hatred for this defenceless and harmless woman, but whatever it was, it was of no concern to him. Even if, in his own mind, no real evidence had been presented, the audience had accepted it, the word of a man of the cloth had confirmed the accusation, and he, himself, had witnessed the 'floating' charade! Whatever his personal feelings were, there was only one judgement he could make...

Richard Beauchamp had resided over trials for murderers, rapists, thieves and robbers. In all cases, he had listened to the evidence and made a judgement according to his conscience. He had always believed that his judgements were fair and justified, his integrity in making those judgements intact. He had no issue with pronouncing judgements that sent people to their deaths, and yet he felt uncomfortable with the verdict he felt compelled to make in this case. This was the first 'witch' trial he had presided over, and he fervently hoped he would never be asked to do so again……

❖

The court was reconvened. Announcements had been dispatched to the local taverns, and markets, where members of the public who had crowded the gallery of the court had repaired during the adjournment to feast and deliberate on the extraordinary events of the day. The discussions had been animated, as citizens debated the evidence, and the character of the accused. Their collective ignorance gave no room for anything other than a guilty verdict, and their macabre deliberations focussed on the nature of the punishment the 'witch' should receive.

Without a single exception, they all rushed back to the courtroom, and bustled their way in. The gossip had spread across the city, and the session designated for the judgement meant that far more people were keen to attend than the previous sessions. As a result, the hall was packed to the rafters, and was far more boisterous than previously. The crowd had been able to enjoy the hospitality of the local hostelries and more than a few of the gathering had consumed more wine or ale than was good for them.

The main characters of the spectacle resumed their places in the courtroom. Beauchamp resumed his seat, de Vere sat at his table with a contented grin on his face, and the magistrate sat down at his table, looking very smug. The purse he had been given during the recess, felt reassuringly heavy on his pocket.

Last of all, Meg was brought up from the cells, and was made to stand directly in front of the presiding judge. Beauchamp stood before the masses to pronounce his judgement.

"Margaret Bowen, you have been accused of the heinous crime of witchcraft. That accusation is exacerbated by the fact that you used your craft for the purpose of murder. A further accusation is that you summoned a demon to perpetrate said murder, which was accomplished. In so doing, an innocent and valued servant of Sir Richard de Vere perished."

The crowd buzzed with anticipation.

"Lord de Vere has provided evidence to support his accusation, and further evidence from members of our sacred church has been submitted. No substantive evidence has been provided from your defenders, that would allow me to make a different judgement about your culpability."

The arousal of the crowd became more animated.

"The evidence presented is incontrovertible. My judgement is the only judgement that I could possibly make in the circumstances."

The onlookers jostled each other, and the atmosphere became heavy with expectancy.

"My judgement is that you are guilty as charged. You are found guilty of acts of witchcraft, and murder!"

The people who were gathered in the chamber cheered and slapped each other on the back. It was clear to Beauchamp, that his judgement was unanimously supported by the people of his city.

Beauchamp paused and placed a black square of cloth on his head.

"As governor of this city, and constable of the county, I hereby sentence you to death for the offence of witchcraft and murder!"

The assembled members of the public cheered the proclamation. Beauchamp banged his gavel on the table in front of him. "Silence!" he demanded.

When the audience had composed themselves and a hush had fallen across the hall, Beauchamp continued,

"My judgement is that you be burned at the stake for your crimes!"

The crowd became noisily animated again, and Beauchamp was forced to use his gavel again.

"You will be taken from this place tomorrow morning and put to death in the place you committed your crimes. May God have mercy on your soul!" he concluded.

De Vere beamed at the additional irony, that not only was his nemesis going to be destroyed, but the site of her death would be her own daughter's grave!

Meg stood in dignified silence. She knew that the judgement had been a foregone conclusion, and that there had never been the slightest possibility of a different outcome.

De Vere left the courthouse in triumph and made his way back to his manor in Oxenton, along with his retinue. A happier man could not be found in the whole of Gloucestershire, and he was looking forward watching Meg Bowen die in excruciating pain the following morning.

❖

At the precise time that the verdict in Meg's trial was pronounced, Isobel de Vere suffered a severe migraine, and muscle pain.

"What is it, My Lady?" the Head of her Household enquired. A worried look creased his face, as he tried to steady his stricken mistress, who was doubled over in pain.

"Maid! Maid!" he cried out, and two young servants scurried into the room. "Fetch some mulled wine!" he demanded, as he gently steered the young woman towards a seat.

"Hurry!" he cried, as the two servants rushed from the room.

They returned quickly with a jug of wine and a goblet.

The head servant poured a measure and held it to the trembling lips of the Lady Isobel. She swallowed some of the wine and relaxed a little.

The Head Servant along with some other staff, fussed around the young woman, but within hours the muscle pain was affecting her abdomen, and she began to vomit. Her staff were becoming more concerned about her welfare.

"My Lady! You are sweating severely!" the servant observed, "We must take you to bed and call the physician!" he stated and ushered to two serving girls to assist him in lifting up the lady of the house. Lady Isobel was almost a dead weight, but they managed to support her to her rooms. The Head Servant left the two maids to help their mistress into bed and rushed down to the servant quarters.

"Send for the physician immediately; and send one of the guards to inform Sir Robert!" he cried. A young man who had been skulking in the kitchens, stood to attention before rushing out of the room.

The physician appeared around an hour later and immediately presented himself to the lady of the manor. When he examined her, he found her suffering from delirium, she was muttering incoherently, struggling to breathe, and sweating profusely.

While the physician was administering to Isobel de Vere, a shattering scream erupted in another part of the manor. He rushed out to be confronted by the wet nurse of de Vere's son. She was screaming and incomprehensible.

"What is it woman!" he demanded.

"The baby, sir!"

Hurried along by distressed member of de Vere's household, the physician arrived at the room where de Vere's son was accommodated. He was taken over to the cot in which de Vere's son and heir lay. He looked down into the cot, and observed that the infants' face was bloated and deep red. He lifted the child and brought its face close to his own. He placed his ear against the child's mouth and tried to discern a breath. He could feel nothing. Desperately, held the child upside down by its feet and slapped it on the back two or three times. There was no response from the child. He felt the child's chest for any kind of heartbeat. There was nothing! He bowed his head in defeat. There was nothing he could do for the infant. De Vere's child was dead!

He immediately returned to Isobel's room. Her condition had deteriorated, she had continued to vomit, and was unresponsive to his ministrations. Her eyes had rolled up into her head, and her breathing was ragged and distressed. Her chest and face were a deep red, and it was clear she was finding it impossible to breathe. The physician realised that he was out of his depth. He did not know how to save this young woman......

❖

De Vere arrived at his manor house late in the evening. Despite the message he had received, during his journey back, all of his thoughts had been occupied by his plans to attend the execution of Margaret Bowen the following morning. He thought about the time he needed to leave, and the arrangements that needed to be made. He thought that the message he had received had been an exaggeration of normal 'women's problems'...

The horses of de Vere and his guard clattered through the gates of the Manor house and came to abrupt stop in the courtyard.

He recognised that there was a problem in the household immediately by the way the stable hands attended him and his knights. Their heads were bowed, and they quickly removed the horses to the stables without delay, as soon as the knights had dismounted. De Vere's joy was tempered with trepidation as he entered his home. He was greeted by his Head of Household, standing next to him was a man who he recognised as the family physician.

Both stood with heads bowed and their demeanour was an immediate cause for concern.

"What has happened?" de Vere demanded.

"Sire…. We have terrible news….!"

De Vere was informed that his son had died in the early afternoon, and that his wife had succumbed in the early evening. The Physician informed him that both had contracted a virus that had come be known as 'Sweating Sickness'. The origin of the illness was unknown; however, it had an interesting convention of attacking the richer people in society, rather than the poor, which was unusual at this time, and became known by peasants as 'Stup-Gallant'.

# CHAPTER 26

## Decisions have Consequences

As the sun was breaking, and the darkness began to recede, Meg was awoken from her fitful slumber. The principal monk entered the cell.

"Meg, I have come to give a final opportunity to repent your sins."

"I have nothing to repent. I have no need for forgiveness from God. Those who have condemned me are the ones who should be praying for forgiveness!" she answered.

"Meg! You cannot say that! We are talking about the grace of God himself!" the monk replied, as he blanched at her words, and was reminded himself that it was his evidence that had ultimately convicted her.

"God is not in this place!" Meg responded defiantly. "The evil of greedy and lustful men infect this place!"

The monk crossed himself but did not reply.

As he led Meg out of the dungeon, accompanied by two guards he muttered prayers under his breath. The prayers were not for Meg, but for himself and his fear for his own immortal soul. Meg was escorted along the corridor and up into the courtyard to be loaded onto a cart, for the journey back to Swindon Village, and her execution.

Meg was lifted up into the cart and two guards clambered up with her. She was made to stand and tied to a post so that she could be seen by everyone. The cart and her escort straggled its way across the cobbles and out through the castle gates onto the main thoroughfare. Because of the time of day, there were few people on the streets to cheer or jeer her. Meg was pleased at this, as she did not want to go through the fuss and nonsense that surrounded her when she was first brought to Gloucester Gaol. She was now resigned to her fate and really just wanted to get the whole thing over.

The cart winded its way along the road to Cheltenham, and Meg felt the pleasant breeze on her face. She thought about all the things that had happened, and her own part in them. Had she ever done anything to deserve such a punishment? She considered that she might have been guilty of the sin of pride, she was proud of her achievements, she was proud of her skills, she was proud of how she had been perceived by the people she had met during her life. She had been proud of her husband and her daughter. Was the sin of pride really so wicked as to bring about the terrible consequences that had been wrought upon her and her family. If there was any justice in life, then surely any retribution should have been hers to endure alone, and not involved the two innocents that were her loving husband and daughter?

She pondered on other aspects of her life. Should she regret the decision she made with Old Mother Sawyer? Was that meeting real anyway, or had she been suffering from delusions? No! she thought, I would make the same decision again, if I had the chance. De Vere had destroyed her life for no other reason than he had the power to do so. He deserved his fate.

She considered her relationship with Old Mother Sawyer, and wondered if she was the source of her woes? She thought about "The Archer" was he really a conjuring from her own imagination and will? She dismissed the ideas; both were decent people, trying to protect those who were unable to protect themselves.

"No!" she thought at length, it was the pure evil in the world that was the cause of her misery.

Greedy, arrogant, self-absorbed, individuals, some of whom already had more than most people could ever dream of, but wanted to take more.

For people like this, nothing was ever enough, and they were prepared to do anything to get what they wanted.

They exerted power over people, they bullied, killed people, and abused their authority, without conscience or care, they lied and cheated, with no thought to the damage they did to others...

"No!" she thought, she, and her friends were not to blame for what had happened.

Once again, she thought about the visit from Old Mother Sawyer and the pact that she had made in the cells of Gloucester Gaol. She pondered her involvement with the Maids of Alney. Was she really a witch, had she done anything to deserve her fate? Were the Maids of Alney also guilty? Were the women she knew really witches? Had old Mother Sawyer really appeared in her cell? Or was it all a figment of a tortured and fevered imagination? She really did not know.

❖

Finally, the wagon arrived at its destination, as they approached Meg stared at the grand tree. The giant Elm, whose growth had been extraordinary, stood tall and majestic. The tree was in full leaf, the branches swayed in the breeze, and she imagined it was welcoming her home.

The irony that this would be the place of her death was not lost on her. In some respects, she was pleased, she would be close to her daughter, and this would be a less lonely place to die.

Did the judge Richard Beauchamp realise this? she wondered. She did not blame him for his judgement, just as she did not blame the monk whose testimony had signed her death warrant. These men were just pawns being moved around the board, by the malevolent character of Robert de Vere. If the Devil truly walked the earth, then it took the form of her brother-in-law Godfrey Bowen, and certainly Lord Robert de Vere!

The cart stopped, and Meg was left waiting in it. She watched the preparations that were being made. A post was planted into the ground, and faggots of kindling were piled around the base.

A small crowd had gathered, made up of some of the villagers, officials, and the people of Gloucester who had the time, money, and morbid inclination to watch the death of a witch... The villagers were not there to gloat, unlike the citizens of Gloucester. They were there to observe and record in their own memories the tragedy that had unfolded- a tragedy which would be told to future generations, and would be visible through the magnificent tree, known as 'Maud's Elm.'

All were present to witness the final chapter of the appalling set of circumstances that had afflicted Meg Bowen and her family, and the travesty that had taken place. They were there to ensure that these events would never be forgotten.

The officials were there to do a job, and they included the Captain of the Guard for Gloucester Goal, together with the six men who formed Meg's escort, Sir Richard

Beauchamp, and the senior monk. The guards, including the Captain, had been quite sombre during the journey, and had not insulted Meg, or abused her during the journey. This was a complete contrast to how they had treated during the previous days. Meg did wonder about their change in attitude but could come to no conclusion. She did not know that Richard Beauchamp had ordered them to show some respect and allow a condemned woman dignity in her final hours.

Surprisingly, Meg observed, Robert de Vere was not present. Surely, he would be here to gloat over her demise? However, she could not see him.

❖

In the small crowd, Old Mother Sawyer, and the other members of the Maids of Alney looked on. She made brief eye contact with Meg. She thought that Meg looked serene and at peace. The grief that she had expressed over the past months was no longer visible on her face, and Old Mother Sawyer wondered if this was because Meg knew that she was about to be with her daughter again.

Out of sight of the group surrounding the pyre, and deep in the shadows of the nearby woodland, 'The Archer' observed proceedings. He knew he was a wanted man, convicted of murder in his absence, and would be hanged if he was caught. 'The Archer' was a man who undertook meticulous planning and was generally averse to risk. However, on this day, he was prepared to make a gamble that could cost him his life.

As he stood in the gloom provided by the trees, he considered his position. He had sworn to protect Meg, even if it cost him his own life. He had been given a second chance to succeed. Where he had failed to protect Maud, he was determined not to fail in protecting Meg.

❖

Finally, it seemed as if the preparations were complete.

The workmen had pushed and pulled at the stake to ensure it was secure beneath the gigantic tree. The kindling had been spread around the base in sufficient quantity to satisfy the officials who were overseeing the proceedings.

Meg was taken from the cart and helped across the faggots that formed the pyre surrounding the stake. After tying Meg securely to the pole, the guards retreated.

The monk stepped forward and gave a short benediction, and then returned to his place amongst the officials.

Meg looked out across the crowd of people who had gathered. Her countenance was serene. She recognised many of faces of people she had shared happy times with, people who she had helped, and people who had helped her when she had been in need. They held their heads bowed, but she smiled her love and appreciation for them anyway.

With Meg secured to the post on top of the kindling and faggots, Beauchamp saw no reason to delay the inevitable. He looked towards one of the guards who held a lighted torch in his hands. He nodded for him to proceed, and the guard moved forward.

In the distance Meg could see dust rising up along the road. The clattering of horse's hooves soon accompanied the billowing cloud, and the crowd and officials alike turned to see what was happening.

Beauchamp held up his hand to halt the guard with the torch, while he waited to find out who was causing the disturbance. The guard stopped where he was and waited for further instructions.

❖

Robert de Vere thrashed his horse, determined to be at the burning in time. The flanks of the horse were lathered with sweat, and the animal was frothing at the mouth from the over-exertion it was being forced to make. It was nearly on its last legs, but still de Vere spurred it on.

During the course of the night, de Vere's world had crashed.

The grief at the loss of both his wife and child had overwhelmed him, and in typical fashion, he lashed out at those around him. He had ordered that both the Head of his Household, and the physician were hanged for their incompetence immediately. He had then raged throughout his home, beating his staff whilst shouting and screaming about the conspiracy that had killed his family, and the part the witch had played.

His entire staff, terrified by the ogre this man represented, fled in terror. Even his men-at-arms had deserted their lord, convinced that anyone who remained would be put to death.

De Vere had portrayed himself as being utterly demented. As a result, he had been forced to stay the night by himself with only his dead family for company.

Without a further outlet for his murderous rage, he sat and drank a significant portion of his wine cellar, before collapsing drunk.

He had woken mid-morning in a drunken fug, and it took him sometime to recall the events of the previous day. When realisation struck him, that this had not been a dream, his rage rose again.

He stormed out of the manor, managed to saddle his own horse, and drove the poor beast close to bursting a blood vessel in his desperation to attend the witch's execution.

❖

De Vere's horse came to a shuddering halt just behind the crowd that had gathered in front of the pyre. He jumped down immediately and began to push his way through tight group of people.

Everyone quickly moved out of the way at the sight of this crazed man, who smelt of sweat and alcohol. His hair was greasy and unkempt, and his clothing was dirty and stained. He looked worse than any common street beggar, and it took some time for the gathering to realise exactly who this was.

He pushed his way to the front and screamed abuse at Meg. "You whore of Satan! you witch! You have killed them with your sorcery!"

The crowd looked on in amazement, the officials regarded de Vere with a level of contempt clearly believing that his highly-strung nature had finally cracked and that the man was clearly insane.

De Vere continued to hurl abuse at Meg, and after a very short time, Beauchamp had had enough, and nodded towards the guard to restrain the demented man.

Before the guards could reach him, de Vere rushed forward and seized a flaming torch from the hands of one of the guards who was holding it. He ran towards the pyre and stooped to light it.

Old Mother Sawyer looked up into Meg's eyes. Meg nodded imperceptibly.

Old Mother Sawyer looked into the deep shadows of the nearby wood, and although 'The Archer' was concealed from sight, her gaze focused on him directly. She nodded her head imperceptibly.

The flames touched the kindling, the kindling ignited.

De Vere screamed "Die! WITCH!"

Meg screamed back so that all could hear. "I have become the Witch you wanted me to be!"

A red fletched arrow flew from the thicket of trees and struck de Vere in the heart, he fell forward into the kindling. The monster was dead.

Old Mother Sawyer muttered something under her breath and stared at Meg, Meg held her stare defiantly.

At the same time as the arrow struck de Vere, the flames around pyre exploded, creating a huge ball of flame, followed by a giant cloud of smoke that appeared and obscured everything from view.

❖

The gathering of people, both peasants, visitors, officials, and guards alike, stood and stared in shock and amazement. What on earth had just happened?

Beauchamp regained his wits and checked to see if the people around him were safe and well. He had determined that the only casualties had been Margaret Bowen and Robert de Vere and he ordered the guards to approach the smoking pyre. There was no point in trying to pursue the man who had fired the arrow, he would be long gone by now.

The guards spluttered and coughed their way through the smoke and tried to beat down the flames and put the fire out. Some villagers came forward to help, and after a while the flames were doused.

Beauchamp heard some shouts of confusion and walked with the other officials towards what was left of the execution pyre. Men were crossing themselves, muttering prayers, and pointing.

He looked down and saw that there were no bodies! Meg Bowen and Robert de Vere had completely vanished!

The monk crossed himself "It is a miracle!" He muttered, as he stared at the massive, unblemished Elm tree.

Two other people also vanished on this day. Old Mother Sawyer and 'The Archer' were never seen from that day forward. As far as local people were concerned neither was ever seen in Gloucestershire again…….

The official record indicated that 'circumstances unexplained' occurred on that day. They noted that de Vere was seen to be in a state of 'high excitement' and possibly even 'probably' been driven insane by the news that his wife and only child had both died from a fever on the night before the execution. They concluded that there was no evidence of 'supernatural' involvement in their deaths.

The disappearance of the bodies of both Margaret Bowen and Robert de Vere were explained by the explosion that had been witnessed when de Vere had caused the pyre to be lit. The persons that investigated the strange occurrence concluded that the explosion probably blasted the bodies to small fragments that could not be collected. They also suggested that de Vere himself might have caused gunpowder to have been secreted in the faggots designed to burn the alleged 'Witch' in order to create a spectacle at the execution designed to show an ignorant audience that supernatural powers were at work, and in so doing prove once and for all, his accusations against her.

This hypothesis was supported by witness evidence about de Vere's obsession with Margaret Bowen from both the trial at Gloucester and evidence from the people who lived in Swindon Village about his treatment of her after the death of her daughter.

A verdict was made that de Vere had been suffering from insanity for some time, and that the unfortunate death of his family had exacerbated his condition and driven him totally beyond reason. His malady had been responsible for his actions against Margaret Bowen, and others who were not named. Evidence regarding his treatment of tenants and other innocents were submitted by his former bodyguard of knights, who were keen to deflect attention from their own actions.

The deaths of de Vere's wife and child were confirmed by another eminent physician as being caused by the strange and currently prevalent virus known as 'English Sweating Sickness' that had afflicted a number of noble families in the country. This physician concluded that it was highly unlikely that supernatural powers were a contributing factor, because of its prevalence across the country.

'The Archer' was still considered to be responsible for a number of murders across the county. The deaths of at least four other citizens were attributed to him. He was not considered to be 'demon' but a real person, and therefore his status as an outlaw was confirmed and the warrants for his arrest, remained in force.  His culpability for the death of de Vere was not provable, and therefore dismissed.

No-one was able to ascertain why de Vere had so much hatred for a much-loved and popular woman as Margaret Bowen, who had never done any harm to anyone.  They could not understand the vehemence of his loathing, which had driven him to seek to destroy her reputation, cause her to become destitute, and demanded her death as a witch.

# CHAPTER 27
## A Death Bed Confession

Robert de Vere was never seen again. With his death his entitlement also died. With the death of his family, and having no other surviving relatives, his own estates were subject to "Escheat" and forfeited, and they passed into the hands of another.

The records of his life and deeds were gradually lost in the mists of time. His status, titles, lands and existence perished with him. The only memory of this man, was in the stories, passed down by word of mouth, from family to family, through the ages, that recounted an evil and arrogant monster, who actions destroyed the lives of an innocent family, and the terrible price he paid, when retribution was finally taken for his crimes.

Many decades later, the story of Maud and her family continued to be passed down through the families of the village. Nothing was written down, as the local people did not have the education or means to record the tale in a written form.

However, the story acted as both a reminder and a warning to future generations about the avarice of landlords, and their contempt for normal people. The cottage itself had remained empty ever since the day of Meg's execution. Although the cottage had been well maintained, and despite its favourable position within the village, it had been impossible to rent it out to potential new tenants.

Richard Moryn and his descendants had desperately tried to encourage new tenants to live there. It had been offered to a number of prominent and well-respected families in the village, with the enticement of a freehold, but all of them had declined. This was despite the fact that it would have provided better accommodation than they currently enjoyed.

The cottage gradually fell into disrepair, and became less and less attractive to potential renters, until it became so run-down, that it was almost uninhabitable.

❖

One day, an old man took up residence in the dilapidated cottage that had once belonged to Meg Bowen. He had appeared overnight and seemed happy to live within its crumbling walls.

At first no-one took much notice of him, and people accepted that this aged person needed a place to live. They did not begrudge him the sanctuary provided by the ancient dwelling. He was not a vagabond and was able to sustain himself. He was able to pay for his provisions, and never caused any problems within the village. He kept himself to himself. He was pleasant to everyone that enquired about his welfare, and soon became just another fixture within the village.

The village landlord collected his rent regularly and was happy that someone was at last providing an income from the abandoned cottage.

People began to take more notice of him, when they realised that he would spend every single day sitting beneath the huge tree known to them all as 'Maud's Elm'. The tree had grown substantially over the years, and now, was a landmark known to everyone in the region.

No-one knew the man's name, and surprisingly, no-one ever asked him. The villagers were content to call him 'The Old Man' or 'Oldie', and he was content to be referred to in that way.

They first began to notice him on their way to the market in Cheltenham.

He was there every single day come rain or shine. He was there in the spring, summer, autumn, and winter. He sat under the tree, and appeared to be talking to it, or talking to someone else next to it, who could not be seen.

People would wave and greet him as they passed. "Good morning. Oldie!" they would say. He would just wave back and say, "Good morning!" politely.

❖

One day the old man was again seen at his lonely vigil. The bright sunny day warmed his aching bones, and he knelt under the massive tree that now stood more than 100 feet tall, and 15 feet wide.

It seemed as if he was talking to it, and more surprisingly, as if the tree was listening to him. Some of its limbs almost seemed to bow down to touch him.

The old man's eyes glazed over, and a small tear escaped from the corner of one of them. As it ran down his weather-worn cheek, he spoke.

"Oh Maud! My Love! You were taken too soon from this earth, from me!" he lamented.

"My heart has been lonely for you, all these years! Although I have travelled far and wide, your moonlight beam has lighted my path in times of sadness!" He cried as he bent forward and placed some flowers at the base of the tree.

"I have strewn your grave in fancy's dream, with wreaths of meadow flowers!"

He looked up into the gently swaying branches, which moved gracefully in the breeze. "When I first met you as a young and careless boy, my heart was yours. I thought our love would have been a thing of joy, that would last a lifetime, until we both declined."

He reached forward and broke off a small budding branch from the tree.

"With a bleeding heart, I pluck a young green bough from this tree, whose obscure root, many years ago, drew dead blood from you to sustain itself." He took the small leafy twig and placed it carefully in the pocket of his shirt.

"Time has placed his hand upon my head, but the thought of being with you once more, makes my heart young again." He put his hand over his heart, above the pocket that contained the specimen from the tree.

He looked down again at the base of the tree and laid himself down, his arms spread wide. "Upon thy lowly grave, sweet love, I fling my weary bones; 'Ere long, we shall both meet before the King of King's, and Throne of Thrones..."

❖

As time went on, the old man was accepted in the village more and more. This acceptance built to such an extent, that villagers started to notice that he was not seen sitting beneath the tree as regularly as normal.

With a sense of community concern, local people visited the cottage and found that the old man was seriously ill and unable to rise from his bed.

Not knowing what to do to ease his suffering, they called on the services of the old woman who lived in the village, and who had provided help and assistance for all ailments, injuries, wounds and maladies that were suffered by its inhabitants.

She was renowned for her abilities, providing potions and remedies for the huge range of problems that were regularly encountered by the local people, and had she had been responsible for the successful births of all the children in the village.

No child had ever died under her watch. As such, her healing abilities were widely sought after, and everyone had absolute trust in her skills.

❖

Known as 'Old Mother' the ancient woman entered the cottage and sat at the bedside of the old man.

"Walter?" She said, "It is you! You finally returned after all these years?

His rheumy eyes looked over at her, despite his failing eyesight, recognition dawned. "I had to come back and end my days here."

"Where have you been?" the old lady asked.

"I have travelled to many places and done many things. But my heart always remained here."

"I know, sweet Walter…"

"I need to make my peace with the world…" Walter coughed as he spoke, his voice was wheezy.

"I need to tell you my story, so that you understand. I have never forgiven myself for not protecting Maud!"

"Tell me your tale, Walter." The old lady said gently.

"I loved Maud. She was my heart and soul!" he sobbed.

"I know, Walter…" The old lady responded with tenderness, as she looked down on this frail man.

"I was captured by Godfrey's men on the day Maud died. I did not know their purpose at the time, and had I known, I would have acted differently." he said.

"I arrived too late…. It was Godfrey and de Vere that attacked her. They had plotted against you and your family, and Godfrey used his men to prevent me from protecting Maud. I killed Godfrey, and I thought that Maud had escaped. That was the second mistake I made that day…." He mourned.

"De Vere got away. I thought he had run, but now I think he tracked Maud, and killed her.... That was my third mistake..." he began sobbing again.

"Calm yourself, sweet Walter." The old lady said, "You could not have done more than you did!" and she stooped to mop his sweating brow.

"I killed Godfrey's men the next day, for the part they played in the plot. It was nothing more than revenge, and it did not change what had happened to Maud...." he continued.

"After Maud died, I vowed to protect Meg..." he said. "I killed Hubert de Crecy when he tried to harm Meg. But I was not able to prevent her suffering at the hands of de Vere..." His breath rasped as he struggled to breath, so desperate was he to finish his story.

"I felt as if I had failed yet again... Until I found out that she lived, but was condemned to burn at Maud's Elm..."

Tears now poured down his cheeks as he recounted his sad tale. The old lady put her hand on top of his and squeezed it gently.

"I was given a second chance, on that day... I killed de Vere, but I still could not save Meg!" he gasped his pain.

"I don't know what happened to her!" he cried.

The old lady looked down at Walter Gray, and gazed deep into his red-rimmed eyes, there was a twinkle in her own eyes as she said.

"Walter, 'The Archer'. After all these years, you have lived with the pain of not knowing." She said gently, as the old man's eyes fluttered and the light in them gradually dimmed.

"You did save Meg!"

# Epilogue

## Winter 1525

A vicious storm raged. Thunder and lightning exploded all around and the rain became a deluge. The deluge created gushing rivulets of water that filled the gulley's and ruts in the road. Large pools of rainwater were formed in an instant, and the road through the centre of the village became treacherous. Violent streams ran down the edges of the narrow road that acted as the main street in the village.

A young woman lifted her skirts as she ran, trying to avoid the worst of the water. She failed, and splashed through puddles that seemed to be getting ever deeper.

She cursed under her breath, bemoaning the fact that she had agreed to attend the meeting at the Old Mother's home.

Clutching her recently born child closely to her breast, she began to wonder at the stupidity of leaving her husband asleep in the safety of her own home, to make this clandestine visit, especially on a night such as this.

Thunder crashed overhead and lightning flashed all around. The lightening illuminated her path, but the torrential rain soaked her. "Goodness!" she cried as she was momentarily startled by a loud crash just beside her.  The horses penned on next to Minty Smith's cottage were distressed and threatening to break out of their enclosure.  The fence shook and a horse reared up.  She could see the terror in the animal's eyes in the light of the unrelenting lightning flashes.  She could see other horses milling around in fear, their foals in close attendance to their mothers.  The horses were clearly unsettled by the storm, and with no where to find cover, they were becoming dangerously frantic.

The young woman hurried on.

It was only a few minutes' walk to the Old Mother's home, but on this night, the journey seemed to be interminable.

The young women's clothes were soaked, and she could feel the cold dampness seeping through to her flesh.

Her skirts were covered in mud, her shoes were sodden.

Another flash of lightning lit up the cottage where the old mother lived.  It was a single storey, tumble-down assortment of wattle and daub, rickety and awry, more of a hovel than a cottage.

The young woman rushed to the door and banged hard.  After a few moments, the door opened by itself.  The young woman hesitated as she tried to comprehend how the door had opened without any obvious physical assistance.  The old lady, who was clearly visible inside beckoned to her, encouraging her to enter. "Come in my child and get yourself warm by the fire."

The young woman once again thought of the folly of her decision to agree to this meeting, but Old Mother had been insistent, it had to be this evening, All Hallows Eve…. No other time would be possible she had stated, and there would be consequences if she did not attend.

The young woman had been perturbed when the old lady had come up to her in the street a few days past.

However, the old lady had been present at the birth of her child and was trusted by everyone in the village.

She had a remarkable record in delivering babies, and no-one knew of a single death at birth when the old woman had acted as mid-wife. The girl was concerned about the health of her child, and that the old lady was going to tell her something awful…

The young woman had hardly ever spoken to her, and although she often greeted her out of courtesy, she did not go out of her way to acquaint herself with the old woman. The 'Old Mother' was as old as anyone the young woman ever seen, and she had lived in the village before anyone could remember. The Old Mother was reclusive, but not unkindly, although she kept herself to herself, she greeted people and people greeted her, whenever she was out.

As a child the young woman and her friends would tell stories and dare each other to go and knock at the door of the rotting old cottage of the wizened old woman, but none of them were ever brave enough to go through with it, usually running off, laughing, having not got closer than 10 yards. They had been frightened by the stories of curses, potions and spells that could turn a person into a frog.

The Old Mother was known in the village and the villages around as a 'sayer' of truths, and to be honest, the young mother was quite frightened of her, but if anyone, and women in particular needed healing remedies, then the Old Mother was the person people came to.

If there were accidents or maladies, then the Old Mother was the first port of call. The Old Mother helped with most of the births in the surrounding villages, and in a time of high infant mortality, the record of deaths of babies was surprisingly low.

In general, the Old Mother tended to keep herself to herself, but she was always friendly and polite to everyone she met. Every now and again, she would summon one of the villagers – no-one knew what was discussed and no-one ever tried to find out in a village as small as Swindon Village that was a rarity, as generally everyone knew everyone else's' business. The old Mother always knew when a new baby was due.

With the weather outside continuing without ceasing, the small dark cottage felt ominous. The Old Mother indicated to a small wooden stool next to the fire, "sit yourself down girl, I have something to say".

The young woman, dripping and sodden pulled back her head shawl and looked at the old woman. "What would you have me know Old Mother?"

"Your child is remarkable!"

The startled and confused young woman did not know how to respond. She stared at the old woman in shock, "What do you mean?"

The old woman smiled "Your child will have a wonderful and remarkable life!"

"But what does that mean? How do you know what is in her future?" said the young woman as she choked with emotion.

"Your child will be loved and protected by everyone in this village. She has a destiny that will surpass your imagination!"

The young woman tried to understand what she was being told. The Old Mother continued "Your child will accomplish many things, but more importantly, she will live a long and happy life!"

"What? Why would you summon me here to tell me this? The young woman asked.

The Old Mother did not respond immediately. She twisted a delicate chain around in her fingers slowly.

She stared over the girl's head, her eyes glazed and opaque. The young woman shivered involuntarily, unsure about what she should do.

Suddenly, a loud crash of thunder reverberated outside the cottage and it seemed to the young woman that the walls physically shook. She looked around startled by the violence of the noise. When she returned her gaze to the Old Mother, the old woman was staring back at her, smiling, her eyes had returned to their normal state.

"I cannot be certain, no-one can" she stated, "Your child was born safely, my vision tells me that in her future, there are forces that will always seek to protect her from harm…. From men, who would seek to do her harm…"

The young woman cried in anguish "But how do you know this? You are frightening me. Who are these men? What can I do!?"

The old woman continued to wind the chain around her fingers "You need not worry. There are powers beyond your comprehension, that will ensure your child remains safe, and fulfils her destiny."

"But what about the men! Can you tell me no more about them?" the young woman demanded "Surely, you have seen them in your vision?"

"They are shadows child, I cannot see them clearly. None of them will ever get near your child. That is a promise!"

"How can be sure she will be protected??" The young woman asked.

The Old Mother looked down at her hands. She began to unwind the chain from around her fingers. "I can do little, you can do even less. Take this and make sure that your child has it with her always. It will help to protect her." She held out her hand, and the young woman could see a small red crystal in her palm, at the end of a silver chain. The young woman took the crystal and chain and turned it over in her palm. "This is beautiful Mother. I cannot take this from you."

"Take it. This belongs to your child, not me. It has been waiting here for a long time, longer than me, longer than I have lived…."

"But how?" whispered the young woman, staring at the delicate and beautiful object in her hand. The old woman looked at her tears welling in her eyes "I do not know, child, I only know that it was meant for your child, and she must have it with her always."

The Old Mother moved slightly in her chair "If you are willing, I might be able to teach you some of our ways. This might help you in the future…."

"But I have no gifts" replied the young woman "I couldn't do it."

"You have gifts child. You are exceptional, and your daughter will be even more exceptional! …even at your young age…I feel you have magic in your fingers…"

"No!" The young woman laughed despite herself "I have no magic! Just the skills I have learned through practice."

"That may be child. Nevertheless, if you are willing, I will try to help you…"

"I will think about it" The young woman responded, "But what am I to do now?"

"Go home, look after your child, and your husband. Love them and protect her, there is nothing more…"

May I see the child, the old woman asked.

"Of course!" Here." The young woman said lifting the baby over to the Old Mother. The old woman held the child and looked into her eyes "Beautiful!" she crooned.

She looked back at the young mother and held out her hand for the pendant. Then she looked back down at the sleeping child, and pinned the pendant pinned to her shawl. She flicked her eyes back to the young mother, smiled and nodded her head. "Have you named her yet?" She asked, gently stroking the few golden wisps of hair, already growing on the baby's head.

"She is called Maud!" The young woman replied.

Old Mother Meg smiled…….

# THE END

## NOTES AND ACKNOWLEDGEMENTS

This book is a work of fiction.

There are various references to real individuals and events, however, the depictions of events and the characters of any individuals involved in any such events are entirely the product of my imagination.

I also make reference to real places. I have researched these places and faithfully believe that they existed during the timeframe that I have chosen to place my story. Any inaccuracies are purely my own.

I have completed an exhaustive research in order to identify a probable timeframe for my story. Records are sparce, and the timeframe I chose seemed to fit with the limited information available.

The timeframe that I chose, also presented dramatic opportunities to develop the storyline for my principle characters, which allowed them to engage in historically significant events. It is also a period of history which which was significant for Gloucestershire and in particular for Swindon Village itself. The characters involvement in such events is entirely fictious, but enabled me to develop their characters and assisted with plot development.

The story is my re-imagination of local folklore, legend and history much of which has been passed down through the ages by word of mouth. I will allow the reader to further investigate the folklore and legends for yourselves, and explore the potential errors in my own research. There are numerous resources that have been published online, but facts and records are extremely limited.

Maud's Elm is a real place, and although the magnificent tree was felled around 1906 because it was considered to be dangerous, the site can still be visited today.

Maud's Cottage can still be seen in Swindon Village, although it is probably not the original building.

I researched various historical figures who could have been my major villain (de Vere), including the Earls of Berkely, who resided at Berkely Castle.

I used the name of de Vere, because it is specifically mentioned in probably the most famous poem recalling the legend of Maud's Elm by Clinton, referenced in Norman's History of Cheltenham by John Goding.

It is interesting that within my timeframe John de Vere, 12th Earl of Oxford, was a major supporter of Margaret of Anjou and was engaged at the fateful battle of Barnet, which was significantly influential in the events that transpired at Tewkesbury. There is no information to suggest that a de Vere held property around Cheltenham – but the mention of the name in Clinton's poem and the timeframe that seemed most probable to me for setting the story, was irresistible.

Walter's oration towards the end of the book is attributable to Clinton's poem, although I have rephrased elements. I used them because the wording was so beautiful and emotional. Unfortunately, I have been unable to identify a full reference for Clinton's original poem, and have used versions published online, most notably https://www.mysteriousbritain.co.uk/legends/mauds-elm/

English Sweating Sickness was a real phenomena and first appeared around 1485, remarkably it seemed to impact rich people rather than peasants, although the first major epidemic started around 1485, it was too interesting to not use it as a plot link...who knows maybe Old Mother Sawyer created it, and it was only recognised slightly later!

It is not my intention to cast any kind of aspersion on any real persons or their families, again, this is purely a work of fiction.

I have tried to remain faithful to the legend, whilst expanding the story and providing a context to for the events depicted.

My depiction of the events surrounding the battle of Tewkesbury owe a debt of gratitude to Nora Day from tewkesburyhistory.org which seemed to be an interesting take on the positioning of opposing forces at Tewkesbury and from the lay of the land as I know it, very plausible.

I am not a historian, but an avid enthusiast of the history of the area in which I live.

My story is meant to entertain, and any historical, or other inaccuracies are entirely my fault.

If you have enjoyed my story, please leave a positive review.

Writing is a time-consuming process, and many authors struggle for recognition. Reviews help to bring stories to a wider public.

Russ Cooper 2023

Printed in Great Britain
by Amazon